Finch Books by Britt Cooper & Erin Dulin

The Chronicles of Fayble
Queen of Shadows

I0689709

The Chronicles of Fayble

QUEEN OF SHADOWS

BRITT COOPER &
ERIN DULIN

Queen of Shadows
ISBN # 978-1-83943-781-6
©Copyright Britt Cooper & Erin Dulin 2022
Cover Art by Kelly Martin ©Copyright March 2022
Interior text design by Claire Siemaszkiewicz
Finch Books

QUEEN OF SHADOWS

Dedication

To our wonderful husbands and families who have supported and tolerated us through everything. Sharing a brain has inspired a uni-person spirit and endless inanity that can be trying for us all.

And to Kaedyn, who insisted she be named specifically. Thanks for reading our work — good, bad and ugly. Without you, Rory would still be trapped in the forest.

Chapter One

Fitful cries from the Carvers' infant son pierced the silence, cleaving away Ella's remaining shreds of calm. Trekking through the village was a dubious task on the most temperate of evenings. Doing so in the biting gales of waning wintertide was sheer idiocy, but she had little choice.

Ella tugged the hood of her cloak, attempting to keep it in place atop her head. The wind swirling around her had other ideas, whipping her mantle with vicious ferocity and nearly knocking her onto her backside as she crouched beneath a narrow window. She gripped the rotting sill, cursing under her breath before digging her heels into the frozen earth.

"Be grateful." Much met her gaze, his eyes alight with suppressed mirth as he observed her predicament. "The weather should provide us a little more time."

It was true. Ella glanced skyward, where the silvery haze lingering above conveniently veiled the moonlight. "Would that it could also grant us more provisions to share," she whispered as Much tossed a small bag of grain in her direction. She wedged it neatly between the pile of cordwood and the decaying shingles sheathing the exterior, the burlap sack catching on the splintered timbers of the ramshackle cottage. "Another?" She held out a gloved palm expectantly.

"We cannot spare it." Much's words were but a breath, born both of necessity as well as grief. "If we double their portion, we'll leave another family with nothing."

Ella rose, making her way toward Much with a muted stride. "I filched an extra sack of grain from the lovely Lady Margaret before we set out." She loosed the pouch from her horse, Monroe, with nimble fingers. "The Carvers will put it to far better use. They have five children now, you know."

"Indeed." Much folded his arms across his chest for warmth. "But Lady Margaret is apt to skin you alive if she catches you."

"Tosh." Ella waved his concern away with a dramatic sweep of her hand. "My stepmother would never sully herself over the likes of me. Doubtless, she'll task you with that burden in her stead." She grinned, waggling her eyebrows in amusement.

Much groaned. "You are as delightfully morbid as ever."

Ella ignored him as she scurried toward the shanty for a second time, pairing the modest sack of grain with its twin nestled beside the kindling. The bags were always well hidden from passersby so as not to be stolen but quickly found by the tenants seeking firewood for their hearth. "It shouldn't make any difference," she groused, mounting her horse as Much followed suit. "It all belongs to me."

"Ah, if only, Lady Locksley. It shall be yet another two years, for until the age of—"

"Twenty, I know. I know." Ella sighed. It was an inconvenient fact she wished desperately to change. Thus far, her finest efforts in evading the ill-conceived lineal law of Llundyn included skulking through her hamlet in the wee hours before dawn, distributing food from her manor.

In the simplest of terms, she was stealing from herself, though with great care so as not to be discovered by her insufferable stepmother — the rightful heir of her lands and fortunes until she was finally of age.

Ella was discreet in her thieving endeavors, pinching items that would not be missed. It didn't hurt that Cooke willingly turned a blind eye. And, as luck would have it, Lady Margaret wasn't much for kitchen duty. It was a task she viewed as too menial for a woman of her stratum, even if she had only managed to achieve her status via a wholly undeserved union with Ella's father.

Heavens, how she missed him, God rest his soul.

"Where's the good in my title if I'm unable to use my station? I'm a member of the gentry with no more authority than that of an entitled rat." Ella urged her mount toward their next destination, gritting her teeth against the brisk air as her horse picked up speed. Plucking an arrow from the quiver on her shoulder, she turned, aiming at the weather-worn door behind her, her drawn bow taut. Her bolt found its mark, despite Monroe's bounding gait, announcing the presence of a delivery — the handmade arrow a telltale sign of her brief visit.

Much scoffed. "Nonsense. A rat would never share the spoils of its domain as you have. Neither would it have your impeccable aim."

Ella glanced at Much, expecting to see him smiling as he often did when he teased her, but his handsome face was surprisingly austere.

No. There was no humor to be found in these circumstances.

Two years of poor, drought-riddled harvests had taken their toll on the kingdom of Llundyn. The dearth of crops had failed to significantly affect the nobility, of course, with many a lord and lady inclined to take advantage of the bountiful imports from neighboring realms. But the paltry yield was nothing short of devastating for the commoners who had little coin to spare. Many had begun to exhibit its brutality outwardly, the sharp planes of their faces and bone-thin frames a startling illustration of the land's insufficiency.

Yet wealth poured into Locksley in the form of generous taxes, collected by Lady Margaret from the tenants surrounding the estate. As residents of the Locksley lands, they paid their due and worked the countryside in addition to their regular employment in the borough of Coventry, some five miles south of the manor.

Shame grieved Ella's conscience as she observed the growing disparity, convicting her of something far worse than her newly established hobby of larceny.

Abundance.

Attempting to shed her sense of guilt was worthless. It merely required action. Thievery paled in comparison to the atrocity of starvation and poverty. And, as far as Ella was concerned, it wasn't truly theft if she were merely pilfering from herself.

Much's eagerness to be complicit in her scheming had been all the sanction she'd needed. She'd considered him the more reasonable of the two of them for as long as she'd known him. If he could rationalize the madness in her subterfuge...well, then perhaps it wasn't madness at all.

As an orphan of some four years now, Much was far from his natural element. His father had been a man of the sea, captain of the king's navy, his young son serving as a boatswain under his command and following in his footsteps. But his untimely demise had left his widow and son at the beneficence of the kingdom.

Ella's father, Robin, had taken them on, providing steady work until fever had suddenly taken him away, with Much's mother following quickly behind. The staggering loss had left Much and Ella reeling, grappling for some fragment of hope, an element of security — qualities that they'd had the great fortune of discovering in one another, bonding them at once in heartache as well as mercy.

Then, in a startling turn of events, tragedy had taken a turn for the positive. Lady Margaret had deigned to agree with Ella, who'd insisted that Much be permitted to continue his employment assisting the manor's only carpenter. Whether due to genuine benevolence on her stepmother's part or some peculiar sense of duty, Ella was never certain. Still, it was a small victory that she and Much readily welcomed.

"Blast this wretched wind," Much grumbled, his complaint a swell of haze in the frigid air. "Remind me to wear several more layers of clothing for our next outing."

"And you dare to deem me the foul-mouthed one between us?" Ella demanded, bringing about a reluctant smile from her surly partner in crime. "Perhaps you should reconsider."

"Your words are well received, milady." He raised his brows in satisfaction, well aware that his use of the highborn term was profane to Ella's sensibilities. While he knew his place in Llundynien society, Ella had never treated him as lesser than an equal and always took his ribbing in good humor.

"Well, you're a fiend, James Much. Cease your peevishness at once so we may complete the task at hand," Ella intoned in a haughty impersonation of Lady Margaret, giggling with pleasure as his features crumpled in annoyance.

"Oh, but you do that too well, my friend." Much laughed, shoving her playfully in the shoulder. "How many more deliveries?"

"Only two." Ella patted the satchel that had been replete with various dried meats, grains and hard cheeses only hours ago. Now it was close to empty, bringing about a sobering reality. "How does it go so quickly? What we have will never suffice."

"You're doing your best. Your father would be proud," Much said with reverence, warming Ella's aching heart. "I don't know of many nobles who give one thought to the peasants occupying their lands, and here you are, feeding yours from your own stores. It's far better than doing nothing."

"Yes, but also not nearly enough," Ella agreed. "And besides, I thought the food didn't belong to me yet." Recalling Much's previous assertions, she couldn't help elbowing him in the ribs, nearly tumbling from her horse in the process.

"Careful!" Much hissed, grasping her arm and righting her before she slipped too far. "What good can you do for your hamlet if you meet your end beneath your horse's hooves?"

"Worry not." Ella resettled into her saddle as she adjusted her grip on the leather reins. "I do believe I'd live forever, simply to spite the lovely Lady Margaret."

Chapter Two

It took from the glow of pre-dawn until noon for Ella to recover some semblance of warmth. The earlier misadventures with Much had been essential, but the chill in her bones had stubbornly refused to abate. Her chambermaid, Alice, was convinced that Ella had fallen ill, as she was never one to lie idly by with daylight pouring through the weathered shutters.

After stoking the fire by her bedside to a perilous level of flame and layering her bed with an extra-downy quilt, Ella was beginning to feel herself once more. She might have considered spending the day that way, were it not for the presence of her stepsisters, Rosalind and Kinsley.

"Must you insist upon roasting us out of house and home?" Rosalind's tone reeked of superiority. Her air of self-importance was the first thing Ella had noted upon meeting her elder stepsister some dozen years before. However, she had not recognized the level of excellence in Rosalind that her stepsister seemingly perceived in herself.

She was beautiful, to be sure, with flowing mahogany hair and bright, crystalline eyes. Her pert nose was set above full, bow-shaped lips that were unnaturally rosy, and she was blessed with abundant curves. But in Ella's estimation, beauty did not an attractive person make. Rosalind was a wicked wench—most assuredly an unattractive quality. Not that Ella would ever tell her that she thought so.

"Have you taken ill?" Kinsley placed a tentative hand upon Ella's brow, having perched next to her at the head of her bed. Kinsley was tolerable, if a little dull in disposition and complexion. Pale gray eyes, ash-blonde hair and skin as fair as freshly driven snow, she was as devoid of color as Rosalind was resplendent. Still, her delicate features made her comely enough. And there was, at the very least, the suggestion of kindness in her smile.

"She is not ill. She's merely punishing us for her clever pet name. Isn't that right, Ember?" Rosalind glanced Ella's way with frosty regard, surveying her reaction from the corner of the tidy room. The carved oak chair squeaked with each shift of Rosalind's slender frame, irritating Ella as much as her stupid byname did.

The moniker was a product of Rosalind's diminutive intellect, with Ella having been likened to an ember from the hearth that refused to be crushed beneath Rosalind's boot some weeks before. It was the taunt of one with a childlike wit—so much so that even Kinsley found her humor to be tedious.

Even now, she rolled her eyes, sighing as Rosalind toyed with Ella. "I shall take no credit for your whimsy, Rose. Leave me out of it."

It had been a familiar game, with Lady Margaret's favored daughters collaborating in the torments they'd perpetrate on their stepsister. Observing the souring dynamics between the duo was a welcome surprise for Ella.

"Oh, Kin, when did you become so stuffy? You'll remain forever a maiden if you neglect to resolve your dreadful temperament. Wouldn't you agree, Ember?" Rosalind tittered like a mad squirrel, covering her mouth with dainty fingers as she persisted anew.

Charming.

Ella glanced at Kinsley, whose face was aflush with color—a miracle for the wan girl—and felt a pang of unexpected pity on her behalf. She turned to Rosalind. "In fairness, dear sister, I did not ask you to join me here," Ella said sweetly, though her patience swiftly waned. "Why are you gracing me with your company this fine afternoon?"

"Our lady mother has prepared yet another etiquette lesson," Rosalind sulked. "Kinsley and I knew your chambers would likely be the last place she'd seek us. As if I need more guidance in the art of gentility…"

It was all Ella needed to hear. She leapt from her bed, flinging her covers aside and nearly toppling Kinsley in her urgency. It wouldn't be long before she, too, would be roped into the infernal lesson. Lady Margaret fervently believed Ella had been raised a troglodyte and made regular efforts to correct her—to no avail.

Today would be no exception.

Her stepsisters observed with an obvious mix of awe and confusion as she made her way toward the armoire. Fumbling through the silken gowns toward the back of the chest where she kept her only pair of trousers hidden, Ella hastily thrust her feet through the holes. Clasping the well-worn leather belt—a hand-me-down from Much that was too large but suitable enough for her purposes—she proceeded to throw on a blouse and a doublet pilfered from her father's wardrobe.

She completed her ensemble with a soft pair of leather ankle boots — the only items from her mother that she'd had the privilege of retaining. They were old and tattered with more trips to the cobbler than Ella could recall, but she refused to part with them. An oversight by Lady Margaret, she'd managed to rescue the boots when her stepmother had purged nearly every vestige of her mother from Locksley Manor.

Ella had been furious with her father for allowing such a display, but he'd found himself newly committed to Lady Margaret at the time and was of a gentle nature. Ella couldn't fault him that, but the act had caused her tremendous grief, all the same.

"Where are you going dressed like that?" Kinsley fanned herself furiously, the effort in vain as the hearth crackled beside her.

"Isn't it obvious? She's off to join the filthy woodcutter she has insisted on befriending." Rosalind sniffed disdainfully. "You should know better. We are nobility, not common peasants."

We.

The word vexed Ella, for Lady Margaret and her snobbish brood had been elevated to the status of the gentry by virtue of marriage alone. It was not that they had attained a highborn position that rankled her. It was simply how they used it.

Ella took a deep breath, unclenching her tightly fisted hands. "He is the carpenter's apprentice. And yes, I would much prefer the task of chopping wood than that of perfecting the inanities of courtly conversation."

"That is why she will never marry," Rosalind chattered as Ella exited her quarters, wisely avoiding the main staircase and opting instead for the servant's companionway at the rear of the household. It was easy to disregard her stepsister's callous words. Marriage was far from her mind, with so many more important duties.

Bursting through the creaky back door, Ella met with all the freshness of a brilliant springtide day — a shocking departure from the ill-tempered weather from the night before. The sun shone brightly in the cloudless sky, bathing the rolling swells of the hillside in a rich and pleasant glow, and the gentle breeze carried a cheerful warmth that had her ready to strip off her doublet.

The manor was bustling with satisfying chaos, while man and beast alike busily accomplished their tasks for the day. Chickens clucked about the grounds, nibbling at the scattered kernels of grain dotting the earth and all the while keeping a wary eye on the overfat tabby that was keenly observant from his perch high above the coop.

The laundress and her girls made quick work of the wash, fastening dresses, petticoats and corsets to the clothesline after each scrub and rinse — a laborious chore that Ella was grateful to avoid. Grooms led horses from the barn to the paddock, with each brushed from head to hoof, her own horse Monroe amongst them. The plowmen walked the fields, methodically working the terrain for the season of planting, tilling the soil in the hopes that it might be fertile.

Heavens… Would that their lands could bear abundance for Locksley once more. Ella prayed that it be so.

Dropping by the barn, Ella collected her bow and quiver of arrows before making for the woods at the edge of her property, pleased that her stepsisters believed her to be chopping wood. Better they did not know her true intent.

Perhaps being beneath their notice has its benefits after all.

* * * *

Much groaned under the weight of their kill as Ella kept pace alongside him. The young buck was close in weight to Much himself, making each step he took an immense challenge. Their journey home was further complicated by the lack of a trail, seeing them through the thick of the king's forest over brambles and scrub with their illegal prize.

"Let's hide him here," Ella said, indicating some hearty shrubbery just at the edge of the woods. "We'll need some supplies before we can prep it for delivery."

"Fine." Much huffed, heaving the carcass into the brush. "Would that you might choose a smaller target next time."

"Oh, please. This will feed many more than the two rabbits you snared last week." She ruffled his hair playfully, amused by his cross disposition. He always sulked when he wasn't the first to slay during their frequent excursions. "You sound a little jealous, you know."

"I am!" He cracked a smile, wiping his palm over his sweaty forehead, his dark, unruly hair standing on end where he'd brushed it from his eyes. "You always manage to best me."

"Yes, but this time it'll be for the good of many." She smiled in return, enjoying their easy banter. He was as dear to her as a brother, with Ella harboring a sense of responsibility for him, though he was several years older than she was. He may as well have been her blood.

The pair exited the forest eager to make quick work of their quarry, only to stumble headlong upon Sheriff Dane and his designated minion, the new Lord of Clun, each making their way toward Locksley on horseback down the packed-dirt thoroughfare.

"*Hell*," Ella sighed, slowing her stride as she shifted her quiver and bow low over her shoulder.

Much followed suit, falling in step alongside Ella. "Perhaps they won't see us."

The sheriff turned as if they'd called his name, spying the duo as they wandered through the meadow separating the woods from the manor. She, along with Much, did her best to wipe the guilt from their faces, affecting an air of indifference as she plodded toward Sheriff Dane and his tag-along with sweaty palms, her heart in her throat.

The timing of the encounter could not have been worse.

Visits from the lawman were nothing noteworthy, for he had been pursuing Lady Margaret for some time. It was not unusual to have him join them for dinners or outings in Nottingham, given Lady Margaret's perpetual quest for unions with a modicum of prominence attached. With each husband, she'd managed to climb ever closer to the upper echelons of Llundynien society, disgusting Ella with her manipulative strategies.

Her father had been the third, with a farmer and a knight having had the grave misfortune of being the first and second. Ella did not know much of the previous men, only that her stepmother's second husband had sired Rosalind and Kinsley.

Still, the sheriff's pursual of Margaret meant regular sojourns to Locksley, which may have been bearable had he not insisted on being accompanied by the loutish Lord of Clun. New to Llundyn, Sir Guy of Gisbourne was flirtatious beyond reason, his adulation over the top and unnecessarily intimate. Of course, some people lapped it up—namely Rosalind—but she aimed for higher prospects still. No mere lord would satisfy. Rosalind was determined to snare a prince.

"Ah, Sheriff Dane. Sir Guy." Ella curtsied with all the femininity her trousers would allow, pinning a false smile to her face as the pair of men came to a stop before her. "To what do we owe the honor of your presence on this blessed day?"

"The pleasure is all ours, Lady Locksley." Gisbourne bowed his head in acknowledgment from high atop his horse. "Are you quite all right?" He furrowed his brow as he puzzled over her attire, along with the bow slung across her back.

"She is fine, Gisbourne." Sheriff Dane waved his hand in dismissal. "For some inexplicable reason, she likes to aid the help." His dark gaze fell upon Ella, full of judgment and something more that felt a bit like contempt. "You are nobility, milady. It would be wise to remember so."

"Indeed, sirs. Thank you for your concern, but I'm a healthy, capable woman. Assisting in the upkeep of my estate is no hardship." Ella tightened her smile, along with her fists. Being criticized for her active role in the management of her property had her agitated beyond reason.

"Undoubtedly, although, if I may… What *exactly* are you doing?" The sheriff narrowed his eyes, accusation evident in his gaze. "Certainly, you wouldn't endeavor to poach within the confines of the king's forest."

"Why, no!" Ella issued a disdainful sniff, her hand itching toward the bow strapped to her back. Stars, they were playing with fire. The dead deer in the bushes, not a hundred yards behind them, felt like a beacon, demanding the surly constable's attention. "I was merely honing my archery skills with my companion."

"The woodcutter? And what does he know of archery?" Dane glowered at the pair, plainly dissatisfied with her explanation, as well he should be. She was lying through her teeth — and not all that effectively.

"I was teaching him." Ella straightened, annoyed by the assumption that it was the other way around. "I've been shooting for years, and he wished to learn."

Much nodded in earnest, even as he remained silent at her side. Speaking for himself would come to no good, with his opinion of little value to the officer of the law.

"What of the blood staining his shirt? Was he your target as well?" The sheriff dismounted, striding toward Much as he scrutinized his appearance, though there was no wound to be found. Would that Dane might leave it at that.

Or perhaps that was worse.

Ella's pulse throbbed a fierce beat in her veins as she struggled for an explanation that didn't lead to the poached creature at the edge of the woods. Dane shifted his focus to Ella, his eyes lighting on the satchel at her hip.

Without warning, he moved for her, grasping the satchel with one hand as he clasped her shoulder with the other, keeping her under his firm hold. She struggled against him, her fury spiking as he handled her against her will. "I didn't —"

"Cease and desist!" he shouted as he strengthened his grasp, seemingly attempting to force Ella's compliance.

Ella battered Dane's chest with her free arm, shoving him with all the strength she could muster as he tore the satchel from her form. Stepping away with his bounty, the sheriff fumbled through its contents, finding nothing more than a couple of apples, some spare twine and the fletchings from a broken arrow.

"I told you, I've nothing of any consequence," Ella spat, snatching the bag from his grasp, and greatly relieved that they had not caught any hares. "And don't think for one moment that I will spare Lady Margaret the details of our encounter!"

"As if she will care," Dane replied, provoked by her insolence. "I should see you to the stocks for your sassy tongue!"

"Please don't." Gisbourne leaned idly over the withers of his steed, tiring of their dispute. "I do hope to dance with her at the banquet this evening, and she can't very well prepare for the revelry if she's fastened in that damned contraption."

Dane huffed, waving Gisbourne off with a flick of his wrist. Still, he made no move to detain her, going instead to his own horse, where he mounted with a grunt of effort.

"I shall look forward to accompanying you tonight, Lady Locksley," Gisbourne continued, undeterred. "May I escort you home so that you may prepare for the night's festivities?"

"I'm afraid I'm unaware of your meaning," Ella managed, straightening her blouse. "What festivities?"

"Why, we are to celebrate the return of Prince Johan and his envoy from the land of Chamelaute, milady,"

Gisbourne replied. "We will attend a banquet in his honor. I'm surprised you hadn't heard of it."

"I am not," the sheriff muttered as Gisbourne pointedly ignored him.

"Thank you, but I will find my way home." Ella took a step backward, colliding with Much in her haste to put distance between herself and the insistent lord. "Until tonight," she said with finality.

"Until then, lovely Ella," Gisbourne uttered, causing her stomach to lurch. He offered a wicked grin before the pair of men turned, tearing off toward her manor.

"Are you all right?" Much stepped before her, looking her over with anxious eyes. "I'm sorry, I—"

"No, Much," she muttered, strapping her satchel back in place. "You did the right thing by doing nothing. Had you stepped in, we would both be headed for the stocks. And besides…" She held out a substantial chunk of gold. There, resting in the palm of her hand, was the good sheriff's signet ring.

Much took it in, his eyes widening with recognition. "What did you do? Are you out of your mind?"

"He keeps it in his pocket because his fingers are too fat," Ella explained, a sly smile playing on her lips. "We'll melt it down and sell the gold, so we can buy more supplies for the village. He'll never know it was me."

"What if he does?"

"What if I don't care?" Ella barked, shaking her head. She patted his shoulder. "I'm sorry. I'm just tired of these games, and I'm sick of pretending I belong within a peerage that only wants me because of the lands and prestige that come with me."

"Well, then." Much attempted to reconcile his own fears with the courage oft exhibited by his most beloved friend. He sighed. "We'll give 'em hell. I'll handle the deer, while you feast with royalty, lovely Ella." He glanced at her sideways, earning a not-so-gentle shove from his friend.

"I should rather die," Ella fumed.

If only…

Chapter Three

The palace halls hummed with a familiar discord as dozens of attendants bustled about in haste, each eager to please His Royal Majesty, King Edward. Preparation for the night's opulent revelry had begun days before, and no expense had been spared.

The corridors were spread with plush runners in shades of burgundy, gold and amethyst, the colors made resplendent by the soft glow of the candlelit sconces adorning the walls. Narrow tables laid with all the delicacies of Llundyn lined the hallway, arrayed with platters of meats and cheeses, freshly baked breads, pastries and fruits bursting with sweetness. Curtained alcoves saw their disparate armchairs and settees embellished with silken pillows, all bathed in the warmth of the setting sun streaming through the freshly washed windowpanes.

Casks of wine and other spiritous beverages were carted into the manor, the finest offerings of the castle brewer. Crystalline stemware was stacked to perilous heights atop the bar, a mere breath away from tumbling to the floor in a shower of splintered shards. It was yet another impressive display in a palace already full of them. Every detail was planned, managed down to the very last crumb.

Yet as Prince Riccard wandered through the foyer, he found himself heedless of the chaos surrounding him. Well-practiced in royal decorum and familial duty, he knew what would be expected of him that evening.

Welcome the guests. Remember each name. Lavish them with praise, that they may feel important. Whisper a compliment in the ear of a beautiful maiden or two, inspiring gossip and fostering loyalty. All an act, to be sure, and a bore—but a necessary charade.

'For the prosperity of Llundyn'. It was his father's mantra.

Ric approached King Edward's chambers, flask in hand, taking a generous swig before tucking it away in the breast pocket of his freshly pressed uniform. As the heir apparent, he knew his father frowned upon imbibing before the citizenry, but it never seemed to be much of a deterrent to the prince.

Where was the value in wearing a title if all it earned him was aridity?

"Mother taught us to share, did she not?" Prince Johan smiled widely, approaching Ric from the opposite end of the corridor.

"Indeed, she did." Ric gripped Johan's arm as he pulled him into a firm embrace. "It's good to have you back. The castle is far too stolid without you."

Johan laughed, clapping his brother on the back. It was the first he'd seen of Ric since his return home from Chamelaute. "Was it my absence that drove you to become such an embarrassment?"

"Please. You mustn't think so highly of yourself. I've been polluting the image of the royal family since birth." Ric plucked the flask from his pocket, offering the pleasure of his liquid ally along with a wicked grin.

"That I cannot argue." Johan tipped the leather-sheathed flacon in tribute before unscrewing the cap. One ample gulp later, he was swallowing hard, forcing the swill down before he could choke on the wildfire blistering the length of his throat. "Blazes!" He coughed the flames from his chest. "Why would you carry such rotgut about?"

"I don't think I need to answer that." Ric seized the flask from his brother's shaky hand, nodding toward the emblazoned door that led to their father. "Shall we?"

"Indeed." Johan knocked on the door out of simple courtesy before swinging it wide, revealing the contents of the elegant room.

The spacious chamber was immaculate, as always, aflutter with His Majesty's attendants. Two domestics made up the goose-feather bed, smoothing the sleek silken coverings and fluffing the many pillows before organizing them squarely at its head. An additional pair of servants scurried about readying the elaborate attire and regalia for the king, a tedious process as only the finest would do for such a lavish occasion.

Beyond the crimson draperies separating the bedroom from the bath chamber, their father grumbled at his long-time manservant, Beardsley, his water having cooled to a disagreeable temperature. The steward worked feverishly to make amends, drawing the rotund king to his full height within the hammered copper tub. His Royal Majesty stood, impatiently shivering droplets of water as he suppressed his temper.

Beardsley offered the king his robe with a sweeping bow. "Your cover, sire."

"Yes, yes! Come now, or I shall die benumbed!" The king held out his arms for dressing as Beardsley draped him in the luxurious garment, offering an arm for support as the king stepped from the burnished vessel with his robe hanging freely.

"Some things, it seems, shall never change," Johan uttered, approaching his father with Ric falling into step beside him.

"For better or for worse, I cannot say," Ric agreed as the brazen king's gaze fell upon them.

"Ah! Welcome home, my boy." Edward closed the remaining distance between them, gripping Johan's forearms in greeting. "I trust all went well with your travels?"

"My journeys were a resounding success." Johan smiled tightly, maintaining as much distance as he could respectfully hold while his father's covering remained undone. Perhaps the years of watchful eyes invariably cast upon his father had caused him to become overbold.

It was no matter. He was well acquainted with the king's eccentricities, but that didn't keep him from breathing an obvious sigh of relief when Edward set his sights upon Ric.

"I see you've begun your celebration." He regarded his heir's besotted countenance, inspecting him from head to foot. "I'm afraid your redolence has preceded you, my son. I detected your defiance from across the room."

Ric sniffed his doublet and shrugged. "Don't expect me to share any more of it." Flashing a wry grin, he retrieved his flask, his bright eyes alight with erstwhile mischief he'd had little use for in years. Heartache had stolen his carefree nature long ago.

Of the two princes, it was Riccard whose visage favored the High King—a man who had been startlingly handsome in his youth. Though he now had age and girth on his side, the king had an arresting quality about him that Ric shared. Johan's features unmistakably resembled those of the late queen of Llundyn, fairer in tress and skin, where Ric and Edward were tanned. Still, it was the youngest, Princess Isla, who had been the mirror image of their mother before their tragic deaths.

The unceasing generosity of Her Royal Majesty and the young princess had ultimately claimed their benevolent spirits, a plague having haunted the lands in those earlier years, robbing the breath from the lungs of innocents throughout the countryside.

And henceforth, nothing had been the same.

Edward sighed, fastening the belt around his robe at last. "Do not embarrass the Crown this eve. You must curry the favor of the people, that they may see you for the successor you are to be. For the—"

"Prosperity of Llundyn, father. Yes." Ric stifled a groan. His father's chiding an ever-present thorn in his side. He knew. He could never forget.

"Worry not about my brother." Johan eyed his irritated sibling with amusement, grateful that he wasn't the subject of his father's ire as Ric so often was. "We shall both be on our best behavior."

"Upon my word, you'd better be. Forget not that this is your final opportunity to appraise the women of the kingdom before the ball in two months' time." The king fixed his stern gaze on each of his sons. "And if you cannot choose a wife for yourselves, I will do it for you."

30

"A *wife*." Ric spoke the word as if it were a curse. Perhaps to him it was, the prospect of marriage bonds utterly revolting. "I find no usefulness in such relations. Why further encumber myself with additional duty when I'm already to bear the burdens of the kingdom?"

"On the contrary, Ric. There is great value in matrimony," Johan reasoned, forestalling his father's objections to his brother's surly tongue with a wave of his hand. "Indeed, a wife is more an asset than a hindrance in the life of a monarch. Would it not be a relief to share the challenges of leadership with another?"

"At what cost? For, doubtless, she will require my attention, my devotion, my favor." Ric scoffed. "I haven't the time for such frivolities." Defying his father's directive, he took another deep swig from his flask, only to have it slapped from his hand by the king, the sharp odor of the numbing elixir permeating the air around them as it sloshed from the ewer.

The smell alone was strong enough to cause Johan to gag.

"There is a lovely duchess in Sundsvaile, and an alliance with the house of Balstad would be more than beneficial for Llundyn. Your unions *will* be arranged, by emotions or politics, I care not which. That is all!" King Edward turned his back, dismissing his sons as he began dressing for the night's festivities.

Ric and Johan departed with a bow, clearly eager to leave Beardsley to the soothing of Edward's nettled sensibilities. Nobody wanted to be present when the king was in one of his moods.

"Well done," Johan muttered, eyeing his capricious brother sideways.

Well done, indeed.

Chapter Four

Ella hated her corset with the fiery passion of a thousand burning suns. She attempted a deep breath without success as Alice bound her into the cursed contraption, the tugging of the cords driving her to distraction as her waist shrank to an inhuman size.

"Ember, darling, you look quite unwell," Rosalind sneered, bracing herself against the sturdy column of her bedpost as her chambermaid stuffed her into her undergarments. "Perhaps you would bear the terrible burdens of wealth with more grace if you ceased scampering about in menswear."

Ella persevered, ignoring the blathering of her stepsister with all the tolerance of an exalted saint. As if attending the banquet were not somehow enough of a punishment, being joined by her stepmother and stepsisters would make it positively dreadful.

"Then again," Rosalind continued, "you could hardly be considered beautiful. Perhaps you are better suited for menswear after all."

"Certainly," Ella agreed as she drowned in a flood of petticoats, her patience waning anew. "Though Sir Guy seems to fancy me well enough. I am unlikely the hideous dog you make me out to be."

Perhaps I'm going mad? Being desired by the likes of Sir Guy of Gisbourne was doubtless nothing to which she should aspire. Yet Rosalind's prodding had Ella tumbling to her level. She knew better than to engage in any sort of mental sparring, well aware that Rosalind lived to triumph, no matter how nonsensical her incitement was. But now and again, she simply couldn't help herself.

"He merely pities you, dear sister." Rosalind tittered, a wholly obnoxious sound that had Ella ready for combat. "Though, it is truly charming that you'd believe his affections to be otherwise." She simpered pathetically, holding her clasped hands to her chest.

Ella took a breath, though the infernal corset diminished its effect. Still, it served to soothe her ever-fraying composure. She would rise above Rosalind's machinations, thoroughly satisfied with the knowledge that her beautiful stepsister was wrong.

For what was beauty in comparison to integrity, anyhow? Strength of mind and virtue were far more important to Ella, though she knew she was in the minority on that front. Being a well-respected proprietor, an approachable noblewoman... Those were qualities that mattered.

"What will you wear this eve, milady?" Alice asked, having completed the torturous process of cinching and puffing Ella's underthings into the customary silhouette.

"I'd like to wear the azure gown." Ella smiled knowingly, and Alice responded in kind, the conspiratorial gleam that passed between them going unnoticed by the room's other occupants.

"A fine choice, miss." Alice nodded, offering a half-bow before departing for Ella's chambers to retrieve the garment. As one of the only remaining attendants from the time of Ella's birth, Alice was well accustomed to plotting with her charge.

"Beware the mice!" Rosalind called after Alice. "They've probably torn that hideous frock to shreds by now. Heavens only know how aged that dress is. I should rather die than be seen with you in it."

"Would you?" Ella asked sweetly, mirroring Rosalind as she clasped her hands to her chest in mockery. "If you swear your demise, I promise to honor you further by wearing it to your funeral as well."

"You are a vile little troll!" Rosalind lunged in Ella's direction, as if to slap her, but was wrenched backward, her maid plainly amused by the exchange. Rosalind stamped her foot like a petulant child. "Hurry up! I shall not be late. The princes will be waiting."

"With bated breath, no doubt, for the arrival of such glorious creatures as ourselves," Kinsley said, ever the arbiter.

"Oh, shut up." Sniffing curtly, Rosalind crossed her arms over her girded bosom. She would make an already-tedious evening feel even longer.

Ella glanced at Kinsley, only to find her returning her gaze. They exchanged brief smiles, with neither unnerved by the ever-fractious behavior of the eldest sister. Remarkably enough, Ella had seen herself forming a kinship of sorts with the fairer stepsister. Kinsley could be a great ally.

Or a consummate deceiver. Ella would never trust her completely, for she was of the same stock as Rosalind.

Alice swept wordlessly into the room with the deep blue gown slung across her arms, moving to Ella's side and slipping it over her raised hands. The dress fell heavily, enveloping her in the unforgiving fabric—a shimmering sea of sapphire. And though Ella despised her formalwear, even she had to admit that the tone of the gown suited her.

Billowing sheets of fabric hung loosely over her legs. The outermost layer was pleated with broad silken folds concealing secret seams within, the pockets inside the full skirt enabling her to slip many goods away for later distribution. A bateau neckline left only the top of her collarbone exposed, making its design considerably more modest than the style at present, and for that, she'd make no complaint.

Cinching her stays, Alice tugged the corset laces, its boning forcing her posture upright. Ella had loved her mother in this gown—her favorite feature always having been the back. Material closed overtop the restrictive undergarments, pearls securing each side at the garment's center, beginning at the neck to below Ella's hips.

After what felt like an eternity, Alice buttoned the last of the numerous pearl clasps on the bodice, turning Ella to face her with a gentle hand. "I remember your father bringing home these pearls for your mother, from all of his many seaside trips. You look—"

"Hideous," Rosalind finished, perched before the mirror of her vanity. "Simply hideous. How am I to be presented alongside you in a garment so timeworn?" She dismissed Ella with a scornful wrinkle of her nose, tending instead to the ruby red gloves adorning her arms as her attendant pinned her dark curls into an upswept masterpiece.

"Our lady mother has had many more updated dresses tailored for you," Kinsley added, though there was no animus in her tone. "Perhaps a more fashionable gown is in order?"

"Worry not, for my rags will only serve to amplify your splendor." Ella smiled, her amusement genuine as her stepsisters shrugged in reluctant assent. How anyone could place so much pride in attire was beyond her.

"Quite right." Lady Margaret stood in the doorway, her diminutive stature perfectly at odds with her calculating intellect. "My lovely girls will be the belles of the banquet as always. I've no doubt you will catch the eye of the future king." She swept into the room, an imposing force despite her size in a gown of emerald green, kissing each of her two daughter's cheeks in turn.

Ella cleared her throat, vexed by her stepmother's disdain. It was no secret that Ella was most despised, but she marveled at how little the noblewoman attempted to hide her contempt.

Lady Margaret rounded on her, cupping her face without any note of tenderness. Her keen gray eyes trailed the length of Ella's body, a furrow forming between her dark brows. "How charming it is that you never wish to improve yourself. Your arrogance is quite remarkable."

Ella took a step backward, shifting into a gracious curtsy. "Thank you, Lady Mother. You do flatter me so." She smiled cordially, grateful for the dual purposes of her controversial gown. For not only could she pilfer a considerable amount of food, but she would also aggrieve her stepmother in excess.

In her mind, there was no disadvantage.

"She's wearing her shabby boots as well, you know," Rosalind tattled like a child, eager to cause more trouble. Ella suppressed a sigh, weary with the thought of any further interrogation over her vestment.

Lady Margaret tutted her disapproval, making her way toward the doorway in a flourish of voluminous skirts. "I suppose we are fortunate that this evening is not about her. It is for the two of you that we shall pursue royalty." Her gaze lingered on Ella for a moment more, censure evident on her comely face as she left the girls to finish their preparations.

Would that Ella could bring herself to be bothered by her stepmother's reproach. Alas, she was too preoccupied with the notion of a royal wedding including either stepsister as the bride.

Indeed, she was quite certain that all her lawful family were mad.

Chapter Five

Never had Ella imagined how relieved she would be to arrive at the banquet. In truth, being forced to spend further time locked away in the carriage with her sisters and the Lord of Clun was likely to cause someone to meet their end. Her stepmother also contributed to her growing headache, offering a plethora of unsolicited advice on everything from manners to dancing, which left her wishing for her ax.

If only she were home, chopping wood alongside Much. She was better suited to chores than foolish revelry.

They exited the coach one by one, setting foot before the grand stairway leading to the reception. The lush green grounds surrounding them were manicured to perfection and so unlike much of Llundyn, which was crisp and dry as straw during the arid season. Ella wondered at the efforts it had taken to achieve such glory.

As the presumptive heir of Locksley, Ella ascended the staircase arm in arm with her stepmother for presentation, flanked by Rosalind and Kinsley and the eternal nuisance Sir Guy of Gisbourne, who moved with pomposity between them. Ever the faux gentleman, he lived for women as much as for prestige. And should the notoriety he craved be in his seductions, all the better.

Avoiding him for the duration of the evening would be Ella's utmost priority. She refused to become the fodder for idle gossip.

Marble statues of royalty past stood tall and proud as they climbed, arranged in orderly spans on either end of the broad stone steps. The alabaster balustrade was festooned with flora in blooms of crimson and plum, while pennants of cream lined in thick ropes of gold streamed gently in the light breeze, hung from balconettes bursting with scores of vibrant dahlias.

Myriad guests adorned in a rich array of textures and colors formed a restless line, eager to join in the merriment taking place within. An enchanting melody spilled from the halls within the castle, flooding the air with energy and fueling the fervor of those gathered.

Approaching the palace herald, Ella noted the stalwart soldiers lining the foyer — an impressive lot in their crisp, dark jerkins. They were polished and gleaming from head to toe with their sabers and bows ever at the ready.

Save for one.

The shabby fletching of unkempt arrows drew her eyes. They belonged to a baby-faced young man, likely many years her junior. He was green, to be sure, and plainly out of his element, his countenance strained —

as if he needed to worry on duty in a castle bursting with an able-bodied regiment.

An hour with the poor fellow would see him far better equipped. Ella had received the blessing of her father's tutelage, his skillful hands forming arrows with ease. In truth, fashioning bolts was one of her most treasured pastimes, bonding her at once to her memories and offering her a welcome diversion from the inanities of Lady Margaret's nagging.

Nearly to the head of the never-ending stream of elites, Ella found herself formalizing her posture and mindset unconsciously. Being amidst the aristocracy of Llundyn was nothing more than a game of pretend — an exercise in frivolity that always left her feeling foolish for playing her part.

"The Lady Locksley and retinue!" the herald called when they reached the edge of the crowded vestibule overlooking the ballroom. Ella curtsied deeply in deference to the king, though he was otherwise occupied by the evening's festivities and paid her no mind. It was merely another formality in a night that would be replete with them.

"Do not shame your sisters this evening," Lady Margaret hissed as they made their descent toward the ballroom, all the while maintaining a dazzling smile. "It is the least you can do."

"You needn't worry, Lady Mother," Ella replied pleasantly. "If a highborn marriage is the quickest way to be free of you and your lovely daughters, I shall do my best to facilitate it."

Lady Margaret sniffed in disgust, dismissing Ella's impudence in the only manner acceptable amongst the gathered nobility. "Leave us. You are too difficult to manage by half, and I will not have you sabotaging your sisters' prospects."

When they reached the mezzanine, Ella forced a polite smile. "My pleasure. I shall find you when it's time to depart." With a hasty, half-hearted curtsy, she hurried away, determined to be well disappeared before Sir Guy could disentangle himself from the clutches of Rosalind and Kinsley.

Weaving between a stout baron and equally plump baroness, who was dressed in a shade of beige that matched her flesh in a most unfortunate way, Ella convinced herself that she had succeeded in her subterfuge. The couple made for the perfect barricade, obscuring Sir Guy's roving eyes for, at the least, a short while.

Free from her relentless shadow and the judgmental gaze of her beloved stepmother, she finally relaxed. The extravagance awaiting her was nothing shy of overwhelming. While she faithfully sought to maintain a level head where luxury was concerned, she found herself to be awed by the display put forth by the Crown.

Ella had attended similar commonwealth affairs for well over a decade, the most memorable of which included her father. Back then, her surroundings had enchanted, but her father's undivided attention had been of far more import. Now, as she struggled with the ghost of her father, she was simply bewildered.

Lavish did not do justice all that she beheld. The food was almost too beautiful to eat, arranged atop mahogany tables inlaid with silver and gold gilding. The balcony overlooking the ballroom floor, which was adorned in similar grandeur as those of the exterior balconettes, held all the dignitaries of Llundyn, with each dressed in finery that could finance an entire township for a year. Their intents to impress His Royal Majesty were evident and absurd...as if King Edward hadn't seen it all before.

Likewise, the magnitude of waste on such an occasion had Ella perturbed. For not far from the palace doorstep lived her countrymen, who were only barely getting by. It was well-known that the king had worried little over the state of his expenditures since the death of his queen—a detail the kingdom had managed to survive as yet. Still, it was unlikely that the empire would persevere in these conditions in perpetuity.

As if by happenstance, Ella spied the only tolerable soul she expected to find amongst the nobility seeking refreshment by one of the buffets. A man who was as likely to agonize over the uncertain future facing Llundyn as she, Friar Tuck was a welcome sight.

Certifying her perceived kinship with the aged cleric, she observed the friar as he pocketed fluffy rolls as well as plums and peaches, the latter two of which were imports from the kingdom of Calaise. Piece after luscious piece, the fruits were slipped into his garment by his covert hand.

Heavens. The space in the pockets of his frock was without end. Ella half expected them to burst, with an avalanche of produce cascading from his robe. She smiled at the thought as she made her way toward him, keeping to the perimeter of the ballroom to readily dash behind the curtains should any unsavory lords appear.

"Thou shalt not steal, good friar," Ella crooned, sidling up beside him.

The man flinched, bobbling a plum between his hands. "Ah, Lady Locksley! You gave me a fright." He released a hefty breath, a mischievous grin forming on his face. "And truly, milady, it is not stealing if the food is furnished freely." He polished the deep purple skin of the plum on the sleeve of his habit before offering it to Ella.

She took it, slipping it into one of the pockets hidden in the folds of her skirt. "You speak the truth. Indeed, I've arrived with the same purpose in mind. I will not see all this food go to waste when so many people beyond the walls of the palace are in desperate need."

The friar shook his head in disbelief. "A beautiful gown with pockets. How very clever! It seems we foster the same ambitions, helping those less fortunate by any means necessary." He squeezed her shoulder before leaning nearer. "Please accept a simple word of advice and avoid the gardens. There are dogs out there, and I learned that the hard way." Turning, he revealed a substantial hole in the rear of his garment.

"I'm sorry for your plight, dear friar. It seems the beasts may have bested you." Ella stifled a laugh, though rather unsuccessfully, covering her mouth with slender fingers as she worked to recover her good graces.

"Not so! For I have no pockets back there. All the mutts managed to nibble was some sackcloth and air, the wicked fools." He chuckled, gratified as Ella giggled freely, his round face filling with color. Snatching a red-gold peach from the buffet, he slipped it into Ella's hand. "I've distracted you from your mission for long enough. Since the days of your childhood, you've harbored a heart for the needy. You are a blessing to the kingdom, Lady Locksley." He clasped her free hand in his own, squeezing her fingers briefly before bowing and shuffling quickly away.

Ella settled the peach in her pocket alongside the plum, puzzling over the friar's rapid departure. She'd been grateful for the lighthearted company of the clergyman but now resigned herself to an evening of monotony.

Turning, she became quite aware of Friar Tuck's urgent desire to part ways.

Prince Riccard stood before her, an impressive feat of humanity in a midnight-blue uniform that only served to intensify the shade of his captivating eyes. His dark blond hair was tousled, striking despite its disarray, and the rakish smile he wore had her altogether weak in the knees.

Stars, she was staring.

And she was not the only one. All around the ballroom, the gazes of eligible maidens fell upon them with looks of adoration for the dashing prince and leers for Ella. Competition for his attention was at a fevered pitch, and any woman who attained his regard scrutinized in kind.

A particularly strident assemblage of women chattered from behind her, with unflattering words concerning everything from her hair and dress to her character, dispensed at a pace so rapid she could not readily discern them.

Yet, this slander was nothing new. Ella had survived criticism from Rosalind that was far more severe. Perhaps living with the most judgmental of sisters had its advantages after all.

Recovering her self-possession, Ella curtsied, bowing her head. "My Lord Prince Riccard, it is a pleasure to make your acquaintance once more." She released her skirt, offering her hand in the customary greeting.

Taking her fingers in his, the prince bowed low before placing a lingering kiss on the back of her hand. "The pleasure is all mine. And who might you be?" His face was earnest, but the devilish glint in his eye gave the cocky heir away.

Ella scoffed. "Who, indeed? I should suppose you wouldn't remember." She feigned disappointment, peeking up at the tall prince through thick lashes as she withdrew her hand. "Perhaps I shall choose to remain anonymous, as you've all the other women of Llundyn to entertain."

"I only entertain the ones worth my time," Prince Riccard said, peering over Ella's shoulder at the vicious gossips. "Or, rather, they entertain me." He smiled widely, displaying a mouthful of straight snow-white teeth.

Tosh.

If this was the infamous Riccard charm she'd heard much about in the village, it was sorely lacking.

"I'm afraid your time is up where I'm concerned," Ella bit out. To think she had swooned at his nearness. Prince Riccard was indisputably as wanton as Sir Guy. Only, unlike Gisbourne, he had every damsel in the kingdom falling at his feet.

Not she.

"If you'll excuse me, please. Many guests are awaiting your inspiring presence, and I should like to return to the festivities." Ella bowed her head, placing a hand on her chest as she backed away from the arrogant prince, eager to return to her evening of dolor.

"Wait!" Riccard reached for her, gently catching her by the hand. "I was only teasing. How could I forget you—"

"Ella of Locksley," Prince Johan finished. He stepped around his brother, greeting Ella with a deep bow. "It seems that my brother is as obtuse as ever. He merely meant to determine what was amusing you so, but it seems, rather, that he has offended, as usual." Johan's features filled with suppressed mirth, his lips tipping at the corners.

"Oh? He failed to mention the reason for his interest." Ella returned his smile, oddly enamored with the freckles dusting the bridge of his nose — an attribute that made the handsome spare heir seem more ordinary, despite his station. Seeing the brothers together had an arresting effect on Ella's sensibilities, keeping her fixed before the pair, though she wished very much to be anywhere else.

"I'm not surprised. Riccard is an oaf around beautiful women." Johan's bright hazel eyes sparkled with humor, the profound bond between the princes evident in his gaze. She'd known them for years, having attended noble gatherings since childhood, but never had they been this attentive.

"Do not speak of me as if I'm absent," Riccard said, though there was no irritation in his tone. He elbowed Johan in the ribs, drawing a chuckle from his younger sibling as he moved to stand beside Ella. "And yes, I did wonder at the exchange between you and the good friar. How did you have the pious fellow so jolly?"

"I'm afraid it's none too compelling," Ella admitted. "We share a similar interest in charity and a unique method of achieving our ends."

Ric laughed. "That's delightfully vague." He leaned nearer to Ella, his voice dropping. "Yet no man may accuse me of meddling. A woman is entitled to her secrets."

"Quite so, but alas, my brother certainly knows *many* of their secrets." Johan raised his eyebrows, evoking a look of reproach from his brother.

Ella smiled shyly, well aware of the truth in Johan's assertion. It was commonplace to find Prince Riccard surrounded by the kingdom's most desirable maidens, and goodness only knew what sorts of secrets he'd obtained.

And where the elder prince's trade was in secrets, Prince Johan traded in commerce. It was a rarity to find him encircled by women. He rather seemed to prefer the company of advisors and the familiarity of his royal obligations, making it all the more unexpected to have him standing there before her.

"Please tell me my enchanting sister is not disturbing the pair of you as she does me," Rosalind said, approaching the princes with an elegant gait. She was undeniably attractive, though the smile she wore was as clearly false as her feigned kindness.

"Ah, Rosalind, is it?" Prince Johan bowed, greeting her in the conventional fashion as she dropped into a well-practiced curtsy. "It is a pleasure to have you join us this eve."

"The pleasure is mine," Rosalind lilted. "I was surprised to find her speaking to not one, but both princes! Perhaps there is some hope for your social graces as yet." She offered a sneer of contempt for Ella alone.

Johan covered a smirk with his hand while Ric cleared his throat in a vain attempt to remain courteous, despite his obvious chuckling. "Might I offer you ladies some refreshment?" he finally managed, gesturing toward the credenza that was bursting with provisions.

Ella inclined her head in thanks. "That is most thoughtful. Indeed, there's more than I could hope to choose from." Her hand strayed toward the pocket full of fruit. A little more wouldn't hurt, though she'd have to leave her company behind to gather more.

"Oh, please ignore her," Rosalind moaned. "Ember can't resist pretending to be part of the help." She laughed to diminish the hostility behind her words but to no avail.

"Yes," Johan said carefully. "The sheriff has made mention of you working alongside the people of your lands—a truly noble endeavor. If only I had the opportunity to do the same."

Not to be undone by her stepsister's savage tongue, Ella simply shrugged, refusing to allow the silence that followed to upset her. For it was not she who had driven the circumstances to awkwardness.

"Ember..." Riccard began, thoughtfully breaking the tension. "What a charming moniker, doubtless a reflection of your mesmerizing eyes. The gold flecks are quite fetching."

Ella met his gaze, convinced that she would find him to be speaking in jest, but she was wrong. Remarkably so, as she'd never seen his expression as tender as it was at that moment. Shaking her head, she relieved herself of her rapture. "That's a very kind interpretation, but I'm afraid the name is not meant as a compliment."

"Consider it one from me, Ember of Locksley." Riccard winked, smiling in a way that left her flushing fiercely.

Blazes. Perhaps he is charming after all.

"It seems your entourage misses you, Ric." Johan deftly changed the subject, indicating the group of vicious gossips still chattering away behind Ella and bringing about a much-needed diversion.

Ella fanned her warm face, giggling alongside the princes, who were amused by the prattling noblewomen, all of whom were scowling in the absence of the highborn gentlemen.

One of the more daring women noted the sudden attention her small circle had garnered and made quick work of the opening. Sweeping toward them, she tugged Riccard away in a flourish of lacy petticoats and citrine satin, issuing a titter of glee that had Ella's skin crawling.

Prince Riccard dutifully followed, though the look in his eyes pleaded for mercy — an appeal for a rescue that neither Ella nor Johan were interested in fulfilling. Instead, they waved, all the while stifling snickers over Ric's predicament. It was an ornery approach, but watching the future king of Llundyn squirm under the eager hands of the busybody was too riveting for intervention.

"He'd much rather remain with you." Johan smiled tightly, his gaze pinned to Ella.

"I've no doubt he would. I make for considerably better company." Rosalind smoothed her skirt before primly peeking over her shoulder at the stolen prince.

Ella met Johan's eyes, a shared sense of irony passing swiftly between them. It would never be said of Rosalind that she was meek — or very bright, for that matter.

"Would that more of the citizenry could partake in the abundance of court," Ella said, politely steering the conversation away from the consuming topic that was Rosalind. Her stepsister often discussed Ella's lack of social grace, yet readily saw fit to make herself the center of all conversation.

Not very courtly behavior. Lady Margaret's warning to refrain from sabotaging her sisters echoed in her ears, and that was a request Ella could easily honor. Rosalind readily sabotaged herself. Even now, she rolled her eyes, irritated by the matters surrounding the poorer class of Llundyn.

"The excess is, in truth, an embarrassment," Johan confided, glancing around the ballroom. "I have proposed reining in our expenditures, though that is next to impossible when I am not fully in charge. Still, it is pleasing to know that there are those beyond the palace who harbor concern for those less fortunate amongst us." He bowed his head, and Ella responded in kind.

His rumination caught her off guard. She never imagined any castle dwellers caring a whit about the plight of the people beyond their walls — at least, not in any capacity apart from what was required by duty alone.

"Yes, my lord, I do care deeply for all the paupers of Llundyn," Rosalind chirped, batting her eyelashes as she simpered anew. "For they are so…*poor*."

"Indeed," Johan agreed, though he furrowed his brow in distaste. "Now, please, if you will excuse me, I've the king to attend. The banquet must go on." He bowed to Rosalind before reaching for Ella's fingers, placing a kiss on the back of her hand. "Until we meet again."

"Until then." Ella beamed, the light stubble of his face tickling her skin. She watched as Johan collected his brother en route to the balcony where his father stood and realized that she'd been caught staring, yet again.

Rosalind stood aghast, judgment evident in her haughty features. "You little trollop. The way you were throwing yourself at the princes was positively revolting! Have you no shame?"

Ella recoiled. "I didn't—"

"As if either of them would stoop so low! Our lady mother will be mortified!" She stormed away, heedless of any explanation on Ella's part.

Not that she owed her one.

Ella dismissed Rosalind's tantrum with an exasperated sigh before wandering around the perimeter of the ballroom. The evening slowly waned, having been an exercise in endurance. But it hadn't been all bad. Her encounter with the highborn brothers had been unexpectedly charming, and her wayfaring had produced a skirt full of fruits, hard cheeses and bread.

And, she'd seen neither hide nor hair of Sir Gisbourne. Would that her luck might continue to hold.

"Attention! Your attention, please!" King Edward called the assembly to order from his perch overlooking the crowd. "It is my pleasure to welcome home my intrepid son Johan, who returned to us from his ventures in Chamelaute just this morning. Join me, son." He reached for Johan, guiding him toward the center of the balcony for his moment in the sun.

What Johan had been doing in Chamelaute was anybody's guess. Official matters of state were never shared with the people, aside from a handful of high-ranking lords. Ella would be among them if she were male, but of course, that privilege would someday fall to her husband instead—a truly antiquated custom.

Johan spoke, and all around, her contemporaries lapped it up, seemingly satisfied in the realm of mere observance rather than action. Ella worked to remain attentive as the prince regaled the gathering with tales of his dealings, though she couldn't keep her thoughts from rambling. He spoke of concepts as foreign as the land of Chamelaute itself, building in her resentment toward her betters.

Why not she?

She was capable, ran her lands. Why should she not participate in the governing of the commonwealth? Stars knew she was already doing what she could for the people of her village.

"You've the look, Locksley," whispered a voice from behind her, his breath kissing her bare shoulder.

She smiled. "What look would that be? Euphoria? Contentment?"

"Death." Lord Marion of Knighton stepped beside her, anchoring his elbow around her neck. "I'd believe your demise to be imminent but for all the produce and dairy goods stockpiled in your gown. Your people are fortunate. I, too, live for rare fruits." He picked an apple from the outermost pocket on her hip, tossing it in the air with a conspiratorial grin before taking a bite.

"If you know who the food is for, why are you stealing it from me? Take from any of the dozens of tables around us!" she hissed, smacking him lightly in the chest, all the while ignoring the glances of judgment from those nearest her.

"Shh!" a stout baroness puffed, her long, gaunt face souring with annoyance.

"Please excuse her. She is unwell," Marion said, indicating Ella with his partially eaten apple. He bowed his head respectfully, earning a *tsk* of disapproval from the woman as he escorted Ella toward the exterior walls of the ballroom.

"Always the troublemaker, you are." He removed his arm from her shoulders, facing her at last.

"Indeed. Minding my own business makes for quite the spectacle. And what about you? I can smell the mead you've sampled from here."

"Mead a merry man makes, darling," he replied, plying her with his affable disposition, curving his lips up into a wily grin.

He was handsome, this Lord Marion, though she'd known him long before lordship — practically her entire life. In truth, he'd become lord of the manor far too young, losing his mother in childhood and his father only four years past to the plague that had taken her father and too many others.

He was a better sibling than either of her stepsisters could ever have hoped to be. She linked her arm through his, leading him along the outskirts of the festivities. "Perhaps merry, but also malodorous."

Marion snorted. "What else was I to do? These soirees are so damn boring!" He raised an eyebrow at an eavesdropping duke stationed before him. "What? Are *you* having fun?"

The duke merely shrugged, returning his attention to Prince Johan's musings as Ella stifled a laugh, grateful for the companionship of her friend. The din of Johan's voice carried throughout the hall, with a processional of gifts bestowed by Chamelaute drawing hearty applause. Emissaries from Llundyn's overseas neighbor stepped forward in turn, presenting the king with delicacies, fabrics and riches native to their lands. Princes Riccard and Johan looked on, flanking their father as he raved over the wealth of goods before him.

"Prosperous nations trading extravagant favors," Marion scoffed. "What a privilege it is to watch them honor one another thusly."

Ella bumped her hip against Marion's. "You sound rather bitter, you know."

"Not at all, for I shall make them share the bounty." He wagged his brows, amusing Ella with his arrogance.

No doubt, he would.

Ella glanced toward the dais where the king examined each treasure, his rotund face alight with joy. The princes watched on from behind King Edward, entertained by the wonder that His Majesty expressed with each passing offering. The trio of men made for a curious assortment of kin, but she was fascinated all the same.

A deafening roar burst forth, shattering the serenity of the eventide fete with a gusting blow and generating a dense cloud of debris that obscured the presentation. Ear-piercing screams followed as panicked nobles clambered away from the balcony, darting toward the numerous exits off the foyer, heedless of their surroundings.

A short, balding duke sent Ella stumbling into a stone pillar, her shoulder colliding with the unforgiving column. She sucked in a sharp breath, willing the pain of the impact away as she righted herself.

"Are you all right?" Marion slid an arm around her waist, tenderly guiding her toward himself and shielding her from further collisions. He turned her slowly, brushing the curve of her collarbone with light fingers. "Ella, are you —?"

"I'm fine!" She bit her lip, stifling the tears that threatened to form, as much due to injury as they were due to dust. "What happened?"

Marion shook his head, clasping her bare arms with gentle hands as he took her in. The sun-kissed skin of his face paled, his lips forming a grim line as his gaze wandered from the tips of her well-worn boots to the top of her newly disheveled hair. "You appear to be whole, at least," he muttered, surveying the chaos behind her. His eyes widened as he watched, even as he failed to veil the sudden horror settling over his face.

Ella twisted within his hold, but his arms were unyielding. So intent was he upon denying her answers. "Marion, please! What's wrong?"

"It's the king," Marion breathed. "I think King Edward is dead."

Chapter Six

Sunlight slipped through the hand-woven threads of the tightly drawn window coverings, forging a path of gold atop the stone floors underfoot to where Prince Riccard brooded. Silently, at the head of his father's table, he considered the many ways in which he'd failed the king—and not only on the night when his heart had beat its last.

He had resisted his father at every turn.

His Majesty's Royal Council had met at that very table only days before. Ric had been there, hungover and disheveled, but he had gone. That same council had met there only hours earlier, this time with none but Ric to lead them. It had been bedlam, with opinions bandied about like badminton shuttlecocks, aimless and haphazard.

Ric should stay. Ric should go. He should declare war, or, perhaps, pretend his father's murder had never occurred. All in the interest of preserving the kingdom, it was. To hell with what was *right*. He'd gotten an earful from a bunch of witless, gutless men with no understanding of what it was to live a life outside the precious confines of nobility.

Disgusting. The whole lot of them.

Ric traced the blood-red veins along the table's surface with his fingertips and he closed his eyes, as if with a wish that it could be undone. Exhaling slowly, he clenched his fists, his knuckles whitening as he struck the tabletop. The sound was swallowed by a suffocating sense of foreboding lurking amongst the shadows of the castle. So much of his time had been spent fleeing duty, and it had finally caught him by the throat.

"My men and I will leave at first light." Ric's words were coated in bitterness and despondency that the wayward nation could not afford. He rubbed his throbbing leg—a minor injury earned yesternight as a result of the blast that had stolen his father.

Marion hesitated, the tension in the room driving him to distraction. "Your duty is to your people."

"Do you believe me so dull that I would think otherwise?" Ric pushed himself from the table, turning his back to his brother and Marion. "My very life belongs to the people, which is why my men and I must make haste and leave at once."

"It would be ill-advised to pursue war before your coronation," Marion urged. "Spirits are uneasy as it is and they're looking to you, whether you wish it or not." He knew the prince's heart to be for his countrymen, but there remained a reluctance in yielding to the divine will of his birthright. A land without secured rule was a vulnerability that could meet with unmitigated carnage.

It was as good a time as any for Prince Johan to voice opposition, but no words were uttered in favor of either argument. Though Johan had often remained impartial to the disagreements between his older brother and the Lord of Knighton in the past, it was hardly the time to keep his mind hidden.

Instead, he shifted uncomfortably, his arm bound tightly to his chest to ease the pain of his dislocated shoulder—more trauma resulting from the butchery the night before. His face remained unreadable as always, the thoughts within a jumble of raw emotions as he measured their alternatives.

"You wish to abandon the kingdom, then, for that's how your subjects will see it. They will think you a coward who ran from his duty to the throne." Johan's words were quiet and sharp, like poison on his tongue.

The elder prince met his eyes, his body rigid with the promise of impending war. "Ah, there it is, brother. Perhaps it's you who thinks me a coward." Riccard laughed without humor at the thought. "Is it not *I* who demands vengeance? Am I not the one who is prepared to lose my own *life* to pursue justice? A dastardly offense, indeed."

Outwardly, Johan maintained control, though his eyes blazed with contempt. The princes were vastly different men—one wearing responsibility as an honor to be revered, while the other did all he could to evade the Crown's expectations.

Long before their titles had demanded obedience, he, Riccard and young Lord Marion had spent their days together. Even then, there was no mistaking any one of them for the other. He was analytical and deliberate in everything he did, while Ric lived with an effervescence that never failed to draw discipline.

Marion was most like the elder of the two brothers — bold to be sure, but always calculated in action. Between Marion and Ric, there was never a challenge left unmet, from thievery amongst the councilmen in broad daylight to tricks perpetrated on the most esteemed members of the court.

And while it had been the lord and heir apparent wreaking most of the havoc, it was the cunning artifice he authored that kept them from meeting severe punishment with regularity.

The brotherhood shared between him and the two had been steadfast, and moments of discord were sparse, despite their contrasting temperaments. They'd been bonded by allegiance to one another — the sanctity of loyalty outweighing any personal interests.

This was different.

"It is commendable to be willing to risk yourself for your people, but it's here you are needed. If you desire a postponement of your coronation, so be it, but I beg of you, be by my side to bury our father." Johan's tone was calm, even as he reasoned with the likelihood that all he spoke was in vain. He rubbed his bloodshot eyes, which had not yet rested since his return home. There was no sleep to be had following the tragedy that had shaken the whole of the kingdom.

"Our foes will expect me to do so, which is why we cannot tarry. Nothing I can do would serve his memory better than avenging his murder." Ric took a deep breath, twining his fingers behind his back as he paced the length of the room. "His soul has passed. He doesn't need me to be there."

"You will meet your death at their shores." Marion dared to utter the words that undoubtedly plagued all their minds. Chamelaute was vast, its populace far outnumbering that of Llundyn's. The forces of their territories nearly tripled Ric's armies, making his quest for retribution a mission of suicide.

"It is a risk I'm willing to accept." Ric regarded Marion and Johan in turn, his demeanor suffused with determination. "For the prosperity of Llundyn."

His proclamation hung in the air—a harbinger of doom, despite the courage of his conviction. Marion averted his gaze while Johan stiffened, his brow furrowed in agitation. They had reached an impasse. No matter the price, the future of Llundyn had declared war.

Riccard retreated to the head of the table in a few short strides, brushing his hands along the embroidered stile of his father's chair. The late king had strategized there and confided in his most trusted advisors. There, His Majesty had sat with the High King Luther of Chamelaute, making plans to further unity and peace between the lands.

Peace.

It had been obliterated with one violent act that would not go unpunished.

"Upon my return, I will be crowned king. No sooner." Ric turned on his heel to leave, unwilling to waste any more precious time before his departure.

"I do believe you a coward," Johan said, revealing the truth of his heart as Ric approached the doorway. "I may well not delight in war, but I do not fear the weight of our titles. Go then to your demise. Wage war against an army that is certain to level you with a mere sweep of its palm."

Riccard turned, his lip curled in offense. "We are, indeed, bound by our blood, but I remain the rightful heir, little brother. You may take the crown when I am lowered into the ground. Until then, I am your king, and you'll regard me as such." Each word was brandished to sting, as if they could be forged into daggers at will. With a final twist of the blade, Riccard reached for the knob, hurling the door open as he stormed away.

Chapter Seven

Sheriff Dane's carriage cleaved the sodden earth beneath its creaking wheels, forging deep furrows along the gravel road leading to the castle gates. It had been dreary and gray since morning. Mist nourished the sapless underbrush of Sherwood for the first time in months, and it seemed fitting enough to Ella for the king to be honored in such a manner.

Guards stood on either side of the entrance, with the towering passage heavily manned since the fateful night of the banquet. Their shadowed eyes revealed overburdened fatigue. Prince Ric's call to arms against Chamelaute and its despicable misdeeds was taking a visible toll. Along with his retinue of advisors and two chiliads of men, he had departed silently shrouded by the blackness of eventide, leaving the Royal Guard crippled by stark numbers in the absence of the kingdom's most superior forces.

"It is sweet that you believe your presence will offer consolation to the prince," Rosalind simpered from beside Ella. "Do you truly think so highly of yourself? As if you could charm a future king."

"Prince Riccard is gone," Kinsley corrected, though she didn't push the statement any further.

"Perhaps I wasn't referring to him." She cast a blistering scowl in Kinsley's direction, smoothing a hand over the bodice of her mourning gown.

Her speech was treasonous.

While Ella, too, had considered how Llundyn might stand to improve under the leadership of Prince Johan, convinced as she was that the younger prince was better suited for the burdens of sovereign rule, the crown was the eldest's birthright. To speak in such terms was a betrayal of the monarchy and the history that governed their nation.

But then again, it was no surprise that Rosalind would be the disloyal type.

Margaret reached across the sluggish coach, pinching Rosalind's cheeks. She swatted her mother's hand away, her face rosy with a counterfeit blush as the women of Locksley waited to be escorted through the abbey into the magnificent cathedral of Llundyn for the king's remembrance.

"Try to behave yourself today, Ember, dear." Rosalind patted Ella's leg in a faux display of comradery, evincing no regard for the solemnity a day such as it was demanded. "Don't think I didn't notice how you attached yourself to those poor men at Prince Johan's banquet. You'll do yourself no favors with self-flattery. They were merely polite hosts."

"How foolish of me." Ella feigned discomfiture, splaying her fingers across her chest. "To think that *I* could seduce a crowned prince. Indeed, they would never look upon a lowly heiress with any esteem. They would undoubtedly look beyond my noble lineage in favor of a villein with no title of her own."

Margaret released an exasperated breath but made no effort to chide Ella. Creases of age across the widow's forehead grew more pronounced as she glowered at her stepdaughter, the thin lines around her lips deepening. Beauty had always served her well, earning her affection and wealth over decades of misuse, but the radiance of youth had abandoned her in more recent years.

High cheekbones that were once enviable had become harsh. Her flesh stretched tightly over the sharp edges as if it would tear at the slightest touch. Wizened skin sagged beneath her eyes, accentuated by the bluish veins visible under her dull pallor.

When Ella looked upon her countenance, she saw Rosalind's future in Margaret's sallow profile.

Would that Ella might age with the grace of her mother, may she rest in peace. She believed Lady Locksley had perished early as a mercy from God — that her work in this life had been completed, and as a reward, she had been granted safe passage to her eternal home.

The sheriff's coachman opened the door, offering a gloved hand to Lady Margaret as she stepped carefully down the iron steps. Sheriff Dane was there to greet them with his fist over his heart as he swept into a somber bow. Ella and her stepsisters arranged their skirts, each making room for the next to exit. The smooth black silk of their gowns had undoubtedly required enough coin to feed a small village.

Her stepmother had hired the royal seamstress in Nottingham not but a day following the banquet, and their dresses were breathtaking. Though she, her mother and stepsisters wore differing cuts, the dark threads of their garments were pure and finely spun. Under the flickering luminesce of the candlelit sconces within the abbey, an understated cobalt shimmer moved within the material, mimicking the skies of midnight. Ella felt selfish wearing such finery, accompanied by unyielding guilt because she also felt beautiful.

Lowering caged veils over their eyes, the women followed Sheriff Dane as he guided them through the austere halls of the abbey, Lady Margaret's arm tucked inside his. The stone corridor was chilling, each step they took echoing between narrow walls as if the ghosts of generations past imitated each footfall as they made their way through.

"I trust you found my coach to your liking?" The sheriff's words cut into the stifling silence, and for once, Ella was relieved to hear him speak. She'd been inside the abbey before, but something about the stagnant corridors had her on edge.

Margaret intertwined her fingers with his, as though their relationship was a secret only the two of them shared. "It was. You were too kind to send for us."

Ella scoffed, for she doubted very much that he'd sent it out of kindness. Every facet of his courtship with her stepmother was calculated. But then again, the same could be said of Margaret. *Perhaps they deserve one another after all.*

The cathedral was as gaudy as Ella had recalled. There was beauty in the intricate designs of the stained-glass windows and the craftsmanship of the wooden pews, but she preferred the quaint chapel just beyond the lands of Locksley. The people there were humble and genuine, always reminding her what a blessing they were to Llundyn.

After what felt like ages, she moved alongside Sheriff Dane and the others to their pew. They were escorted to the proscenium of the cathedral, joining the company of the most high-ranking citizens of Llundyn.

"To think he thought it appropriate to leave before his father could be buried!" a plump woman seated behind them uttered. Her words were spoken to her husband alone, but her whisper was like a toddler's during a Sunday service. "With any fortune, he won't return."

More treason. Ella understood why the elder prince had left so hastily. Even as the sanctuary filled with those who came to offer sympathy, it was a gathering void of any honest fondness for the royal family.

The man next to the buxom woman grunted in agreement, and Ella's stomach lurched. She wasn't impressed with the heir, either, but to articulate such cruelty in the wake of tragedy was unseemly.

A wave of empathy for the prince emboldened Ella as she turned, recognizing the pair as Lord and Lady Greer. She remembered the whispers at her mother's funeral service from callous women hoping to gain title through her father. The same was true at his funeral, with many noblemen attempting to convince her to become their bride when she came of age.

"In Calaise, those who speak treason against the king are hanged without a trial." She smiled tightly as her remark met with a glare from Lady Greer that could've charred her to ashes. For Ella, it was only fodder for the flames.

"Or perhaps our new king simply desired to avoid a citizenry that wishes to use his father's untimely death as a foothold to gain position in his court," she continued, undeterred. "Do you think it possible?"

"Put away your serpent's tongue, or I will cut it off for you." Lady Margaret fixed Ella with a piercing scowl. Ella quirked her lips, offering a shrug of indifference as her stepmother's eyes narrowed in warning. Yet she knew the threats were hollow. Lady Margaret wouldn't push her any further, not in the presence of Llundyn's most prominent.

The cathedral doors groaned, and light from outside spilled into the center aisle of the sanctuary. Lowering her head in reverence, Ella kissed her fingers, pressing them to her heart as King Edward's uniformed pallbearers entered, carrying his coffin between them.

Even with eight men ferrying the ornate box, the weight of it looked ponderous. Prince Johan led the processional with Marion opposite him, each of them bearing a pole upon their shoulders.

Hushed criticisms of Prince Riccard's absence followed the cortege as they marched in tandem past the packed rows of pews. The youngest prince was the only remaining member of his family in Llundyn to honor the former king, and he looked very alone, even with Marion by his side.

His blank expression had Ella's heart breaking anew, knowing of the grief that he faced firsthand. It was easy to think of the sovereign leadership of Llundyn as other—inaccessible, hardened, detached. The nature of their positions had them all so utterly superior that it was easy to forget that they, too, had feelings.

Following the service, the assembly relocated from the cathedral, trickling into the banquet hall where they had all assembled days before in celebration of Prince

Johan's return home. Being there once more caused a flood of conflicting emotions. Indeed, it was as though the explosion that had stolen the High King from Llundyn had never occurred, with every vestige of damage erased in only a few days' time.

That was a blessing and a curse, in Ella's estimation, for moving forward was essential in the face of all that had transpired, but remembrance was also imperative. The kingdom had already lost so much during the plague and continued to feel the desperation of famine. The loss of King Edward was yet another blight on a country already struggling for survival.

Ella glanced at the prince as they drifted ever deeper into the sea of mourners—an undulating mass that vowed to hold them hostage with refreshments and small talk well into eventide. His dark eyes caught her gaze, lingering long enough for Rosalind to take notice.

"Stop ogling," she spat. "You're certain to thwart any further conversation for the rest of us by doing so."

"Is that meant to be a deterrent?" Ella's eyebrows rose in mock curiosity. Rosalind rolled her eyes, dragging Kinsley along with her to distance themselves from any persisting humiliation their stepsister might inflict.

Sheriff Dane had swept Lady Margaret away the moment they'd shuffled through the receiving line, so Ella was left to herself. Her only remaining objective was the avoidance of Gisbourne, who had somehow managed to creep nearer, despite her efforts to maintain a firm barrier between them. Still, his attention span was like that of a whelp, easily distracted by all the distressed maidens. It wouldn't be that difficult.

And if they were stupid enough to seek comfort from the likes of him, they would sooner regret it.

Ella found the cavernous space of the banquet hall to be nothing short of stifling as she made her way to a curtained alcove — a semi-private anteroom that would allow her to be alone with her thoughts. Full of the supposedly bereaved, the atmosphere struck her as more a celebration than any sort of last rites. The kingdom was as stocked as it had ever been with those who aspired to higher positions and loftier gains.

Peering through a corner window, Ella fervently wished to be anywhere but there. The pretense of cordiality was a bridge too far, with the familiar sense of loss threatening to eat her alive.

"My lady."

Ella turned to find Prince Johan. His broad shoulders brushed the curtains on either side of him as he entered the modest space, his countenance weary but warm.

"I wanted to thank you personally for being here today." The words were like velvet, his breath softly brushing her cheek as he leaned nearer.

"There are no words to express my sympathies, Your Highness." She curtsied, dropping her gaze to the floor between them.

"Please, call me Johan." He reached for her hand, his mouth tipping at the corners. "The weight of title is laborious enough, is it not, Ella of Locksley?"

"That it is," she agreed, smiling at last. "And you must also call me Ella."

"Very well then, Ella." He brought her hand to his lips, pressing them against her knuckles. "I only hope this day has not caused your own painful memories to resurface."

"My heart has mended with time, as will yours." She was both surprised and flattered that the prince would be concerned over her loss in light of the grief he'd suffered. He seemed to be handling himself far better than most would under such circumstances.

"The world is far more resilient with a soul like yours treading upon it," Johan said. "Perhaps you could lend me a portion of your strength until I am graced with the good fortune of your company again?"

Ella's smile grew, for the prince had a canny way with words. "You're too generous with your compliments, I fear. I endure solely by God-given impudence that I've not been able to rid myself of, despite my stepmother's greatest efforts."

Amused by her candor, the prince laughed, drawing the attention of many noblemen and women who gawked as they struggled to sight the pair hidden just beyond the crimson draperies.

"I thank thee," he managed, having recovered himself. "You've done unfathomable good for my soul. Until we meet again..." He offered a shallow bow before backing away, a hint of a smile on his face as he returned to the aggrieved within the hall.

Ella curtsied, though too late. She was foolish to believe that he'd meant anything by singling her out, yet she hoped. He was casual in a way that made him seem almost common — thoughtful beyond measure, with a wicked sense of humor she'd never have guessed a man of his stature would possess.

It also didn't hurt that he was beautiful to look at.

Chapter Eight

Nottingham.

Visiting the shire was an unfortunate necessity at times. Ella preferred to frequent the establishments run by her villagers, but there was no blacksmith among them who could forge a weapon like Little John.

'Little' was a bit of a stretch when it came to John, for he was as formidably built as a plow ox—and churlish as one, too. The junior John of the family Smythe, he kept the kingdom in fine armament alongside his father, who was also John.

Their shop was a modest one near the center of town, filled to bursting with tools and tackle in various stages of completion. The scent of smelting metal and sweat hit Ella powerfully as she neared, the doorway leading to their workspace thick with hot, stagnant air. She was steeling herself for entry when she noticed the sheriff sauntering into the town square.

The arrogant bastard. His hubris was evident as he strode, his hooded cape flowing lightly in the breeze as he ascended the steps of the dais oft used by the town herald. Indeed, he might've been mistaken for royalty if one didn't know better — and Ella *did* know better.

His self-assurance in public was a far cry from the scorned servant to the Crown she witnessed in the privacy of her own home. Courtesy of his frequent visits with her stepmother, Ella was well aware that he felt under-appreciated and overworked by his betters in the castle.

Pity.

Sheriff Dane raised his hands, a bland expression affixed to his unpleasant face. "People of Nottingham, your attention, if you please!"

Blowing out a huff, Ella paused once more in the entryway. It was as fine an excuse as any to enjoy a little more fresh air before journeying inside. She leaned against the frame, crossing her arms in impatient expectation as she prepared for what would surely be another tiresome sermon from the idiot sheriff.

The villagers gathered, offering the man their attention as they squeezed nearer to the platform. In an act that was quite unnatural for the boorish lawman, he smiled, taking a deep breath.

"The citizenry is fortunate, for we've the blessing of unequaled leadership in a time of great trial. Where lesser kingdoms would crumble under the weight of tragedy, we've flourished. Yes, we have grown!"

More than a few brave pragmatists grumbled their dissent from the crowded square as Ella rolled her eyes. In truth, a rousing speech from the constable was the last thing she expected. The sentiment was absurd.

"Good people," Dane continued, "the fight for restoration in the face of such adversity stretches beyond our borders to Chamelaute, but the battle will not be won there alone. Here, at home, our support is imperative. The very life of our future king depends upon it!"

"Riveting, no?" Little John stepped through the doorway, both hands occupied with the polishing of a finely crafted rapier — a peculiar choice of weaponry for a Llundynien. "Methinks ulterior motives are afoot."

"You don't say." Ella eyed the sheriff warily. "Heavens, John. Would he dare to mislead the commonwealth?"

"Never," John gruffed, drawing a giggle from Ella. John wore his contempt for the sheriff on his sleeve, just as she did.

"Have you defected?" Ella brushed light fingers over the hilt of the savage sword. "It looks like the blade of a Calaisean."

"In fact, it is. At least, I think so." John furrowed his brow in thought, but he shrugged it away. "A small band of them passing through. Their coin is solid, at least."

Dane's features blazed with urgency when he resumed. "Prince Riccard requires our assistance now more than ever. My fellow citizens, the only aid we may grant the future of the Crown, is that of our financial offerings. Thus, we are redoubling taxes to cover the wages of war. It is a small price to pay for the safety of our king and kingdom."

The goodwill of the people collapsed in an instant, agitation evident in the form of angry faces and clenched jaws. A collective grumble burst forth, shattering the calm of an otherwise mild afternoon as the gathered villagers seethed.

"Redoubling?" someone challenged. "Preposterous!"

"You are out of your mind!" another man yelled, pumping his fist. Ella recognized him as the village butcher, ordinarily a man of spare words. Not today. The crowd around the firebrand reeled with barely contained fury as he continued. "We cannot afford our current levies. How are we to produce double?"

The false mask of Sheriff Dane's compassion slipped, revealing the serpentine smile of a man with too much power and little restraint. "You will find a way. And, if not, perhaps you shall die trying!"

"Shame!" the crowd wailed as one, the chant of reproof rising above the burgeoning fray. Onlookers wasted no time in making their displeasure known, scaling the columns supporting the dais as they made their way toward the sheriff. His men struck the rebels away one by one from their lofty stronghold, easily besting the blindsided villagers.

Unmoved by the animus of the townspeople, Dane indicated the butcher with a steady finger, sending his entourage into action. Fists flying, the man was brought to his knees at the center of the platform in a whirl of thrashing cloaks, with Sheriff Dane standing triumphantly over him.

Ella's heart thumped a riotous beat in her chest as she observed. The people were simply overwhelmed — in desperate need of hope even before the untimely announcement. Would that she could speak some reason, bring about some resolution that would save them from this burden. And the butcher... If only she could rescue him from his fate.

As if he'd read her mind, Little John placed a comforting hand on her shoulder, his face grim. "He should know better, Elle. We all do."

She shook his hand away, soured by the defeat evident in his tone. "Courage, John. Lord help us if we cannot muster enough fortitude to combat the likes of Sheriff Dane. We shall not yield to corruption—his or anyone else's."

Little John sighed, nodding soberly. "Indeed. Leave it to a tiny noblewoman to remind me so."

She sniffed haughtily, elbowing the strapping blacksmith in the ribs. He cracked a tight smile, and Ella reached for his hand, giving it a squeeze that did little to make either of them feel any better.

"I take no pleasure in your plight, good people of Nottingham," the sheriff boomed, regaining the attention of the restless crowd. "Yet, as any respectable lawman would, I must put an end to the impudence of those who would dishonor the Crown. Thus, I shall have Robert's ear pinned to the stocks, the better to help him listen. Heed this warning, one and all, for insolence will result in far worse." Dropping his head to his chest in an act of insincere melancholy, the sheriff stepped aside, gesturing his men toward the kneeling butcher.

"Please!" Robert pleaded, his eyes wide with panic as the mob keened anew. "I will pay my fair share! Please!" His feet slipped beneath him as the sheriff's men dragged him upward, his struggle in vain against the four mammoth enforcers.

Sheriff Dane watched, his eager eyes trained upon the butcher as a smile tugged at the corner of his foul mouth. He savored violence as much as he relished power.

Ella turned away, burying her face in John's chest.

* * * *

Surveying the mountain of straw Ella had managed to shred did little to assuage her sullenness. While chores often did wonders for her spirit, this occasion left her with nothing more than blistered hands and an angry, bitter heart.

"Will you please eat something?" Much sopped up the remains of his stew with a crust of seedy bread. "Your stepmother will never know of your private hunger protest. Why let it go to waste?"

"It won't." Ella flopped dramatically onto a hearty pile of hay, wincing as an errant end stabbed her thigh. "Give it to Jasper or Tom."

"Already gave them twice your portion," Much answered around a mouthful of supper. "The whole of the manor has been fed a double portion, all from the leavings of Lady Margaret's table."

"It seems we continue to evade the plight of so many in Llundyn," Ella spat, pushing herself up onto her elbows. "How is it that so many suffer hunger and poverty while our wealth abounds?"

"You are a fierce patron for the needy, to be sure, but you know the rules that govern our ranks as well as I." Much silenced Ella's emerging rebuke with a single raised finger. "We are expendable, and you are worthy. It's that simple."

"It's anything but simple!" Ella cried. "My father would never have stood idly by as I did today. It's shameful! Enough is enough!" She rose to her feet, thundering toward the open barn door where she peered at her residence. The sheriff's carriage remained, bathed in the warm glow of candlelight streaming from the manor.

"The gall of that man. Will he never leave?" Ella had been relegated to the barn since she'd returned from town, knowing that a run-in with Sheriff Dane would not go well after all she'd witnessed that afternoon.

"What's to be done, lovely Ella?" Much raised his brows in question. Though his attempt at levity was well-meant, there was little he could do to quell the growing desire for action that burned within her.

Ella stilled, feeling hopeful for the first time in ages as a plan of attack took form. "Plenty. And we needn't wait any longer." She slid the barn door closed before gathering her parcels from the afternoon. "I'll sneak up the servant's companionway and change my clothes. Our deliveries tonight will be as bountiful as we dare, Much. Perhaps Lady Margaret's next feast will be more modest."

"Blazes, you're scaring me." Much grinned wickedly, slapping his hands together in anticipation.

Ella smiled in kind, grateful for a partner in crime who understood her better than the closest of brothers. "Good. A woman can be an excellent ally or a dangerous enemy. My stepmother has made her choice clear, and our people will not suffer for it."

"Indeed." Much anchored his long arm around Ella's neck, giving her a squeeze of approval before sending her on her way. "I'll prepare the horses and begin gathering rations while you dress."

"I'll bring you a spare cloak," Ella called over her shoulder as she made her way through the rear doorway. "Goodness knows what a baby you are when the wind picks up."

Much bowed low, issuing a sniggle of amusement. "Ever the altruist. I thank you, milady."

"Hurry up!" Ella demanded, deeply gratified in her renewed purpose. Idleness would never suit her the way it seemed to for so many nobles. And, perhaps her station could be of use after all, even if it were as a result of subterfuge.

She would see it through, come what may.

* * * *

Ella tucked the spare cape under her arm as she rounded the outer corner of the barn, a clever remark at the ready for her ardent companion.

The words died on her lips as Much came into view, his hands raised skyward. Sheriff Dane stood before him, sneering as he pressed the tip of his dagger into the soft flesh beneath Much's chin.

As if he sensed her presence, the sheriff's head snapped toward Ella. "Ah, dear girl. It seems you've a thief in your employ."

"What are you doing?" Ella's fists clenched as she moved toward the scuffle. Upon further scrutiny, it was apparent that she'd missed out on more than a little chaos as one of Dane's soulless eyes blackened before her. Much had remained unscathed thus far, though the vicious end of the blade at his throat promised the odds were not in his favor.

Setting her shoulders, Ella adopted the condescending air oft displayed by her noble peers, narrowing her eyes as she lifted her chin. "Good sheriff, I've no need for your services on my lands. I'm convinced this is only a misunderstanding."

"I am not." Lady Margaret stepped from the shadows, her imperious gaze falling upon Ella. She smiled in smug satisfaction, confident that she'd bested her charge in their constant fight for authority. "And these, my lovely daughter, are not your lands. Not yet."

Ella simply frowned, though her entire being blistered with fury. She wished very much to lunge at her stepmother and pound her to bits but was careful to conceal her wrath, knowing that the spiteful noblewoman would only have Much punished further in excess.

"The penalty for theft is the loss of a hand, while penance for thrashing an officer of the law is left to my discretion, including forfeiture of life." Sheriff Dane beamed, digging the point of his dirk into Much's jugular. "Death by gallows. A shame, is it not? Such a strapping fellow." He patted Much's shoulder in patronizing fashion, snickering all the while.

Ella knelt, bowing her head in deference to the volatile lawman. "Please, sir." Her words were a breathless plea that left her more bereft than before, servile to blooming desperation that was swiftly overtaking reason.

Her eyes met the dark stare of the sheriff when she lifted her head. There was no remorse there, only mirth — an ugly loathing that seeped into every facet of his being, producing a man who had no business enforcing his own self-serving form of law.

"Without a trial, Sheriff Dane?" The words had left her mouth before she'd fully weighed them. Challenging the man with a dagger was foolish, convincing Ella that her stepmother was right. She was an arrogant little girl, gambling with her meager influence in a system built against her.

Valid, though, as that assessment might be, she would not lose.

Ella rose, smoothing her damp hands over her trousers before squaring her shoulders. "The princes will be displeased, no doubt, when they learn of your arbitrary justice. Indeed, I believe they will find it quite distasteful." She held his stare, willing him to bend.

The sheriff snorted, grinning as he reveled in her candor. He was toying with her, with Much, and she was powerless. Would that her father was here, stoic and imposing. The sheriff would not laugh in his presence.

"Perhaps the hand, then, as an untimely death, no matter how deserved it may be, does require more explanation." Dane gathered a fistful of Much's shirt in his hand, yanking him nearer before shoving him toward the ground. "Kneel! I shall make it quick and clean if you cooperate."

"His hands are his livelihood!" Ella cried, clambering toward Much only to be warned away by the incensed sheriff as he turned his blade upon her. She pulled up short, raising her palms in submission. "Please, sir, grant mercy!"

"Perhaps the life after all, then, if it is mercy you desire." Dane drew his saber, the metal wicked and cold as it shone in the eventide moonlight. "For putting this poor fellow out of his misery would be merciful indeed."

Ella struggled in vain to control her shaking. "But—"

"Choose!" the sheriff bellowed, piercing the eerie quiet with his command. "You are the aggrieved party, after all. Choose, or I shall decide for you!"

"His hand," Ella breathed as the tears she was desperate to hold at bay streamed over her cheeks. A bleat of despair tumbled from her lips, a vulgar note in the frigid air and wholly unladylike. It was the sort of reaction that would have Much in fits of laugher, were he not in dire straits.

Her fault. It was all her fault.

Ella's gaze found his, wide and frantic, carving her heart in two when he found the fortitude to smile. Ever the model of obedience, he extended his arm, the only hint of his fear vaguely evident in his trembling fingers.

She bowed her head, determined to stay conscious as the sheriff's sword found its mark.

Chapter Nine

Ric approached the beaches unaccompanied, and while there was a possibility that he was being set up, a greater part of him still believed that Chamelaute remained an ally. Though he thought it wise to have brought his men as a show of force, reason had overtaken the demand for justice until clarity was obtained.

Anchoring his boat, he tucked away the oars, shedding his boots and hose for carrying as he waded barefoot through the waters to dry land. The scent of the sea air and the breeze skirring off capped waves served as reminders. He knew these territories and the people they held.

His very soul had been conflicted since his father had been murdered, and reconciling the struggle between instinct and fact was a galling trial of logic. What had begun as a crusade to avenge his father had quickly shifted into an errand to understand the motives behind a seemingly indiscriminate attack.

The words of Marion echoed in Ric's ears. If there were to be a war, then the fight surely would have greeted them on the beach where he now stood. Instead, Ric locked eyes with those of an esteemed denizen of the region—a highly sought individual who was known for his wisdom and professed foreknowledge.

The man was raving mad.

He stood alone on the shores of Chamelaute with nothing more than a walking stick crafted from the barbed wood of a blackthorn tree in his hand. A snow-white beard shrouded deeply tanned skin, and his hooded eyes shone with lambent citrine hues of honey as he stared intently at the prince.

In years past, when Riccard had come to train with King Luther's men, he'd seen the odd fellow roaming the bustling streets of the square. Whispers had followed the wanderer, and people throughout the villages gossiped about his peculiar ability to see beyond the present. Even his brother, Johan, had been allured by the illustrious Seer's claims of what was to come.

"Am I to believe it pure coincidence that I would be met here by the All-Knowing himself?" Ric's tone was thick with mockery while his posture exuded affability, his arms outstretched genially. He never had himself believed in the Seer's alleged abilities, but there was no question that King Luther did. It seemed unlikely that the king would risk someone so valuable to him if he had, indeed, provoked war with Llundyn.

"All-knowing, I am not," the man replied. His strange eyes lifted skyward as he raised his head toward the heavens. "I have been entrusted with a gift beyond my comprehension. It's a simple courtesy to do my best in helping others when I'm granted the opportunity."

Ric nodded, his eyes scanning the grounds beyond them both for foes. A half-smile formed on his face. "Very well, then. Might I ask your business here, sir?"

"I've already stated my intent, Your Highness." Gentle winds swept off the vast waters, and the man tightened his long robe around himself. "And your business is retribution, is it not? Yet, you've left your men behind. You must believe Chamelaute innocent in the crimes committed against your king." Planting his staff in the ground before him, he set off, following slowly behind it as if it were the rod guiding him rather than the other way around.

Ric watched as the Seer shuffled across the sand, and before he could question his sanity, he found himself keeping stride alongside him. Together, they made their way into one of the outer villages without speaking another word. While he didn't believe the man a prophet, he was also convinced that he'd already be dead if King Luther had so intended.

He'd been foolish to have gone ashore alone without any further proof of Chamelaute's innocence, yet there he remained, unscathed. It was impulsive, but better he learn the truth before sacrificing the lives of his company.

"If you know as much as they say, then who is to blame for my father's death?" Ric's inability to hold back the only question that mattered shamed him. Here he was, utterly skeptical of the Seer's supposed abilities, only to issue a desperate plea for answers, despite it all.

The man's steps halted. Swirling dust from the well-trodden footpath came to rest at his feet as the two men regarded one another. His gaze held empathy but betrayed no knowledge of what may have unfolded, no promise of vengeance for the prince or his people.

Though Riccard hadn't trusted the Seer's visions as a premonition, he had dared to hope that maybe, somehow, he could lead him in the right direction. In truth, he was as lost as he'd ever been. There on foreign soil, and without the guidance of his father to reassure him, he felt completely powerless.

"There are consequences to what I share, Your Highness," the Seer replied slowly. "When first I discovered that I possessed certain insights, I betrayed them, and many have suffered as a result."

"Or maybe you're nothing more than a skillful liar, as I'd suspected," spat the prince.

"Is that why I alone anticipated your arrival on this day of all others? Would not the king have sent his most capable defenses to receive you, had he been awaiting retaliation?"

There was no use questioning the soundness of his point, much as Ric wished to deny his claim.

"I have not made him aware of your circumstances," the Seer continued, wandering onward as he dispensed his wisdom. "I thought it best you do so yourself. He thinks very well of you and will be grieved to learn of the great trauma you've endured."

Ric groaned, following the foolish man, nonetheless. The trek leading to the palace gates was not but a few miles from the beach, so perhaps it was his nerves that made the journey feel like an eternity. Now, it wasn't so much that he believed King Luther had committed the nefarious crimes against Llundyn, more that his presence made it evident that Chamelaute's innocence had once been in question. To offend such power could instigate the very war Ric wished to avoid.

Luther had a vigorous reputation. He was just, but by all accounts, possessed a temperament best left untried.

The prince's chaperone was a welcomed guest of the kingdom, but, to Ric's knowledge, was a foreigner himself, having fled his home and offering his gift as indemnification for the keeping of his true identity. Chamelaute had been the Seer's sanctuary, but from what or whom, Ric wasn't certain.

As they were escorted through the courtyard and the elaborate halls by the royal guards, Ric's heart thundered in his chest. Gifts from distant emissaries lined the walls—all tokens of goodwill between nations. But Ric knew better. Leaders had showered King Luther in an effort to encourage kinship, fearing the far-reaching influence they held.

Llundyn's influence was second only to that of Chamelaute's, creating an unassailable might once the two nations had leagued. To break the confidence maintained by their formers would mean the end of decades of peace—and abject failure before the crown had even set upon Ric's brow.

Upon entering the throne room, Ric walked to its northernmost end where the High King sat, elevated above the few members of the council who remained present. Prince Philippe, the heir to the throne, sat beside him. Both wore capes of amethyst velvet suitable only for sovereignty. The finery was embroidered with strands of shimmering gold and lined with the softest of all ermine fur, as pure and white as freshly fallen snow.

"Forgive me. We were not expecting guests." King Luther rose to his feet, addressing Riccard and his prized visionary. Prince Philippe joined Luther at his side.

Ric took a knee before the royals, his gaze downcast. "I would have sent word, Your Majesty, had my visit been planned." He hesitated before meeting the king's eyes.

Evidence of guilt had been the motivation propelling Ric's travels. He had left his country behind, intending to obliterate as much of Chamelaute in retribution as he could manage, knowing beyond any reasonable doubt that he would never return home once war had been declared. Yet, even clothed in all their finery, standing before him were men that he knew he trusted — men his father had trusted.

"My father is —" His words caught in his throat, the bitterness of their reality so stifling, he had to pause. He took a fortifying breath. "My father is dead."

King Luther glanced with urgency at the Seer, who nodded solemnly.

"I was given only glimpses, Your Majesty," the man admitted. "There was nothing to be done once I became aware of the High King's fate."

"Mere words cannot adequately describe my sympathies, Prince Riccard," Luther began, his countenance suddenly drawn with sorrow. "I've learned to keep my questions to myself when it comes to my Seer's insights. Edward's passing must have been quite recent, for my emissaries not to have sent word of his demise."

Prince Philippe cleared his throat, lips forming a grim line. "I, too, would like to offer my condolences, though I believe recent developments demand a change in title for you, King Riccard."

"Of course, Your Majesty. Please rise," King Luther uttered apologetically.

Riccard rose to his feet. It was the first time anyone had addressed him by his new title, whether it had been formally given him or not. He was the rightful heir, but the use of the term felt like bathing in a trough of acid.

"Unfortunately, it is never under good circumstances that we have the privilege of welcoming a new king. On behalf of the kingdom of Chamelaute, I offer our deepest regrets." Luther bowed his head, his fist clutched against his heart in tribute. "And while we are most pleased to have you here," he continued, pinning Ric with his piercing gaze, "I must inquire what has brought you to our shores. Truly, it seems a time when your country would be most appreciative of your leadership."

His words stung, pointed and canny as they hit their target. Ric shifted, squaring his shoulders in a fabricated show of confidence that felt as though he was no more than a child, playing the role of his father as he prepared to answer King Luther's question.

And answering the question would be a trick, indeed. It was a moment that had the potential to obliterate an alliance that had been maintained for decades.

As a boy, Ric's mother had scolded him for tugging at a loosened thread on his riding scarf, that pulling on that single string would unravel the entire material. Destroying his scarf hadn't been his concern that day, but rather the risk of being sent home early from the annual hunt.

There were consequences that came from trifling with sensitive things, and he was terrified. In stating his business, he could destroy his kingdom, even before having the opportunity to rule.

"Your Majesty, if I may, would you permit me to offer some light?" The visionary stepped forward, allowing Ric a chance to gather himself.

Luther nodded, a gracious smile forming at the corners of his mouth as he urged the mystic onward.

"Prince Riccard has set out to avenge King Edward's death," the Seer began.

Ric clenched his jaw. Would that the strange fellow might help him. It was a hell of an introduction. Perhaps he would've been better off speaking for himself.

"There were several unfortunate casualties," the Seer continued. "He intends that these crimes not go unpunished. There was evidence surrounding the loss that would suggest it was, in fact, Chamelaute that planned the assault. The use of materials attained from our *Potash* mines caused an explosion that ultimately took the life of King Edward, along with one of his guards and the two emissaries sent on your behalf to deliver your gift."

There was a sharp intake of breath, with those gathered in the chamber hissing amongst themselves in earnest. Ric was heartened, for he had not yet been arrested or executed. It seemed the Seer's words were held in high regard by everyone in Chamelaute — a true blessing in disguise.

King Luther and Philippe remained silent as they surveyed one another, their faces crumpled in bewilderment. Finally, Prince Philippe managed to articulate what they shared in the wordless exchange. "We sent no messengers or gifts, Your Majesty."

"I believe your claim as truth, but the question of who might have had access or motive remains," Riccard replied, his tone even, despite his uncertainty. "Though I arrived on your shores this day with my men prepared to fight for our nation, my better judgment assures me that our alliance stands firm. For to have martyred intermediaries is not your way, as I've learned in the months spent under your supervision over passing years. I wish to ask your forgiveness for doubting the fealty our nations keep."

"You are duty-bound to question every situation as a king." Luther placed his aging hand on Ric's shoulder, smiling with the kindness the prince remembered from his time among Chamelaute's court. "I would question your rule if you didn't."

"I thank you for your understanding, but I also must correct you. I chose to postpone my coronation ceremony to expedite my arrival here. I departed as soon as my men could be gathered to me."

"A bold statement of courage, to be sure, but you mustn't leave the throne unattended, Your Highness," the Seer interjected. "Your reluctance to accept the crown will only lead to ruin."

Luther watched as the man spoke, considering his words carefully before addressing him. "What is to be done, sire? We know there must be limits on what you share, but we require your aid."

Ric fought the urge to roll his eyes at Luther's naivety and fascinations with the bearded oracle's professions, though hesitantly, he too was intrigued by some of his observations.

"It's clear that we have been pitted against one another by a force that seeks to end our peace," Ric began before the Seer could respond. "It seems it would behoove us all to, by all appearances, convince whoever wishes to divide us believe they've been successful."

"Yes." Philippe thumbed at his manicured beard, contemplating the strategy. "To do so would likely stave off further attacks for a time."

"I agree, but I do not think it prudent to keep His Highness from claiming his rightful seat on the throne," King Luther added.

"Your Majesty, you are correct that he mustn't remain in Chamelaute," the Seer continued, his voice grating on Ric's patience as he proceeded to discuss him as if he were incapable of plotting matters of artifice himself. "He should return home at once, but he must keep his travels secret, even amongst his people."

The Seer approached Riccard, and he allowed the visionary to grasp his arms. Creped skin stretched across his boney hands, cold to the touch, while long, speckled fingers curled around the prince's wrists.

"You must trust your intuition and take the road less traveled into your kingdom," the mystic muttered, his eyes wide with the urgency of his mind's revelations. "If you heed anything I tell you, let it be this. Leave alone, and we who stand with you now and your second-in-command will be the only beings who will know you've left these lands."

With a raised brow, Riccard sighed. These mutterings were nothing more than what he'd already intended. It was smart to travel without an entourage. Nobody would anticipate the future ruler of a nation such as that of Llundyn to face the seas or woods alone, and it would allow him to investigate not only neighboring territories but his home as well, undetected.

"Before daybreak, I will take my leave," Ric settled. "I will return to my men offshore until then, and by all appearances, our actions will be perceived as negotiations of war."

As the prince attempted to free himself from the solid grip of a man over twice his years, the pressure of their meeting flesh intensified. When he leaned nearer to Ric, the warmth of his breath brushed against his stubbled jaw. "Remember," the visionary whispered to him alone, "all friends were once strangers. Do not ignore the musings of your instincts, or you will lead your lands to ruin."

His words were harsh and cryptic, causing the hairs of Ric's forearms to stand on end. Releasing his hold, the Seer stepped away, his eyes alight with warning. Refusing to let the eerie attentiveness shake his confidence, Ric bobbed his head in acknowledgment.

"We will stand beside you, son," Luther said, his brow creased with worry as the Seer wandered without another word from the throne room. "Let not our alliance falter." He reached for Ric, shaking his hand firmly before dismissing himself.

"Worry not, my friend," Prince Philippe added, offering a half-bow before following his father through a side door.

Well, then. In Ric's estimation, it could have gone better but it also could have been far, far worse. Now, all that remained was escaping his second-in-command without an entourage of soldiers for his journey home. Ric excused himself, exiting the palace as his thoughts raced in circles. Too many unanswered questions yet remained, but the union between Llundyn and Chamelaute stood firm.

For now, that would have to do.

Chapter Ten

The trees hung lower that day, lamenting alongside Ella as she moved through the lush foliage of Sherwood alone. Her thoughts warred, blaming her for the events that led her deep into the thicket without her steadfast companion.

It had all happened so quickly that she'd scarcely realized what had been taking place. The idea that any person could be so readily capable of mutilating someone without just cause had not crossed her mind. In truth, she'd thought it a display meant only to frighten Much into compliance, having naively assumed that an officer of the Crown would've intended only to make a point then show mercy as a mark of goodwill.

The sheriff was the embodiment of systemic partisanship. By blind chance, he'd been born into wealth and, therefore, position. It was a privilege gifted to an opportunistic wolf, a curse that had revealed the unsettling composition of his character.

She would never make the mistake of underestimating him again.

Nottingham square was conducting business as usual when she finally reached the edge of town. People carried on with their day, oblivious that her world had been severed at the seams.

Ella's first stop was a little-known healer, a woman who lived just within the tree line outside the common. A rival of the town apothecary, Clara was a wonder with elixirs, and her remedies were often far superior. She swore by a combination of willow bark and valerian root to ease the pain and aid in sleep. Her recommendation was a far cry from the topical treatment offered by the druggist, but she had not yet steered Ella wrong.

She left Clara's home with a satchel full of linen cloth and strict instructions for the brewing of the two curatives for Much's pain. Would that the remedies she'd procured bring him relief. Ella only wished she could do more.

A flurry of activity near the old tavern caught her attention as she made her way through the center of town. Approaching the source, she was surprised to find none other than Prince Johan himself.

The prince stood amongst his people, talking and laughing with them as if he belonged. It was nice to see spirits so high. To have a royal take the time to simply hear the thoughts of his subjects was uncommon, at best.

Beside Ella, a young boy broke free from his mother and ran to Johan, whispering something into his ear. He smiled at the boy, squeezing his slight shoulders before leaning down to share with the child a secret of his own. The boy beamed before running back to his mother, the prince's gaze following his trail with a crooked smile upon his lips.

The spare's hazel eyes lifted, catching Ella's. His smile grew, and she took it as an opportunity to approach. Nobody stopped her. Instead, people moved from her path until she stood before him.

"Your Highness," she greeted, holding her cloak as she dipped into a low curtsy.

"Hello, Ella," the prince offered warmly. Extending her hand to him, he pressed a kiss to her knuckles, and she suppressed a shiver as he brushed his mouth across her flesh.

"It's an unexpected pleasure to see you here today." His eyes gleamed with good humor, and she regretted not having the time to engage in casual conversation.

"For me as well, thank you," she began politely, but coy flirtation had not been what had brought her forward. She hesitated for a moment more before recovering her courage at last. "I'm afraid I've not come today in high spirits. Rather, I wish to bring to your attention the actions of one of your men."

Johan's brows knitted together in concern. "Please, do not feel as though you can't speak freely with me," he urged.

Ella nodded, her gaze falling to the dusty ground separating them. "Sheriff Dane, he—" Her voice shook as she struggled to force words into existence. Speaking of the horrors of those dark hours unleashed their harsh truth as reality.

"The sheriff accused a young man of Locksley, my dearest friend, of thievery from the estate. It was I who had asked him to assist me with the supplies, only your sheriff wouldn't hear it. As punishment, he demanded I choose—my brother's life or his hand." Recounting

Dane's alternatives made her seethe, her chest rising and falling in tandem with her quickening heartbeat.

She remembered Much's smile before cold steel had crippled his future, the way his lifeless hand had dropped to the ground. Prince Johan had the authority to invoke change, and if he wouldn't do it, she vowed to find a way to punish Dane herself.

His expression darkened. Drawing a deep breath, he closed his eyes

"Your position affords you the jurisdiction to strip Sheriff Dane of his standing, does it not?" Ella pressed, willing the prince to meet her gaze.

"As regent, my charge is limited." He took Ella's hand in his, his sympathetic eyes pinned to hers.

She puzzled at the gesture, but her frustration grew with his lack of response. "If you're trying to tell me you'll do nothing, then I have no more to say." She removed herself from his gentle hold, turning to leave. Just as she began to walk away, he reached for her, grasping her arm.

"Wait," he said with an urgency she hadn't anticipated. She hadn't expected him to say anything more at all. His hold shifted from her elbow down to her fingers. "Forgive me for being so forward, Lady Ella, but I cannot allow you to leave thinking I will not do my best to correct this grievous crime."

She scoffed, her eyes narrowing. "There's no correcting what happened, don't you see?"

Gasps and murmurs from the surrounding onlookers reminded her that they were not alone, and even further that she was not conversing with an average commoner. For anyone, much less a woman, to speak in such a vulgar manner to a crowned prince was inconceivable, but her words had met the day, and she regretted none of them.

He drew her nearer, his thumb slowly moving over the curves of each knuckle. "I will call the council together to determine what can be done, though I cannot promise action with my brother away," he said quietly.

Ella nodded, her heart fluttering with his touch. She cursed herself for letting it do so. And while his solution wasn't the retribution she sought, it was better than nothing, at least for the moment. She didn't deserve Johan's kindness, not after the way she'd disrespected him before the rest of the square, but he'd offered it just the same.

Someone cleared their throat from behind her, calling her attention away from the prince's touch. She glanced over her shoulder, finding John tapping her repaired ax against his open palm as he watched her intently.

"Thank you, Your Highness," Ella managed, all the while scrabbling to recover her poor social graces. She curtsied, her head dipped low in deference. "Will you excuse me?"

"Indeed." Johan bowed, departing with a roguish half-smile playing on his lips, and she found herself suddenly mindful of the missing heir. It was much like Prince Ric's. *Very much like his.*

It seemed her consciousness was replete with thoughts of men these days. She cursed herself again, irritated by their persistence in her mind. Turning, she prepared to engage with yet another male, this one grinning from ear to ear in a knowing way.

"My father said he'd seen you wander over here, so I thought I'd help you on your way," John said, only to waggle his eyebrows.

He had her temper flaring already.

She snatched the ax from his massive hand, stalking off without a word as he chuckled and kicking pebbled sand back at him for what his amusement implied.

At least with her back to him, he wouldn't see the flush coloring her cheeks.

"Someone, stop him!" a man exclaimed. Near the well stood Sir Thomas, a former vassal of the late king, pointing a fat finger in the way of a pickpocket. Ella's eyes followed the scoundrel as he cut through the modest assembly with ease. The hem of his dark cloak whipped, trailing after agile strides and taunting his target with the growing distance he set between them.

At least a man of Sir Thomas' standing could afford the loss and was, himself, a louse at best, having faked an injury to dodge his duty to the Crown. No more than a coward, he sought to reap the benefits of title without any intent to earn honorable regard.

Ella watched along with the rest of the square as the thief hurtled over an empty cart, striding toward a narrow gap between structures. But instead of disappearing and continuing through the opening, he scaled the vertical surface of the building, effortlessly launching himself from one wall to the opposite as he scurried up its side with deft precision.

Upon reaching the rooftop of the local cooper's shop, he thrust his seemingly weightless form atop it before continuing along the roof's edge, chunks of decrepit stone crumbling beneath his feet. The man was making sport of Sir Thomas, mocking him with every step.

But something was wrong.

He stumbled, teetering precariously on the disintegrating perimeter as he laughed, looking upon those gawking from below. As the man chortled, an individual similar in stature breezed by Ella. She noted the figure's attire, matching that of the fellow above them as the miscreant's double quietly fled the square.

It was a clever diversion if that was, indeed, what it was, and the duo seemed well-practiced. Ella knew she'd been away from Much for too long, but her instincts urged her to follow the man who'd slipped out of sight. He was now beyond the smokehouse and headed straight for Sherwood Forest.

She smiled, glancing back at the jester who moved as though he could walk on the clouds while he hollered down at his growing audience, and as much as she wanted to see how the performance ended, she quietly made her way out of town.

It wasn't long before Ella caught the duplicate's trail, following crumpled leaves and the branded soil he'd left behind. A light breeze had gathered strength enough to confuse her pursuit, using its gentle breath to sweep the earth of his feathery tread. Like a phantom, he eluded her until the flapping of wings betrayed his position. Ella peered around the trees, but the cloaked figure remained hidden.

It was only then that she realized how far she'd traveled.

To her knowledge, very few were privy to the secret of Major Oak—a mammoth tree at the heart of Sherwood where Ella and her companions had played in their youth. As children do, they had sworn one another to silence, that it might remain a haven for the rest of their lives. One of the four children had fallen victim to an infection that later took his life, and only three remained. Much had been there as well, but certainly wasn't now, given his recent condition. That left one final member of their oath unaccounted for.

Soundlessly, Ella edged over to the primordial timber, softly touching a thin layer of moss covering aged bark. Still, she heard nothing and feared that perhaps the potential accomplice truly had gotten away. Slowly, she pushed back the thick cords with her heart in her throat, finding the unexpected staring her straight in the eye.

Will Scarlet…with a dagger in his hand.

As a boy, it had always been Will of the four who'd kept a level head. He was reserved and cautious in everything he did, but times had changed.

"Ella?" Recognition colored her old friend's features, and his tensed stance relaxed, though the tip of his dagger remained at the ready.

Taking a careful step toward him, she dropped her small sack of supplies, tossing her ax at his feet as she raised her hands to show she meant no threat.

"I—I'm sorry." He tucked his blade into the waist of his woolen trousers. "I never meant to—"

"Don't apologize." Ella's mouth quirked into an amused smirk. "But I must say, I never thought Will Scarlet the thieving type. You're very good at it, you know."

He grunted. "Not good enough apparently, as you didn't have any difficulty catching onto our ruse. I'm surprised you're alone, not that you're incapable of looking out for yourself." He regarded the freshly sharpened blade lying in the rooted dirt before him. Pausing for a moment, his countenance darkened. "Please tell me it wasn't Much you were referring to in the square."

"It was." Ella cast her gaze toward the supplies she'd collected, her face troubled. Each time she recounted Much's fate, she was struck with grief.

"I know you well enough to know that you blame yourself for what happened. You said as much to the prince today."

Of course, he'd heard. She stiffened, considering how her rant must have sounded to all who'd been present, yet regretted none of it.

"What was said to be his crime?" he asked, leaning casually on the hollowed trunk of the oak, peeking beyond where she stood in its narrow opening.

"Stealing." Ella spat the word as if it were profane. "Though he's committed no real crime at all, nor have I. The goods we've distributed belong to me, and everyone knows it, but they're clinging to every second they can before I take full possession."

"Not many are as charitable as you, Elle. I've heard whispers of the villagers receiving aid, but none have known from where it came." His smile was familiar, reminding her of simpler days when they hadn't a care in the world. Running calloused fingers through thick black curls, he retrieved from his tattered cloak the pouch pilfered back in town. Metal clinked together as he handled it, sounding of a healthy loot.

"I haven't done a lot in the way of looking after others in a long time. But I remember what the sisters at the priory taught me about the Lord remembering the needs of those who fear Him. I trust you know where this could be used well." Extending the weighty bag to Ella, he dropped it, only to have it snatched away.

"Is this what I get for sticken' *my* neck out back there?" Will's flamboyant accomplice appeared out of nowhere, the coin jangling as he tossed it into the air above his palm. "Over my dead *rottin'* corpse, you'll hand hard-earned coin over to a harlot!"

His personality matched the excessive production he'd executed back in Nottingham. Ella stood aghast, attempting to come to terms with the thief and his insults.

Will cleared his throat. "Lady Ella, meet my abettor, Alan a Dale."

Ella turned, facing her new acquaintance. Piercing blue eyes appraised her, when awareness struck, the white-hot flames of his scrutiny shifting to Will.

"Are you completely daft? She's fair, I'll give her tha'. But she's nobility!" Alan fumed, pacing as he aired his every thought. "We'll be dragged to the pillory or secured in the stocks by noon tomorrow! No. *No.* That pompous swine'll see to it we're fed to the gallows, he will. All due to your tryin' to impress a lady!"

"She won't turn us in, and she's no prostitute, either. Ella and I are old friends. She may well be nobility, but she's been the one leaving food in the villages." True to his character, Will remained composed as he sorted through the confusion of their encounter. He'd always served as a peaceful intermediary, even as a boy.

When Will had been abandoned as an infant, the nuns who had raised him at Kirklees Priory had instilled in him the value of remaining even-tempered and diplomatic, a skill which seemed only to have matured with time.

"I was trying to share what we collected to help her cause along," he continued calmly. "Another friend of ours has been punished for what they've been doing. You know that we're better off than most."

"Aye, tha's true," Alan agreed, inclining his head toward Ella. "It's very kind of you, trying to help where you can, miss."

She shook her head, averting her gaze. It wasn't enough. She'd never be able to sustain all those in need with only her own means for scattering.

* * * *

After daylight had faded, Ella tended to Much's wound, doing her best to clean it and protect it from infection. Tuck had also been by after receiving word from Will of the unfortunate circumstances forced upon them. He'd prayed over Much as he rested, the discomfort quieted by swigs of the smelly brew and tranquil words of truth spoken by the friar.

The injury had begun to clot, but Ella remained diligent in tending to it. Rags soaked with blood littered the loft of the outbuilding where they'd stationed themselves, away from the prying eyes of Margaret and her stepsisters.

As Ella rinsed and boiled the soiled linen cloths, a new reality took shape. To filch further from Locksley would mean Much's life, and she would never risk him again.

Still, too many people were hurting, and she couldn't ignore the ever-growing need. She thought about her encounter with Will and the man named Alan. They were thieves, yes, but they only stole from those blessed enough not to want.

The solution, she knew, was risky, but doing nothing was no option. Indeed, her own little insurrection might be just what Nottingham required.

Chapter Eleven

Ric was being followed.

The bloody fool likely thought himself fleet of foot, but to the well-trained ears of the practiced hunter, it was as if a drunken elephant tailed him. The presumptive king had spent the balance of his youth in the woods, whether with King Edward's men or his close friends, locating their oft-invisible prey with nothing more than a keen sense of hearing.

Many times since he'd first noticed his clumsy shadow, Ric had altered his course, but the chase never ceased. His tag-along was no accident.

Still, Ric would give credit where it was due. The cretin was adept in staying hidden, needing only to grasp the exalted art of silence. Being pursued by the indiscreet nitwit was the least of Ric's concerns, at any rate. Or, perhaps, it warranted more attention, given his whereabouts.

Traveling alone through the forsaken territory of Wylewoode was less than ideal, but the only credible option given Ric's tenuous circumstances. Fording the fierce Bournesmouth Sound separating Chamelaute from Llundyn would've proven dire in his solitary state, lacking the expertise of the sea captain and his crew, though it would have had him home more quickly.

Instead, he was braving a woodland labyrinth brimming with peril, full of menaces as yet unknown to the intrepid young prince.

A blessing, indeed, that Ric's advisors were not privy to his exploits. And his father — oh, his father would see him thoroughly rebuked, though not without a hint of a jaunty smile upon his face. The king was a mischievous sort, always intrigued by the impulsive escapades of his boys.

But that no longer mattered. The realization was unwelcome, bringing with it another objectionable truth.

Edward was no longer king. Soon that would be Ric's burden to bear.

Sighing, and suddenly fed up with his uninvited companion, he paused. "Come out! I've no intention of leading you any farther. Show yourself at once!"

The silence was deafening, his rival having abruptly gone still.

"We're shy, are we?" Ric called, his tone thick with ire. "Well then, if you will not reveal yourself, I shall come to you." Wasting no time, the prince began to backtrack, stomping petulantly in the direction of his adversary. The idiot would regret his shenanigans, for Ric was in no mood for trifling.

To his great satisfaction, the fool was sent scrambling, no longer making any efforts to remain covert. He couldn't have asked for a more natural hunt.

Ric picked up speed, eager to bring the game of cat and mouse to an end.

There.

Mere meters ahead, his shadow appeared, cutting through the wild underbrush and knotted tree roots toward the decrepit pathway, mantle whipping behind him. The man was quick, but Ric was sure he'd be quicker.

Gaining on his foe, he took a flying leap, linking his arms around the scrawny stalker before tumbling to the packed soil beneath them. The clod took the brunt of the damage as Ric's large body landed atop him, forcing the wind from his lungs in one fell whoosh.

"Who are you?" Ric turned the would-be assailant onto his back, all the while keeping him pinned tightly between straddled knees. He was a wisp of a man—a boy, more like—short in stature and more bone than brawn. An ornate broadsword inlaid with amethyst hung at his side, confirming Ric's suspicions.

Spitting mad, he wondered at the gall of Chamelaute, annoyed that they'd had him followed after all they had discussed. They'd reached an understanding—or at least he'd thought so. And further, they'd retained the services of a truly unfortunate little man, perhaps with the belief that he'd be stealthy, but their tactics were utterly flawed.

"Answer me!" Ric grasped the spindly arms of the stooge, stilling his flailing form with great effort and all the while laboring for breath. The diminutive fellow was stronger than he looked and reeked as if he hadn't bathed in weeks, his head whipping from side to side. The prince struggled to maintain a hold, and when the lad's gray woolen cap slipped from his crown, Ric froze.

For *he* was, in fact, *she*.

"Blazes!" Ric scrambled away as an avalanche of hair poured from beneath the woolen cap. "You're a girl!"

She bowed low, her movements laced with contempt. "How observant, Your Highness, though, in point of fact, I am a woman." Rising, she smiled tightly, her dark hair falling in waves over her shoulders.

Ric stepped back, raking a hand over his stubbled face in disbelief. "They had me followed by a girl?"

"A woman, yes, and followed…? Well, not exactly. I was sent by the Seer as a companion, for your protection." She stepped toward him with her hand extended. "I'm Rory."

"Are you, indeed?" Ric scoffed, shaking her hand as his mind raced. Insult wasn't entirely accurate for what he felt.

Outrage. That was it.

Sighing, Rory nodded. "The Seer thought it unwise for you to travel alone, though you and King Luther thought nothing of it." Her tone dripped with scorn as she prepared herself for confutation.

"And clearly, you agreed with him." Ric folded his arms across his chest, a bemused smile forming on his face as he eyed her weapon. "He even gave you a sword, I see. To *protect* me."

"This is *my* broadsword, and I know how to use it." She reached for her sword just as Ric brandished his own. "Truly, my lord prince, you do not wish to challenge me."

"I do not wish to…?" Ric prowled in a slow circle around his unwelcome counterpart. "Did the Seer reveal this to you as well?"

"I did only as he requested of me." Rory turned, blade at the ready as she followed Ric's every step. "All to keep you safe for some inexplicable reason." She huffed, sweeping aside a thick tendril of hair with the back of her gloved hand. "But if you are of import to the Seer, then I shall see my mission through. He is never wrong."

"I don't need your protection, regardless of what your blessed Seer says. I'm a trained soldier, and I lead an army. Stars, I'm about to be king!" His voice cracked, a betrayal of all the pent-up emotions behind the unpleasant revelation. "Go home and leave me to my duties."

"I've already saved your life — twice, as a matter of fact, and maybe more." Rory watched as the prince paused mid-step, his face a blank mask as he considered her words.

"Do tell," Ric demanded, certain that the young woman was every bit as delusional as the Seer himself. How any person or nation could put so much stock in one random madman was beyond his comprehension.

"Fine." Rory sheathed her broadsword before wandering toward the roadside. She indicated a bramble covered in blood-red roses. "Poison. You were headed for an entire thicket of them before I warned you away with my hefty tread. One prick of the thorn and you're asleep for life. Might as well be dead."

"Ah. Your inability to silently follow me was for *my* benefit?"

"Well, you did alter course, so I shall consider my method a success." She smiled in smug satisfaction, meeting the steely gaze of the prince. "I also steered you away from a pit of quicksand, though you'd have to venture off the road to encounter it. I wasn't willing to risk it."

Ric sneered, eager to be rid of Rory and her steadfast devotion to his safety, but also mildly intrigued by her assertions. There was a good chance that she was lying, yet something about her confessions had him hooked.

It was grief. It had to be. For Ric was an eternal cynic, prone to inquisition and never trust. She was merely taking advantage of his impaired state of mind — the sudden absence of his father and his status as heir apparent having damaged him, breaching his carefully constructed wall of cynicism.

Damn her.

"How is it that you've come to be such an expert on the perils of Wylewoode?" Ric challenged, eager to poke holes in her authority. "And further, precisely how do you expect me to trust you when our affiliation began with you sneaking along behind me? Any potential for kinship seems unlikely at best."

"My mother." Rory's voice was low and free of hostility when she looked away; her thoughts lost to the forest around her. "She escaped these woods many decades ago and the stories she told… Let's just say you'll be much safer with somebody to watch your back."

Something about the reverence with which she spoke tempered Ric's anger. Perhaps loss was a part of Rory's story, too, though he did not wish for any details. His faith in her was still sorely lacking.

"She escaped, did she?" Suspicion punctuated each word, though Ric's resolve was wavering. "Why didn't she simply leave?"

Rory shook her head. "That tells me how little you know about this place."

"I've made it this far." He smiled in an attempt at levity, but she refused to meet his eyes.

Mercy. How Ric possessed the capacity for guilt at this moment was mystifying, but there it was. And, as absurd as it seemed, given Rory's insistence that she would protect him from the horrors of Wylewoode, he now found himself feeling responsible for her as well.

Ric thought for a moment, determined to remember if he had somehow offended the Seer, wondering if this was the madman's means of getting even. If so, it was a wicked ploy indeed.

Sighing, Ric resigned himself to his lot. The steward of the people who lived within every royal demanded his compliance. He would not leave Rory to an uncertain fate at the hands of their untamed surroundings.

And, having a companion could prove to be of some use. For while he would never admit it aloud, traveling solo through the feral woods was unsettling. "All right. We travel together, but only after you rid yourself of that nauseating scent."

"It's that odor that's been keeping you safe," Rory replied, pleased to have another opportunity to reveal her savvy. "Part of the reason I had to trail you so closely."

Ric took a deep breath. "Despite my better judgment, I'll bite. What exactly are you saving me from with that putrid stench?"

"Crocodiles." Rory bent, adjusting her boots in turn before facing her charge. There wasn't an ounce of humor in her countenance. "You've the roots of globe thistles to thank for that, and me, for braving the smell to protect you."

"Ah, crocodiles. Of course," Ric agreed, confident he was nearing insanity as an errant chuckle escaped him. This woman was trying his patience. Still, arguing the idiocy of repelling crocodiles would only cost him more time in a journey that already felt as though it were taking a lifetime. "Well, then. Keep the ridiculous odor but swear to me that you will travel in silence, and you may have yourself a deal."

"I'll be joining you for the duration either way," Rory asserted, carefully tucking her hair into place beneath her woolen cap. Retrieving her cloak from the dusty vestiges of their scuffle, she clasped it in place at her throat, smiling broadly. "Shall we?"

"By all means," Ric grumbled. "Lead the way."

Chapter Twelve

It was almost too easy.

Almost.

The last thing Ella wanted was to become complacent. Yet even with the myriad rumors floating about regarding the mysterious Hood, the noblemen patronizing the marketplace were nothing short of careless with their coin pouches — irrefutable evidence in her mind that they were too accustomed to the privilege of plenty.

Doubtless, the day would arrive where they would be more cautious, but until then, Ella and her merry band of accomplices would make the most of their negligence.

Her new life of criminality had begun innocently enough. All Ella had ever wanted was to see to the needs of the people of Locksley. Lady Margaret had made that a near impossibility after Much had been caught and relieved of his hand. She'd locked down the cellars and taken over the ledgers, keeping a watchful eye over every bag of grain and turnip that entered the manor.

As if the four women occupying the homestead needed such wealth. The greed made Ella mad with temper, prompting her to pack up and head for the woods, eager for the peace to be had outside of Lady Margaret's fortress of avarice.

Easing her mind over the impetuous decision was her ever-present conscience, Much, who, upon hearing her hasty plan, had revealed that he'd already packed.

It was all the reassurance she had needed.

Will and Alan had also readily followed her, fleeing swiftly in the eventide and leaving everything behind without question. It was exhilarating and daunting all at once, for she felt very much responsible for each of her three companions.

The ringleader and instigator of all their recent exploits, she knew she was putting everyone in potential peril. It wasn't the way she'd wanted to do things, but it seemed the best way forward, affording the lawless quartette a means of provision for not only the people of Locksley but many other townships as well.

A heavy burden to bear, but one each of them freely welcomed. It was merely the right thing to do.

"The Hood's a slippery bugger, he is!" the tailor hissed, all the while failing to suppress a deep chuckle. "Why, he left me a bag of coin just this morning. I hope he'll keep giving the constable what for!"

"Quiet down, you idiot! He cannot rescue you from prison should the king's men overhear ye!" a fellow merchant cautioned, glancing about warily. The whole village was buzzing with news of the charitable thief who robbed the rich to save the poor.

"Who says the Hood is a man?" Ella inquired as she wandered by the vendors.

"Well, he sure as hell ain't a woman, ma'am," the tailor asserted, blushing when he realized he'd been speaking to Ella. He bent at the waist. "Pardon my language, Lady Locksley. I meant no offense."

"Indeed. None taken." Ella smiled brightly, patting the man on the shoulder as she passed. "And no doubt you are correct. We are the fairer sex, after all." She bowed her head in parting, giggling as she lifted the hood of her cloak over her head and thankful that he hadn't seemed to notice the menswear she wore underneath. Moving into the crowded town square, she set about hiding in plain sight as she picked her next target.

Her new moniker as the vaunted Hood had given rise to many jokes at Major Oak, her dwelling alongside her brothers in arms, with Much alleging that the hood was its own being, saying no man or woman even need wear it.

Their teasing had reached a fevered pitch upon the introduction of her very own wanted poster—a ragged piece of parchment pinned to the dais in the center of town featuring Ella's likeness in the form of a faceless, hooded cloak of green.

Ridiculous, it was, as all of them wore capes at times. Most of the town's people did, in truth. Ella had argued that the poster was a generic rendering meant to depict each one of the crew, but the boys were adamant. The cape was green, and therefore, Ella, in all her moss-hued glory.

Living with boys was harrowing.

Posting herself next to the entrance of the town cobbler, Ella leaned against a crumbling pillar, watching the everyday chaos of the lively borough. The cobbler was located near the center, offering a view of the various shops, enabling her to keep an eye out for each of her allies.

As Ella idly nibbled on a sour apple, her stomach turned to knots, though the apple was only partially responsible. Every day of thievery had her on edge, and while she thought it would only get easier, it seemed the opposite was so. The gravity of what they were doing came into stark relief, with each stolen bag of coin and precious jewel adding to her unease.

Yet the good that was coming of their escapades could not be denied. The people they were helping appeared healthier daily and smiled more, their joy slowly returning. There was a sense of solace in place of the previous distress. Things were looking up.

It was worth it. It *was*.

After several minutes of searching, she spied Will on the opposite side of the square near a clothier, blending into his surroundings as though he were nothing more than a shadow in his dark cape and cap. His ability to acquire information was uncanny, providing the crew with a wealth of knowledge as they selected their targets.

High above, the fleet-footed Alan skipped from roof to roof on the outskirts of the common. Squatting low on a truss jutting from beneath the eave of the butcher's shop, he resembled a gargoyle more than a man, still as a stone as he observed the bustling below.

Mere meters away, Much took up position next to a gaudy statue of the dearly departed King Edward, armed with nothing more than a tin cup and a few copper coins. Waving his wounded stump in a show of misery, he called for their assistance, shoving his mug into the faces of each passerby.

She met each of their eyes in turn with a nod of assent, blessing their impending heist, heaven help them all.

"Oye, there! Can you spare some alms for the poor?" Much wandered into the fray of the market, sprawling forward as if he'd tripped and sending the few coppers in his cup scattering to the earth.

"Lord, help me, I've lost my coin!" he cried, scrabbling about in the dirt in a well-practiced fit of faux dismay. As expected, it was bedlam, with the poor amongst those gathered in the square diving toward his carefully crafted distraction.

It was time.

Ella moved, identifying a richly dressed noble on the outskirts of the uproar. Filled with the adrenaline that preceded each theft, she drew nearer. "Out of my way!" she bellowed, her tone shrill and feminine. For if the world around her was so sure the Hood was a man, she would use their faulty logic to her benefit.

Launching herself into the man with ferocity, she made as though she were eager to join the struggle underway before plucking the satchel tied to his belt with ease. "Move!" she shrieked, covertly tucking her prize into the deep pocket of her trousers. She scowled at her mark from beneath her hood, features filled with a mix of madness and desperation.

"Relax, lady!" He backed away, hands raised as he was jostled to and fro by the gathered masses. The crowd was more turbulent than she'd hoped, offering exceptional cover for her game of deception. He would never know it had been the frantic woman who had separated him from his coin.

Stars knew a woman would never be responsible for that.

Chapter Thirteen

The operation was bloody brilliant.

It was by a stroke of luck that Marion found himself in town at all on an errand for Prince Johan, who had developed an ever-growing need for trusted couriers. And like a scripted production, Marion watched in awe as the Hood accomplished his daily thievery.

He hadn't been aware of the Hood's efforts at first, oblivious to everything that stood between himself and his delivery. But the chaos was heady, drawing him to the unfolding spectacle and the presence of the figure shrouded in green.

Suddenly the pandemonium made sense, with the startling plea of one who sounded too vigorous to be a beggar ringing clearly through the market as a battle cry—a call to arms. Marion laughed. He couldn't help himself, as it was all too perfect. Crisp as a well-rehearsed drama, he watched the Hood execute a flawless pocket-picking, freeing Lord Ambrose of his wealth with a single shove.

The arrogant bastard deserved it—and Marion wanted to help.

His mission all but forgotten, Marion set his sights on the cloaked man, falling in step several dozen paces behind him as he made his way toward the edge of the square. The Hood was alone, or at least he seemed to be as Marion followed him through the throngs of townspeople. He was also quick, walking at a clip that had the lord struggling to keep up.

A piercing whistle like that of a dove rose above the fray, drawing the attention of Marion and the man he followed. In an instant, the demeanor of the pilfering do-gooder changed, the set of his shoulders collapsing as he slowed his stride, merging ever further into the anonymity of the crowd around him.

Though he tried to keep pace, Marion found himself falling hopelessly behind and losing sight of the thief, who was smaller than he'd envisioned and well adept at escape. Certainly, the crowd around them gave the man an advantage, but Marion wondered at the ease with which he'd disappeared before his eyes.

Irritated by the turn of events, the lord made his way toward a small staircase, slinking up the steps as he sulked over his near brush with greatness. The outlaw was rapidly becoming a legend in the shire, and Marion was an admirer, even in spite of his own lofty position in Llundynien society.

Perhaps that made him daft.

Perhaps he didn't care.

Reaching the top, he turned, scanning the crowd for any signs of the thief. The coolness of the day worked against him, as he spotted an abundance of hooded villagers. Capes were as commonly worn as hats and shoes, damning him to a fruitless pursuit.

Unless the diminutive form he spied at the edge of the shops was his aim. It was his best guess, at any rate. Marion set off, scurrying along the periphery of the square, avoiding the hordes of bodies as his back slid against the splintered surface behind him.

Just as he broke free from the crush of humanity, his arm was caught, stuck hard and fast to the timber that was grating his jerkin to shreds. A roughly hewn arrow pierced the linen of his shirt sleeve, pinning him in place.

"Blast!" Marion burned with anger as his target hastened away, leaving him flustered and feeling every bit a fool as he wrested his damaged sleeve from the wall. What was he thinking anyhow — that he'd simply mosey up to the infamous bandit and congratulate him on all his successful heists?

The sheer idiocy.

Recovering what remained of his dignity, he straightened his jerkin, eyeing the crowd around him with suspicion. The arrow was no accident, having nicked his arm. Marion scoured the square for signs of his attacker, only to light on a fellow who wasn't in the common at all.

High above, another cloaked man stood, slinging a bow over his shoulder before draping his cape over the top to conceal it. Had it not been for the sun winking off the fellow's ring, Marion wouldn't have noticed him at all.

Of course. It all made sense now.

The whistle. The disappearing. The arrow. The Hood was wise, and people were watching his back.

Marion wasted no time, bound and determined to follow his assailant. Winding through the rolling masses, he watched as the man leapt from the rooftop with ease, nimbly landing on the lower roof next door before jumping again to the alley below. The fiend was more feline than man in Marion's estimation, agile in a way that made him jealous, though he was loathe to acknowledge it.

Following at a distance, Marion watched the man as he prowled to the outskirts of town, readily blending into the background as he altered his pace and presence to match his surroundings.

He scoffed. It was little wonder that the Hood had found such success with the likes of the cat-man watching his back. The sheriff would have his hands full in bringing this crew to justice — if justice were, indeed, what it was. For though he was rife with fury over his wounded arm and ruined shirt, Marion couldn't deny the good that the Hood was doing for the shire.

It was no trouble following the man as he made his way into Sherwood Forest. He might be a slippery sort, but Marion was well versed in tracking, keeping a respectable span between himself and his quarry. His silence was another matter, however. He could only hope that the fellow was far enough ahead to be out of earshot as he struggled through the thick underbrush, stumbling over half-buried roots and jutting bedrock. Dusk was quickly falling, and he was finding it challenging to muffle his heavy tread.

It seemed his years of leisure had taken their toll on his hunting skills. He would have to amend that, should any more opportunities to chase criminals through a darkening forest arise in the future.

Absurd. It was all genuinely absurd.

Marion tripped again, cursing under his breath as he caught himself on a thick bough. *Mercy*. He'd narrowly avoided a collision with a thorny shrub, saving his ego as well as his handsome face. Perhaps he was more out of his element than he'd realized, with the creeping darkness as much an enemy as his assailant.

Er…

Scanning the grove around him, Marion was utterly perturbed. After all his flailing about through the woodland nightmare, he'd lost sight of his target entirely, damn him. "Bollocks!" he hissed, righting himself before bumbling his way toward the edge of a modest clearing to gather his sanity.

Only he wasn't alone. A small fire burned at the base of a mammoth oak tree on the far side of the clearing, the smoke drifting into the darkening sky. Slipping into the forest's edge, Marion skirted ever closer, his eyes pinned to the hollowed core of the aged trunk.

His heart beat a fierce tempo in his chest as he watched, hoping that the massive timber was a dwelling. There were rumors enough that the outlaws lived in the wilds outside of Nottingham, but he'd never believed it. Why should they, wealthy as they had to be with all the stolen coin?

A burlap bundle flew from the cavern, landing just shy of the slowly burning embers, followed by a lanky fellow in an umber cape who had to duck as he emerged from the tree cave. A second man materialized, stepping out from the protection of the arbor, his green mantle pulled tightly around his narrow shoulders as he moved to untie the bundle.

Could it be? Marion desperately wished to be nearer but feared he would make himself known if he moved. Still, he was confident he'd found the Hood. What were the odds of another caped crusader in these parts of Sherwood?

His suspicions were all but confirmed when a third man appeared, this one in the same dark shroud his assailant had worn. The man had made impressive time through the woods, looking very much at ease despite his having loped through the thicket only mere moments ago. Again, Marion found himself jealous of the sheer athleticism displayed by the damn cat-man.

Funny, though, as he'd have sworn his attacker was broader. It was no matter. Marion had made it after all. He stood statue-still, observing the trio as they set about making camp, pulling bread and cheese from the sack. The one in brown fussed over the glowing coals, prodding them into flame as the man in green stripped the low-hanging limbs of their branches. The cat-man, however, looked right at Marion.

Bloody hell.

He steeled himself for confrontation. His arm ached, all thanks to the mercurial chap, and he wasn't one to shy away from conflict. Besides, he was a lord. Even a bandit should know better than to do him harm.

Striding from his useless hideaway, he took a fortifying breath, only to have it cut short as he was violently seized around his waist. The sharpened edge of a blade pressed into his throat as the heathen behind him forced him forward step by step.

"Look at the loot I dragged home," called the savage man. "A lord, he is!"

The trio of thieves drew their weapons in unison, and each wicked armament pointed in Marion's direction. He raised his hands in submission, his throat working as he attempted in vain to swallow with the dagger thrust at his gullet.

His captor released him, shoving him forward into the circle of marauders. Marion straightened his jerkin with shaky hands, eyeing each of the veiled men warily. He'd never felt so vulnerable in all his life, the uncertainty driving him to distraction.

The one in brown moved toward him sword in hand, and he knew he was dead, heaven help him.

But the man didn't stop, never struck, advancing instead to the dagger-wielding man behind him, smacking him on the ear with the stumpy end of his arm. "We like this one, you blockhead!"

"Well, he followed me here, the fool," dagger man groused, rubbing his ear with a scowl. "Terrible tracker, in truth. Must've snapped a dozen branches as he neared the cave."

"Why'd you come here if you knew you were being followed?" asked his twin, also cloaked in black. So, there were two dressed in shadows, then. Marion watched as the shrouded double moved toward dagger man.

"Lords make for excellent ransom," he said, only to be cuffed by his twin. Dagger man fought back, the pair of them tussling like a couple of children with each of them losing their hoods as they pounded one another.

Not twins. Not even brothers, Marion realized, with dagger man fair of hair and skin, and the other tawny, his midnight waves falling over his forehead as he sparred.

"Quite an operation we're running here, fellows."

Marion turned, shocked to find that the voice from the one covered in green was that of a woman — a woman he knew, no less. "Ella?"

She removed her hood. "Hello, Marion. My associates — Much, Will and Alan." She indicated each man in turn, an indulgent smile for her ragtag crew fixed to her beautiful face.

He was aghast and somewhat speechless. "And Much? Your hand is—"

"Is fine," Much finished, pushing his hood from his head. "I'll do." He greeted Marion with a bow before pulling Will away from Alan. "These two, however…"

"Indeed." Marion eyed the duo as his adrenaline began to abate. "Which one of you shot me?"

"I did," Alan said, his tone prideful. "And I'd do it again. Nobody follows the Hood."

That earned him another shove from Will, but this time they were grinning.

"Ah. Well, thank you for your honesty." Marion smiled tightly, determined to complete his jaunt with no additional injuries. He turned to Ella. "It seems we've some things to discuss."

"If you wish," she replied, as though her recent transformation into a criminal mastermind were an everyday occurrence.

He nodded, feeling greatly unsettled. "So, the indomitable Hood is none other than my lifelong friend. When did you start stealing without me?"

She linked her arm through his, guiding him over to the fire. "This is a bit more serious than stealing a coin or two from Lady Tolbert when she was into her fifth sherry."

He chuckled at the memory, seating himself near to her, fireside. "Lady Tolbert, the old hag. She's still alive, you know."

"Must've pickled her insides with all the rotgut she drank at those dreadful council functions. She'll be forever preserved." Ella laughed, bringing a genuine smile to Marion's face.

The other three men joined them, passing around several loaves of crusty bread and a couple of wedges of cheese—their presence a reminder of the severity of the situation. Marion cleared his throat. "I was excited to meet the Hood—until I found out he was you."

"I'm sorry to disappoint," Ella groused. "It seems everyone expects the Hood to be a man."

"No, Locksley. It isn't that." Marion took her hand, giving it a reassuring squeeze. "It's just an awful lot of danger. It's too much risk."

Ella sighed, meeting his eyes. "I've no choice in the matter. Taking great risks is the only way to help my people. They're starving, Marion. These taxes…"

"Are out of control," Marion said, his gaze earnest. He shook his head, stroking his thumb over the back of her hand. "But—"

"But nothing," Alan hissed, throwing a scrap of bread at Marion's face. "She's doing what she must for her people, and she ain't got time for romance. So please, sir, begone!"

There was a moment of uncertainty over Alan's irreverent treatment of the influential lord before the camp burst into laughter, with all but Marion finding the remark amusing. "Why is that funny?" he demanded, his tone sullen.

Ella wiped a tear from her eye, patting her highborn companion on the shoulder. "Worry not. There's always time for you." She smiled, her cheeks cheerfully pink in the dancing light of the fire. "But if I may, why *are* you here?"

It was a fair question, and one he suddenly felt self-conscious answering. Silly, really, given his stature in the shire and beyond. Yet, he couldn't simply walk away. "I want in," he admitted, donning an arrogant grin. "I could be an asset—and here's my first contribution." He pulled a bag from his belt before launching the hefty pouch over the fire, hitting Alan squarely in the chest.

The bag dropped into his lap with a *clink,* and Much issued a low whistle. Will grabbed Alan's arm, determined to hold his friend back, but he hadn't seemed to notice Marion's incitement at all.

Instead of firing back, he grasped the satchel, ever entranced by the prospect of riches. He opened it with a gasp. "Dirty rotten lord! Always knew you was robbin' the people blind!" He hefted the prize into the air, and Will and Much jumped to their feet to examine the pouch.

Marion chuckled. The irony was thick and even more profound than Alan realized. "It's not mine. That coin is a bribe."

"You ain't bribing your way into our crew, you foolish lout," Alan grumped.

"A bribe from whom?" Ella was well aware of Marion's penchant for his riches. Not that he wasn't willing to share, but the gift appeared robust.

"Prince Johan is bribing the lords of the shire." Marion watched Ella for understanding. She didn't disappoint, sucking in a deep, shaky breath.

"What?" Much demanded. "What does that mean?"

"Prince Johan is lobbying for the kingship. It's a plea for support," Marion said, his voice low. Speaking the words out loud felt dangerous, and he'd wished very much to be wrong, but the evidence was mounting.

The posse fell into silence, the trio of men opposite the fire scowling at the flames as if they held answers. Even Alan and his smart mouth appeared to be at a loss for words.

"You mustn't speak this way, Marion. It's treasonous," Ella cautioned, her words but a whisper, as if the wilds of the woods around them had become full of covert ears eager to report on their sedition. Her wide eyes met his, full of innocence despite her new profession.

His breath caught. He wanted nothing more than to shield her from the uncertainties of the kingdom's future and the perils of her thieving and carousing. It wasn't a life for a lady. It should never have come to this.

"It is the only possibility, Locksley. That pouch was intended for Lord Remington, and I was on my way to him when I spied you." Marion sighed, shaking his head. "I've one to match at home, a bribe I couldn't refuse for fear of appearing disloyal. Johan is positioning himself to take the place of King Edward in Ric's stead. In truth, I fear for Ric's life."

"No. No." Ella shook her head, as if to shoo away the burden of his revelations. "What if you're wrong?"

"I'm not." Marion tossed an errant stick into the fire, watching it sizzle away into ash as his thoughts raced anew. "I didn't want to be right. Everything would be much easier, but, Elle, the proof is everywhere. Have you noticed all the foreigners?"

"I..." Ella paused, her brows furrowed. "Yes, I have. Little John has been fashioning a wide array of exotic arms of late. Men of Sundsvaile, Calaise, Debrecyn... He didn't realize—I didn't— Oh..."

"Oh, what?" Alan demanded, throwing his hands up in frustration. "Can't someone please speak the king's English!"

"An army, it is," Will replied, frowning. "He's raising an army with our taxes, and he's bribing our betters with our own blood, sweat and tears."

Marion nodded, relieved to be free of the secrets he'd been harboring. "Let me in. I'll be your eyes on the inside. I'll make all of Johan's bribes yours. In truth, my only solace in possessing his blood money in the first place was in the fervent belief that it would one day soon be stolen by the likes of you."

"It's too dangerous, Marion!" Ella burst, her eyes sparkling with moisture. "I won't have it!"

"But you may endanger yourself?" he challenged.

"It's my choice!"

"As it is mine. The kingdom is being bled dry, and I must do something!" Marion regarded his stubborn companion in frosty silence. Ella returned his gaze, her features filled with defiant disapproval.

"Do we really have to include him?" Alan's features crumpled in distaste. "He's too loud, and he's even bossier than you are."

Ella's attempt to remain stern vanished as she began to snicker, undone by her ill-mannered accomplice. In short order, the whole band was laughing—a welcome respite from the severity of their new reality.

She reached for Marion, taking his hand in her own. "Are you truly prepared to lie, cheat and steal from those you've been raised to honor, my friend?"

Marion grinned. "Indeed I am, darling. Come what may."

"Well, then," Ella replied. "Welcome to our circle of thieves, Lord Knighton."

Chapter Fourteen

Traveling under the Seer's instruction had proven daunting. Rory had chattered incessantly, repeating much of the nonsense the old fool had told her. Ric would have completed the two-week journey much more quickly had she not attached herself to him, replete with orders that had them taking a winding, senseless path. Heaven forbid the musings of a lunatic not be followed to the letter.

Rory also loved to sleep and didn't like to be rushed. Moody and unpredictable, the girl made him long for his soldiers. Even after the calamity he and his men had experienced in the hills of Calaise, where his captain had assured his entire company that the water was always purest near the bluffs beyond Lyona, they were a far more favorable option. Their stomachs had writhed, their tents having become chambers of anguishing fetor, but still, Ric would've chosen them over his raven-haired companion.

The weeks of posing as wearied newlyweds fleeing their homeland had reassured the prince that a wife was more a nuisance than an asset. While women in the minor territories they'd passed through had been enamored by the passionate tales of forbidden love Rory had spun, their swooning was of no benefit to Ric if they all believed he was spoken for.

She'd been given shawls, cloaks and jewelry as gifts from romantics along the way. All Ric had managed to obtain were some garments he'd bought off a merchant's back in Garstowe and a beard he'd grown himself.

The route they'd taken made a wide berth around the main road leading into the heart of Llundyn, but still, the wilderness of Sherwood was home. Though he'd rarely seen these parts, the aroma and foliage surrounding him were welcomed and familiar. Mist filled the woods, the gloom of the day compounding the chill in the springtide air.

It was no matter. He was nearly home.

Behind him, the rhythmic pounding of hooves had halted. Heaving a sigh, he tugged the reins of his steed. Rather than asking to rest, Rory had made a habit of merely stopping without warning wherever she saw fit.

"Where are you going now?" Ric groused. "We'll make it to Nottingham before sundown if we keep moving."

When he received no response, he retraced his tracks, finding where their paths had diverged. Following the strides of her horse, he spotted her through the trees. She smiled and waved, kneeling at the edge of a modest pond as she filled her canteen. Jamming the cork into place, she let the container swing, hanging at her side as she rose using her mare to steady herself.

"She was thirsty, and I decided I was also." She shrugged, unapologetic as usual, before reaching into her satchel. When she held out a palm-full of oats to her horse, the animal reared, sending Rory stumbling backward.

It hadn't taken long for them to understand why they'd been able to finagle such a bargain for the creature. She was as high strung as they came, but Rory took to her instantly. Rory was thrilled with the exchange, but Ric knew without question who had received the better end of that transaction.

"Something's not right." Rory's eyes swept their surroundings as the horse moved anxiously, crunching the dried leaves underfoot.

"You just now noticed?" Ric dismounted, securing the leather reins to a nearby branch. "The farmer practically begged you to take that thing."

Her features darkened as she gazed above, nodding upward with a careful tilt of her head. "That's not what I meant. There's something in the trees, Ric," she hissed through clenched teeth.

The prince laughed, all the while exuding a detached air, but he too felt the crush of a presence closing in on them. With Rory's horse on edge, a quick escape seemed out of the question. He motioned to her, and she drew quickly to his side, each of them alert and poised to meet opposition.

She wasn't a soldier, but she had the stance of a warrior. Ric was confident that together they would stand their ground against whatever lurked nearby.

"The Seer spoke of this," Rory said quietly. "He told me we were to trust our captors when the time came, and this is it." Her words were earnest but firm.

Ric suppressed the urge to groan. While he questioned her judgment concerning the intrinsic faith she placed in the madman of Chamelaute, she couldn't be foolish enough to allow them to be destroyed by a silent, invisible foe. He gave a hasty nod to put her at ease, his hand slowly finding its way to the hilt of his blade.

With his pulse racing, Riccard readied himself to fight. Battle was in his blood. He'd trained since he was a boy, his innate instincts paired with the superior direction he'd received as heir apparent.

He felt eyes upon him, but whatever, or *who*ever stalked them appeared in no hurry. Beside him, metal *clinked* off the hard earth. Glancing beside him, he found Rory with her hands up in surrender. Taking several steps forward, she reached for her boots, withdrawing two more knives that hit the ground next to her sword before lifting her hands skyward once more.

"We want no trouble." Entirely unarmed, she dropped to her knees, daring the threat to reveal itself. "Take all we have if you must. We won't fight you."

"Like *hell*, we won't," Ric spat, eyes continually scanning the hazy forest for signs of threat.

"How exceedingly generous of you." A shrouded figure stepped from behind a tree not more than four feet from where Rory knelt, with an arrow nocked and readied for flight. "Although you and your husband seem a bit at odds with how to proceed."

Ric was shocked, for the voice of the hooded ghost belonged to a woman. If he'd learned anything during his travels with Rory, it was the principal truth that women were not to be trifled with. He glanced at Rory's discarded weapons, lunging for the sword.

A man dropped from his perch overhead, landing between the prince and Rory's blade. "Oh, no. I don't think I'd do tha'."

Staggering backward, Ric stumbled directly into the chest of a third brigand, and before he could regain his footing, the man had his elbow braced tightly around his neck. If the bandits had wanted to kill them, they certainly could have, but the pressure around his neck never threatened to crush his throat.

He struggled against the man's hold, his feet unable to gain the traction needed to free himself. In his periphery, a final form emerged to pilfer through the few supplies they'd had strapped to their horses. There wouldn't be much to find, but perhaps it would be enough for them to carry on their way.

None of their faces were visible, the thieves seemingly making artistry of their crime. Deftly, the same man who had blocked Ric from Rory's sword tied the prince's arms together behind his back, stripping him of further defenses before dragging him to a thick trunk to be restrained beside his companion.

"They won't hurt us," Rory whispered. "We can trust them."

Ric scoffed. The girl was delusional at best, with no regard for the monumental implications her flippant submission might have. Ric was to be king, only to find himself at the mercy of common criminals. He would already be dead if they'd played any role in the atrocities that had ended his father's rule, but he wasn't naive enough to believe they were to be *trusted*.

The prince held his tongue while the marauders circled their captives, though his notorious temper threatened to unravel his composure. He observed each one with bitter scrutiny, his annoyance ever-growing with the realization that he'd been bested by a clan seemingly led by a woman.

The petite woman stopped before him, her stature exuding confidence. Her face, however, remained shadowed by the hem of her hood. "From where do I know your face?"

Smirking, he shook his head at the captivating stranger. "You think me so daft that I would reveal anything to you?" The prince laughed as the woman turned her back to him, the other members of her gang continuing their assessment of his meager belongings.

The woman wandered over to her companions, only to again glance toward the captured prince. Ric congratulated himself on a job well done, for he'd once had one of the most well-known faces in all Fayble. His beard and clothing had done their duty, despite Rory's insistence that he wasn't nearly disguised enough. Yet, he'd managed to puzzle the lady thief very adequately.

A light breeze gusted through the bosk, offering an unexpected gift to the restrained heir as it lifted the edges of her hood, betraying her identity. Ric had found familiarity in her voice, but without seeing her face, he'd been unable to place their association. The delicate outline of her profile gave away the enigmatic daughter of Lord Robin.

Ric's smile widened with the revelation, and at that moment, he agreed with Rory. They would, indeed, remain captives, at least until the prince could make some sense of their circumstances.

"You look like Prince Riccard," Ella muttered, adjusting her veil as she broke the silence hanging in the space between them.

"Tha' ugly bloke?" one of the cloaked men interrupted. It was the same man who had remained hidden above them in the trees moments before, moving skillfully across their branches. He stormed over to where Ric and Rory remained bound, taking a closer look. He grimaced. "You best not insult the Crown like tha', Hood, or you'll get us all hanged."

He took no care to conceal his face and seemed not to worry in the slightest over being recognized. Ric surveyed his features, but to his knowledge had never made the man's acquaintance.

Ignoring the fair-haired wag, Ric leaned toward his woman captor as much as his bindings would allow. A wry grin formed on his face as he raised a single brow. "You also strike an uncanny resemblance to an acquaintance of mine, Lady *Ember* of Locksley."

Chapter Fifteen

Ella felt as though her legs might collapse from underneath her. Had they well and truly captured the future king? Lord help them, they were barreling toward disaster.

Perhaps Much and the others would still have a chance if they left before the prince and his lover had more opportunity to note their appearances. But Ella knew better than to believe they would ever leave her behind to handle their unwitting plight alone.

Much had already lost a hand in exchange for her impulsive yearning to help those in need. It went without saying that they would all stand to lose much more when the prince disclosed the true identity of the infamous Hood.

How pompous he looked, sat beside his striking mistress. A perfectly white smile stretched across his handsome features as if to mock her, implying that she was, in fact, the silly girl Lady Margaret always said she was.

"It is I, Lady *Ella* of Locksley." She removed her hood, taking a step toward the prince and his beautiful companion. He already knew who she was, but if he proved to be anything at all like his younger brother, he might be willing to listen. His current position left him with no other option.

"Hooves in the distance!" Alan called out. With a few graceful strides, he heaved his weightless form out of sight into the trees. Will, too, vanished from view.

Ella's heart pounded with a wild thrill as she followed Much deep into the thicket, leaving the Llundynien heir helplessly bound to an old tree. The kingdom would undoubtedly demand her head for this error, but they would have to catch her first. Within seconds, the prince bellowed for aid, attempting to attract the attention from whatever savior might be galloping through the woods.

Ella and Much crept silently to the roadside as horse and rider drew nearer. They spied a darkened form, approaching the ruckus as he dashed along the well-trodden path. Closer, he came, and soon Ella could just make out the man's features. Her heart sank.

Marion.

She needed to warn him before the prince learned of his involvement with the notorious thieves of Nottingham. Ella ran into the road, her arms raised in her desperation to prevent any further complications.

He slowed his horse, dismounting before her. Much stepped out from the surrounding foliage, joining Ella as she motioned for Marion to keep quiet. She wasn't certain how much distance they'd gained from Riccard and his lover, but his voice was ringing through clearly enough.

"You must leave before you're discovered," Ella whispered to Marion. His brow furrowed, concern evident in his gaze.

"What have you done?" Marion took her by the shoulders, his gaze scanning the woods behind her. Prince Riccard's voice echoed through the night once more, and the lord paled. "Is that—" Marion stopped himself, pinching the bridge of his nose between his fingertips. "Tell me I am mistaken, Ella. It cannot be."

"They were traveling alone, and we realized too late. He knows not of your involvement, and you mustn't be seen with me again." It pained her to say so, but she wouldn't risk him more than she already had.

"You've shown me what it means to be willing to abandon every comfort, every semblance of affluence to do what is right for those who have nothing. Ric will pardon your crimes, Locksley. He's your best chance at achieving prosperity for those who deserve it most." Without delay, Marion turned, mounting his stallion.

"Marion, please!" Ella raced toward the lord, only to have him sidestep her with ease, setting off toward the prince.

She followed Marion's trail with Much hot on her heels, hoping, praying that Marion would come to his senses before finding the restrained heir to the throne.

They'd tied the future of Llundyn to an old oak tree. Heaven help her, but she was as good as dead.

Prince Riccard and his companion were right where they had left them when Marion found the travelers secured to the gnarled trunk. Ella caught her breath with Much close behind as they watched Marion approach. He wasted no time in removing the heir's restraints with a blade he'd retrieved from his doublet.

"Why are you here?" Marion asked, moving from Riccard to his partner. "And without your men in a time of warfare?"

The prince wrung his hands together before pushing himself from the ground, stretching his limbs with each movement. "I was left with no other option, I'm afraid." Crossing his arms over his chest, the prince waited while Marion cut through the ropes tightened around the woman's midsection and wrists.

Ella remained tucked behind the brush, accompanied by her comrades, all shielded by the foliage around them. Not one of them moved, but each was prepared to act for their friend if need be.

"There is no war, Marion," Riccard continued. "Chamelaute sent a man they claim to be a Seer to meet me upon their shores. If indeed they had meant for war, the sea would have surely lapped at its bloodied sands that day. Instead, I was received with sympathy and kindness from a long-time ally."

"How certain are you?" Marion's question mirrored Ella's thoughts. It was true that the lord harbored developing suspicions of heinous schemes rooted deeply within the council. Ella knew without question that he hoped for nothing more than to be mistaken.

Would that Prince Riccard might prove Marion's theories wrong.

"If Chamelaute wanted to take Llundyn, they'd have done so," the woman interrupted, her slight accent giving her away as a foreigner every bit as much as her broadsword did. She massaged her narrow wrists where they'd been chafed, confidently meeting Marion's gaze.

"You know this?" Uncertainty colored his speech, with everything about their circumstances throwing him off balance.

The woman was indignant, pursing her lips as she considered her argument, though Marion would need little convincing. "The agreement shared between the nations benefits both territories immensely, but Chamelaute would never seek to burden its system with land not only so distant but also lacking agrarian fertility."

"And you are?" Marion was seemingly amused, the woman's candor having clearly surprised him. Ella considered the many other foreigners who'd come to occupy the barren state, though this was the first female among them she had noted.

The sudden influx was unsettling, to say the least, partnered with Marion's suspicions about the younger prince. Men from the surrounding kingdoms of Fayble had arrived in force, readily replacing many of the soldiers of the Llundynien army that had remained.

Marion already feared for Riccard, and with his return, Ella knew the concern would only grow. It hurt her to consider Prince Johan capable of treason, but the information they'd continued to piece together only further indicated a betrayal of the highest order.

"My name is Rory." The stranger stiffened in defiance before continuing. "The Seer sent me to aid His Highness in his travels. Without my assistance, he was as good as dead as far back as Wylewoode."

A guttural laugh escaped the prince. "Oh, yes. Truly, the most perilous threat I faced was that of your horrifying odor."

Rory turned to meet his mockery. "You're very welcome." She gave an exaggerated curtsy, her full-lipped pout forming a wily smirk.

Alan snickered to himself, earning an elbow in the ribs from Will, which he quickly shrugged off. Ella, too, appreciated the woman's ardor, steadfast despite the noble company she kept. Still, she wondered at the sharp remark from the prince toward his companion. The lovers formed an odd union, to be sure.

"That may well be so," Marion asserted, his brow furrowed as he contemplated his next actions. "But I cannot allow you or Prince Riccard to continue until I can be certain of his safety moving forward." He whistled the trill of the Hood — a few notes that Ella and her outlaws used to communicate discreetly amongst themselves. With his call for support, they emerged from the trees, pressing in around the prince and his female counterpart.

"You needn't bind me," Rory insisted, seating herself on the ground. "We won't run. We'll comply with your demands, for the Seer spoke to me of this. We are to remain with our captors."

"Not this again," Riccard mumbled, rubbing his eyes with the heels of his hands. He seated himself upon a nearby boulder, his demeanor creased with annoyance.

"Forgive me, Ric, but I fear your life may be in danger." Marion paced as the prince watched. He didn't look pleased but appeared willing to listen, which was more than any of the thieves deserved, in Ella's estimation.

"Johan seeks the favor of the council, offering gains and favors to those who side with him. He has increased financial pressures, overwhelming your people under the pretense of what I now understand to be a nonexistent war," Marion continued. His features knitted together as he shared his insight, undoubtedly feeling the sting of an old friend's duplicity.

"What is it you mean to tell me, Marion?" spat the prince, his speech blistering with each assertion of potential treason.

"I haven't enough evidence to say for certain." Marion ceased his overwrought pacing as the gravity of circumstantial exigence threatened to crush him. "But until I possess it, we cannot risk your brother learning you've returned."

"We have much yet to learn, as it's still possible the prince only intends to provide for you and your men. But if he is indeed guilty of treason, it would likely mean your death if you're discovered." Ella removed her hood, approaching Prince Riccard slowly. "You must consider the welfare of your people, should the wrong powers rise to abscond with the authority that is your birthright."

He nodded, examining Ella's face as if he sought to memorize each contour of its structure. She looked away, wary under his scrutiny and knowing fully that she and Marion were left to his mercy.

"Well, then... Now you know why we are here," Riccard said, gesturing between Rory and himself. "But you've neglected to explain why we yet sit here surrounded by two members of court and handful of grifters."

"The taxes inflicted on your people are too heavy for them to manage. Poverty is more prevalent than the very air we breathe, and we've found a way to relieve some of the strain." Ella shrugged, her admission enough to end her legacy with a swift blade to her slender neck.

"We steal from the rich and give it to the poor," Alan clarified. Dropping some kindling he'd gathered from around the thicket, he knelt to construct the makings of a fire to warm away the chill of Sherwood nights.

"It's not been achieved without consequences." Will moved forward, patting Much's shoulder. "Though I suppose at that point, it wasn't even considered theft, but the good sheriff doesn't miss an opportunity to make an example of anyone who might threaten the opulence maintained by the wealthy."

"I've put it to good use, I think," Much said, grinning as he nudged Will with his stump, its bandages tattered and frayed.

"The hope they've spread throughout the villages is palpable, and the Hood's notoriety burgeons by the hour." Marion smiled at Ella, who was quick to give one in return. "Ella and these men have the respect and support of the people, more so than even you or Johan. I believe your best defense is to join them until we can uncover the truth of your brother's intent."

"Wait. What?" The smile disappeared from Ella's face as she waved the suggestion away with a dramatic sweep of her hand. "Absolutely not."

"Your Seer did tell us to stay with them," Riccard said, turning to Rory and all the while pointedly ignoring Ella's objection. Rory nodded, offering a half-smile in agreement.

"He can't do what we do!" Ella's fists tightened at her sides. "He's —"

"I'm what?" Ric's piercing blue eyes met hers, full of challenge and undisguised amusement.

"You're—you're *you!*" Ella turned away in an attempt to clear her mind. Looking at the prince did strange things to her sensibilities—and arguing with him made it even worse. She took a deep breath before facing him anew. "We are *stealing*, Your Highness, from *your* subjects! You can't."

"I can," Ric returned, rising to his feet. "Why not?"

"Is this a ploy?" Ella demanded, suddenly considering how he could be entrapping her and her posse. "That you and your lover may join us in thieving only to indict and hang us?"

"I'm not his lover," Rory groused, her features twisted in disgust.

"Heaven forbid!" Ric added, eyeing his companion with disdain. "I would sooner die than tie myself to the likes of her."

"Likewise," Rory agreed, the pair of them smiling at one another as if they hadn't each been insulted in excess.

Ella watched the exchange, furrowing her brow in confusion. She shook her head, as if to clear it before continuing. "Fine. I care not about your attachments. But please understand the dilemma you face. Any entanglements with us will surely see you to regret and eventual penalty for each one of us by your hand. It can be no other way."

"I'm to be king, am I not?" Ric took a step toward Ella, then another, as though moving too quickly would cause her to bolt like a frightened hare. "Upon my word. If you welcome us into your band, we shall fight alongside you to right the wrongs my people face, until which time I can recover my position in my kingdom."

Ella gulped, her eyes fastened to the dauntless heir before her. His self-assurance was inspiring, his presence equal parts thrilling and unnerving. She found herself nodding against her will, slowly surrendering what little leverage she'd maintained in her argument against him.

"And when I am king," he continued, "you shall be pardoned of all wrongdoing, for it sounds very much to be no violation at all. If my people hold the Hood in such high regard, then so shall I." His lips tipped at the corner with a coy, almost nervous smile forming on his handsome face. He extended his hand, and she took it, signing all their lives away with a single shake of their adjoined hands.

Ric bowed his head slightly before stepping away, appearing to at last realize how near he'd been to the vaunted Hood. "But we must also send the news to my brother that I meant to deliver myself. If there's a chance of his innocence, I wish to allow him to prove it."

"Very well then," Marion settled as he moved to the satchel kept on his steed. Rifling through it, he retrieved a folded piece of blank parchment, a small vial of ink and a quill. "In your own hand, you can pen a letter to inform him of your experience in Chamelaute."

"His actions following will either prove his innocence or convict him," Ella agreed, recovering her senses. "Marion, you will need to ensure the delivery of the message without being associated at all with its delivery."

He nodded solemnly. "I have access to do so without raising suspicion. We will have the answers we seek soon, but we need to prepare ourselves for what that may mean for the future."

Riccard had already begun writing, his quill scraping frantically over the blank surface. Once completed, he blew on the ink, watching it dry as the glossy sheen of his script took root in the material.

Marion handed the prince a stem of red wax, which Riccard melted over the flames. He held the scarlet stick above his folded missive, the scalding liquid falling onto its opening. From within his jerkin, he pulled a golden chain that held his royal signet ring. Pressing it firmly to the parchment, he sealed his letter before handing it to Marion.

"Remain on your guard, my friend," Marion said, clasping Ric's forearm firmly. "And know that she is very much in charge." He indicated Ella with a wave of his hand, his faith in her implicit.

The attention of every lord, prince and thief fell upon her, causing her to squirm. Ella smiled, projecting an air of confidence that she did not feel.

What in the world have I done?

Chapter Sixteen

She was every bit the stubborn woman that Rory was, if not more so. A day and two nights with the lady thief had taught Ric many things, not the least of which being that Marion was right. Ella was *very* much in charge.

Watching the men she commanded about with the proficiency of a seasoned soldier had him reluctantly impressed. Even Marion, a man who had been his fiercest ally and most wicked enabler, had fallen over himself bending to her whims.

He'd been gone for only a handful of weeks, and everything had changed.

She'd rounded up her crew and taken off the day prior on one of their daily heists, striking the king's highway — *his* highway — with impunity. They'd left him alone with Rory at Major Oak, only to return with a chest full of coin, several swords and a well-made wheel sheathed in steel that would fetch a handsome sum when they sold it at the market.

It was a test, in Ric's estimation, defying him to either leave of his own accord, else have Ella and her merry men arrested.

He wouldn't bite. In truth, he was hopelessly intrigued, for Ella was risking much more than her name. Her very life was at stake. The knowledge that such measures were necessary for the survival of his kingdom drove him to distraction.

How had everything become this desperate?

"Breakfast," Ella said, leaning into the cavernous hole that formed his shelter. "Won't you join us out by the fire?"

Ric groaned, stretching as he rose from his bedroll. He'd been oddly comfortable in the yawning oak, surrounded by the sounds of slumber and the warmth of the gathered band packed together in the heart of the tree.

Stepping outside the large trunk, he observed the fellowship of Ella and her posse. Even Rory had been readily absorbed into the family of bandits, with each of them huddled about the modest fire quietly chatting as they ate their morning meal.

Ella handed Ric a wooden dish as he approached, seating himself beside her. "Eggs and ham. It was Alan's turn to cook, so it might be a bit chewy." She smiled brightly, ignoring Alan's scowl.

Glancing at his plate, he could see that it was true. The ham was charred beyond recognition, and the eggs resembled some sort of yellow grain. *Blazes*. It was anything but appetizing, but he was determined to choke it down. He knew beyond any doubt that his beautiful new master was watching, ready for him to fail.

He was not a coddled prince, nor was he a scold. As a part of the Llundynien army, he'd seen worse, at any rate. "Stolen?" he asked around a mouthful of egg shards, lifting his bowl in question.

"Of course, although we prefer the term 'pilfered'," Ella replied, her keen amber eyes alight with mischief. "You don't mind, do you? Not everyone can stomach our lifestyle."

Her words were full of challenge — something he found utterly thrilling, his gaze dropping to her sassy lips. "Not at all. I confess it makes them all the more savory."

Ella scoffed. "Well, then... Since you've developed such a proclivity for the spoils of our crime, perhaps it's time for you to help. You will be an asset, I trust?"

"I will, indeed. But first, more scorched pig and sandy eggs." He held out his plate as Alan served up more grub.

"Aye, eat to your heart's content," Alan chirped. "The old chap ain't so bad after all!"

"We'll see." Ella eyed the heir beside her, a hint of a smile on her face as she set about fashioning the pile of branches she'd gathered into arrows.

Ric's mouth tipped at the corners. He could get used to this, sparring with the queen of shadows.

* * * *

"Is this entirely necessary?" Ric sulked as Rory and Ella streaked his face with grime, each of the women delighting in fouling him up. "I've masked my features enough already with this fine beard."

"Oh, yes. I scarcely recognized you." Ella splashed some mud onto the shoulders and chest of the borrowed cape, giving the impression of a timeworn traveler.

"Agreed. Why, it makes you practically invisible," Rory added, drawing a giggle from Ella and a long-suffering sigh from the future king.

Ella regarded her efforts before lifting her hood onto her head with a nod. "You'll do. Remember, you are only to observe. I wouldn't be able to save you if you got caught."

"Nor will I." Rory bent, tucking a blade into her boot.

"Ah." Ric folded his arms over his chest, feeling mildly perturbed. "And each of you just *assumes* that I shall be our downfall in the market?"

"Of course," Rory said, shrugging her shoulders.

"Doubtless," Ella agreed in unison. She stepped before Ric, grasping either side of his hood. Rising on tiptoe, she managed to slip the covering over the top of his tousled hair. "But keep your head hidden, and don't meet anybody's eyes. We wish to remain anonymous."

"Right," Ric muttered, confident that the day would be a long one. Will, Alan and Much had gone on to Worksop, a township several hours away, to hawk their various pilfered treasures and snag more coin if it were safe, while Marion continued his deceptions within the walls of the palace. When Ric was told that he'd be joining Ella and Rory, he'd thought he was getting the better end of the deal.

Never in his life had he imagined that spending time in the company of two attractive women would be so trying. How they had become such quick friends was beyond him, their tag-teaming testing his mettle at every turn.

Women. He would never understand their ways.

The trio spread out when they entered the borough, keeping an eye on one another as they made their way through town. And despite all the pains they'd taken to disguise him, Ric felt nothing short of conspicuous — like a gilded turret amongst a sea of shanties.

It was his snobbish nobility. His upbringing had necessitated a sense of ease with the constant attention of multitudes. Somewhere along the way, esteem had become an expectation. That truth offended him deeply.

Perhaps, then, this detour into crime and anonymity was in order. It was proper justification in Ric's mind, at any rate. And if his treachery happened to be perpetrated alongside a woman he found utterly fascinating, then so be it.

Ric watched from afar as Ella worked the market, swiping jewelry from a distracted merchant and tripping into gossiping noblewomen, relieving them of their purses and fleeing before they'd even realized she was there.

Skirting along the edge of a pushcart, she lifted two loaves of seedy bread as the baker haggled over price with a patron. Watching her slip the boules into the pockets of her mantle, Ric found himself wondering how much more she could carry.

He wanted in.

It didn't seem that difficult. He'd been observing her for nearly an hour and hadn't seen a hint of the law. Rory had also disappeared, leaving him to his own devices.

Sidling up to an overfat nobleman, Ric set his sights upon the pouch hanging at his side. Gently tugging the leather thong attaching the satchel to his belt, he bumped against the man, only to be hit from behind himself. The blow sent him stumbling into the noble, the man blustering over Ric's incompetence.

"Please forgive my brother. He is quite unwell." Ella tugged Ric away, her eyes shining with anger as they fell upon him. "He meant you no harm, my lord. He's simply delirious with...plague."

"Plague!" the noble cried. "Plague! I never!" Tutting his disapproval, he waddled away as quickly as his stout legs would carry him, all the while wringing his hands. Those gathered around Ella and Ric also dispersed, casting dark looks in their directions.

"Perhaps a different false illness would have been advisable," Ric groused, noting the dirty glances he garnered. "And besides all that, I had it! That pouch would've been mine if only you'd let me finish."

"That is Lord Archibald," Ella hissed. "His satchel is full of pastry!" She stormed away, towing the prince by the hand as she made her way into the shadows of an alleyway.

Ric followed, feeling every bit the scolded child he'd been in his youth. He'd gone through tutors like water, pushing their patience to the limit with his antics, as well as his inability to follow orders.

Mercy. He was an *ass.*

Ric ducked into the darkness, turning to face the wrath he richly deserved. "I'm sorry, Ember. I—"

"Ella." She pulled her hand from his. "My *name* is *Ella*, and I should've known. I cannot give you orders. You're the king!"

"I'm not the king. Not yet." He huffed a sharp breath. "Maybe not ever. But you...you *are* the queen." He reached for her, tucking a stray lock behind her ear as he puzzled over his thoughts.

She was suddenly robbed of breath, her eyes meeting his. "What?"

"This is your kingdom, more so than mine. You know the people, their needs. You know the streets and the towns. Indeed, I cannot think why I ever would've second-guessed your judgment." He folded his arm across his broad chest, a hand fisted over his heart when he dropped to one knee, drawing a gasp from Ella. She covered her mouth.

"Please accept my humble apology as well as my solemn vow. I shall follow you to the ends of the earth." He grinned at her in earnest. "*Ember*."

She sighed, rolling her eyes as she suppressed a giggle. "Ella. *Ella!*"

Ric rose to his feet, welcoming a playful shove from his counterpart. "As you wish, Your Highness." He bowed deeply, when something over her shoulder caught his eye. He tugged her behind himself, stepping around her before reaching for his sword. "Show yourself."

"Relax," Rory said around a yawn, hands raised in submission. "I only saw the last part of your dressing down. If it had been me, you'd have received far worse."

"Doubtless. Perhaps a laving in the sap of globe thistles?" He quirked a brow, earning an exasperated groan from his perpetual tag-along.

"We need to leave." Ella's insistence had both him and Rory on edge, each of them retreating farther into the shadows of the corridor. Ella kneeled, tucking herself behind a sizeable barrel and observed the chaos moving through the thoroughfare. Rory followed suit while Ric stood at their backs, giving them cover.

"What has alarmed you so?" Rory took in the scene, though nothing struck her as out of sorts. It was the typical pandemonium she had come to expect in any town.

"Over there." Ella indicated a man a few short meters away. He was heavily engaged in conversation with another local, his features grim. "That is Sir Guy of Gisbourne, the new Lord of Clun. He seems to wish very much to make a wife of either one of my sisters or me. I think he cares not which, and he has an uncanny knack for finding me, no matter how well I hide. I don't want to give him the opportunity."

Her tone was full of an animus Ric had not yet witnessed from the patient thief—not even when it came to him and his juvenile behavior, which was most deserving of her ire. Following her gaze, he was confounded by the man's mere presence. "I know this man. What did you call him?"

"He is Lord of Clun," Ella grumbled, rising from her perch, her hands itching toward her concealed bow. "Sir Guy of Gisbourne. A loathsome creature if ever there was one. He's—" She paused, taking in the nettled countenance of the prince beside her. "My apologies, Your Highness. I have overstepped. If he is your choice for—"

"He is my choice for *nothing*," Ric seethed, his mounting outrage catching the two women off guard. "He accompanied the treasures of Chamelaute, arriving here just over a week before Johan returned from his expedition. Lord of Clun?"

"Yes, for well over a month now," Ella replied. "Were you unaware, my lord prince?"

He took her gently by the shoulders, the tenderness at odds with the fury clouding his face. "You must call me Ric, Ella, for I am plainly undeserving of anything greater. I'm not even aware of the most banal details of my own kingdom, it seems." He glanced at the unwelcome lord. "How could my brother possibly bear this man's continuing presence here after our father's death?"

Ella and Rory remained silent as a harsh new truth came to bear. Ric prowled the corridor like a caged cat, his shoulders stiff with the mounting pressure in the escalating revelations. "He, himself, accompanied the elements that were later presented to my father — the materials that blew him to bits before my eyes. The gifts that Chamelaute was not aware that they had sent!"

"This man, Gisbourne…" Rory began, her words tentative. "I know of him as well. He used to run the *Potash* mines of Chamelaute until he disappeared — before your brother left."

Ric ceased his restless pacing, his back ramrod straight as he weighed their words. "He knew. My brother knew. He must have." He turned to face Ella and Rory. "Marion was right to be concerned, for it seems my brother has been plotting against me."

His words were quiet — full of resignation, but also laced with danger. "And if he was conspiring against me, then perhaps my father's death was not merely an act of war. It was an act of treason."

"What you insinuate is shocking," Rory said. "But the evidence only grows. Bribes, the mounting presence of foreigners, Gisbourne…"

"He wants your throne," Ella whispered.

The proof was all around them — standing only meters away from him. His brother, Johan, had been skillful with his deceptions, hastily coordinating allegiance through payoffs and guarantees.

It was an insurrection, funded on the backs of the people of Llundyn. And nobody was any the wiser.

"You cannot let him win, Ric. You must fight!" Ella moved before the prince, fueled by a renewed determination born of burgeoning wrath and remorse. She reached for his hands with both of hers, pouring her desire for reprisal into her hold as she met his stormy gaze.

"I have nothing here, no way to fight back. My men are in Chamelaute, and I cannot trust the ones who remain for fear that their loyalty has fled." He shook his head, his eyes falling closed when he issued a grunt of frustration. "Johan has played me for a fool. He always swore he would make a better king, but never did I imagine that he would force his will upon us all. *Dammit!*"

Ric moved to pull away, desperate to resume his frantic pacing, to *think*. Only, Ella held fast, his hands shaking within her grasp as he regarded her earnest countenance. Her wide amber eyes blazed with conviction, her courage serving to fortify his own. What was it that she saw in him that had her so certain of this course?

"You have us," Ella breathed. "The Hood and her merry men. We are no army, but we are a force for the reckoning." Sinking her teeth into her lower lip, she peered up at Ric, melting away his reservations.

He stepped nearer, closing the distance separating them with their joined hands between them. "Show me the way then, queen of shadows, that we may restore the kingdom. The people deserve our best, and I swear I shall bring it." A half-smile tipped the corner of his lips, matching the one upon Ella's face.

"Let's give 'em hell," Rory added, a single brow raised as she grinned at the pair before her.

Seemingly mindful of her proximity to the prince, a lovely rosy flush stained the swells of Ella's cheeks as she inclined her head. "Consider it done. I look forward to our coming exploits." Clearing her throat, she stepped away from Ric, salvaging her composure and looking eager to begin the recovery of all that the people had lost.

"I make for a wicked enemy on a good day. For the sake of my brother, I'll be certain to be at my finest." Ric glanced at the pompous lord of Clun, resolute in the path at hand.

He was grateful for his formidable companions, their victory a foregone conclusion in his mind. The lord—as well as his brother, who was now a thief in his own right—would never know what hit them. Turnabout was fair play, after all.

Chapter Seventeen

Strange as it was, the life of a thief did not excuse one from everyday tasks. Morning light brought with it a whisper amongst the treetops as they swayed to the soft rhythm of dawn while Ella's friends slumbered within their hollowed oakwood shelter.

Having been relieved of her night watch, she began gathering the few garments she'd brought from Locksley, bundling them into her leather satchel, careful not to wake any of the men snoring at her feet.

"Are we ready, then?" Rory smiled brightly, her own meager belongings tucked under her arm.

"Have I mentioned how refreshing it is to no longer be the only woman amongst these brutes?" Offering a light laugh, Ella wrapped her cloak tightly around herself, kicking her legs over a large fallen trunk blocking their route to the creek. Rory followed after her, the new friendship as comfortable as their own company.

At the water's edge, Ella retrieved from her sack the only luxury she'd refused to leave behind when she'd left home. Plunging the thick bar of soda ash and lye into the creek along with her trousers, she scrubbed the panels of stiff material together, lathering them as she massaged the filth-encrusted fibers. Handing the slick soap off to Rory, she wrung out the fabric before fully submerging it once more.

"Do you miss home?" Ella asked, wondering at the ease with which Rory had integrated herself into a foreign land and people.

A humorless snort passed Rory's lips, her features knitted with indifference. "At times." She paused, her gaze wandering off into reveries of a life left behind. "But I suppose we share the same tiresome compulsion to do what is right, no matter how it might affect our own futures."

"So it seems." Ella sighed, draping her freshly washed breeches over a low-hanging branch, the weight of them straining the integrity of her makeshift line.

"I hope you won't think me too bold…" A hint of mischief filled Rory's dark eyes, and without waiting for Ella's response, she continued. "But what exactly is your opinion of Ric?"

"What of him?" Ella couldn't hide her emerging smirk, readily betraying her intrigue.

"Watching him with you yesterday, he was more…*attentive* than I've seen him. I can't help but notice the way his gaze follows you." Her words were sincere, filling Ella with a long since forgotten appreciation for idle gossip, though she did not at all wish to be the subject of it.

Rory's informal reference to the crowned prince reminded her of the peculiar bond the two of them had formed throughout their travels. Though Ella had initially believed them to be lovers, she knew that, in truth, they'd merely struck an unusual camaraderie, thriving upon lighthearted insults and rebukes laced with immense mutual respect.

And, while Rory had spent enough time with him to better understand the inner workings of his mind, surely she had mistaken his sentiments.

"He was prepared to fight the four of you when first we arrived until he saw your face. Since then, he's made every effort to be at your side. Did you know he held affections for you?" Rory's tongue was running away with her, bringing Ella up short.

The truth was, she had not yet processed the possibility.

"The poor man!" Rory snickered as she twisted excess moisture from her tunic, casting a wry grin at her reflection within the rippling armlet.

The prince.

He had been unexpected, not only in presence but character. Ella had long thought him caddish and irresponsible, but underneath his aloof exterior, he was far more complicated than the witless rogue she'd surmised him to be.

He had a reputation, as did she. Were she to be held only to the baseless opinions others had formed of her, she too would be branded as one far more despicable than who she truly was.

"I'm still forming an opinion," she replied diplomatically. "Though, I fear I've misjudged him."

"You're not alone," Rory added. "I thought him an awful wretch when first we met, but he is far more complex than he lets on."

"Are not we all?" Ella took Rory's freshened items, stretching her tunic over a sun-warmed boulder, laying out trousers beside it.

"He's rather confounding," she continued, relishing the rare opportunity apart from the men to lay bare her confusion to a female ally. "In all our years at court, it was the younger prince, Johan, whom I had always admired. He wasn't one to spend nights in the company of fawning young women, while Riccard never failed to have a swarm of hopefuls around him. I suppose I never considered whether or not he cared for the attention, but here in Sherwood, I see the burden he bears. Yet, heavy as it may be, he remains steady."

Ella shook her head, unable to staunch the flow of her thoughts as they trickled from her lips. "I'd once believed that calm to be conceit. Now I can see that he doesn't revel in title or birthright as so many do. Rather, like the soldier he is, he will meet the challenge fated to him with resolute courage."

"Indeed." Rory smirked but said nothing of Ella's numerous insights. Sprawled out atop the forest floor, she braided together blades of grass, her head resting upon Ella's bag. "It's no surprise he's found such refuge in your trade."

Scoffing, Ella seated herself on the dampened earth. "He will better understand the vast difference we can make for his people come sunset. This Calaisean emissary Marion spoke of should prove to be a fine target. I look forward to sharing with His Highness what it means to the villages when we redistribute the profits."

"No doubt, he will enjoy watching you take charge of your men." Rory raised her eyebrows knowingly.

Ella smacked her shoulder, snickering at the subtle innuendo buried deep within her companion's assertions. She was relentless, this mysterious woman of Chamelaute.

And Ella was so pleased to share her company.

* * * *

Stood alone in the center of the king's highway, Ella watched, her breaths even and calm as she absorbed the silence of the forest surrounding her. The balance of her crew lay in wait in quiet expectation, hidden amongst the trees as they listened for the carriage that harbored the potential to be their most excellent haul yet.

At last, the groaning conveyance came into sight, chewing through the sodden earth as it approached with a team of swift Friesians at the lead. Ella turned, an arrow nocked and ready as she drew her bow, her aim fastened to the speeding coach. It was a risky maneuver, but she was prepared to leap into the woods should her machinations fail.

The driver huffed, gesturing wildly toward the hooded obstacle in his path, only to find that he was the target of the archer stubbornly lingering in the roadway. But he refused to slow, prodding his animals onward as they picked up steam.

Perhaps he'd not heard of the Hood. Soon, he would never forget.

Ella released the arrow, shooting the flat feathered cap from the head of the coachman, who sputtered in panic from high atop the carriage. She nocked another bolt as she was joined by Much in the road.

"Stop! That was your warning," Much hollered, the hood of his cape concealing his face as he stood alongside Ella, each fearless in the face of the thundering horses.

"Whoa!" cried the driver, tugging the reins as he urged his steeds to a standstill. They stamped and lunged, cuffing the ground before Ella and Much. Neither moved, their cloaks rustling lightly in the breeze as they waited for their accomplices to fall into place within the trees.

The stuffy emissary exited the coach, his sour face a mask of irritation. "What is the meaning of this? You cannot—" He paused mid-bluster, finding the mysterious archer's drawn bow pointed right at his heart.

"Don't mind us," Alan replied, stepping from behind a great oak as his compatriots filtered out from the thicket. "We only mean to separate you from your wealth." He moved toward the gruff envoy, prodding him to the roadside.

"Is something the matter?" A second figure emerged from the conveyance.

"*Marion*," Ella uttered to Much alone. "That's rather a surprise." She grinned from beneath her hood, noticing the lord's struggles to restrain a smile of his own as he puffed about in faux dismay.

"Unhand me, you wicked knave!" he shouted as Ric took to his side, nudging him toward the Calaisean ambassador, whom Alan was busily confining with rope.

"I shall see you all captured and brought to justice!" the emissary howled, spittle from his overfat lips pelting Alan as he cinched the man's bindings. "Do not simply sit there, Brewster! Do something!"

The coachman waved his hands, vigorously denying the man's directives. "I think I'll stay put, my liege. No sense in me gettin' involved in this."

"Aye," Will agreed. "Stay aloft, and I see no need to shackle you further. Just keep out of our way."

The driver nodded his assent in relief, the envoy rolling his eyes as Marion was sat and secured at his side. The lord's restraints were slack, and Marion would easily give them the slip when the time came, but for the moment, he was more than pleased to observe the infamous antics of the Hood and her merry men.

When each of them was suitably subdued, Ella and her team got to work, making a quick sweep of the carriage and retrieving a trunk filled with gifts and coin for Calaise — yet another bribe from the indomitable Prince Johan.

"It seems my brother has taken some liberties with the treasury," Ric groused, hoisting their prize from the coach's interior with Ella's assistance. "And this feels like a fitting way to repay him for his crimes."

"I couldn't agree more." Ella patted the heir's forearm, a broad smile lighting her face as she met his gaze. "We'll do what needs to be done until we see you safely to the throne."

Ric grinned, feeling very much at ease in his new role within Ella's syndicate. Their words were low, spoken only in the confidence of one another as they completed their task, each feeling wholly contented despite the burdens they bore.

"Are we ready, then?" Rory asked, poking her head around the backside of the carriage where Ella and Ric remained. "We should get moving before Marion blows our cover. Indeed, he's a bit too dramatic for our purposes."

"I've no doubt," Ella said, shaking her head indulgently. And while his theatrics amused her, he was a mite absurd. She took up one end of the chest while Ric grabbed the other. "Let's get moving. Tell the others."

Rory nodded, disappearing as Ric and Ella headed for the woods with their bounty hanging heavily between them. Their crew fell in around them, making a beeline for the safety of their woodland home.

"You've made heisting a pleasure today," Alan said, offering a haughty bow to the trio of victims they left behind as he backed away. "Thank you for your assistance. Good day!"

Ella and her bandits vanished every bit as quickly as they'd arrived, reveling in their loot as she laughed and they bantered their way home, even as the voices of their marks echoed into the distance behind them with vows of revenge.

Chapter Eighteen

The pub was bursting at the seams, which was all the better for hiding in plain sight. People milled about in various states of drunkenness outside the squat alehouse, some playing a subdued game of dice while others looked to be half asleep as they lounged in rickety wooden chairs, late as it was.

For a night of celebration, the grubby tavern on the outskirts of Edwinstowe would serve them well enough, being both far enough from Nottingham to avoid recognition and near enough to home. Major Oak was only a quick jaunt away.

Over a week's worth of heists had seen Ric through the throes of betrayal, though it could never entirely erase the sting of Johan's treachery. His duplicity was no longer in question. While there had been some vague optimism surrounding their ploy, Ric's letter had served its purpose, with Johan ignoring the content in favor of his continuing sedition.

He had readily claimed that the circumstances of war were grave and that Ric had demanded yet more funding. And following a heartfelt plea to the people of Nottingham, he'd told them how very much it grieved him to add more strain to the already dire state in which so many had found themselves. He'd been given no choice, forced to yield to Ric's authority.

Johan was turning the kingdom against him, setting the stage for Ric's demise with talk of a failing war from which he might not return. Being mistaken, it seemed, had been too much to hope for. The spare heir was not dealing in indecision. His intent was as plain as the setting sun.

But the same could be said for Ric. Thieving suited him in a way that no other enterprise had. Indeed, he was a natural with an eye for spotting riches that nearly rivaled Ella's. Pinching the wealth of the most affluent in Nottingham had become as familiar to the elder prince as any inane courtly duties but provided him with much greater reward.

In truth, he was *good*. Willing to take risks that made his comrades queasy, Ric had readily taken his place amongst the most prolific producers in their band. And, while on occasion, a thorough tongue lashing had been delivered, the exquisite Hood had only taken issue with his safety but never his involvement.

She was more patient with him than he deserved, offering him an opportunity that brought him greater fulfillment than anything he'd ever undertaken as a worthless royal stooge. He was a part of a vital undertaking, an oddly honorable endeavor.

Finally, he felt useful.

Enriching the people of Llundyn with the spoils of their thievery felt like he was doing something, with the added benefit of disrupting his brother's endless swindling. Johan was bleeding the people dry in the name of a nonexistent war on the other side of the continent. Taking advantage of the ignorance of the citizenry was nothing short of appalling, in Ric's estimation.

He'd determined it was time for action on another front as well, having written his second-in-command. Though not soon enough to satisfy his desire to immediately wrest control from his brother, Ric's army would quickly return. Meeting him at the border of Llundyn and Wylewoode, so as not to raise suspicion amongst Johan and any spies living in their midst, Ric would gather his men to him once again.

They'd taken great pains to ensure that, by all appearances, it would seem Ric and his men had never left the shores of Chamelaute. Would that their subterfuge might hold. It was time for a reckoning, and Johan would be none the wiser.

Ric followed behind his crew, eager to be off his feet after the chaos of the day. It had been an overwhelming success, orchestrated in large part by Marion and his insider knowledge from within the palace.

Rory angled her arm around Ric's neck as they entered the seedy pub, a sly smile upon her face. "Oye there, I've found the prince amongst us!" she called, offering him a wink as her only explanation. "Imagine! The future king poking about right here in our own little borough!"

What is she doing? His heart beat a fierce rhythm in his chest, each of his associates turning to observe whatever charade she'd launched. Ella furrowed her brows in confusion, though she wore a subtle smile. Dumbfounded, Much and Alan's mouths were agape in horror as they took in the manic woman with her arm around the prince, while Will simply grinned.

Had he misplaced his trust yet again? Ric's mouth went dry as he cleared his throat in vain, searching for something, *anything* he could say to rescue himself from the ensuing fiasco. "What are you doing?" he muttered.

"Saving your life, as usual," Rory replied, tugging him into the warmth of the pub.

"He ain't the prince, you rube!" Will hollered, catching onto her ruse. "That bloke is far too ugly to be Prince Riccard."

"He is the prince, I tell you!" she roared, eyes sparkling with mischief. "Found him outside, wandering about like a little lost lamb."

"Why would he be all the way out here in Edwinstowe when he could be at the palace?" Little John stepped from the crowd, a wave of mead sloshing over the lip of his mug. "He's in Chamelaute, you blockhead! Prince Riccard, my ass!"

A few curious stares and chuckles met them as they made their way toward an empty booth alongside Little John, though most in the ramshackle tavern were too preoccupied with their ale to pay them any mind. Rory's stunt seemed to have had the desired effect, making a mockery of the prince's presence, even in spite of its validity.

"I overheard a few suspicious fellows outside who thought it was you," Rory said. "I thought it best to ridicule their presumptions."

Ric nodded. "Effective. My thanks, despite the irony."

"It's nothing." Rory patted his shoulder before moving to slide into the booth beside the rest of their gang.

"Marion could've blown our whole operation, the foolish lout," Alan griped as the barmaid arrived, offering each of them a fresh tankard of brew. "Who smiles when they're bein' robbed?"

"Who *doesn't* smile when they know the whole thing is a sham?" Much took a hefty gulp, wiping his sleeve over his mouth in a show of ill manners. "We'd never have had a tally like that without his tip, and him being there to witness it was a stroke of pure genius, in true. Nobody will ever suspect him now!"

"Shove it, will ya?" Will smacked Alan and Much in turn. "Everyone will suspect if you don't shut up!"

"Sounds like I missed out on quite the heist today." Little John had the good sense to keep his voice low, though his grin could light the whole of the tavern. "I've some news for you, though, Elle."

"Do tell, John." Ella sighed deeply, relaxing against Ric as their legs pressed together. The booth was a tight squeeze, with four of them on one side and three on the other, though Little John might well count for two with as brawny as he was.

Ric's gaze drifted toward Ella, his fascination with the lady thief without end. She took a sip of ale, her manners elegant and refined. At times, it was easy to forget that they ran in the same lofty circles. They weren't born for a life lived in hiding, in criminality, yet here they were.

And he had never felt more at ease.

John leaned forward, resting on his forearms. "There're more foreigners everywhere. I can scarcely keep up with their demands for arms. They aren't all

Calaiseans, either." He shook his head, reconciling the peculiarity of all his recent requests. "I can make any sword, any dagger, sure, but it feels wrong."

"If you refuse, you will be counted as a traitor." Ella nodded toward Much, where only a stump remained at the end of his arm. "Maybe not in public, but certainly in the privacy of Prince Johan's mind. You cannot risk it."

"She's right," Ric agreed, frustration building within him. He was the rightful heir with no power to speak of. Still, his brother hadn't crushed him completely. If deception was the commodity in which Johan wished to deal, then Ric was happy to oblige.

"I've heard of your mastery with weapons. Doubtless, you take pride in your trade. Perhaps a little less is in order." Ric raised a brow in challenge, knowing fully that such a request would be distasteful to an honorable fellow such as John.

Ella nodded slowly, coming to terms with his proposal. "It could work."

John puzzled over his intent. "You don't mean…"

"I do. Finely made weapons can be brittle, no? Break with use and degrade over time?" A roguish grin formed on Ric's face when Ella giggled, her levity a welcome reprieve from the tedium of their never-ending strategizing. Her mirth may well have been as a result of exhaustion, something that plagued them all, but it was refreshing just the same.

John was aghast, his eyes wide in a face that looked too boyish for his years. "I suppose I could, but—"

"But nothing, my friend. It takes courage to stand tall when braving the forces of tyranny. I swear to you that your sacrifice will not be in vain. Your integrity will remain intact in the eyes of the king and kingdom."

Ric reached across the table, extending his hand, the depth of his pledge hanging in the space between them.

It was what he hadn't said that seemingly brought John up short. One day, Prince Riccard would become king, and with any luck, it would be soon. He shook Ric's hand. "I'd be honored to be of service. I shall not fail you…any of you," he added, tossing a meaningful look Ella's way.

Rising from his seat, he bowed deeply before catching himself. "Forgive me, sir, but looking like a prince does not make you one. You may get your own ale!" He grimaced, backing away with an apologetic shrug as he headed for the bar.

Ella shook her head, an indulgent smile upon her face. "Poor John. I do believe he finds himself rather awestruck in your presence."

"If anyone here is awestruck, it's me." Ric reached for her, lacing his fingers through hers before pressing his lips to the back of her hand. He settled their joined hands on his thigh, meeting her sparkling gaze. "You have the most incredible support throughout the kingdom. People follow you, and their faith in you without question. The confidence you inspire is nothing short of admirable. I am duly impressed, lady thief."

"Do not call me that!" She wrinkled her nose, bumping her shoulder against his, though she made no effort to pull free of him.

He chuckled, enamored by her indignation. "Do you not wish to be called 'lady'? Or is it 'thief' that offends you?"

"Yes. No… I don't know!" She covered her face with her free hand, her cheeks bright with color. Tucking a loose curl behind her ear, she gathered herself once more. "I suppose I only wish it weren't necessary. Becoming a criminal was never my intent, but it seemed the only way to affect change. I can help the people that my stepmother refused to acknowledge, people well and truly in need. If I'd been born a man, I would've had so many different choices."

"You handle the freedoms you do have better than any man I've ever met." He squeezed her hand, their eyes meeting in earnest. "And when I am..." He shook his head, lowering his voice. "When I am king, I shall see to it that you have many more."

They observed one another in silence, bound at once by their confessions and the risk therein. Their dreams had been laid bare with a few daring words, each of them receiving the other's desires for safekeeping without question. They were allies...accomplices — and it all felt so very *right.*

The bawdy sounds of the tavern swirled around them, enveloping the pair in an odd sense of sanctuary, and Ric found himself more at peace, perhaps than he had ever felt in his life. He smiled, enraptured by the conundrum that was Ella of Locksley. "Where'd you learn to shoot as you do? You're quite accomplished."

"My father," she said without hesitation. "It was our reprieve after the loss of my mother. The wilds were our refuge, and he'd have me out there for hours. It was nock, shoot, breathe — an endless loop of actions that served as a welcome distraction for us both." She sighed, her eyes heavy with fatigue.

Ric frowned, never imagining her mastery of archery having come about in such a peculiar fashion. "A worthy pursuit, indeed. I'm profoundly sorry for your loss, twice over."

"As am I for yours." She leaned nearer to him, tucking herself tightly to Ric's side. "But our grief can also make us stronger. Were it not for my father's marriage to the delightful Lady Margaret, I may never have found myself to be useful with a bow."

"How do you mean?"

Ella yawned, resting her head upon his shoulder. "After they married, the woods were my closest companion — at least, aside from Much. We spent every day out there in hiding. She is the reason I can shoot an apple from atop Much's head from fifty paces off. Sometimes more." There was a smile in her voice that brought Ric consolation, despite the dolor of her tale.

"I should like to see you do that."

"So you shall," she murmured, her breathing slow and even.

Ric took a sip of mead, using care to avoid disturbing the now-sleeping beauty at his side. Smiling, he wondered at how a crown prince could find himself in a filthy pub on the edge of the kingdom with a lovely thief in his arms and be happier than he'd ever been in a palace filled with plenty.

Chapter Nineteen

Ella skimmed her razor-sharp blade over the shaft of her newly formed arrow, gingerly testing its lethal tip in the palm of her hand. Each stroke of her knife was deliberate as she manipulated the bolt.

Ric visibly marveled at the precision with which she labored. "This isn't going as planned." For in the time it had taken him to skin a stick to little more than a curved shard, the enigma that was Lady Locksley had successfully crafted three pristine pieces of weaponry fit for the finest archers of the Crown's army.

With earnest eyes gleaming, Ella slipped her new arrow into the filling quiver at her side before taking Ric's from his hand. Her widening grin belied her efforts to encourage him as he attempted to justify his place among the infamous outlaws.

She examined the prince's workmanship, turning it over in her hands, but before she could suppress her amusement, laughter burst from her lips. "I'm so sorry. I didn't mean—" Ella covered her mouth in a futile struggle to keep herself from causing any further offense. After considering the less than subtle camber of the prince's design, she conjured what she thought to be enough diplomacy to respond. "It's quite good for your first try."

The prince chuckled, a wry grin forming on his face. Ella placed the arrow at her feet, snatching a long twig from the ground beneath her. Leaning toward him, she took his hands, and though her own barely covered half the size of his, she began to show him in more detail her refined skill.

"If you hold the blade at this angle, it allows longer, cleaner strokes." Guiding his hand, she peeled away the weathered outer layer in an unbroken ribbon, revealing the fresh blonde wood underneath. "You see?" She rotated the stick in Ric's fingers.

"Perhaps you wouldn't mind showing me again?" The prince drew nearer still to Ella, catching her gaze when he spoke.

She was surprised by how quickly her opinion of him had shifted, from believing the heir a self-serving egotist to seeing firsthand the way he cherished his kingdom. Further, she was increasingly caught off guard by how her body responded to his attention to his touch. His mere presence was intoxicating.

"I'll show 'im, Elle," Alan offered, shocking her out of her reverie. Ric and Ella parted as he approached. He stopped short of the pair, a loud *crack* sounding from beneath his weight.

Ella looked on in horror at the prince's arrow, snapped in half at Alan's feet.

"What was that for?" Ric gawked at his splintered endeavor lying uselessly on Sherwood's floor.

"I thought it was a snake — the way it was all curvy an' such." Alan shrugged, bending to pick up the bolt. Scoffing, he tossed the pieces over his shoulder, discarding them just as he did his emptied walnut shells.

"Marion has arrived," Much said, loping through the trees. On his heels was Rory, with Marion close behind on his graying horse. Rory and Much had taken the most recent watch, with every member of the band on high alert since Ric had arrived. Protecting him had become their utmost priority — a shame indeed, as they were nowhere near adequate when it came to the security of Llundyn's future.

"Are you well, friend?" Ric clasped Marion's forearm, welcoming him to their woodland home.

"As well as expected," Marion said, dusting the vestiges of the road that had gathered on his clothing away with persnickety hands. "I'm afraid I've bad news."

The band fell in around Marion as he collected himself. His face was grim — unusual for the blithe fellow — and everyone was duly concerned. Their combined efforts had been unexpectedly successful, bringing joy and a dose of contentment to the people of Nottingham. For everything to go awry at this point would be crushing.

"Johan was joined by Sheriff Dane this morning, the pair addressing the citizenry. 'A development', they called it." Marion paused, taking a hefty breath before continuing. "He proceeded to share that the Council of Lords has had enough of the vigilante referred to as the Hood and bids he be seized and tried immediately. Anyone caught aiding or accepting gifts from you will be punished as well."

"Ah, so now he's not only stolen my birthright, but he also deigns to issue edicts." Ric laced his fingers behind his head, the gesture refreshingly casual despite the blow they were being dealt.

"That isn't yet the worst of my news. Prince Johan has so graciously offered to free any prisoners held for such crimes should the Hood turn himself, or I daresay *herself*, in."

The profanity that burst forth from Ric's lips was unmatched by any sailor as he let fly his discontent, kicking at the dirt. He was joined in his outrage by all the members of the crew, save for Ella.

It was as if an ass had kicked her in the gut. Her only intent had been to aid those who were unable to help themselves. But to punish the needy for *her* crimes was cruel beyond measure—a clever scheme indeed, turning those loyal to the band of thieves against them, solely in the name of self-preservation.

Her mind ran a mile a minute as she turned the alternatives over in her head. For the first time since embarking on this endeavor, Ella felt the sting of hopelessness. "Who would even believe me if I did?"

"You won't," Much ordered, taking her firmly by the shoulders. "We will find another way, and you mustn't blame yourself for any of this. Do you hear me?"

"I was reluctant to share with you what I'd learned for this reason." Marion caught her gaze, her eyes sparkling with moisture she refused to give in to.

"Much is right, though, Elle," Will added. "You cannot turn yourself in. You would not be taken seriously but would still be kept as a criminal for exposing your allegiance to an outlaw."

"She will not, no. But someone else will," Ric said, having recovered his civility.

"I'll not sit by and allow someone else to confess to my crimes." Ella's frustration spiked, her tone dripping with bitterness. The suggestion that she might permit anyone else to take the fall to save her own skin was insulting.

"Hear me, I beg you." Riccard held his hands before him as though praying for mercy. "We draw straws between ourselves. Whoever draws short turns himself in at the palace gates clad in your famed green mantle." He took a step nearer to her. She was profoundly dishonored, and he likely just wished to offer comfort, to steal the burden of guilt she need not feel.

Ella raised her chin as if to dare him, and he would not disappoint.

"I know the castle better than anyone, better than my brother. If Johan does what he claims, releasing those already incarcerated upon the Hood's surrender, then we need only extract our own man before dawn. I would not risk any longer." Ric watched as his words sank in, with some of the enmity draining from her countenance.

"It could work," Marion agreed. "I'm confident your brother will be true to his promise, for he will not miss the opportunity to sway the loyalties of Nottingham with such a bold display of clemency."

Ella watched as Will wandered several paces off, plucking a small handful of hay from the bundle meant for the horses. "I say we try it," he said, returning to the group. Taking three stems from his collection, he threw the rest aside, clutching the varied pieces in his palm.

"Bu' there's only three to pick from." Alan nodded toward each individual, noting the number in attendance. Much cocked an eyebrow, disgruntling him all the more. "There're seven of us, genius."

"But only three can reasonably pass as the Hood," Will reasoned. "Ella and Rory are out, and Marion must maintain confidence with Prince Johan."

"How convenient that His Royal Highness has only to show us the way when it's *his* plan puttin' our necks on the line." Alan snatched a straw from Will in a huff, and Much followed, choosing one of his own.

Ric twined his fingers behind his back, unwilling to speak any further on the matter. Alan wasn't wrong, but they were running low on options.

Ella fought to see another solution that wouldn't jeopardize any of her friends, but Riccard was right. Unless someone claimed the Hood's identity, innocents would remain trapped within the dungeon indefinitely.

"Who will it be then?" Much opened his palm, showing his straw.

Will followed, revealing the longer straw between the two. Alan was next, his straw a mere stub by comparison. He stiffened upon the realization that he'd be giving himself up, but when he looked at Ella, he smiled.

"I'm proud to do this for you, milady." Alan dramatically bowed his head. "Jus' get me out before they string me neck tomorrow."

"You'll be free before dinner." Ric clutched Alan's forearm as he did with his own men.

"But maybe jus' after dinner, then?" Alan asked, returning Ric's hold. "I've never been served a meal in a castle before."

"Very well then, but no longer." Ric's visage was stern, the mien of a commander, but Ella still noticed how the corner of his mouth rose with Alan's request.

* * * *

It was late afternoon, the beginnings of the eventide nipping at their cheeks as they silently treaded through town. Each of them took a different route to quell suspicion from onlookers. For now, they could trust nobody but themselves.

Together, the outlaws had determined it best to take up posts surrounding the castle gates for Alan's surrender. Some of them were hidden while others remained in plain sight, each equipped with weaponry fit for their designated positions.

Much's blades were discreetly tucked in his boots, with more at his waist as he shuffled pathetically into place, his character ever the maimed beggar. To his enduring credit, he had earned nearly a month's wage out of sympathy the week prior, proving that there was still generosity and hope to be had.

Ella observed everyone from her perch atop the farrier's shop, obtaining a direct line to the castle in the event the spare's men attempted anything foul. To the south, she nodded at Will, who was poised for action with a bow and bolt readied at his side. Ric and Rory milled about the square, each with their own saber and broadsword concealed.

Ella waited expectantly, for any moment the Hood would make his appearance. She missed her own cloak, its lining far more insulating than the warmth of Alan's, the coolness of the day settling deep in her bones.

Finally, she saw him, ambling confidently down the center of the cobbled road leading to the iron gate.

Her hood covered his face as he wandered by the few remaining individuals in town, all finishing up with the day's chores. One woman gasped when she recognized the notorious mossy green material shrouding their friend, stumbling after him as she begged him not to give himself up.

Gently, he shrugged away from her grasp, only to turn and clasp her hand between his own two. With a flourish, he bowed, pressing a kiss to her knuckles before moving on his way, undoubtedly appearing eager to get his unfortunate errand over with.

Alan's weightless steps slowly garnered the attention of the people, their eyes following his form all the way to the castle wall. More citizens gathered, whispering to their loved ones while others ran into village shops, telling of the Hood's arrival.

So far, everything was going according to plan. With many witnesses to the Hood's surrender, Prince Johan wouldn't risk going against his word, especially if he wished to earn the allegiance of those he continued to bleed dry during his reign.

Alan stood before the gate with outspread arms, while all who were present waited with bated breath for his arrest. Some yelled for him to run, while others thanked him for all he'd done for their families. None among them cursed the Hood's deeds, nor did they urge him to cave into Johan's manipulations, showing nothing less than wholehearted devotion for their efforts.

True to his nature, Alan couldn't resist the thrill of having garnered the attention of the town. "I received your message, Your *Highness*," he called, his hand to his mouth to increase the range of his voice. "It's me, the robbin' Hood!"

He dropped the covering from his head in dramatic fashion, the people cheering with the confession of his identity. A small fraction of those gathered began chanting the moniker, their fists pumping the air.

Ella surveyed the growing crowd, when her sights fell upon Riccard below, watching her as those around him shouted the Hood's praises. The smile upon the heir's face stole her breath as she met his gaze, his pride evident.

Heat built rapidly behind her eyes, forming tears she had no prayer of stopping. The outpouring of support from the people she cared for more than herself was overwhelming, and seeing how valued she and her band of misfits had become to Nottingham was heartening, indeed.

Her small moment of victory was cut short when the palace guards appeared, making their way toward the gate. The towering doors of the castle entrance opened behind them, with Prince Johan standing at their center. Hastily descending the steps, the handful of royal guards split to either side, letting him through.

"You've made a noble decision coming here today," Johan said loudly enough for most to hear. "Many will be released because of your persisting selflessness this eve."

"Free the Hood!" a man yelled from beyond the square, hidden behind fellow onlookers so as not to be discovered.

"I'm afraid his release is not within my power," the prince responded genially. "Though I am pleased to have been granted the authority to send your loved ones home."

It was hardly something for anyone to grumble over and masterfully played by the prince. He'd designed a situation in which there were no winning sides, but a victory meant only for himself. While families appeared happy to see unjust imprisonments remedied, the price for their liberation was to be paid for with the pending slaughter of one who'd fed them when they couldn't feed themselves.

"Take the *Hood* and get him settled so that we may reunite friends and family." Johan's wry grin resembled that of a demon boasting the sabotage and waywardness he wrought, without any show of regret for the murder of his father or decimation of his only brother.

Ella kept her sights on Alan until the palace doors closed behind him. He was escorted by five guards, whose faces she did not recognize. If these men were some of the foreigners that had begun flooding the streets of Llundyn, her only solace was to think that their weapons might fail should they attempt to use them against her friend.

It was time. They had only one chance to free Alan, or it would mean all their heads. Slinging her bow and quiver over her shoulder, Ella set off to the location she and Ric had agreed to meet outside of the priory, praying that her faith in Friar Tuck's willingness to bend his vows would be justified.

Chapter Twenty

Tucking the free tendrils of her hair into the bun tied at her neck, Ella steeled herself for the task at hand. With nobody inside the castle's connecting chapel, she waited with Ric for the friar to arrive. He wasn't late. They'd simply come nearly an hour early, anxious to release Alan before Prince Johan thought up any ominous plans for his new guest.

"You're nervous…all your fidgeting." The heels of Riccard's boots tapped quietly against the limestone floors as he moved nearer to Ella, the echo of each step whispering from one wall to the next.

The spare had remained true to his word, releasing all other prisoners in exchange for the Hood. Yet the thought of Alan trapped in the dungeon plagued her consciousness. "We can't fail him, Ric." Glistening eyes lifted to meet those of the prince. "It's my fault he's in there, and if we get caught…"

"We won't. While my brother was attending council meetings and private lessons, I was doing my best to avoid all responsibility. In doing so, I found passages and cellars that have been long since forgotten." A sheepish grin crossed his face, his embarrassment evident to Ella with the admission. Still, it was courtesy of his youthful carousing that they were able to do what they were about to do. It hadn't been all for naught.

Ella rewarded Ric with a weak smile of her own before blotting a fallen tear from her cheek with the linen sleeve of her father's old tunic. Heaving a cleansing breath, she opted for a change of pace. "What was it like, growing up within the palace walls?" Setting her shoulder casually against the gray stone behind her, she allowed herself to look, *really* look, at the heir next to her. Decorum did not allow for such things, but in the dimness of the sanctuary, she studied him.

The lines of his tall form were powerful, brawny with his many years of training. Broad shoulders rigid with muscle set atop his taut frame, funneling lower into his narrow waist and hips, his presence ever-royal, even amid his newly acquired role as prince of thieves. In the planes of his face was a startling youthfulness, despite the fine scruff stretching from cheeks to chin deceptively marking him as a tradesman older than his twenty-one years. His tousled mane grew in disheveled fashion, giving him the appearance of an unkempt child — an unexpectedly endearing sight.

The future of Llundyn was not at all what Ella had anticipated.

Riccard leaned his back against the same wall, pressing the sole of his boot against it, as if to keep it upright. "Not as different as you might think." He paused, chuckling to himself while he riffled through memories that had long been stowed away, covered in the dust of willful abandon.

Considering his words, he remembered the many reasons for neglecting reveries of his past. It had been too painful to remember the rapture of his youth—a time when the world gave more than it spoiled. But somehow, he savored sharing the intimate details of his history with the woman beside him.

"I was so blessed, though, of course, I could not see my fortune then," he began again, nostalgia flooding his mind. "My parents were king and queen, yes, but their children always came first. I never appreciated the value of a loving mother and father as I should have, but I understand now what they gave my siblings and me."

"No child recognizes the benefits of their upbringing, no matter how significant they might be." Ella placed her hand on Ric's forearm, the gesture utterly without thought.

Unclasping his own hands, he turned to face her, mirroring her stance against the cold rock. She skimmed the tips of her fingers over his wrist to his palm, lacing them within hers, their gazes fastened upon one another.

"Tell me of your mother," Ella inquired as he closed the little space that lay between them.

"She was beautiful in body and soul," he offered without hesitation. He traced rhythmic halos within her palm with his thumb, her skin silken and soft as the feathers of a dove. "My mother was stubborn as a mule when she wanted to be, but her heart was golden. She stood in the gap for me when I least deserved it, urging me toward my destiny before I knew what it really meant to be king."

Silence hovered between them, the ardor of Ric's regard for the lady thief ever-growing as they stood a mere breath apart. "You are much like her, you know." He cupped her cheek with his free hand, and she readily nestled her head into the warmth of his touch, though she no longer met his eyes. She was beautiful without question, her grace and allure far exceeding the confines of physical desire alone.

The prince's thoughts drifted to his father, and for the first time, he understood. Edward had allowed the kingdom to suffer while his grief had secretly torn him to pieces, but he hadn't been a fool. He'd simply lost his will to lead after the deaths of his beloved wife and daughter.

While the marriage had been arranged years before, the adoration between Edward and Eleanor had developed rapidly once they'd wed. Their affection had undoubtedly been the motivation behind the king's entreaty on the final afternoon of his life, beseeching his sons to seek wives for themselves.

Ric had laughed at the notion of pursuing a life of forced monogamy, unable to identify the advantage in tethering himself to another.

His doubts had fled.

"My parents were married in this chapel," he said abruptly, taking in the architectural grandeur that it was. Moonlight trickled into the space through the ornate stained-glass arches above the pulpit, shining more brightly than most nights. "In fact, in the last conversation I had with my father, he expressed his hopes for my brother and me to do the same."

"No." Ella feigned shock at his confession, a wry grin upon her lips. "The fabled Prince Riccard married?"

"I'm afraid so." He cocked a brow, affecting insincere disappointment.

The doors of the back entrance creaked open, the prince and Ella reacting quickly to the sound as they sprang apart. The good friar entered, ambling to the center aisle where he knelt before the image of his savior. Marking himself with the sign of the cross, he bowed his head in reverence before rising to his feet.

"Brother Tuck!" Ella hastened to meet him. "We are in your debt."

"Nonsense, my child, for what we are doing is the work of the Lord." He pressed a kiss to her hand.

"Even so, if there is anything I can do for you when I take the throne, consider it done," Ric said, inclining his head in a show of gratitude.

"I may well hold you to that, Your Highness," the friar jested. He reached underneath his habit, retrieving two fawn-colored garments identical to his own. "But until then, we mustn't tarry."

Grabbing her bundled bow and quiver from where she'd stashed it beneath a pew, Ella crossed it low over her back, a short sword already attached to her belt. They were prepared to deliver a fight if necessary. Would that it never come to that.

Ella and Ric hastily draped themselves in the thick material, knotting the accompanying golden chords around their waists.

"How do I look?" Ella's nose scrunched in amusement as she dipped into a stiff bow.

Ric grinned as he stepped before her. "You look thoroughly pious, milady." He reached for the cowled hem of her robe, lifting it onto her head like a hood to cover her hair.

"Indeed, you both do," Tuck confirmed, moving nearer as he addressed them in a hushed tone. "Now, neither of you need speak if we are met by anyone at the palace. You've made a vow of silence, hindering you from doing so. They will not question your commitment. We will likely move about the halls without drawing attention, but if our presence is questioned, I will inform them that we've come to bless the daily provisions."

"Ever the conman, I see," Ella teased. "Though I suppose there's no dishonesty to be found in your plan."

"Correct as usual, my dear." He rambled over to check the entrance through which he'd just arrived. Motioning to them, they followed his steps, stopping behind him side by side. "Follow closely and keep your heads down."

Ric and Ella kept their gazes downcast, keeping stride as they were disregarded within the friar's shadow. When the guards posted at the southern entry saw Tuck, they ushered them through without dispute. The prince recognized none of the guards, assuming only that his brother had swept the vast estate of any guardsmen who'd been formerly stationed on that side of its gates.

The familiar hum of servants tending their chores welcomed them, each eying the trio with disinterest as they passed through the maze of corridors with ease. It was strange for Ric to return. It was home, yes, but he knew he would no longer be openly received by the staff with whom he'd once shared history and connection. Johan had planted seeds of doubt, gripping their steadfast conviction with cords of ambivalence as he'd shepherded them directly into his snare.

Each time Ric acknowledged the spare's duplicity, his heart lurched. All their lives, they'd maintained a steadfast kinship, and he struggled to make sense of Johan's actions. In the years spent by each other's side, he never would have assumed his brother capable of such heinous treachery.

By Johan's wicked design, their father had been murdered in cold blood, and the usurper intended to put an end to Ric's life as well, leaving the throne unoccupied for the taking.

Rounding the corner to the eastern wing, they reached the stairway. It was shockingly undermanned — the entirety of the palace was — but Ric was grateful for the shreds of luck they'd been dealt amid their pursuit.

Down multiple flights, they descended, the air thick with the pungent redolence of stale moisture and feces. Ric remembered the odor well, having trod this same path in his younger years as he endeavored to secure a smooth but cutting flask of old Sheriff Benedict's aged brandy. For lower still than the accused were kept ran a series of overlooked tunnels leading to neglected cellars and secret chambers beneath the town's center, while the opposite side opened to the woods. It was said that they were installed by the original architect as protection against invasion.

Musty passages, crumbling from time's unrelenting decay, would serve as Alan's unobstructed route to deliverance.

"Finally, then!" Alan bellowed, overhearing the footfalls of his rescuers. "You've decided I can have some supper! I was beginning to believe you migh' leave me starving in here with nothin' more than chicken bones and dirt to fill my belly."

Ric saw Ella's features brighten at the sound of his voice, and his freedom within their grasp. It was likely he was entirely alone from the way he spoke, which seemed quite possible, considering how few men seemed to be posted about the property.

She picked up speed, hastening deeper into the depths of the dungeon following the trails of Alan's bellows. Ric stayed on her heels until they reached the dank cell. The friar was close behind, sucking in rapid, shallow breaths as he grasped an iron bar for support, having exerted himself beyond his traditional standard. He nodded toward the heavens, offering thanks for safety in their toil.

Alan was perched on a boulder, biting at his fingernails when they spied him. He'd been stripped of the infamous green cloak, left wearing only the boots on his feet and a filthy tunic and vest paired with moth-eaten trousers. It was cold, wedged between damp stone walls stories beneath ground level, but he displayed no indication of discomfort.

"Come, Alan!" Ella beamed at the sight of him. "It's time to go, and if you hurry, there may be some dinner left for you back in Sherwood."

"I hadn't expected you so soon!" Jumping from where he'd planted himself, he ran to the metal barrier separating them, clinging to it with both hands as he grinned from ear to ear. "And you've even gone and become a monk since I last saw you. How things do change."

"Have you been hurt?" Ella snaked her arm through the bars, taking his face between her thumb and fingers to examine him for injury, while Riccard retrieved two long, narrow picks from a pouch he'd kept tied at his hips.

"Don' fuss, Elle. I'm fine," Alan assured her, chuckling as he ducked out of her reach. "The only thing hurtin' me is my starvin' gut. Those bastards never fed me!"

Tuck pressed toward him, digging a fresh roll from within his habit pocket and handing it to Alan.

Ella patted the friar's shoulder. "To think I believed you carried the holy word in those pockets."

"That's what the other pocket is for, my child," the friar said. "I was saving it for later, but he needs it more than I do."

"Thank you," Alan managed through a mouthful of bread as Ric set to work maneuvering the slender pieces of metal within the keyhole of the rusted lock. When he carefully twisted and shifted the picks, its internal mechanism clinked with the deliberate movements, and with a final *click*, the prince had successfully unlocked the prison door. As he pulled it open, the hinges protested with an ear-grating shriek, and Alan slipped out.

"Well done, sir!" the good friar chirped, each of them gratified that the most uncertain portion of their journey had been conquered. "You are quite handy with those instruments."

"While my brother learned the strategies of war, I conquered the exalted art of lock-picking." Ric tucked the tools into his satchel. "Being trapped in the castle was too tedious for my liking, so I found ways to avoid such fates. That's how I found the door at the end of this passage. Once through it, continue down the length of that hallway until it divides. It's the leftmost corridor that will feed you out into the northern woods."

"But you're coming with us, aren't you?" Concern laced Ella's tone.

"There's something I need to find while I'm here." Ric bowed slowly, his gaze never leaving Ella's. "I'll be fine. I know how to get to what I'm looking for without being detected, so worry not."

"I shall join you," Ella replied, drawing a smile from the heir, who was perfectly happy being told what to do when it was she who was doing the telling. "Alan doesn't need me, and Tuck is better off not being seen with us more than he already has been."

The friar nodded in agreement, while Alan shrugged behind him.

"We'll see you back at camp then." Ric clasped Alan's forearm with a nod. "And to you, Brother Tuck, thank you for all you've done this night. Your courage will not be forgotten."

Ella embraced the friar and Alan quickly in turn, before watching their retreating forms alongside Ric. Pulling at her hood, she arranged it atop her head, shielding her face for their adventure. "Ready when you are."

* * * *

Ric led Ella through the palace without incident, only once nearly crossing paths with a chambermaid and her second. Together, they silently passed the meeting hall where last Ric had seen Johan. Upon his journey across the sea, he'd hoped to mend what had been severed between them. Now, it was evident that the contempt the spare had expressed had not been the result of tumult or sorrow.

"In here." Ric motioned to Ella, opening the door and ushering her inside, before barricading it shut behind them with a nearby chair.

Once he was confident they were alone, he crossed the room to the opposite wall, removing the late King Jerothan's framed likeness. Setting the portrait aside, he pulled on the handle hidden within the vacant space, and the wall split from floor to ceiling, revealing the secret access to his father's chamber. Riccard secured the painting back into place, leaving it as though it had never been handled. The pair entered, Ric sealing the doorway as the blackness of the passageway enveloped them.

He held out his hand, barely visible in the space between them. "Join me?"

Ella reached for him without hesitation. Again, he was awed by the fearlessness she exhibited in her pursuits, never relenting in her passion for serving. Defeat was not known by her, neither self-seeking diversions of fleeting frivolity. Lady Ella of Locksley was a force of unmitigated determination and had earned not only the prince's most profound respect but his admiration as well.

Hand in hand, Ric walked them through the darkness using the stone wall as his guide. Mice squeaked at their feet, scurrying about the ground. It wasn't much farther, but he slowed his steps unconsciously, keeping her close for a moment longer.

"What is it?" Ella whispered as they slowed. "Is something the matter?"

"We've made it." He released her hand, feeling along the wooden barrier ahead of him. Gripping a carved hold within the smooth finish, he struggled against its weight until finally, it broke free, shuddering to the side enough for them to squeeze through the opening.

Riccard entered first, ensuring the chamber was not presently occupied, before nodding Ella in.

"Is this the king's…?" Her voice trailed as she stood motionless, observing.

A modest glow illuminated the trinkets and grandeur within the bedroom. Ric moved about, realizing that his father's chambers, the room meant to be his own, had already been claimed by another.

"Indeed, it is, though it has not remained so." He glanced at the table where a single candle flickered, a harbinger of Johan's intent to return. His evening meal set upon the same surface — further warning that they did not have time to linger. "My brother may steal my throne, but he cannot have all of my memories with it."

Ric set about his search, roving around the dimly lit room but careful not to disturb anything. Buried deep within a bureau, he retrieved a sturdy-looking chest. "I'll just be a moment," he said, his voice low.

Quickly, he sorted through its contents, with everything he'd hoped to find still there. The box had belonged to his mother, and in it rested her most treasured pieces. Snatching up the items for which he'd come, he slipped them into his waist pouch for safekeeping, relieved to have them within his possession. He closed the chest then, moving it into the bureau once again as though nobody had touched it.

"That's settled." He turned to Ella, who explored the space with wide-eyed fascination. For a moment, he watched her, eager to know her thoughts.

"I'm sorry for your loss, Ric," she murmured, brushing light fingers over a portrait of Queen Eleanor, framed beneath an elegant tapestry adorning the east-facing wall. "She was very beautiful. Your sister, too."

"Thank you. We've all lost much," he replied, joining Ella before the painting. He reached for her, grateful for her grace under pressure and her gentle sensitivities. "Would that we begin to right these wrongs."

She met his gaze with a smile as he towed her toward the passageway. They were both ready to be far from the danger that the castle and its many soldiers and spies posed.

The chamber door flung open, the knob bouncing off the stone wall as it clashed against it.

"Who are you?" Johan demanded, a familiar moss-colored cloak draped over his arm as he stepped into the chamber. A large man flanked the younger prince, though Ric did not recognize him.

With the cowls of their habits still shrouding their faces, Ric's and Ella's identities were impossible to discern, and when neither of them answered, the spare's fury boiled.

"Kill them," Johan muttered, directing the goon at his side toward the pair of interlopers.

Ric dove between Ella and her pursuer, pushing her to safety as the burly sentinel collided with him. Ric's fist connected with the brute's jaw, but not before the wicked sting of cold steel sliced through the flesh of his own forearm.

Ignoring the sudden pain coursing through him, he drew his elbow back, executing an unyielding strike to the gut, knocking the wind from the thug's lungs. The man staggered backward, folding in half when Ric followed up with a swift kick to his abdomen.

Johan huffed, likely frustrated by the sentry's lack of prowess in battle, though the imbecile had at least recovered his feet. Watching the man grapple with the shrouded intruder, Johan made for the smaller of the two trespassers, dropping the famed cloak as he moved toward Ella.

Ric landed another hit on his opponent, an uppercut jolting the man's head back. The maneuver gave him just enough time to force his brother off Ella, kicking Johan in the ribs before being pummeled from behind himself. "Run!" he called to her, feeling nothing short of helpless as he brawled with the relentless sentry.

Ella crawled out of Johan's reach, only to be grasped around the ankle by the incensed prince. Flipping onto her back, she slammed her other foot into his face with the full force of her body. His grip loosened as he clutched his throbbing jaw, groaning on the ground as she scrambled to her feet.

Racing toward the open doorway, Ella scooped up her cape while Ric kneed his adversary heartily in the groin, immobilizing the hired ruffian once and for all. He ran for Ella, sparing a quick glance for his brother, who writhed on the floor in agony.

"I'll see you both hanged for this!" Johan sputtered through blood-stained teeth as the pair dashed through the doorway.

Running for their lives, Ella and Ric sprinted through the empty hallways, only to be spotted by a handful of guards patrolling the southern wing of the palace. The meager squad quickly noted their presence and pursued them from both sides of the connecting archway, bridging the living quarters to the heart of the castle.

Ella peered through one of several open-air windows, overlooking the courtyard below. They were at least a story high, but there were numerous straw-filled carts beneath, only a handful of feet from the castle wall. With a vigorous leap, they might just make it.

"We have to jump!" she cried, climbing into one of the archways. "Tuck your knees and head to your chest." She stood on the lip of the opening, leaning forward as she threw herself from the structure. Ric gaped, watching her plummeting figure as she swiftly curled into a tight ball, her arms wrapped around her tucked legs. She hit the cart, sending a burst of straw dust into the air before rolling to the edge unscathed. Nimbly leaping from the cart, she waved him forward.

Wasting no time, the prince thrust himself into the archway, hurling himself from it just as Ella had, but with far less aplomb. Flipping mid-air, he landed with a harsh *thud* flat on his back, knocking the breath from his lungs. Frayed stems of hay billowed around him as he wheezed, the air entering his chest with a fiery gust. Pushing himself to the cart's edge, he rolled out, steadying himself with a hand on Ella's shoulder.

"Let's go," Ella breathed. Nodding toward the archway, she noted the gathered guards, none willing to exhibit the same level of commitment to their duty as they stood impotently by.

Together, they made for the palace walls, sprinting toward the barricade that was much too high to ascend without help. Ric knelt, lacing his fingers together. "Let me boost you."

Ella quickly stepped into his adjoined palms. He rose with her weight clasped between his hands, lifting her just high enough to reach the edge of the gray stone walls. Using the gaps between the stacked boulders, she scrabbled the remaining distance to the top, hauling herself over with a final burst of effort.

Turning, she straddled the rampart, squeezing her legs against the cool stones as she reached down for Ric. "Hurry!"

He retreated several paces, allowing himself a sprinting start. Clambering against the rough surface, he gained just enough traction to take hold of Ella's outstretched hand, heaving his body upward before vaulting off the wall. "Jump," he rasped. "I'll catch you."

Without a second thought, Ella leapt into his awaiting arms. After he settled her on her feet, the pair took off hand in hand, feeling nothing shy of sheer exhilaration. They'd broken into the palace and lived to tell about it.

The synchronicity between them was unmatched, an alliance made of necessity and something far more profound.

Destiny, it was. Johan would never know what hit him.

* * * *

Major Oak was a welcomed sight, alight with the pulsing blaze of a campfire weaving ribbons of smoke into the star-filled sky. Ella and Ric had returned safely, the midnight canvas of stars overhead their guide with their brilliant, scattered clusters marking the path.

Much greeted them as they galloped into camp, dismounting the horses they'd secured at Little John's shop. Enveloping Ella in his embrace, he looked her over for signs of harm while the prince excused himself, allowing the two of them a moment to speak as friends alone for the first time all day.

"What took you so long?" Worry creased Much's brow as he stepped away.

"We were held up unexpectedly, having the misfortune of encountering Prince Johan and a handful of his men. We evaded them without much difficulty, though not entirely without incident." Ella was hesitant to share what had happened, but to have kept it a secret would have felt far worse. Her eyes followed Ric as he ducked into the mouth of Major Oak, removing the brown robe from his back and revealing a crimson stain on the sleeve of his tunic.

"What have I asked of all of you?" Shaking her head, she exhaled slowly. "It's too dangerous, and you — "

"I'm *fine*." Much offered a comforting smile. "You must realize that this is a path we've all chosen for ourselves. You neither coerced us nor promised us anything other than a chance to make a difference."

His words silenced her, but the memory of Sheriff Dane's wicked attempt to ruin Much and his future remained as alive in her thoughts as the present, haunting her dreams nightly.

"You're the only one who hasn't moved past what happened," Much added. Perhaps her gaze had lingered too long on his stub, as he had pinpointed her guilt with absolute accuracy. "You couldn't have changed this, you know. I've learned to live with it, and in no way do I blame you. We are only responsible for the choices we make individually, and I chose to change my life for the better by risking it for those who cannot. *You* gave me that." He nudged her genially as across camp, a light stringed tune fluttered through the still air.

Ella looked toward Much, and he chuckled at the evident confusion lighting her features. "Alan lifted a mandolin from the palace before he left," he explained. "Said he used to be a minstrel, if you can believe that."

"He *what*?" The shock in her voice made him laugh even harder before she continued. "So, he didn't even leave after we got him out?"

"He set off to find his dinner before he left and made off with that instead." Much shrugged. "Pretty good, though, don't you think?"

She scoffed, realizing that she was not in the least surprised that he might have done something so reckless.

Much led Ella back into camp as the chipper tune grew louder. Rory welcomed Ella home wordlessly with a nod opposite the campfire where she sat near Little John, who had joined them as well. Will grinned, acknowledging her safe return while Alan began singing alongside his capable strumming. Much took a seat beside him on the ground, with Ella finding her place on a nearby stump. The song was unfamiliar, but she loved the sound of it, enveloping them with the warmth of a soothing blanket.

Ric emerged from the tree cave, leaning his back casually against it and donning a fresh tunic. Alan finished his song, following up with a second. This one was slower — smooth and peaceful. Ella closed her eyes, relaxing in the familiarity of her woodland home as the day's events drifted away into the confines of her memories.

"Lady Ember." Ric stood before her, formally extending his hand. She met his smiling gaze with one of her own, the moniker having won her over at last. "Might we share this dance?"

The obligations of the court had been tedious to Ella with their balls and lavish finery, but dancing was something she'd always adored. Something in the way the ladies' skirts swept across the gleaming floors or the way a man would seek a woman he fancied for a fleeting moment of subdued intimacy. She'd watched from the balcony as her father had guided her mother across the ballroom, all the steps in perfect harmony while the guests' movements mirrored one another, syncing flawlessly with the melody.

Ella rested her hand in Ric's and rose. All eyes were upon them, gliding over the dust at their feet. Soon after, Little John invited Rory to join him alongside them, each respective couple reflecting the steps of the next. It was one thing class had never dictated, a shared comprehension of tradition and grace expressed through dance.

The tempo increased, the music reaching its crescendo as Ric drew Ella near, his arm wrapped tightly around her waist. With their hands still joined, they moved effortlessly in circles, breaking apart while they faced each other. With the descending beat, their shoulders met, each stepping around the other with the choreographed strides of the times.

"I remember watching you with my sister, Isla, when she was still just a girl," Ric began so only Ella could hear. "You asked her to dance, and she was overjoyed to oblige. It remains one of my most treasured memories, the two of you laughing together as you whirled through the hall."

Their forms continued through the movements, each motion so deeply ingrained in their minds from years of experience that no focus was needed to recall the steps. She spun toward him, his arms coming around her when her back met his brawny frame, only to be twirled away from his strong hold. She felt silly completing the steps in breeches, a wholly laughable image when a full skirt was the typical fashion—but she wouldn't change a thing.

"I never thought anyone had noticed that, apart from Marion." Returning the heir's smile, she thought back to the ball he'd spoken of, surprised by the fondness with which he reminisced of it. "She had a free spirit, your sister."

Ric clasped her hands in each of his, their arms crossed between them. Lifting them high, they stepped toward one another, their faces but a breath apart before they stepped away once more. "I didn't stop thinking about you for weeks following that night," he confessed, leaning toward her again, his words but a whisper in her ear. The song quieted, finishing softly as the notes carried off into the night. The tip of his nose softly brushed the flesh of Ella's temple, and for a moment, they were all that existed.

Reminded of their present company when Will cleared his throat, she fell back a step from Ric, distancing herself so as not to further tempt her self-restraint. His crooked grin was proof enough that they had, indeed, made a spectacle of themselves. Searching for something, anything that would sever the growing tension between them, Ella remembered his wound.

"You—you were hurt tonight," she managed, reaching for his arm as she lifted it for inspection. Carefully slipping the linen material over a makeshift bandage, she noticed that it, too, had bled through. "I could mend it for you. Meet me down by the water. I'll bring my supplies, and we'll get you cleaned up."

"If you wish," Ric said. "Though I assure you, it's nothing to fuss over."

The others among them carried on with their own tasks, while Ella went for the small sack of belongings she'd taken from Locksley, along with the remaining linen she'd purchased for Much. She'd brought a small number of sewing materials, unsure of what to expect from living in the wilds. She had little experience with a needle, but a gash like Ric's would not soon clot without assistance. Setting a soft blaze to her lantern satisfied her need for light as she made her way to the creek.

The rippling water was not but a dozen meters from camp, flames from the fire yet visible through the surrounding foliage. Standing at the water's edge, Ella found Ric, brilliant moonlight reflecting off the creek's surface, illuminating his imposing countenance.

"There you are." He strode toward her, offering his arm in assistance.

"Why didn't you tell me you'd been harmed?" She knelt beside the stream. Patting the earth, she bade Ric sit, and he stretched his long legs toward the water, dutifully following her instructions as he extended his arm for examination.

"It's of no matter—not given the danger I put you in." He observed her careful hands as she rolled his sleeve back, revealing the soiled cloth he'd used to protect his injury. "I hope you'll forgive me for that."

With great attentiveness, she untied the knot holding the bandage together, unwrapping it slowly. "You needn't apologize at all. Indeed, you have endangered yourself more than anyone." Dipping a linen cloth into the creek, she wrung out the excess, blotting the cut upon his forearm. He winced as it touched the flayed flesh, and Ella pulled away.

"I'm all right," Riccard promised, guiding her healing touch to his arm once more. "And how do you mean? I've endangered myself no more than any of you have."

She retrieved a curved needle, threading it before dousing the gash with whatever it was that Alan's flask contained, knowing it to be far more potent than mere water. Sucking in a sharp breath, the prince took the small container, swallowing a hearty gulp of its contents.

Just in time, it seemed, as Ella's needle pricked his skin, pushing through one side of the damaged area to the other and back. "Though the chamber was only dimly lit, there was a moment where I believe your brother may have seen your face."

"Then he shall know I've returned to take my rightful place," Ric replied, grateful for their idle chatting and the distraction it provided. Ella continued closing the wound, her attention focused on the making of a tidy row of stitches. He bit his lip as she reached its end, giving the string a little tug to tighten the final suture. "No doubt he will be off-put by my presence this eve, especially to have been spotted coordinating efforts with the notorious *Hood*."

"It's dangerous," she said quietly. "The last thing I want to do is endanger you. You're our future." She tucked her head, holding the string taut as she used her teeth to slice its fibers.

"That's why doing what I am is so important. You've shown me what my people need, and more importantly, how to provide for that need." He watched as she dressed his stitches with linen, wrapping it neatly around his forearm. Fastening the two tails end over end, she tightened it, creating a knot of her own making to keep it in place.

"I haven't done anything you couldn't have figured out yourself," she said, a shy smile gracing her face.

"Well, you certainly make it more enjoyable. Thank you," he added, waving his newly adorned arm. "Much better, that. Now, I must insist that you close your eyes."

Ella offered a suspicious glance, her nose wrinkled in a manner he found altogether endearing before she finally obliged. Removing the pouch from his waist, he rifled through the contents. "I know you will likely object, but I wish for you to consider accepting a small token of my appreciation."

"What is it I'm to reject, Your *Highness*," she teased, her mind turning with the possibilities of his meaning.

He drew nearer to her, close enough for Ella to feel the warmth of him as he maneuvered his hands behind her neck. The weight of his intention settled onto her collar bone.

Feeling the coolness of metal against her skin, she opened her eyes, surveying the opulence of an emerald stone gilded within a mounting of gold. Glinting with light, the necklace was made radiant by the stream's reflecting glow.

"Do you like it?" Ric's eyes shone with eager anticipation as she examined the gemstones.

"It's too much," she breathed.

"Before you refuse, consider all you've done for me. Indeed, all you've done for our kingdom, queen of shadows." He tucked a free-hanging strand of her otherwise-bound tresses behind her ear to better see the gift displayed across her slender neck. "I couldn't help myself when I saw it. The color resembles so closely everything that reminds me of you—your cloak, the moss of the trees among which you thrive. When I think of you, I'm awed by your contentment in calling the shrubbery of Sherwood your home when you were destined to sit upon a throne."

Rendered incapable of speech, Ella met his gaze, the intensity in his ocean blue eyes weakening her resolve to remain detached from his advances. He lifted his hand to her chin, running deft fingers over its gentle curve before tilting her face upward.

"You are my every thought, Ember of Locksley." He leaned nearer, brushing his lips gently over hers.

Remaining still, she savored the raw sensations of his affections, his mouth colliding with hers. Unwittingly drawing her toward himself, she deepened the kiss and her whole body responded to his touch, weaving through the tousled ends of his hair as she submitted herself to the encounter.

Time ceased as she found herself utterly beguiled, allowing herself this one frivolous measure of desire as she melted into his embrace. Ella parted her lips with his, and he explored her tongue with his as she drew nearer still, her arms bound tightly around his neck as she breathed him in. He smelled of earth and spice, smoky and rugged, and something more that was distinctly male.

He dropped his hands to her waist, the heat of his caress setting her soul alight. She stroked lazy fingertips over the length of his broad shoulders, enjoying the way he trembled at her touch. Ella wished to commit every detail, every facet of their stolen moment to her memory, longing to indulge in him for far beyond the reigning hour.

While it was possible that lying in the arms of a future king was the most negligent management of her heart, the way he'd shared his sentiments of persisting adoration had struck her in a way for which she'd not been prepared. Alas, it was not a matter that she would trouble herself with that evening, for the dawn would bring with it new worries. Such was the vow it pledged to the twilight each time it departed.

Or, perhaps, it was merely the reality that for one single night, she wished to be at peace.

Chapter Twenty-One

The sounds of combat floated through the crisp morning air, rousting the few who remained asleep within the hollowed timber of Major Oak.

"What's going on?" Rory appeared at the mouth of the tree, her hair a tattered nest from slumber. She raised a single brow, her features burning with displeasure. Waking the foreign woman was amongst the stupidest things that could be done in their camp — and everybody knew it.

"I only wanted another crust of bread," Alan hollered, his face pressed into the dust. Will leaned upon him, his elbow thrust between Alan's shoulder blades. "He's so stingy with *our* food! Let me have it!"

Alan flipped Will from his back with a twist of his hips. Will landed with a yelp, only to be set upon by his mad bandmate once more, Alan ripping the bread from his hands. He held it triumphantly above his head before taking a massive bite.

"You are ridiculous," Will spat. He clambered to his feet, beating the filth that remained from his scuffle off his arms and trousers. "All of us are hungry, but we don't steal from our stash."

"I had to do it," Alan said around the remnants of his stolen roll. "For if I had not, I might've eaten Much's other hand. Sorry, Much." His penitent gaze met that of his singlehanded partner in crime, who quietly observed the chaos with a smirk.

"Carry on," Much said with a wave of his stump.

"What more is to be said?" Alan grumbled. "Perhaps I should go live in town so that I may reap the benefits of our work. The townspeople are better nourished than we are!"

Rory groaned, dragging her palm over her face. "Do *not* wake me again!" Heaving expletives, she returned to her bedroll, casting herself into its warmth once more.

"You could've died." Ric emerged from their den, his eyes squinched against the brilliance of the morning sun. "I could've died, for I was trapped within our lair."

"Rory will not kill you. Indeed, I do believe she's sworn to protect you." Ella smiled shyly, peeking up at the handsome heir through thick lashes. The last thing she wanted was to be silly, to lose her mind like many of the girls in town, gawking and whispering as their paramours wandered about. But she did feel flustered, her first kiss taking place with the future king of Llundyn, of all people. It was preposterous.

And exhilarating.

Still, she knew not where they stood, and she refused to become foolish over a boy — or a man or a prince or whatever he was. She handed Ric his portion of breakfast as he seated himself next to her, fireside.

"Don't tell me you believe the Seer's musings, too." Ric took a bite of bacon, careful to consume it slowly. Nobody was starving, but the food was scarcer than he was accustomed to. While it was by choice, with each member of the band eager to donate as much of their daily haul as possible, it made for meager portions within their camp.

"Who's to say? And Alan isn't wrong, loathe as I am to admit it. We cannot do what needs to be done if we are half-starved." She glanced at the most outspoken of their bandmates as he huddled with Will and Much, the trio having reconciled in short order.

"We're fine." Ric took her hand, interlacing their fingers as he offered a reassuring squeeze. "I've no qualms with our arrangement. Hell, I shall give my portion to Alan if it will assuage your conscience." He grinned, bumping his shoulder against hers and drawing a derisive scoff.

"You'll do no such thing." Her smile grew, becoming genuine at last. "But it is a benevolent proposal, nonetheless. You shall make an excellent king, much as you make an exemplary criminal, Ric."

"I thank thee, milady." His eyes met hers, a thrill running through him with her casual use of his name. She championed him at every turn, supporting him in ways that not even the most committed of courtiers or advisors within the palace had managed. She was confounding and ardent...challenging.

Beautiful.

As if she could sense his thoughts, Ella averted her gaze, her cheeks pinking as she rose to her feet. "Remember me when you become my sovereign, dear prince. I've no doubt many pardons will be in order for all my covert activities." She pulled the hood of her borrowed cloak over her head, tucking the loose ends of her hair within its cover before moving toward her horse.

He scrambled along behind her. "You've no need to ask my pardon. Where are you going?"

"I shall remedy our meager provisions today." She mounted her horse in one smooth motion, settling herself upon the bare back of one of three mares they'd purchased with some spare coin. "I'll not be joining you in heisting, but you've far outgrown your need for me. Please, do be careful." Patting the heir on the shoulder, she urged her horse forward only to be halted after a few paces by the troubled prince.

"Wait!" Ric grabbed the reins, the broody mare stamping in disagreement until he released her. He moved to Ella's side. "Let me join you. Whatever you're up to, I'm certain you could use some help."

"You cannot help me — not where I'm headed. My stepsisters would eat you alive. Well…" She paused, her features a mask of reluctant amusement. "Kinsley might, but I believe Rosalind harbors designs for your brother."

"Ah, Rosalind. Yes. I remember the delightful creature." Ric waved a hand in dismissal, his brows pinched in distaste. "She may have my deceitful brother if she likes. No doubt they'd make quite the scurrilous duo. But why go home at all? I'm afraid that's much too perilous."

"It's the quickest way to amend our circumstances." Ella sighed, though she remained resolute. "It isn't what I want, but it is mine — at least, more mine than all of the other things we've been helping ourselves to."

"No good can come of this. A repeat of yesterday's misadventures would be devastating." Ric raised his bandaged forearm as evidence, and Ella winced. She didn't need a reminder of the strife they'd barely escaped, yet there it was. She had her own wounds as well, all superficial but remembrance enough.

And not everything about the previous day had been rough. The necklace hidden beneath her tunic was evidence enough of that. So, too, the lingering sensations from Ric's fervid kiss. Shaking away the irrelevant musings of her mind, she sought to make her case. "At least, in this case, I've some leverage to speak of."

Ric crossed his arms, awaiting her compelling proof.

"My stepmother can do nothing to me or she will lose our lands — *my* lands. Were she to turn me in, my estate would return to the care of the kingdom for redistribution, and she would become homeless. I'll be fine, I swear it. Worry not."

"I will worry." He peered up at her as they regarded one another in silence, and there was no insolence — only a sincere spirit of concern. "While I've no doubt you can take care of yourself, your stepmother is a wild card. And you..." Shaking his head, he looked away. "Just be careful."

"She has no reason to suspect me of anything more than running away from home, at any rate." Ella brushed light fingers over Ric's stubbled jaw, coaxing him into meeting her eyes. His unease gave her more than a little pause and an all too peculiar sense of desire.

She swallowed hard, her eagerness to complete the task at hand dwindling with each passing moment. "Nobody believes the Hood to be a woman. And besides, I've got the future king on my side. At least, I hope I do..." Her lips tipped up at the corners, brows raised in uncertainty.

A bemused smile formed on Ric's face as he observed his counterpart — a woman willful and lovely in every conceivable way. He took her fingers in his, pressing his mouth to the back of her hand before stepping away. Bending at the waist, he offered a deep bow. "As you wish. Come home soon, my love."

Ella inclined her head in parting, taking her lower lip between her teeth as she galloped away, his words settling over her with all the warmth of her favorite green cloak. Peeking over her shoulder, she found Ric with his keen eyes yet trained upon her, his hands clasped behind his rigid back.

He had the posture of a king and the presence of one who knew how to make his impulses a reality. And, as if his mere companionship weren't miraculous enough, he was every bit as staunchly committed to the band as Ella was, even unto sleeping in a primordial tree alongside snoring, farting, blanket-thieving allies.

She was perilously close to swooning, with the handsome heir having caught her off guard once again. Perhaps there was something more between them than she'd allowed herself to believe.

Ella had half expected for the better part of her adult years that she was meant for Marion — not at all as a result of any sort of passion or undying love. Mostly because she'd never imagined herself having any real interest in the lords of their kingdom. It was more of a means to an end — an inevitability.

She loved Marion dearly, and he was one of her most devoted companions. Marriage was a necessity, an essential part of survival in a land that refused to evolve, to allow women the privilege of true independence. If she had to be tied to a man for the remainder of her earthly life, it stood to reason that one who loved her, even if only as a friend, was better than the alternative.

Better by far than all the Gisbournes of the world.

Filled to bursting with the promise of new possibilities, Ella made her way toward Locksley for the first time in weeks.

Chapter Twenty-Two

Arriving at Major Oak always effected a duality of feelings in Marion. For while he found himself profoundly grateful for the lavish comforts that his home and title provided him, he was also guilty, never having taken on the burden of living with the bare necessities as Ella and her crew had managed.

Even Ric — the bloody future of Llundyn, no less — had managed to bear the affliction that was a life lived in a hollowed-out tree with an abundance of grace, and heavens only knew what sorts of comforts he'd sacrificed to do so.

Marion was fascinated by their level of commitment and eager to do his part. While he wouldn't partake in the thieving of the day, he had come equipped with news and targets for their ever-growing ventures.

He strode into camp on the back of his faithful piebald, Apollo, a steed that was becoming older and grayer by the day. But he had broken the aged fellow alongside his father, and time spent with his enduring ally brought him many fond memories.

The grounds were abuzz with activity, each member of the band prepping for a day of heroics on behalf of the citizenry. Will and Alan, the inseparable duo garbed in cloaks of black, readied their rations and weapons as they chatted fireside, while Much gathered his belongings into a satchel, tossing it into the mouth of the cave.

Even Rory was up and at 'em. Much brought her cape, lifting it onto her shoulders in gentlemanly fashion without difficulty, having become well adept in the use of his singular remaining hand. Rory smiled, squeezing his arm in thanks for his thoughtfulness.

It was all so quaint, the familiarity the crew shared every bit as close as a family. Perhaps, after all this time, that was what they'd become, thriving despite their various disagreements and the harshness of their circumstances.

Marion shifted, throwing his leg over the silvery neck of his horse as he dismounted, leading Apollo by the reins as he entered the fray.

"What've you got for us today?" Alan demanded, popping a handful of blackberries into his mouth. A dribble of juice leaked from the corner of his lips and Marion shuddered at his repulsive lack of manners.

"Hello to you, too." Marion dropped the reins, patting Apollo's rear as he sent him toward some brush at the edge of the clearing. He pulled his riding gloves from his hands before retrieving a message from the pocket within his doublet. "A message from John. He'd like to assist you in your efforts today. It seems he's not nearly as busy now that he's reduced the precision with which he crafts his weaponry."

"Or he just wants in on the action." Will winked, jamming a dagger into his boot in a way that made Marion flinch, for it wasn't sheathed. These people were daring, to be sure, and possibly a little mad. "Anything else?"

"A coach will leave Nottingham at noon, headed for the road that cuts north through Sherwood, bound for Yorkshire. Don't attack."

"And why the hell not?" Alan planted his hands on his hips, his contempt for the Lord of Knighton without end.

"Because you will die." Marion sighed, weary with the monotony these reunions often produced. "It's no ordinary conveyance. It seems Prince Johan has grown tired of your successes. He's loaded the carriage with the same materials that killed his father — saltpeter and sulfur from the *Potash* mines of Chamelaute and coal from right here in Llundyn. He's instructed his mercenaries to mix them and set them alight, should they meet the likes of you. Not even the soldiers within know what will happen to them when they do. It's a deadly combination, indeed."

Alan looked befuddled. "What will happen?"

"It'll explode, you idiot." Will shoved Alan in the shoulder, sending him stumbling to the side. "Just like what happened to King Edward."

Marion grimaced, the conversation rather boorish and indelicate. Much and Rory appeared to be similarly stricken, Much grinding his teeth as Rory averted her gaze from the insensitive pair.

"Where is Ric?" The exchange had Marion on edge, knowing that his friend had to be near, though not within earshot he hoped.

"He's down by the river, moping. Ella wouldn't allow him to accompany her," Will said, wandering back toward the old hollow tree. Alan turned away with a shrug, their discussion evidently having come to an end.

Much made his way toward Marion, shaking his hand. "Thank you for the information. We'll see to it that no harm comes to anyone."

Ah, civility. Marion nodded once, handing the note to Much. "Which way?"

"Through the trees, just there." Rory indicated a copse of budding oaks, a muddy pathway visible between them.

"Thank you." Marion bowed in parting, striding down the marshy footpath forged through knee-high grass and reeds. The woods were alive with the blessings of springtide, bringing about fresh colors along with the gentle aroma of flourishing blooms. From above, the sun was in all its glory, refreshingly warm and easing away his emerging annoyance. The day was not yet lost.

Upon the riverbank, Ric carved a rut into the sodden earth with incessant pacing, his thumb and index finger clasping his forehead. To say that he was distressed seemed a gross understatement. Indeed, Marion hadn't seen him this troubled in ages. Not even with the loss of his father. Ric had readily buried the rawness of his sentiments deep within as he always did.

This was different. And over a woman?

"What's wrong with you?" Marion stepped from the tree line, causing the prince to jump out of his skin.

"Knighton." Ric dismissed Marion's intrusion with a shake of his head, his frantic striding ceasing. "Nothing is wrong. I only needed some space."

"Of course. Yet something tells me that the whole of the forest would not be enough for you when you are in one of your rare moods." He raised his chin in challenge, earning a scoff from the heir before him.

"You would know. Nobody broods quite so well as you, my friend." Ric grinned while Marion laughed, each welcoming the levity that their verbal sparring always wrought. "And I'm not in a *mood*, as you so flippantly put it. I'm simply concerned."

"Over what?"

"Ella left for Locksley not long ago for supplies," Ric said, renewing his pacing, only to pause once more. "Did you see her?"

"I'm afraid not." Marion suppressed a smirk, finding that he was profoundly amused by Ric's fretting. Never had he observed his dearest friend express more than a passing interest in any woman before Ella.

It was an interesting turn of events, providing a much-needed diversion from the dullness of all the tasks that Johan produced without end. He moved nearer. "Why do you worry so?"

"She shouldn't be alone. Not now. Not after last night. Things are becoming more perilous by the moment, with each risk we take fraught with evermore to lose." Ric rubbed his eyes with the heels of his hands. "I wish to honor her request and do not desire to smother her with my presence, but I cannot ignore the feeling that she may find herself endangered."

"You couldn't have gone even if she'd wished it," Marion pointed out. "How could you explain your presence alongside the heiress of Locksley? Nobody knows you're here."

"They may." Ric sighed, watching the crystalline waters of the river rush by as if they could deliver the answers to all of his nagging questions. "Ella thinks Johan may have seen my face during our escapades last night."

"You did make quite the impression, it seems," Marion admitted. "You aren't certain?"

Ric merely shook his head, the object of his focus miles away en route to Locksley.

Suddenly, Johan's developing interest in luring Ella and her crew into thieving a rigged coach made sense, enraged as he was over the Hood and *his* companion escaping the clutches of the hired mercenaries only yesternight. Marion had heard all about it over brunch, with Johan incensed as he regaled him with tales of the heroic manner in which he had earned his blackened eye.

It was a sight to behold, with fully half of Johan's face a startling purple-black.

"Was it you who kicked Prince Johan or our beloved Hood?"

"It was she," Ric said, grinning once more. "A hell of a kick, too."

Marion smiled in kind, feeling a surge of pride over Ella's triumphant exit. "Quite a woman, she, though Johan continually refers to the Hood as a man."

"Ella doesn't mind that anymore. Indeed, the fallacy keeps her safe." Ric clasped his hands behind his back, his humor growing serious as he regarded the forest surrounding him, seemingly without seeing. He closed his eyes, heaving an impatient sigh. "Lord, keep her safe."

"Good heavens, man." Marion stepped beside Ric, the teeming river licking at their boots as he watched his consort in astonishment. "I never thought I'd live to see the day. You're in love with her."

"Yes." The word was pained and spoken without hesitation. Ric's pacing began anew, treading a fresh furrow into the saturated earth. "Deeply and irrevocably. I do believe it's driving me to madness."

"Her love is hard-won, but if ever there were one worthy of her affections, I daresay it's you. Brother…"

Marion's hand fell upon Ric's shoulder, stopping him in his tracks. "Fear not. Ella is strong, her guile a match for any man." Releasing his grip, he chuckled slightly. "But I will go to her if it will ease your mind."

Ric gripped Marion's forearm, his eyes bright with expectation. "I will think of nothing else until I see her safely home."

Home. The word held a variety of meanings, each of them significant and full of possibility. Marion bobbed his head, sliding his arm out of Ric's steady hold and shaking his hand. "Home, indeed. I shall see to it, my friend."

Chapter Twenty-Three

The day had taken an unexpected turn, and not for the better. Ella had hoped to be on her way back to Ric, hidden away in the refuge of Sherwood, but fate, as usual, had made other plans.

Having only managed a small loaf of bread, a sack of oats for the horses and just short of a dozen potatoes, Cooke had caught her looting her own supplies. She'd been thrilled to see him after being away for so long, but the smile that dimpled the fine lines of his features vanished as quickly as it came.

Her home, her lands, neither were safe any longer. While Locksley Manor had never regained the calm it had once boasted, at least it had still been hers.

"Elle!"

Tugging on the mare's reins, she drew her to a halt, surveying the road behind her. Squinting, the form of Marion became clear, his own animal thundering toward her with a quickness.

"Are you all right? I worried when I didn't find you back at Locksley, but one of your help told me I might find you here."

"I'm fine." Her words were terse as she suppressed a groan, again urging her horse toward Nottingham. It wasn't Marion's fault he'd come across her just as her future had crumbled to bits.

He followed on wordlessly at her back, steadily guiding his trusty beast to her side, and her temper melted alongside the silent understanding shared between them. Only years of familiarity could yield such harmony, but then again, Marion had always been as considerate and close as a blood brother.

"What is it that's made you so delightful this afternoon?" Marion smirked, his tone playful, despite her foulness.

Releasing an exasperated sigh, Ella refused to meet the lord's gaze, instead further considering the information she'd gathered. "She took it." Tears misted her eyes as her new reality took shape. "Margaret has succeeded at last. I knew well before I left that this might happen, that she would find a way to strip from me my rightful inheritance. Indeed, she's been plotting to do so since my father died, but I dared to hope…"

"You needn't worry, Locksley. She has limited control over your lands, and only until you are of age. You know this," Marion reasoned as he puzzled over her anguish.

"Yes. But that was before the jezebel accepted Sheriff Dane's proposal of marriage." Glancing at her long-time confidant, she watched as the rippling effects of a union between lady and sheriff sank in.

Now, it was he who could not meet her gaze.

"You cannot go back there." His eyes remained focused on the gravel path before them, the earth crunching beneath the weight of their animals' hooves as they neared town. He was only confirming what she already knew, but to hear it articulated with such certainty only perpetuated the malaise crippling her spirit.

"Thus, my trek into Nottingham?" Instantly regretting her sassy retort, she softened, shaking her head. "Forgive me. Once, I'd thought I might find a way to prevent this very day from occurring, but now nothing is stopping her from turning on me altogether. She will have her own lands through that pig, Dane, and she will find a way to accomplish the redistribution of Locksley before I can rightfully claim it as my own."

"You've not yet lost," Marion reminded. "But maintaining distance is wise. If she suspects you of anything, you can be sure she will use those suspicions to ruin you."

"Yes. Then I would be left at the mercy of Prince Johan." Ella scrunched her nose in disgust.

"Ah. No need to submit yourself to such trials." Marion chuckled, his imposing posture like that of the aristocrat he was born to be. "Though, I don't believe he'd be so friendly toward you if he knew it was your boot that blackened his complexion," he teased, loud enough for only Ella to hear as they entered the square.

A reluctant smile covered her face, the good humor of her oldest friend a balm to her weary soul. "It was well deserved, believe me."

"I've no doubt." Winking as he dismounted, Marion secured his horse to a post outside of the market. "Now, choose whatever you wish to bring back with you, and we will help our local merchants the legal way today."

"Very well. If you insist." Ella slid from the back of her mare with a chivalrous hand from Marion.

"Perhaps we'd do well to start with some pastry to satisfy Alan's insatiable demand for sweets."

"Then pastries you shall receive, my darling." He swept into a bow as he excused himself, setting off for the bakery two doors down.

It was pleasant moving around town without the concern of being caught thieving looming over her head. She had grown so accustomed to keeping watch over her shoulder that she hadn't remembered how relaxing a day milling about could be, causing her to long for a future when her new lifestyle would no longer be a necessity.

Outside of tailor Graves' establishment, a familiar face was revealed through the bustle of a warm springtide day. Her father's beloved attendant, Dietrich, beamed with Ella's approach. His skin was more wizened than when last she'd seen him, with faded speckles covering the thin flesh spreading across large knuckles that were frail from age.

Her heart sank, but her smile remained as she took hold of the hands that revealed more honesty than Lord Robin's trusted confidant would dare. With Ella away, the staff of her estate had suffered neglect, a sin of which she, too, was guilty. Mistakenly, she'd thought that the household would run as it always had, but a single glimpse of Dietrich proved otherwise.

"You'll not wish to speak with this old man for long," he advised, squeezing her fingers as he stepped back to examine her. Since the death of his lord, he'd taken it upon himself to look after her — at least until she'd run off to become the notorious purveyor of precious gains.

"Lady Margaret and your stepsisters are visiting Mr. Graves and his seamstress for their final fittings. They're sure to be finished at any moment," Dietrich persisted. It was his second warning, and Ella nodded her understanding.

At his rear was a cart she knew well. It was one she'd often filled alongside Much with freshly chopped firewood and many other goods they'd hauled to and from the neighboring villages. That her stepmother had forced this aged man to drag it all the way to Nottingham in service of her feckless demands was unseemly.

"What's all this?" She looked about the neatly packed contents of the old wagon. It came as no surprise that Margaret had expected Dietrich to wheel every spoil of her frivolity all the way back to Locksley, but she was disappointed just the same.

"For tomorrow's ball, milady." Ever dutiful, he made no complaint, only offering a half-smile as an acknowledgment of his mistress's folly.

"A ball? Whatever for?" Ella was baffled when Dietrich merely shrugged. A celebration amid such brutal devastation was absurd, making a mockery of the desperation most Llundyniens faced.

Still, it was an intriguing opportunity to consider.

Ella began rummaging through the cart. New shoes, hair adornments, shimmering jewelry, masks… The list grew with each package she unearthed from the mounting pile. She scoffed. "Could they not instead have stored their treasures in the carriage?"

"Stars, no." A shrill titter she knew all too well rang in her ears as Rosalind approached. "We don't need our belongings jostling about next to us."

"Of course. What a hassle that would be for you," Ella spat, the trio of ingrates closing in on her.

The tailor's little boy shuffled along behind them as voluminous tiered panels of silk rustled within his faltering hold, his arms trembling under the load. With a fat sack packed with pastries in one hand, Marion scooped the dresses from the child's grasp as he fell in step beside the lad. Sighing with relief, the youth wiped his perspiring forehead with his sleeve.

Having laid the gowns away, Marion turned to the boy, extending a generous tip to him for his efforts. The young assistant scampered off with a yelp of glee as the lord offered a cordial bow to Ella's loathsome family, ever the gentleman though not one of them deserved his civility. "Ladies, a blessed day, is it not?"

"What a wonderful surprise!" Margaret lilted, lowering into a well-practiced curtsy. Rosalind and Kinsley mirrored their mother, batting their lashes like harlots in pursuit of wealthy prospects.

"The pleasure is all mine." Marion grinned, his smile winning more admirers with each appearance. Ella glowered at her friend, his charms dazzling the women who had abused her lands and help with reckless abandon. They cared for nothing more than themselves, and even a sliver of flattery was too great, in her estimation. Marion's eyes fell upon Ella's dark gaze, his mouth twitching at the edges.

"Lady Ella has been gracious enough to spend the afternoon with me after much coercion. I hope you'll not find me rude for stealing her away," he continued as each of the women's smiles vanished from their faces.

"Forgive me, my lord. Do you mean to imply that you're spending the afternoon with *her*?" The confusion coloring Rosalind's tone was almost enough to break Marion's composure, but he held fast, his earnest grin setting her further off balance.

"Yes, in fact," Ella announced, her hands fisted tightly at her side as she weighed her words. "He's kindly offered to purchase food and supplies for me to take to Much, that we might not starve. Indeed, he was appalled that a lady of my standing should find herself homeless. Of course, I was left with no other option as Much had been banished from Locksley." Her eyes blazed with contempt as she watched the three women squirm under her scrutiny.

"Homeless! Whatever gave you that idea?" Margaret laughed, though it was as contrived as her faux sympathy. "Why no, dear girl. Only the thief was banished from our lands, protecting us from his greedy hands. But Locksley is your home and your birthright. You know that."

"She may not be homeless, but she certainly looks it." Rosalind pouted, her features filled with distaste. "Where did you even find such rags? You have dresses at home, yet you choose to embarrass us all by wearing these tattered togs?"

Reaching out, she took the loosed hem of Ella's borrowed mantle between elegant fingers, twisting it between them as she frowned with revulsion. Rosalind tugged, fibers of worn fabric bursting at the seams as she yanked the cloak from Ella's neck.

"She always liked wearing trousers," Kinsley said, breaking her silence with a weak taunt.

It was their typical fare. Ella had grown used to the inane humor they shared, though Rosalind's was far more tiresome. Marion took the cape from her grasp before stepping nearer to Ella. He draped it over her petite frame, his eyes harboring intense anger when they met hers.

He understood, at last, her inherent frustration with Lady Margaret and her stepsisters. "Perhaps I will have the royal tailor fashion you a new one before the ball tomorrow night—one to match your gown and another for daily use." Marion pointedly examined the torn cloth. "Until then, you will use one of mine."

"*You're* going to the ball?" Rosalind demanded as Margaret squeezed her daughter's hand, preventing any further harassment from slipping off her poisoned tongue.

Before Ella could speak for herself, Marion answered. "She will accompany me. But worry not about her transportation. I will send my coach for her alone. That is, if it suits you, milady."

"Very well," Ella agreed, smiling as he took her hand in his before pressing a kiss to it.

"How lovely." Her stepmother clapped, simpering as insincerely as ever. "We shall look forward to seeing you both, but we have many preparations yet to make before the day's end."

Marion inclined his head, nodding to both sisters as well. "Until tomorrow."

Holding her head high, stately as she was, Margaret motioned for Dietrich to follow, the wheels of his cart screeching with each step. The girls fell in stride alongside their mother.

Kinsley leaned toward her sister. "I didn't know Lord Marion to be courting her, did you?"

"Shut up!" Rosalind hissed, their forms fading off into the busy square.

Ella had never needed aid in fending off the vitriol of her sisters, but it had been pleasant nonetheless.

"They're worse than you let on," Marion admitted, tossing a pair of apples to Ella from a stand beside him. "Ric's favorite."

She nodded, collecting several more. Pacing the length of the displays throughout the market, they gathered everything they wanted and more. There would be no more growling bellies at Major Oak.

* * * *

They returned just after evening fell, dim moonlight glistening atop freshly sprung greenery as Ella and Marion entered the camp carrying satchels bulging with food. Little John was first to greet them, handling their steeds as each of them slung a bag over their shoulders.

"I see the day was not met without success." Catching the sack of oats Ella tossed his way, John grabbed a fistful, bits falling to the forest floor while the horse eagerly accepted her dinner.

"One hardly has to try when the goods are paid for." Ella bumped Marion's elbow with her satchel, a grateful smile upon her lips. "Join us, will you? For supper?"

"I would love to accept your offer, but it seems I have a ball to prepare for." Marion delivered his bag, laying it fireside.

"Ah. Yes." Ella's mouth pursed, a rebuke forming on her lips. "One you'd somehow neglected to mention."

He answered her scrutiny with a wry grin. "Correct me, Locksley, if I was wrong to assume you might again willfully risk your safety to somehow make an example of the evening."

He knew her well. Of that, she was certain.

"Johan is going through with the ball, then." Ric appeared, his mouth set in a grim line of anger. "Is that where you've been all day? Making ready for the festivities, while I remained here at my station, praying you'd not been harmed?"

Ella dropped her bag to the ground at her feet. Standing before him in equal fury, she suddenly lost any feeling of guilt she'd harbored over his concern. "I did what I set out to do, did I not? And yet you accuse me of galivanting about Llundyn for something as ridiculous as a ball. You have surely outdone yourself with your preposterous conjectures."

"Indeed, you're mistaken," Ric pressed, fortifying his stance in the center of her path as she attempted to push past him. "You weren't at Locksley as you said you'd be."

"You *followed* me?" She met his eyes, her own narrowed in disbelief as she stormed past him. Without sparing a glance for her friends, who sat gaping after her, fireside, Ella ducked inside of Major Oak. Settling herself, she removed Much's ripped mantle, resolving to mend it come morning light.

"I told you that you shouldn't have followed her," Rory chastised from without the hollowed tree.

Ella listened as the band passed food about. Though her world had been ripped to shreds, at least her Sherwood family would be well cared for. Laying out her bedroll, she resigned herself to an early evening.

Gravel crunched beneath heavy footfalls as Ric's face came into view. Alone, he entered the oak, maintaining what felt a painful distance, even despite Ella's anger.

"When you didn't return..." he began, only to pause, his mind rife with remorse. "I was distressed by your prolonged absence, but I should have trusted your judgment. You know these lands, these people, better than I could ever hope to, and I beg your forgiveness for today's indiscretion."

His sincerity was disarming, his words shaped by obvious regret. Yet his contrition was not at all what Ella sought. The blow she'd been dealt by her stepmother smoldered in the back of her mind. The inevitability of loss loomed like a black cloud of doom, promising that all she'd hoped to achieve, all she'd fought for would never come to pass.

"Well, you needn't worry over me ever returning to Locksley again. My estate will assuredly by redistributed when my stepmother weds Sherriff Dane. As I cannot hold my claim given the risks in my criminality, your brother will have more than enough cause to approve its reassignment."

Ric's brows knit together with the sting of Ella's words. "I'm still to be king. Perhaps you've forgotten that." A flicker of betrayal shone in the intensity of his stare as he bowed, leaving Ella to wallow in her heartache.

Chapter Twenty-Four

The ball was to be held at the palace come sunset, and Much had left camp, pursuing the solution to all their dressing woes. Though Ella had not asked questions, she was curious as to how he planned on acquiring enough suitable wardrobe for the night's endeavors. Still, she also knew that he'd never before have fallen short on his word.

It was to be a masquerade, with a guest list full of golden opportunities for the thieves hidden among them.

Will shared the scriptures of his Lord as the band conquered menial tasks about camp, quoting parables and portioning words of encouragement that he often studied only in private. It was as hope-filled as the blossoms of spring, sprouting around them as if confirming the validity in his conviction. A once-abandoned boy delivering God's living word with the certainty of a priest was the boost they all needed, waiting for Much with eager anticipation.

To Ella, this doctrine was received as a vital reminder of how little control she had in a world where she was merely doing her best. It was a relief when she considered the ever-increasing weight of rising tensions surrounding her. She had blamed herself at every turn for events that she had no way of altering. In truth, it had nothing to do with her at all.

Will's recitation had awakened a far different response within the prince. Ric quietly excused himself from the gathering, and Ella watched as he wandered into the trees. Their interaction the night before had not set well with her, and she'd been unable to put it from her mind since. Nodding to Will, she followed after him, hastening her stride to catch up.

Ric had not made it far before he'd noticed her tailing close behind. He paused, and she reached him, not quite knowing what it was she even meant to say.

"How is it that one can find themselves so devoted to a God that allows desperation to rule?" Ric met her gaze, interrupting the lingering silence that had fallen between them.

"Tribulation inspires people to become who they were meant to be, does it not?" Ella took a step nearer, closing some of the space that felt vaster than the few feet separating them. "It's no different where faith is concerned. Without hardship, a person cannot possibly determine what it is they truly believe. Whether in the holy trinity, or nothing beyond what is seen, how can one know until they are first held to the flame?"

"I'll admit I've never considered that." The heir scowled as he scratched the line of his stubbled jaw. "But to see the people, *my* people, toiling day after day for scraps while my brother has taken it upon himself to separate from them what they cannot afford…"

"You're doing what you can in an impossible situation." Ella approached him as his thoughts trailed, resting her hand gently upon his wounded forearm. "There was no way you could have predicted his intent."

Riccard scoffed. "Indeed, I'd never known him to be so duplicitous as to usurp the throne from not only our father but me. Though, he had always made it known that he never believed me deserving of my birthright."

Ella had undermined his authority, as well. Not only had she ignored his plea to steer clear of Locksley a day earlier but she had also inadvertently implied that Prince Johan might well maintain his hold on the throne.

"Last night." She paused, meeting his gaze at last. "You *will* be crowned king."

"Is that so?" Ric's mouth quirked in a weak acknowledgment of her efforts to mend the rift that had driven them both toward a restless night.

Unsatisfied, she persisted. "It is not a matter of if, but when. The only question yet to be answered is, what kind of king will you choose to be?"

A genuine smile lit his face as he pulled her to him, wrapping her in his warmth. He pressed his lips to her forehead, the rift between them silently reconciled. She rested her head against his chest, wishing she could remove the burden set upon his shoulders as his heart beat in tandem with her own.

"I'm sorry to interrupt," Rory said, emerging from the rustling bushes, her eyes cast to the ground as if she was not witness to their embrace. "Much is back, and he's brought a man named William with him. Says he was a friend of his father's."

The three of them hurried back to camp where the man was stood next to an ass-drawn cart that was bursting at the seams. Ella made out trinkets, amongst many other miscellaneous items, but she still had her doubts that this William would be able to outfit all of them before the night's festivities. The ball was but a mere two hours' time from beginning, and they were still dressed in filth and rags.

Mr. William was a jovial sort, ecstatic to have been sought out by Much. He'd not yet noticed that Ella or Ric had joined them as he dug through his wares, splaying them out on top of the mound filling his cart. Sidling up to Much, Ella nudged him with her shoulder.

"Indeed, you do not disappoint, friend." She giggled, taking in the scene before them.

Alan helped himself with unabashed delight to the collection of assorted pieces, while Little John and Rory sorted elements they thought worthy of the festivities.

With keen eyes trained upon Mr. William, Ella watched as he raised a stunning crimson gown from a sack that had seemingly materialized from thin air. He held the dress to Rory, whose bronzed features looked all the more remarkable when paired with its cherry tones, the glossy sheen of the billowing fabric deepening the rich ebony of her cascading tresses.

Grinning, she accepted the dress, clutching it to her chest. There wasn't a wrinkle to be found on the garment, a miraculous truth given how it had traveled to them within a satchel.

"You must be Lady Ella," William said, motioning her toward him. His speech carried a pronounced lisp, undoubtedly a result of the teeth she noted missing from his smile.

"I am." Ella curtsied as he took her hand, pressing cracked lips to her skin.

"For you, I have just the thing." Shaking his finger, he mumbled to himself, half of his form bent into the same bag from which Rory's gown had surfaced.

A peculiar man, he was, not far beyond where her father would have been in years, and his energy was infectious, having lifted the spirits of everyone at Major Oak. The creases of hard living branded within his features were coated with grime, his lightly salted hair unkempt, and sprouting from his scalp in wild curls coiling in every direction. Perhaps he might have been considered handsome had life not been so cruel and unrelenting.

"If you haven't already guessed," Much inserted, "my friend is a connoisseur of rare goods, most of them donated involuntarily by those who no longer require them."

"*Tsk!*" Mr. William hissed playfully, clapping Much on the shoulder. "I've simply found a way to make a living! Seems you have as well, although I do hope fate will see us both back to the seas someday."

"Perhaps so, old friend," Much agreed with a grin.

Ric chuckled at the exchange, his gaze landing on Ella as their guest approached her. Emerald satin draped over his elbow, requiring the assistance of his other arm to tame the fullness of the dress's skirt.

"You'll find no condemnation here, sir," Will assured him, plucking a vest from among the man's stash. "And I daresay, we could not have found a gown more suited for our Ella than what you have brought."

"I do believe you've captured her very essence with your selection." Ric beamed, watching Ella hold the intricate design out before her. She caught his lingering stare, feeling the familiar thrill that always accompanied his attention.

The tone was more vibrant than that of her cloak, but still a tribute to everything it had come to represent. With golden embroidery hand-stitched throughout the corseted bodice and a dropped waist which dipped at its center point, the staggering garment was beyond its time. A contoured neckline complimented the V-shaped midsection, while finely embellished gold edges defined the silhouette. Within the painstaking adornments were glittering gemstones picking up the surrounding light at every angle, the delicate pattern continuing into cuffs that transitioned into soft flowing sleeves which belled at the ends.

And how the dress had emerged from Mr. William's bag of tricks with nary a wrinkle was yet again a mystery. Indeed, how it had even fit within the sack at all was magic enough.

"Hurry now," Mr. William urged, ushering Ella into their hollowed oak alongside Rory. "You ladies assist one another in dressing while I clothe the men. Go on then." He shooed them off, turning to tend to the remainder of their crew.

In short order, Rory and Ella had peeled free of their daily wear, each of them helping the other step into their gowns. It was as if they were climbing into clouds, the ample layers of delicate fabrics swelling around their petite forms as they slid them up into place.

Ella tightened the laces of Rory's corset, tugging the string forcefully as Rory, with her hands firmly on her waist, aided the process. Tying the ribbon off at the small of her back, Ella turned as Rory returned the favor. Each yank of the stays forced the breath from

Ella's lungs, but if she looked half as brilliant as Rory did, it would be worth it.

"Do you wish me to pin your hair for you?" Rory offered, reaching for a small pouch she'd kept in her breeches. "I'm well-practiced after having tended to my sister's unruly mane for years."

"I'd be delighted if you would!" Ella knelt, reluctantly excited to be dressed in the finery she'd been free from for several months. "Just one thing first." Ella removed the emerald necklace, with all its broad gold leaves and stones, handing it to Rory.

She pursed her lips, running slender fingers through Ella's strands. "I suppose it can't be worn as intended with Prince Johan lurking about." Rory turned the extravagant piece over in her hand. Gold metal held together a chain of diamonds which bled into larger precious stones, matching Ella's dress flawlessly.

Nimble hands worked through her hair, tacking pieces into place as she twisted the locks. Rory skillfully secured the necklace, allowing its tear dropped emeralds to dangle delicately just above Ella's neck beneath the curls she'd loosely woven together into a low bun. Feeding the diamond-studded chain through her arrangement, she used the remaining length to create a shimmering headband resting across the part atop Ella's crown.

Deftly braiding her own hair, Rory knotted the ends together, leaving it hanging long over the front of her shoulder as she picked and pulled at the overlapping shocks. Her beauty was effortless and anything but simple, awing Ella with her comely mien.

Outside of Major Oak, Alan complained, his familiar bickering causing squabbles amongst the men as they finished dressing. Rory gave Ella a wary glance as the pair ducked out of cover, wondering at what had caused the fuss, only to get an earful as Ric scolded Alan over his wardrobe choices.

"We're meant to blend in, not bring attention to ourselves," Ric said, his frustration bordering on amusement. "Your attire is far too...*posh* to achieve the stealth we rely upon."

It was a masterfully articulated critique, both complimentary and commanding, leaving Alan befuddled as a result. As he considered whether or not he was offended by the prince's analysis, Ella and Rory fell into his line of sight.

"Then what of *them*! As if *they* won't enchant the whole lot of 'em?" Alan huffed, stripping the garish red and gold brocade vest from his body. He tossed aside the offending garment, along with an obnoxious feathered cap, retrieving a more modest jacket from the pile of goods.

"They are meant to shine." Ric approached Ella, dressed in the regalia meant for a nobleman, resplendent in shades of gold, cream and deep blue. "You look..."

She smiled, averting her gaze and offering Ric a view of the back of her hair. The gleaming necklace caught his eye. She hadn't taken it off since the day he'd gifted it, and he was clearly pleased that it suited her so.

"I see Mr. William has come prepared with masks for tonight's theme." Ella nodded toward Ric's hands, where he held two such disguises for the masquerade.

"In fact, he did," Ric said, holding a half-mask out by its stem. "I took the liberty of choosing one for you while you dressed. I hope you don't mind."

"Not at all. It'll do perfectly." She held the sweeping, gold-gilded affair to her face, the anticipation of the ball having built excitement within her she could no longer suppress. "Surely with this, nobody will know me," Ella teased.

"On the contrary. Perhaps Alan is right to be concerned." Donning a dashing grin, Ric leaned nearer, his next words spoken low to her alone. "You're very *distracting*."

Unable to hide her smile, Ella marveled at the man beside her. Despite his royal lineage and his upbringing, he was startlingly normal. Since he'd arrived in Sherwood, he'd worn his heart on his sleeve, forging a path directly to her soul and inspiring sentiments within her that long lay fallow.

"Promise me you'll be careful tonight." Ric twined his fingers with hers. "My brother feels something for you."

"What he feels is false," Ella replied quickly, embarrassed by his assertion. Why it bothered her so, however, escaped her scattered thoughts.

"I beg to differ." Ric met her eyes as if to will her into accord. "He will not be taken for a fool if he suspects anything. He's always been shrewd and acutely aware of his surroundings. Be certain not to underestimate him."

Ella nodded her word, the apprehension in his tone enough to shake her confidence. Still, his warning was prescient. It had been easy, falling prey to the mentality that they had become almost mythical in their ability to avoid disaster.

But that by no means exempted them from consequences. They were all victims by flesh or by bone, no more immune to the repercussions their actions might prompt than anyone else. Much was more than enough proof of that.

Marion's arrival brought with it a welcome intrusion upon Ella's plagued musings. He rode in atop a carriage, reins gripped tightly as the horses at its lead halted. At last, they seemed to be set for departure.

"How are we to be taken seriously in *that*?" Alan groaned, releasing an exasperated sigh of disappointment. "Looks like a blasted gourd, it does!"

Climbing down from the bench, Marion quirked a brow. "My uncle's discarded coach was the best I could manage on such short notice. My apologies for not acquiring something more to your liking." Sarcasm coated his every word as he turned his attention to Ella. "If Locksley and I are to quell speculation as to how we might be acquainted with the rest of you, we must arrive separately using my own carriage."

"Well done, brother." The prince made his way to Marion, clapping him on the back while gripping his arm in greeting. "Shall we then?"

"Upon your ready." Marion smirked, glancing from Rory to Ella. "It seems there will be little risk to the rest of you, as these two will doubtlessly hypnotize everyone in attendance."

"Ah, yes, they will," Mr. William agreed, motioning Ella forward, his blackened nails encrusted with dirt. She obliged, and, standing before him, he held out to her a final donation. "I have these for you, a token of my thanks for all you've done."

She hesitated, the slippers lovelier than any she'd ever seen. Made of glass, the smooth surface reflected an iridescence from the retreating sunlight.

"As much as I wish to accept, I'm afraid I am unable." Standing in the comfort of her mother's worn leather boots, she knew she could not. "They are beautiful, and I thank you for all you've been willing to share with us, but if I need to run, I will require something more practical."

"Not at all, miss. But, you'll keep them — for another occasion." The man placed the shoes back into the velvet box he'd pulled them from, holding up a single finger to stay Ella's emerging protestations. He tucked them into the mouth of the old oak tree, before urging them onward. "Go then, all of you! You have a big night ahead."

"We will be on our way now, as well," Much replied, as he and Little John mounted their horses. "Many thanks to you, William. I will be sure to set aside a portion of our earnings for your kindness."

Marion opened the door to the pumpkin-shaped coach, bending in a modest bow. "Your invitations are within. We will stop off behind my own estate so as not to be seen, and Ella and I will depart together. Until then, I thought it wise for Will and Alan to act as our coachmen." Offering his arm, he helped Rory inside. Ella followed and then Ric, Marion latching the door behind him.

"A job meant for the vermin of society. I should 'ave figured," Alan mumbled, earning a solid smack upside the head from Will as he scaled up the side of the aged carriage.

"It's completely honorable," Will scolded before taking his place next to Alan. Grabbing the reins, he wrapped them firmly around his fists. "Get your wits about you before I decide it best to leave you behind."

Alan's only response was a huff of aggravation.

Little John and Much set off through the woods, dressed to blend with the help where they'd take up post outside the castle, prepared to catch the spoils of the thieves within. Will drove his passengers down Old North Road into Nottingham, the carriage jostling along the uneven terrain.

The night was young, the nerves of each of the Sherwood bandits frenzied with anticipation for what they hoped to be the heist of their lives.

Chapter Twenty-Five

Marion's coachman brought the carriage to a halt directly before the palace steps. A line of guests had formed in the entryway, donning masks and costly attire that revealed no shortage of extravagance, even amid crippling taxation.

Offering his arm to Ella, Marion helped her step from his coach, waving it off with a flick of his wrist. He carried himself with all the arrogance expected of a lord, confident and indifferent as he led her up the steps where they joined the company waiting for entry.

The others were already safely inside, having entered through the servants' quarters as Ric had suggested, avoiding the receiving line where Marion and Ella found themselves. For them, it was expected, given their titles.

Guests were welcomed inside quickly enough, though Ella dreaded the moment when she'd be expected to look Prince Johan in the eyes without exposing her disdain. With her fists clenched, they moved forward, the prince's voice echoing off the surrounding stone as he cheerfully addressed each individual.

As if reading her thoughts, Marion pulled her closer. "The night will be over soon enough, Locksley."

Feigning shyness as if he'd just uttered secret flatteries, she smiled, raising her mask to her face. They were one couple away from Johan, and Ella's veins pulsed with revulsion. Being forced to breathe the same air as the murderer standing before her was a trial, to be sure, though she did find satisfaction in the strategic placement of his own mask. Covering both eyes, it curved low over his right cheekbone where she'd kicked him.

Good. She hoped it ached and throbbed, causing him no end of agony. It was the least he deserved. Johan's presence alone was suffocating, with more knowledge than she wished regarding his ruthless manipulations. Still, Ella dipped into a low curtsy while beside her, Marion bowed.

"I hoped you might come, Lady Ella." Prince Johan reached for her hand, his lips lingering a moment too long upon her flesh. "I had not known that you and Marion were—"

"We're old friends," Marion interrupted, casting a sidelong glance at his stormy companion. "I have come as Lady Locksley's escort, as it seems no other ladies were willing to tolerate me for the evening. All in the hopes of finding favor with the prince, I suppose."

"Not at all." The prince clapped Marion on the shoulder. "Who's better than you, old friend?"

"You, I suppose," Marion said with a chuckle, only to draw laughter from Johan as well.

It was all so familiar, a comfortable friendship that fit like a well-worn glove. Once, Ella had enjoyed Johan's laugh and the sound of his voice. She had dared to consider that, perhaps, they might have shared further regard for one another as well. But the merciless man that lay below the genial exterior was almost too much to bear. He was false and more insensible of feeling than anyone that Ella had ever met, and she burned with indignation, for Marion and Ric as much as for herself.

"Would you be so kind as to take a walk with me?" The usurper's eyebrows rose as he awaited Ella's response, when she realized she'd been scowling. Thank heavens for her mask.

"I'd be delighted, Your Highness." She inclined her head, taking his arm. They left Marion behind amongst dozens of others who yet waited to greet the tyrannical prince.

Johan paid them no mind, guiding Ella through the grandeur of the large hall. The ballroom was abuzz with music, and guests danced to the exquisite composition moving elegantly as one beneath candlelit chandeliers. Even the flames of the elaborate candelabras swayed in time with harp and violin as they created the resonant melody heard throughout the grand hall.

Weaving together toward the broad-paned doors, they kept to the outer edge of the floor where twirling forms had congregated into wide circles. One within the next, the dancers moved in opposite directions, turning to one another as they took new partners with whom they repeated the steps once more. The movement was complicated, and one of Ella's favorite dances, but the company beside her ensured no pleasure would be had this eve.

Ella surveyed the area, searching it for her friends. Rory was the first she sighted, surrounded by three young men. Two were lords Ella always had herself avoided due to their insolence. The foreign woman played her role well, doubtlessly charming the men into simpering fools. Of course, Ella had already known it would be simple for a woman so disarmingly beautiful as she.

In her hand, Rory held a sparkling beverage with brightly colored fruits floating atop effervescent bubbles. The three hopeful suitors sipped their glasses to the last drops while Rory slowly nursed her own, all of them offloading empty flutes onto a tray held by Will, who happily replenished wanting hands.

Flirtatiously pawing Lord Edmonton, Ella knew precisely for what Rory had reached. A golden pocket watch glinted from between her fingers as she slipped it to Will, who passed by without notice. Throwing her head back in insincere amusement, Rory beamed while the lord leered at her.

Blazes, but Rory was a treasure. How she managed all the loathsome men surrounding her was a mystery. Her grace was truly without equal.

Tearing her gaze away from the one-woman show, Ella gasped. Ric was directly in their path, his back turned to them. With a partial mask obscuring his features and his customary freshly shaven jaw covered in stubble, he would not be as easily recognized.

Still, her unease chipped away at her counterfeit poise. Perhaps only because she knew of his presence did he seem so obvious, standing there quietly disengaged from the goings-on around him. To Ella, he was a beacon, her soul ever captivated by his luminous bearing.

Within a few paces of his brother, Johan stopped. Ella waited, ready to scream for Ric to run as the youngest prince gestured to a nearby servant.

"Would you like one?" Taking hold of a stemmed glass, Johan offered the shimmering refreshment to her. Well-mannered, he most certainly was, thoroughly skilled in the fine art of decorum.

"Very much, thank you." She accepted the pale pink beverage with as much courtesy as she could muster while Johan took one for himself. Ric turned toward them, watching as they continued their journey to the balcony and befuddling Ella further.

Had he no sense of self-preservation?

The spare took no notice of Ric, despite him being little more than an arm's length from his reach. Indeed, they narrowly avoided exposure as Ella's shoulder brushed Ric's, the heir's fingertips lightly running across the back of her hand as she passed. When she caught his gaze for a brief instant, her pulse thundered at the intensity of his stare, only to be ushered outside by his odious brother.

When she cast a final glance behind her, it was not Riccard who caught her attention, but Rosalind, whose scrutiny followed her every movement.

"Won't you be missed?" Ella asked, peering up at the darkened sky. Stars shone brightly over Nottingham, their sparkling light very much at odds with the gloomy thoughts swarming within her mind.

Johan stepped beside her, his hand landing on the small of her back. "Beautiful, is it not?" he countered, ignoring Ella's inquiry as he took a sip of his drink.

When she didn't speak, he continued. "Are you aware of the purpose behind the ball tonight?"

Uncertain of how to respond, Ella met his eyes — the same ones she had once wished to lose herself in. Now they reflected only deceit and greed. He was a hollowed man, vile in his pursuits and unwittingly staring his greatest adversary in the face.

And while she did know what the late King Edward had intended in arranging this lavish affair, she wasn't about to confirm her awareness. For, in Ella's estimation, the occasion was in poor taste, given the deceased king's violent end a mere two months past. Even worse when one considered that he'd met his demise by the hand of the man beside her.

"I confess I've heard gossip in recent days, though I'd not known quite what to make of it. Given the grave misfortune of your circumstances, a declaration of matrimonial intent would be most inappropriate," Ella declared, the tilt of her chin the only evidence of her contempt. "Do you not agree?"

"Yes," Johan conceded, his laughter dubious as he gazed at Ella. A wry grin crossed his lips. "Though, I suppose that even if I had chosen this occasion, I'd be rather ill-prepared. It seems that my brother made off with our mother's ring."

"I'd have thought it would be his as firstborn," Ella said quietly, all the while her thoughts racing. Ric had gifted her with the emeralds adorning her hair, of course. Had he also taken his mother's ring from the chest that same night?

"Certainly, it is," Johan clarified, dancing around the truths regarding his utter disdain for his elder brother. "Though Riccard has never been the sentimental type. Likely, he will never marry at all. Would that the Lord safely return him to us from the ravages of war." He kissed his fingers, pressing them to his heart in a false show of concern, which only served to further embitter Ella.

"It is quite an opulent gathering," she managed, hoping for a change of subject. The rebuke hovering on the tip of her tongue was a fiery arrow she wished very much to discharge, but she swallowed her disapproval, forcing a smile. "A night such as this could feed the whole of Llundyn for weeks, I would imagine."

"I'd thought the same myself." Johan sighed, placing his glass atop a nearby pillar before taking her hand. "Truly, you perceive the frivolity of court with a canny translucency. Most are happy to disregard it altogether. It was not my desire to host a ball in the wake of tragedy or war, but the council demanded it be carried out as planned in a show of resilience to our enemies."

His ability to transfer responsibility from himself didn't come as a surprise. "Ah. How difficult this must be for you." She went to withdraw her hand, but he only held faster.

"I knew you would understand." He took a fortifying breath. "It would be you, you know."

"What?" She met his gaze without thinking, shocked by his assertion, by his tender regard. He didn't mean...

"If I were to choose tonight, I —"

The doors opened behind them, golden light from the ballroom flooding the overlook. "Oh! I beg your pardon, Your Highness." Rosalind bowed her head in apology. "I only sought fresh air, but I've interrupted you both. Forgive me."

She had very much intended to intrude, Ella was more than certain, and she couldn't have chosen a better moment. Dressed in a deep royal blue, Rosalind was a vision as she lowered her mask, revealing an unblemished complexion and doe eyes framed with long, thick lashes.

"No matter, sister. How wonderful it is to see you tonight," Ella said, hastening away from Johan. "I was about to go find Marion, at any rate. Perhaps you might keep our prince company in my absence?" She turned, only to offer a brisk curtsy to Johan. "My lord prince."

"We will speak again soon, I hope," the prince called after Ella, who was already making her way to the door.

She slipped by Rosalind, who fought to suppress her annoyance with a sneer, offering only an obligatory curtsy before closing the monstrous pair outdoors.

Leaning against the broad oak panels, Ella fanned herself, having had enough chaos for one evening though the night had scarcely begun. The spare had not seemed suspicious of her in the least, despite her rather obvious scorn. It was a small blessing, but even more so to be away from him. She longed to scrub herself raw, to remove the chilling sensation of his contact, but there was still work to be done.

Steeling herself, she discovered Marion following through with his task for the evening, aiding in the imbibing of anyone and everyone.

"You wish for me to take tha', miss?" Beside her, Alan held out a tray where she placed the untouched cider, her palm sweating from the tight grasp she'd kept on it.

"How is everyone doing?" she asked. His only reply was a wide grin before he carried off his libations, encouraging the furthering of inebriation and easy loot.

Marion made his way toward Ella, having excused himself from a young woman she had never met. With his departure, the poor beauty was set upon by none other than Gisbourne. The man was unendingly insufferable, a blight on all the eligible maidens within the kingdom.

Ella shook her head, accepting Marion's offered arm with a smile and feeling somewhat whole at last in the presence of her dearest old friend. A stringed refrain filled the hall with an upbeat air as she followed him to the center of the dance floor. "I don't know this one," she admitted, earning a smirk from Marion.

"Then you'll have to follow my lead. But pray, darling, try to keep up." Propelling her forward, she rotated around the back of him in time with the lively tune. Meeting face to face once more, they laughed, having spent the balance of their years together dancing, as well as hiding from the obligation of it.

The footwork was simple enough, but quick in motion. Ella attempted to match the lord's movements with only moderate success. "Now you're just showing off."

"Perhaps if you hadn't left me alone during so many affairs, this wouldn't prove as difficult," Marion jested, pulling her nearer as they continued about the room one couple after the next.

"If only you'd been better company." She grinned up at him, the retort catching him by surprise. Marion's brow quirked in amusement, his mouth curving up at one end.

"If only..." His words trailed as the song came to a close, the violin's final notes drifting away, fading into the spirited bustle.

Ella parted from Marion, curtsying as was the accepted custom before taking his arm once more to make their way to a glowing Rory. She stood before a long table set with hors-d'oeuvres, exotic fruits, and an assortment of sweetened pastries.

"The getting is good this eve, is it not?" Rory mused, her cheeks colored with a delicate flush. "Why, I must've plucked more riches from the arrogant rubes of Llundyn tonight than in all of our previous adventures combined! Celebrate with me." She gestured toward the lavish spread.

"I've heard the duck is exceptional," Marion said, pleased to take a break from the rigors of their duplicity. Refreshments were always a good excuse. "Shall we?"

The next hours consisted of plentiful bounty, which was dropped from designated windows into the receptive clutches of Much and Little John, their stashes growing by the minute. They'd even obtained a small cart to carry the overwhelming plunder, the efforts of those within the palace having been successful beyond measure.

Ella began spreading the word to her party that they would soon disperse. Their thievery was shockingly elementary, almost an insult to the level of skill they'd acquired, but they were thrilled. Tossing her final collection from the window's edge, she gave the signal to Little John that he and Much could leave their posts.

"You promised a dance to your sovereign." Ric caught her by surprise, his warm breath caressing her ear. "You haven't forgotten, have you?"

"I don't recall giving such assurances, dear prince." She felt the length of his taut frame at her back as he drew her to his chest, his fingers lightly tracing the flesh of her bare forearms.

"Surely you don't mean to force the future king to his knees," Ric uttered, the whiskers of his jaw skimming over her temple as he teased her to within mere inches of her sensibilities.

Turning within his embrace, Ella met his eyes, his penetrating gaze commanding her very will. "That would be cruel, would it not?"

"You are many things, Ember of Locksley, but cruel is not one of them." Her heart thundered as he leaned nearer, the tip of his nose grazing the side of her own. He took her by the hand. "Come."

She obeyed without objection, teetering off balance from their encounter. Sweeping her across the ballroom floor, he was all that existed, and she was fully surrendered under his charge. Lost in the strength of his hold, she floated weightlessly in circles through the hall. With one arm tightly fixed around her waist, Ric held her hand tenderly within his own, her very presence his personal lifeline.

Never had she felt so much herself, even as she was yet lost entirely to another. Enveloped in the commanding possession of a man she'd believed not only negligent but reckless only a few short months ago, Ella gave in to the longing of her soul. Riccard was not a prince, not heir apparent—he was everything she yearned for, and with him, she was who she was meant to be.

Their improbable journeys brought them together, unveiling all they'd lacked before fate merged their futures irreversibly.

Ella was content to dance with Ric for the duration of the evening, the music carrying fluidly into a new melody. But when she recovered herself enough to look beyond his mesmerizing company, all the other guests had fallen away. "Ric…"

He pulled her closer still. "Yes, my love?"

She nodded subtly to their surroundings, stirring them from their rapture. High above, Prince Johan observed them, his masked face as rigid as stone.

Twirling Ella away in an elegant spin, Ric and Ella bowed to the prince, deep and deferential, in spite of his crimes.

Johan nodded his approval, even as recognition sparked within his stare. Donning a false smile, he bade the revelers resume their pleasures with a wave of his hand, all the while keeping a watchful eye upon the enamored pair at the center of the hall. At his entreaty, the gala continued in earnest, the ballroom floor filling with drunken dancers once more.

"We've been made," Ella whispered, falling in step with Ric as they continued dancing alongside the gathered masses.

Ric nodded, easing them toward the outer edges of the great room with each movement. Peering over Ella's shoulder, he noted the mercenaries congregating around his brother, undoubtedly collecting their orders for his capture.

And hers.

"Follow me." Ric tugged Ella along, their fingers intertwined as they darted toward the grand foyer. Up the stairs and through the vestibule they rushed, with nary a soul paying them mind as they hastened through the doors and down the palace steps.

Picking up their pace when they'd left the sight of the gathering, they reached the footbridge, Ella's foot catching on the lip of the trestle. She pulled and tugged to no avail as she struggled to free her foot from the crevice. Ric bent to aid her, but before he could find her ankle beneath the countless layers of fabric, she pulled free, her shoe fastened tightly within the cleft. With no time to waste, they continued on, leaving behind half of the only two items Ella had managed to retain from her mother.

Reaching the pebbled drive beyond the bridge, they came upon dozens of horses tied up alongside myriad coaches awaiting the return of their celebrating masters. After they made their way to the nearest steed, Ric quickly untied the beast. "Up with you," he gasped, boosting his encumbered accomplice onto its back. Mounting the horse, he settled before Ella, her arms encircling his waist.

"Go," she breathed, resting her face between his shoulder blades as she tightened her hold. The great clock of North Tower struck midnight just as they took off, Ella's skirts billowing in the breeze while clouds of dust rose in their wake.

Chapter Twenty-Six

The beating hooves of the unfamiliar horse sounded beneath Ella, matching the pace of her scuttling heart. She turned, examining the path that lay behind them. "I don't see anyone at our backs."

"We'll ride for a while," Ric said, urging the animal onward through the trees. Though it was difficult for her to see, she knew the horse would find its way through the woods without difficulty. "I wouldn't want to lead any pursuers to Major Oak. You don't mind, do you?"

"Not at all." Ella shifted, moving nearer to the prince. His proximity filtered through her with the heat of a blazing pyre, doubtless a result of their harrowing escape. "In truth, I cannot think of anywhere I'd wish more to be."

He slowed the beast to a canter as they reached the bank of the stream that would eventually lead them home, wandering along the shore. "Nor I." His voice was low, smothered as he was by the burden of his actions. Moving to the river's edge, he dismounted before reaching for Ella. "May I?"

She placed her hands upon his broad shoulders as he grasped her waist, lifting her from the back of the horse with ease. He settled her soundly on the earth beneath them, his long fingers lingering before sliding to the flare of her hips where he held tight, as though he were afraid she might altogether disappear.

The silence stretched between them, neither sure of what to say. The chaos of their escape caught up with them, along with the realization of what had occurred. It had been closer than either would ever admit and would change their operation in ways they could not yet understand.

Ella slipped to her hands to Ric's chest as he closed his eyes, resting his forehead against hers. "I shouldn't have…"

"What?" She nudged his nose with her own. "Tell me."

He took a fortifying breath, pulling away only enough to look her full in the face as he opened his eyes at last. A storm brewed within them, turbulent with unease. "I never should've endangered you like that."

"I gave you little choice when I waltzed into camp, announcing that I was going." She smiled, knowing well that she was a difficult ally with which to keep stride. "I seem to remember you were none too keen on the idea."

"We all make choices. And my decision will always be you." He trailed the tips of his fingers up her spine with one hand, eliciting a shiver born of both his touch as well as his admission.

Ella gazed up at him, entranced by his candor. She was quite undone. "I don't deserve such consideration."

"You do." He kissed her forehead, brushing his thumb along the curve of her neck. "You must understand what I felt, seeing you with him—my deceitful brother." A short, humorless laugh escaped him, and Ella wondered at his troubled countenance.

They were safe. *She* was safe—free from harm after all they'd risked.

"I was mad with jealousy," he continued, pulling her nearer still, their bodies pressed together in a way that had her flushing. "I nearly lost it when he led you outside, all alone with him...with a murderer." A muscle in his jaw ticked as he clenched his teeth, the memory driving him to distraction. "I was mere moments from charging the balcony. The whole of Johan's purchased army could not have kept me from you, determined as I was to rescue you from his clutches. But I stopped."

"Why?" Ella's voice was but a breath, lost to the forest around them

"You're your own woman. I confess it's tempting to interfere—a regrettable product of my upbringing, as you well know." He arched a brow, a wry grin forming on his face. "But I would never presume to doubt you again. It's your independence, your strong will that leaves me in endless awe of you. From here on, I shall endure at your word."

"You're the king of Llundyn," Ella uttered, wrapping her arms around his neck as she closed the little space remaining between them. "I quite imagine it should be the other way around."

"Never." He kissed the tip of her nose. "Following you has been the greatest adventure of my life. Ember. *Ella.* I'm very much in love with you."

"*Ric.*" She rose on tiptoe, her lips grazing his, then said, "I love you, too."

Ric circled her waist, his passion unfettered as he drew her to himself, fitting his mouth to hers. At that moment, there was no close enough, no fear of consequences or capture—and, fortunately, no observers.

Only a prince and a thief who had stolen his heart unequivocally.

* * * *

It was just before sunrise when they wandered into the camp hand in hand, the borrowed horse rambling along behind them. The attention of every forest dweller fell upon them, their eyes trained upon Ric and Ella's joined hands. Much and Rory grinned, while Will chuckled. But it was Alan who would not allow the moment to pass without comment.

"Took you long enough," Alan offered with a wicked smile.

"Indeed," Ella agreed, fanning her overwarm face as Ric laughed without any sense of shame. "We fell asleep while we waited out the search, not wanting to lead anybody here to our refuge."

"Aye. Just as you say." Alan bowed his assent though his face reflected barely contained humor. He continued about his business, preparing a large breakfast, and everyone followed his lead, moving on from the spirited encounter.

Ric pulled Ella toward him, kissing her cheek. "My dear, you are blushing. Sleeping with your head upon my shoulder should cause you no disgrace."

"Perhaps that's not the portion of our evening I was recollecting." She bit her lower lip, suppressing a full-blown smile. *Have I truly just admitted that?*

He stepped toward her, closer than was altogether appropriate as he cupped her face, his mouth deliciously close to her own. "Go," he breathed. "You are entirely too enticing for your own good."

Ella backed slowly away, delighting in the roguish grin he wore, his gaze pinned to her retreating form. She offered a prim wave, eliciting a chuckle from her beloved as they parted ways, with Ric moving to tend to the horse while she ducked into Major Oak, desperate to be free of her frilly dress. Reaching for the laces of her corset, she managed only to untie it. Loosening the infernal thing would be another matter altogether.

"Would you like some help?" Rory entered the hollowed fortress, finding Ella in a huff as she strained without success against her bodice.

"Please, if you wouldn't mind," Ella groaned, grateful that at least one person within their camp understood her plight. She couldn't very well ask for assistance from any of her male companions, at any rate.

Rory freed her from the grips of the cursed contraption, and Ella could finally breathe again. "Thank you! I shall never choose to sleep in a corset again."

"I should think not," Rory agreed. "A terrible way to spend an evening, I suspect. Though, I'm sure it wasn't entirely lost."

"No, indeed," Ella quietly admitted. In truth, it had been an unexpectedly pleasant way to spend the remainder of the evening, nestled in Ric's embrace as they'd dozed against an old ash tree. They'd had only his cloak for cover, but she had been more than comfortable, despite the chill of the night.

Ella turned to find her only female companion grinning from ear to ear. She felt bare in more ways than one, quickly dressing as the truth poured from her lips. "He told me he loves me...last night."

"I am shocked!" Rory said with a giggle, tossing Ella her trousers. "Shocked that it took him so long."

The woman was more of a gossip than Ella would ever have guessed upon meeting her a few short weeks before—and a welcome friend. Ella beamed, filled to bursting with contentment she had not known for some time.

"I'm happy for you." Rory made her way toward her, folding her into a suffocating hug before pulling away. "Look at you. In love with the king." She patted Ella's shoulder before departing, offering her the first shreds of privacy she'd had in days.

She set about scrounging up some appropriate footwear, down to only one shoe after the ventures from the previous night, and all the while wondering over Rory's words.

In love with the king.

She was. Profoundly so. Ric was a pleasant surprise in a life that had become one of mere survival, and not at all what she had expected him to be. He was devoted and affectionate beyond any measure, charming her endlessly with his good humor and quickly becoming her closest confidant.

To Ella, he was not merely the king, not a prince. He was her soul, winning her heart in a way she never thought possible.

Settling on a pair of boots that were several sizes too large, she added a few more layers of stockings to fill them out before joining her fellow bandits, partaking in a feast of eggs, bacon and biscuits. Alan had become increasingly accomplished in his culinary feats over the fire and made more of their meals than anyone else in their woodland home.

They laughed and chatted as they ate, enjoying one another as they recounted all their triumphs from the ball. They'd returned with more loot than anyone had expected, and it would take many hours to parse it out for delivery. Still, that was a task that nobody minded, knowing that they'd be delivering healthy satchels for the citizenry.

Will paused with a forkful of food halfway to his mouth. "Someone's coming."

"Hide," Ric hissed, sending the gathering into disarray as everyone made for the trees. It was too early for the likes of Marion or Little John to be arriving, leaving only sinister alternatives. And while it would be clear that somebody had been there, given the discarded food and fire, at least they were no longer sitting ducks.

Ella and Ric tucked themselves behind a sizeable rock, while Alan scaled the trunk of a nearby oak with ease. Will followed him up, the pair camouflaged within the branches, as Much and Rory dove behind a felled timber.

"Oye, it's only Little John," Alan announced after a few moments in hiding, dropping from the limbs above, only to land nimbly on his feet as John entered the clearing.

"Where is Ella?" John leapt from his horse, searching the camp in earnest. "Is she here?"

"Where else would I be?" Ella rose from cover as her crew converged on John.

He went to her, grasping her by the shoulders. "Elle, I was so worried." Pulling her close, he wrapped her in his steady arms.

"What's going on?" Much demanded.

"Her face is all over Nottingham. Wanted posters everywhere," John said. "The prince knows that you're the Hood. I came here straight away, hoping to catch you before you left to deliver the spoils."

"Posters? How does he know?" Ella paced the forest floor, thinking over the previous night. Never had Johan indicated that he had any inclination of her alter ego.

"That is not the worst of it," John added. He glanced from Ella to Ric, dreading his next words. "Marion was arrested just after you left."

"Whatever for? He didn't steal a thing last night!" Ric's temper was quickly running away with him. It felt as though they were destined to remain one step behind Johan at every turn, and he was growing tired of their lot. Would that they could somehow finally turn the tables on his arrogant brother.

"I can't say for certain," John began, fidgeting under the scrutiny of the many eyes upon him. "All I know is that I saw you run away with Ella, sire, followed closely by Marion himself. He stopped at the footbridge, where he picked something up. I saw him tuck it in his pocket, only to be seized on both sides by Johan's mercenaries. Did you drop some coin?"

"No, nothing of the sort!" A startling sense of dread gripped Ella, settling in her chest like a cold stone. "Why would they detain him?"

"We both know my brother had me dead to rights at the ball," Ric seethed. "Marion should not have followed us, for I fear he only fanned the flames of suspicion by doing so. Indeed, even you were endangered the moment you left with me." He issued curses so profound they'd have made his own army blush, the implications of their antics crashing down around them. "I gave our hasty exit no consideration. How could I have been so stupid?"

"I couldn't very well have stayed!" Ella's throat tightened with each declaration. "Leaving was our only choice! It was only a matter of time before my identity was made."

"That doesn't explain the wanted posters, I'm afraid," Rory said. She was deeply troubled, having become attached to each member of their band. "How does he know of Ella?"

"That's easy," Alan spat. "Marion must've tol' them. Always knew we shouldn't trust the bum!"

"No. Marion would never do that. Not to Ella. Not to *me*." Ric paused, eyes widening with realization. "Your shoe. That's what Marion picked up."

"My shoe…" Ella pinched her eyes closed, willing away her unease. It wasn't possible. "Certainly not."

"I daresay Johan got a good look at your footwear when you kicked him in the face, and the shoe would only serve to confirm his suspicions." Ric sighed, his brows furrowing as he turned the possibilities over within his mind. "Or perhaps it was merely being seen with me. My presence here would alone be cause for him to question Marion's allegiance. Why not yours as well? Maybe that is enough."

It was an unmitigated disaster. After the triumphs of the evening, they'd awakened to a nightmare. The crew silently milled about the clearing, each captive to their thoughts as the sun rose, illuminating the wilds around them.

Ella took a fortifying breath. The whole of their circumstances were her fault and doubtless her responsibility. She had begun the damned quest for justice, for reconciliation. It would end with her, as well. "I will go."

"You won't. I mean…" Ric shook his head, his eyes falling closed as he scolded himself. She was not his to command, nor did he wish to. He only meant to keep her safe, but he'd be as good as his word, letting her lead the way.

Ella met his gaze, her eyes blazing in a mutinous manner that had him prepared to fall at her feet, begging for forgiveness. He reached for her, taking both of her hands in his. "I only mean that we do not know enough. We must find out why Marion has been detained and understand Johan's intent. It may be how he intends to draw you to him."

She groaned, torn between her eagerness to simply do *something* and Ric's sound reasoning. He wasn't wrong, but she also didn't want to tarry. The fate awaiting Marion was unknown, and she was unwilling to gamble with his life for fear of her own.

She nodded once, turning to Little John. "Can you find out more?"

"I will," he agreed. "I'll go at once. I can question people at my shop without raising suspicion. Word of scandal travels quickly."

"I'll go, too," Will added. "The shadows of the town square always harbor many secrets. We won't let you down, Elle."

"This is not for me," Ella said, her tone even and fierce as she observed her fellow thieves. "Marion is one of us. Make no mistake, my friends. I would do the very same for any one of you. We are a team, a family. Not one will perish without a hell of a fight from the rest of us."

"Hear, hear!" Much shouted, pumping his fist, only to be joined in voice and action by the whole syndicate. A loud cheer rose within Sherwood Forest, the promise of retribution echoing in its wake.

Chapter Twenty-Seven

Would that there might be another way.

Ella scrabbled up the surface of the palace wall, forcing herself to look up rather than down. Scaling the outer wall surrounding the castle had been a breeze by comparison, as it wasn't nearly as high. Sneaking by the few guards rambling about the courtyard had also proven an easy task, with most of them mead-addled enough that they may as well have been dead on their feet.

This was different. Each span she managed to cover brought her nearer to a decision she could not take back, and Ella wasn't yet certain it was the right one.

But dawdling in the safety of Sherwood felt wrong, and no amount of news or gossip would suffice when there was an actionable pathway forward — at least, not for Ella when she had one.

After a day spent parsing out the spoils of their thievery, which had decidedly not included Ric or Ella following their debut at the ball and Ella's subsequent fame from her wanted posters, the evening had passed in tense contemplation. Each member of the crew attempted to plot a way out for Marion, but there had been no progress.

Little John and Will had been unsuccessful in their quest for information, finding that nobody had heard a word regarding the lord, not even the people of his manor. It was as if he'd simply vanished.

Of course, he had. Were it not for Little John's knowledge of his detainment, not one of them would be any the wiser.

Ella had stolen away in the dark of night after leaving a note with Much and Rory. Her missive was not well received, but they understood her plight, promising to say nothing until dawn. It was not, perhaps, the most honorable course, but she knew that she'd never have been able to leave otherwise.

Her heart ached. She hadn't lied to her band, to Ric, but taking matters into her own hands was the only way she could do what she felt was right.

She neared the window leading to Johan's quarters — rooms that should belong to Ric — straining as she pushed herself upward. The edges of the stone jutted only enough for Ella to gain the purchase necessary to hang on by the tips of her fingers and toes, digging them into the crevices between the boulders.

It was precarious, indeed. One false move would have her tumbling two stories to the earth below, and there was no convenient cart of hay this time. The exercise was necessary, however. She couldn't very well go knocking on the portcullis for entry. She needed to speak to Johan directly.

And from there, the remainder of her plan was…well, rather vague.

Her whole body was slick with sweat, and she wished very much to wipe the moisture from her hands but didn't dare. With a grunt of exertion, she heaved her frame toward the open window, wrapping her damp hands over the ledge as she clambered higher with her feet.

Ella's hands slipped, setting her legs flailing as she scrambled for a foothold. Pausing, she took a shaky breath, attempting to calm herself as she hung freely from the window ledge.

Her blasted hands grew clammier by the second, and she felt her fingers sliding. Digging the toes of her boots into the mortar of the wall, she splayed them, clutching the sill as she willed herself up and over the lip of the window frame.

With great effort, she managed to crawl into the room, sinking to the floor as her nerves abated. She'd been more or less silent, which must've been good enough, as she'd not yet been captured.

Glancing around the quarters, she noted only a small fire lighting the space from the hearth — no candles or lanterns. It was the best she could hope for, seeking to catch the treacherous prince unaware as he slumbered.

Ella rose to her feet, creeping toward the sprawling bed enveloped in a crimson velvet canopy. She'd been there once before with Ric, but navigating the vast space by herself felt more daunting.

What did it matter, though, really? She was about to feed herself to a wolf, and she was doing so voluntarily. Still, maintaining some semblance of control over the situation calmed her considerably.

She drew the heavy curtain back, expecting to find the sleeping prince alone, but he wasn't there. Peeking over her shoulder, she spied the portrait of Queen Eleanor she'd seen some days before, as well as the bureau that Ric had plundered. It was the right room. She was sure.

Perhaps Johan wasn't staying there after all.

"Lady Locksley."

Ella startled, nearly leaping out of her skin as she turned around. Johan stood before her, having risen from the chair that sat before the dwindling embers in the fireplace. He hadn't made even the slightest sound, leading her to believe that she'd been very much alone.

How wrong she'd been.

Johan's face was unreadable, displaying no hint of betrayal or even surprise. Dressed in fine riding clothes, he seemed more apt to mount a steed for a jaunty hunt through the king's forest rather than head for bed, despite the late hour. He took several steps toward her, moving as slowly as a jungle cat, with a glint to his eyes that was every bit as predatory.

"Or perhaps you'd prefer I call you *Hood*." His voice was smooth and commanding, even as he scoffed. "Though I find the moniker positively daft. How do you tolerate it?"

"Very well," Ella replied, determined to stand her ground, even in spite of her instinct to run. She lifted the edge of her cloak, only to drop it once more. "I believe you're familiar with its origins."

"I am, although I must admit, I'd never have guessed it belonged to you." He smiled warmly, his countenance perfectly at odds with his dangerous air. "You confound me, Ella. Why did you do it?"

"Because of you!" she spat. "Why else? You were bleeding our citizenry dry. You still are, though we both know there is no war!" She moved toward him, suddenly filled with courage. "What is your game with Marion?"

Johan's eyes narrowed, his lip curling in distaste. "It is no game. He's been working with my own brother against me, and after last night's discovery, I know you are, too." He pulled her missing shoe from behind his back, displaying it in the palm of his hand before tossing it aside. "If you're going to make such a splashy exit, you really shouldn't leave any belongings behind. And, if you're going to kick a *prince* in the *face,* it's best not to wear the shoe you used to do so in his presence!"

"I'm sorry about your eye." Ella managed enough grace to look contrite, even as she relished the sight of his bruised cheek. It was deserved—that and much more—but further vexing the man would only work against her.

She was at his mercy, much as Marion was.

"Did you come to finish me off?" Johan closed the distance that remained between them, standing far too close for her liking. They were breathing the same air as he peered down, analyzing her.

"I've come to offer a trade," she murmured, struggling to meet his gaze. "Myself for Marion. For now that you have the Hood in your possession, there is no need to keep him locked away."

"Now why, pray, would I do that?"

She swallowed hard, looking him full in the face. "Eventually, you will have to explain his absence. He's a lord with his own lands. He will be missed. But I—"

"You're an infamous bandit now known throughout the whole of Llundyn! What good are you to me?" He reached for her, gripping her forearms with his cool hands as he studied her anew. "The people adore you, putting any sort of punishment out of the question.

Perhaps I shall stash you both away. I've some clever minstrels in my employ who can spin fantastical tales. I daresay you won't be missed for long." He raised a single eyebrow as if to dare her to defy him.

She was rapidly losing ground in a battle of wills where she had little leverage to speak of. Yet the truth he had voiced had given her an idea, Lord help her. "Certainly, they could devise tales of my demise—or maybe of my treason. But there is a far better story they could share."

He grazed his hands up her arms, coming to rest upon her shoulders. "Do tell, my love."

Ella suppressed a shiver born of pure revulsion as he spoke the words oft uttered to her in intimacy by his brother. With Ric suddenly occupying her thoughts, she was in danger of losing her nerve.

But she had to buy time. Ric's men would not be far off now, and with any luck, he would be along soon enough for her to avoid making a decision that would ruin many lives.

She forced a smile. "Marry me, and your bards may forge legends of our love. Is that not just the thing for a people in desperate need of hope?"

He laughed, his reaction not at all what she had expected. "You're serious? What's in it for you?"

She pressed her hands to his chest, fighting against the urge to shove him away as she met his eyes. "You will free Marion, and you mustn't pursue Ric."

"There it is," he hissed, releasing her as he retreated in disgust. He cast a sidelong glance her way as he paced, looking very much like the man she loved with all her heart, but with none of his virtues.

It robbed her of breath, her soul longing in vain for its other half, still asleep in the wilds of Sherwood. Ric would be devastated by her decision, by her suggestion of *matrimony*. Heavens, but she'd hatched a colossal mess of a scheme.

Yet Ric would understand. She knew he would, and she knew he trusted her instincts. He'd said as much more times than she could count, and he would not fail her. She need only perpetuate her hastily planned ruse until the king's men returned.

Ella would hold on, playing her wonted part in this struggle for power that had become a battle of wills. Finally, she was on the right side of the law.

"I should've known, really," Johan growled, his manic striding driving her to distraction. "Has this anything to do with Marion, or is your lone concern the safety of my brother?"

"A passing fancy," Ella said with a dismissive wave that made her burn with anguish. *Lie.* She *had* to lie. And convincingly.

"I can hardly imagine." Johan stopped before her, his shrewd gaze pinned to her face as he assessed her sincerity. "I watched you at the ball. Indeed, you seemed quite taken with one another—a shameless display. Affection can only lead to ruin."

"I agree," Ella continued. "That is why I refused to leave with him. He wished for me to follow him to Calaise, but I would not. My heart is fickle and belongs to many, not the least of which is the people of Llundyn. Being his in any capacity could never suit me. I am my own woman."

"Yet here you are, willingly sacrificing yourself for not only Ric but Marion as well." Johan's skepticism only grew, and Ella suppressed the urge to panic. "Do explain this conundrum, for I am mystified."

"It's quite simple." Ella leaned casually on the wall behind her. "I can do more good for the people and even for you by remaining here in Llundyn — far more than being the mistress of a man with no power in a foreign kingdom."

"Your words are bold, perhaps even persuasive," he added, moving toward Ella as he caged her in with a hand firmly planted against the wall on either side of her. "But I don't believe you."

Without another word, he leaned toward her, his mouth meeting Ella's in earnest as he pressed his taut frame against her. There was urgency behind his kiss, the fervor with which his lips explored her own both nauseating and startling.

Ella squirmed, despite her best efforts to satisfy the cruel prince. She closed her eyes, conjuring false enthusiasm as she pulled him nearer. Revulsion did not do justice the depths of despair Ella experienced at that moment. He was a vile, soulless creature who would stop at nothing to ruin his brother and kingdom for his own selfish gains, and she had just become a willing participant in his machinations.

At last, he pulled away, searching her eyes. *Calculating. Always calculating.* "Not a chance in hell." He laughed once without humor. "You're in love with my brother. You may as well admit it."

"Love is not enough," she managed, ignoring the pain it caused her. "I can do more here. The people mean everything to me. That's why I became the Hood." In desperation, she reached for him, grabbing hold of his doublet to force his attention upon her. "You wish to be king, but you will never be such without the goodwill of the citizenry."

He shook his head, and she jerked his collar with shaking fists, determined to help him understand. "I have their loyalty, Your Majesty," she purred when she'd recovered his full regard. "By marrying me, their allegiance would be yours. The power you seek is within your grasp."

"Maybe you're more ambitious than I'd surmised. You would be at my mercy, you understand," he asserted, the words hanging in the stifling air as he wrapped his arms tightly around her waist, drawing her body flush with his. An involuntary shiver slid down her spine, born of anxiety that promised she would lose her very life should it ever come to that.

He was a menace—lethal and wicked.

"I do." Ella met his piercing gaze. "But together, we'll be unstoppable." She reached for him, stroking his cheek with faux tenderness and all the while feigning strength she did not feel. "Imagine what we can do."

He grasped her wrist tightly, abruptly thrusting it away from his face, and she braced herself, preparing for an outburst that never came. Instead, he slid his hold from her wrist to her fingertips, kissing the back of her hand.

"You surprise me, Ella of Locksley. We are agreed...for now."

She took a step backward, affording herself just enough room to drop a curtsy, a genuinely absurd gesture in trousers, but she could think of no better way to hail his assent. That, and she was in dire need of distance from the handsy prince. "I'm honored, Highness."

"Indeed, I should think so. Marion will be freed when we are wed and not a day before. As for my brother—"

"He's gone," she cut in, kicking herself for the eagerness she'd revealed in her haste to shield her beloved. She took a deep breath, recovering herself. "You know he never wanted to be king. We can leave it at that."

"Yes. So, we shall." Johan smiled tightly, offering a single nod. "Well, then...follow me." He offered his arm. "It seems we've some preparations to make."

Ella straightened, adopting a dignified air as she walked arm in arm with her reprobate fiancé out of the king's quarters and down the corridor she'd escaped through with Ric mere days ago. The hallway was empty, save for two guards who trailed behind them, their footsteps echoing through the eerie quiet as they bounced off the stone floors.

She refused to ask where they were going, hoping to convey her zeal for their accord. Pausing outside of a doorway not far from Johan's, he opened the door. "Your chambers, my dearest Ella."

Waiting while their escorts bustled about the room, lighting a fire in the hearth and several lanterns, Ella smiled. "I think our agreement is quite suitable. Thank you for your generosity."

"We are both well-served, and you may continue your abundant charity at my side. The sun rises early, so please, get some sleep. We will announce our nuptials in the morning." He took her hand, kissing her knuckles before bowing. "Until tomorrow."

"Until then." Ella inclined her head in parting, nodding as the two goons exited her quarters. Closing the door behind her, she leaned against the knotted oak panel, releasing a sigh of utter exhaustion.

She'd done it.

Now all she had to do was survive.

Reaching for the handle, she pushed, only to find it locked. She scoffed, rolling her eyes. Nothing she hadn't expected, but idiotic nonetheless, given that she'd climbed her way into the palace and could just as easily do the same on the way out. There were four windows in the seating area alone, and she hadn't yet seen the bedchamber.

It was no matter. She wouldn't be leaving at any rate—not until Marion could be safely removed from the dungeon. She shuddered, remembering the dank depths of the castle prison far below where he surely waited. And here she was, alive and well, jailed in a cell of opulence and finery.

It wasn't right.

Ella had managed an alliance, shaky though it was. Would that it might be enough to see them all through. But the tide had turned too quickly with Johan for there to be any genuine assent on his part.

He was lying, but so was she.

And both of them knew it.

Chapter Twenty-Eight

The morning sun had not yet winnowed away the darkness of night, but some latent portion of Ric's subconscious had awakened him. Searching the slumbering figures huddled inside the ancient oak, he knew before he'd counted them.

Ella was gone.

Crisp pre-dawn air chilled his bare chest, his heart thundering frantically in her absence. Retrieving his tunic, he climbed over one, then two resting souls before emerging from the timber.

Outside, Rory and Much whispered between themselves, not yet having noticed the prince as he slipped the linen garment over his head, adjusting it across his broad frame. Beside Rory, sat on a fallen trunk, was a folded parchment.

Ric steeled himself, harnessing his temper before it could run away with him.

They knew she'd left, and neither had stopped her.

"When? When did she leave?" Ric demanded, striding over to where they murmured their hushed secrets. Rory handed him the hastily scrawled note without a word, each of them watching in silence as he poured over its contents in Ella's elegant script.

Please, do not follow me. You speak of your pride in my efforts and of the respect I've secured amongst the people. You call them my people and me, your queen of shadows. Show me that you trust me. Allow me to lead in the way that I must. I seek only to buy us time, and when your men return, I hope then you will come for me. Marion mustn't be permitted to suffer for my actions, and together, we can see him through to freedom. Love me enough to allow me this, Ric. I'll see you soon, my king.

Ever yours, Ember.

Riccard fumed, his mind spinning with dire scenarios that had him ready to combust. "She cannot believe I will sit idly by while she submits herself to the devil incarnate! I will not — *she* will not!"

"It is the only way." Rory's words were firm and unwavering, only causing his fury to spike further.

"Surely, you disagree." Ric looked toward Much, awaiting his response. He was met with silence. Of all the people he would have expected to join him in a mission to save Ella from herself, it would have been her childhood confidant, and yet…

"With which one of you did she entrust this?" the prince demanded, tossing the note into the lightly misted earth with a flick of his wrist. "Which one of you sent her to her death?"

Much rose to his feet, meeting Riccard's penetrating scrutiny. "Royal, you may well be, but I will not have you accuse me of such an atrocity. Neither Rory." He mirrored Ric's stance. "I don't like it, either, but Ella has always known her own mind. I will not stand in her way, only to have her torture herself for not following her instincts, which, mind you, up till this very moment have been sound."

Ric sneered. "Better then for her to be kept for my brother's entertainment and used to *mock* me until he decides he's had enough. He will end her, and that will be on your head!"

"He cannot sentence her without causing an uprising," Rory objected, planting herself between the two men. "Prince Johan is canny, is he not? He will not kill her unless he wishes to destroy any goodwill he's earned within the villages. There are eyes everywhere."

There was validity to each of their points. But more importantly, each of them loved her. While Ric would not go so far as to tell them they had been right to let her go, he knew that even he couldn't have kept her from what she'd set out to do. He didn't have the strength to argue, only hope that his men would come before the sands of fortune were funneled fully through the hourglass.

Ric sighed, nodding his assent in defeat. There was nothing more to be said, and being at odds with his crew — with *Ella's* crew — was not the way forward. Besides all that, he did trust her. Everything she had said in her letter was so.

Blazes.

He hated that it was through such grim circumstances that he would prove his faithfulness, for every piece of him wished to run after her, no matter the cost to himself.

Fresh sunlight cast radiant beams through the thick canopy of foliage, the promise of a glorious spring day entirely at odds with Ric's sullen temperament. The new day would begin as always, no matter the toll its hours might take.

"Hold on, man," Much said, clapping Ric on the shoulder. "I learned to relinquish the reins to Ella long ago. She will prove herself worthy of the task at hand, just as she always does."

Ric clasped his forearm, giving it a singular shake as he did with his men. "Thank you, Much. You're a good friend."

Much offered a tight smile before moving to join Rory in arrow making while Ric retrieved the frying pan, his mind set upon making breakfast. It would be a welcome distraction, and better by far than trying to help Rory and Much. He had never mastered the skill, despite Ella's best efforts to guide him, and spending time with her best friend and his traitorous travel companion was more than he could handle at the moment.

Ric was cracking eggs when a shadowed figure that could only be Little John galloped into camp, the radiance of dawn creating a halo around his advancing silhouette. He dismounted, blissfully unaware of the despondency he'd ridden into. "Good morning, all. Where are the others?"

Rory rose to her feet, prepared to run interference. "Alan and Will are still sleeping, and —"

"And Ella has turned herself in," Ric finished, his tone bitter.

"Come on." John smiled, certain they were pulling his leg. But one look at each of their sober faces, and he clearly knew it was so. "*No.*"

"There's more to it than that, but yes, she did. She has a plan." Rory's statement felt like an effort to convince herself of its truth, and all of them desperately wanted to believe it.

"Then perhaps the prince's announcement relates to our Ella more than Marion," John said carefully. "It was heralded throughout Nottingham, not but an hour past. I came to relay the message immediately upon hearing."

"When?" Ric's mind raced with possibilities. They needed to be prepared for anything, and they had next-to-no resources. But Ric did have one advantage over his brother. For if it came to losing himself or the throne for Ella's sake, there was no question of what he would choose.

Her. Always her.

"If we leave now, we will not miss what he has to say," John said, moving toward his horse. He was as eager as the rest of them to take action.

Rory went to roust Will and Alan, as Ric and Much prepared the horses. While there would be danger involved for Ric in attending, it was well worth the risk. He was done simply following Johan's lead and ready to make moves of his own.

* * * *

The square was abuzz with townspeople whispering about the prince's pending statement, so it was no trouble blending into the seams of their movements. Having tied their horses at the edge of town, a quick escape was well within reach, though Ric actively considered an outcome wherein he'd make no exit at all.

"Remember why we are here," Rory admonished, the hood of her cloak resting upon slight shoulders. Wild, raven coils fell around her face, her eyes blazing with caution.

Acknowledging her with a silent nod, Riccard pushed his way past the outermost edge, noting the sun's position overhead as time dragged onward. Finally, the late king's herald took to the stand to announce his brother.

"Hear ye, hear ye!" Shouting over the assembly, his words were but a murmur as the people persisted in their gossip. Attempting to garner their focus, he began again, louder still. "I say, hear ye, Nottingham! Your prince has arrived!"

A hush fell over the square as Johan made his way onto the platform, only he was not alone. Ella followed closely behind, moving to his side center stage as the usurper spread his arms wide in welcome.

Ric burned, a mix of anger and envy as he watched his brother alongside his beloved. He couldn't bear it, straightening as he prepared to act without a thought for consequence. Much rested his hand on Ric's tensed shoulder, shaking his head as if he had read the heir's mind.

Perhaps he didn't need to, as Ric's desperation was plain.

Johan greeted the town with a false smile as if it belonged to him, reaching for Ella, whose presence beside him he'd yet to explain. She was made up entirely as a well-esteemed member of the court, dressed in a manner that would bring any man to his knees. Quiet chatter began again, the women at Ric's back verbalizing their shock at seeing the newly revealed Hood joining the youngest prince.

"Today is a special day," Johan bellowed, his gaze flashing toward Ella. "As you're all aware, our own Ella of Locksley has made herself known to be the notorious Hood. I was as surprised as you when she arrived at the palace to give herself up before dawn, this very day." Johan drew closer to her, her eyes meeting his as a shy smile played upon her lips.

Taking her hand in his, he paused, regarding her tenderly for the sake of those around them. Ric's jaw clenched at the sight of her, merely an ornament, a cherished darling of the townships forced to lose herself in a life of inspiring counterfeit loyalties.

She'd left to buy time for the arrival of Ric's men, but at what cost?

It was not jealousy that made Riccard struggle against the urge to reveal his identity but utter contempt for the wretch who sought to take everything of worth from him. His brother had seen them together the night they'd fled his foreign mercenaries and again at the ball two nights past. Johan had seen enough to know that for Ric, Ella was his very soul — and therefore evermore useful for his wicked schemes.

"She confessed her crimes to me, though they are known well enough across the whole of Llundyn," Prince Johan continued, persisting in his attempt to win the steadfast favor of the Hood's following. "However, in my eyes, I see no crime, no offense — only a woman who loves her people. Beside me stands a woman of noble birth who was willing to sacrifice privilege to ensure the villagers were fed." Pressing his mouth to Ella's knuckles, Johan returned the air of restrained delight she wore on her face. "Under the law of the crown, she should be disciplined, but I cannot allow it."

"Wait," Little John growled, his large hand braced on the heir's forearm, sensing Ric's torment as he unwittingly moved forward.

Ric ripped himself from his grasp, the action catching Ella's eye, judging by her movement. A hasty motion in the distance would have been precisely the sort of thing she'd trained herself to mark. Her gaze met Ric's, her focus on him alone.

Johan thumbed over the curves of Ella's knuckles adoringly before his voice cut through the final remnants of Ric's self-control. "Lady Ella of Locksley — your Hood," he amended, his lips tipped up at the edges as he regarded her with affection, "has agreed to become my wife."

Ric seethed, and he balled his fists at his sides as his pulse raged within. He should have seen it coming, for it capped Johan's endless treachery flawlessly. A king cannot succeed without an heir and is scarcely considered legitimate without a wife. A queen who carries the adoration of the people would be an immeasurable asset.

Tentative applause penetrated Ric's hollowed thoughts, his gaze yet locked with Ella's, tethering them together and keeping him whole. A single tear slipped down her cheek, her countenance pained, but Ric seemed to be the only one to notice. For those surrounding him, clapping and cheering for their new princess, their hero, all was as it should be, fortifying Ric's resolve to right this catastrophic turn of fortune.

Johan stepped toward her, using the pad of his thumb to tenderly blot the moisture from her flushed complexion, and Ric braced himself to move, forcing his way forward with a sweep of his arm. For but a moment, Ella seemed to welcome his approach until a subtle shake of her head warned him off. Almost imperceptibly, she'd ordered him away, but it wasn't enough.

Tipping her delicate face toward himself, Prince Johan demanded her attention. "My love, in only a week, we will be one for the rest of time."

Ella closed her eyes, managing a weak smile as she nodded her enthusiasm. Johan drew her nearer, wrapping possessive arms around her waist as Ric watched on resentfully.

A week. *One* week.

He wouldn't allow her to sacrifice more than she already had, not for him or anyone else. His men were on their way, due for arrival any day, but what if they were too late?

He knew what revealing himself would mean. Johan's sins would be pinned to him, and he would die. It wasn't a risk, but surrender, one that might allow Ella her freedom.

Shoving past the outer edge of the gathering, he drew more attention with each step, and with every footfall, he considered his vastly errored logic without care. His vision filtered crimson, stained with the blood on Johan's hands—the blood of his father. It was Much's severed limb, and even his own blood, which would surely blemish the earth before nightfall.

Curious whispers followed his steps before the commanding form of Little John stepped before his senseless pursuit.

Then there was nothing.

* * * *

Startling into consciousness, Ric rested against a cold, flat surface. Vaulted planks angling skyward came into view, reaching a sharp peak at their center. An array of vibrant colors filtered across the vacant space in narrow rays as particles of dust floated weightlessly atop radiant beams.

It might've been a dream had his head not throbbed with ceaseless intensity, matched only by the savage aching of his jaw. Bruised, not broken, he had determined, as he tested the range of injury.

Propping himself on angled elbows, clarity resurfaced. He'd awakened in the quiet refuge of the palace chapel, with only Friar Tuck to greet him. There was little worry of being found, as the space was traditionally reserved for the royal family's personal use. Johan wouldn't be using it anytime soon. At least, not for another week.

Ric massaged his temples as Tuck looked him over, his brows knitted together. "You seem well enough."

"I suppose I am. In body, at least." Ric groaned, using the wooden pew he'd been left upon to pull himself up.

Tuck replied with a solemn nod, clutching the cross he wore over his heart. "You mustn't lose hope."

"You don't know him as I do." The words had left him more harshly than intended, but the good friar paid no mind to his manner.

"I know him well enough, and I know he is not to be trusted," Tuck stated simply. "He has been gifted with a silver tongue, but make no mistake... He too will be judged."

Ric scoffed, a humorless breath of doubt and rage as he shook his head. "What difference will that make once he has taken my kingdom and my future?"

"The breath has not left your lungs, Your Highness. You've not yet completed the task for which you were designed." Offering a sympathetic smile, the friar stood. "I will let your friends know you're awake."

As he shuffled out of sight, Ric's thoughts returned to Ella. He knew why Little John had stepped in, and though part of him still wished he hadn't, it was better this way. He would have been useless dead, but with life still coursing through his veins, there remained an opportunity to remedy all that Johan had set into motion.

He waited there, alone in the chapel he'd always avoided in his youth. The queen had often encouraged him to join her when she had gone there to pray, yet more often than not, it would be only Isla who had accompanied her.

How he wished he had obliged. They'd both been taken far too soon.

Indeed, Ella shared their sense of sincerity and spirit, and a world without compassion could not thrive. A soul like hers should never be compelled to harden for the sake of survival.

Dropping to his knees, Ric submitted himself to a being more significant than himself, a foreign God that he did not know, nor had he ever wished to know before desperation and fear had settled.

"If it's a life for a life, Lord, let it be mine, lost for the sake of hers," he begged, his heart thundering within his chest. "Surely, it is a corrupt nature like my own that is meant for such a fate. If you are just as it is said you are, then she will not only live but flourish. And if it is a sacrifice you require, then it shall be me who gives it."

His words were strained, caught in his throat as he forced them into being. But they were all he could offer. "Lord, please protect her."

Rising to his feet, he was quickly joined by familiar faces, each of them exhibiting the anxiety he, too, shared.

"Your Highness, I—" Inclining his head toward the prince, Little John stumbled over words of regret. "I never would have... More I—I never meant—"

"You did what was necessary, brother." Smirking, Ric winced, cautiously assessing his stiffening jaw. "I left you with no choice."

John extended his arm, which Riccard firmly took as a symbol of their comradery. John was more a friend for landing him on his back than if he'd watched the heir give up his birthright along with any potential of saving the kingdom, or Ella. In truth, Ric was grateful.

"We mustn't tarry." Rory peeked through the doorway, making sure they'd not been followed. "Your brother will surely send men after you for the display you created, so I do not think it wise to remain so near the castle."

"We would do well to move on to Benthamshire. It'll be over a day's journey, and we've no time to waste," Much agreed, for the Llundynien army was due to return in short order. With their assistance, they would surely guarantee freedom for Ella and Marion.

It would require a day and a half to journey to the border, meeting at the edge of Wylewoode. Ric had no desire to return to that forsaken wilderness, but for Ella, he would do anything. With the time robbed from them due to their travels, they would be left with a brief window of opportunity, but it was not entirely insurmountable.

Johan had given them one week—one week to conceive of a strategy, to reclaim a nation. In seven days, Ella would be expected to wed Johan, and she had entrusted her extrication as well as Marion's to Ric.

He refused to fail her. Whether his men arrived or not, he would find a way.

* * * *

Benthamshire was a quiet village, seated at the outermost edge of Wylewoode. There was no question as to its sparse populace, given the proximity to the minacious lands just outside their town.

Together, Ric and Rory had met several villagers during their previous travels, and the citizenry of that shire had been particularly hospitable. Utilizing their established relations, they'd been fortunate enough to secure private rooms with beds for the first time in months.

It had been determined through Ric's correspondence that he would meet with his second-in-command upon his arrival at the modest brewery owned by their host. He'd not known at the time he'd called for his men of the generosity they would encounter but was grateful for it, nonetheless.

They had spent two nights in the sleepy town, a full day longer than the heir had dared hope, and his patience was running thin.

"What's taking so long? At the very least, Will and the others should have been here by now." Pacing the length of the tavern, Ric pinched the bridge of his nose between his fingers. At Will's suggestion, he had stayed behind with Little John and Alan to recruit able-bodied villagers to assist Ric and his men when the time arose. Will's ability to organize and plan ahead was a blessing, to be sure, but Ric was becoming eager to see them.

"They'll be here," Rory assured him, though there was no denying that some doubt had begun to take root.

The day dragged as hours passed by, the waning sunlight peeking over the tops of humble shanties as it moved to take its leave. Much had fallen asleep, his head resting upon his stump as he hunched over a sticky tabletop. Rory had spent the day taking advantage of the kindness offered by the friends she'd made a month earlier, reveling in an opportunity to bathe.

But the prince, his temper short, was not of a mind for company. Even the barkeeper had left them, as they were his only customers. The door of the hostelry parlor creaked open behind Ric, and, expecting Rory, he motioned her off.

The footfalls of more than one individual drew near. "Your Highness," came a gruff, weary voice.

Glancing over his shoulder, Ric saw his second, Thorne, at attention. His eyes were rimmed with fatigue, much as the men to either side of him—one Thorne's young squire and the other a man with whom the heir was not acquainted.

Ric was on his feet in an instant, and in his periphery, Much had awakened as well. Greeting Thorne, he took his arm in hand, clapping him firmly on the back. "You took your time, man." Ric smirked, nodding acknowledgment to the squire, Massey, before waving Much forward. "This is James Much. Much, Thorne and his squire, Massey. There are others as well, whom you'll meet soon."

"Aurora is among them, I trust." It was the foreign man, flanking Thorne, a man with whom Ric was unfamiliar. Indeed, he knew of no Aurora, either. Ric exchanged a questioning glance with Much, who simply shrugged in confusion.

"Nobody calls me by that name." Rory stepped through the doorway. She had been pampered and washed, her garments freshly laundered, with raven strands knotted neatly down her front. "Who are you, that you would inquire of me? I do not know you." Placing her hands at her hips, she waited expectantly.

"Artyrus of Romsey," he replied stoically, inclining his head.

Rory rolled her eyes, her face a mask of indifference as she strode nearer. "What a name you have. Your parents were lamentably creative."

"I have no parents." Artyrus' voice was low, his brow raised in contempt. "The Seer sent me to escort you home."

Much whistled through his teeth. The woman was uncommonly obstinate, a trait that somehow suited her beautifully. And while she revered the Seer's insights, they all knew this was hardly the time for her to be plucked from her current station.

"Perhaps once you've helped us restore Llundyn, I will consider leaving, but no sooner. And I have no need of an escort." With a wave of her hand, she dismissed his commission.

"I will not have traveled all this way to return to Chamelaute empty-handed. I'll grant a few days before we depart, but that is all. You will accompany me home," Artyrus asserted with finality, meeting her defiant gaze with one of his own.

Ric grimaced, stifling an errant chuckle. Artyrus gave as good as he got, a rarity when it came to the headstrong Rory. If anyone were familiar with the whirlwind of conviction that was the foreign woman, it was him.

She must've known that it was time, too. Otherwise, she never would've stayed silent following such a demand. Ric was more than aware of the esteem with which she regarded the Seer, and that hadn't changed. He knew she would follow the man home.

Or, perhaps, she would lead him herself.

Ric observed Artyrus, a tall, broad-shouldered man with a sullen countenance. While his own bond with Rory had been slow to develop, he would miss his friend. For his sake, the heir hoped Artyrus was as patient as he was Herculean.

"How many have you brought with you?" Anxious to pre-empt Johan's scheme, Ric returned his focus to the situation that had brought them all together, doing his best to ignore a sulking Rory as she slouched into a nearby chair.

"Two hundred and fifty of our best, Your Highness," the general replied. "There are more units on the way, approximately one day behind, and additional men trailing, three days at the rear."

"We have not a day to spare. Your two hundred and fifty will have to suffice, alongside however many more our friends have rallied." Clenching his jaw, Ric took up pacing once more. "Rory and Much, you must stay behind to greet Will and the others when they arrive. Thorne, deliver me to my men."

"Right away, sire," Thorne said with a bow.

"I trust you can lead the remainder of my crew to us when they arrive?" Ric asked Artyrus.

"Indeed, Your Majesty," he agreed with a hasty bow of his own, his eyes drifting toward Rory as she stewed in the corner.

"Well, then. Let us take our leave." Ric smiled tightly, eager to get moving. With yet another day lost to them, time was a dwindling commodity.

It was a short ride to a large clearing outside of town, twenty minutes at most. The beginnings of campfires were being forged, flickering to life as vibrant amber ribbons streamed toward the darkening sky.

Ric had seen these men fight—but better, he had seen them triumph.

Chapter Twenty-Nine

The days passed in a blur of activity, and Ella had struggled in vain to numb herself. She was prepared to own her decisions and made every effort to justify them within the privacy of her own mind, but to no avail.

She would never forget Ric's face.

His smoldering visage was etched into the very recesses of her memory, his eyes burning with displeasure as he attempted to reconcile the announcement made in the square with what he knew to be true in his heart.

He understood. She knew he did. His abiding love for her was evident from the start, their eyes meeting in earnest as Johan had droned on. She hadn't paid his musings any mind, her focus interminably upon the man who held her soul in his capable hands.

That was, until Johan had made his fateful proclamation.

And while Ric was well aware of her love and devotion for him, she knew that wouldn't make their separation or the prospect of her impending nuptials any less painful.

Would that Ric and his men render that future null.

"Milady."

"Oh." Ella sighed, her mind restored to the present by the mild urgings of her lady's maid. She took in her appearance in the tri-fold mirror as Queen Eleanor's wedding dress was fitted to her body with pins and thread. "Yes, that will do very well."

"Only a few more adjustments, Your Grace," the seamstress muttered, her gnarled hands busily executing last-minute alterations to the timeless gown.

Against all the odds, the fabric had remained as white as freshly driven snow, refusing to succumb to the discoloration that so often yellowed antique fibers. The neckline hugged Ella's shoulders, exposing the gentle curve of her collarbone, while breezy sleeves of sheer silk covered her arms, splitting just below her elbows and spilling into floor length bells. Yards of finely spun crimson linen accentuated the dropped waist in the form of a sash, settling on the flair of her hips and flowing into the full skirt. Accents of gold filigree sheathed the bodice, completing the whole sumptuous affair—unequivocally the most beautiful thing Ella had ever had the privilege of wearing.

It was a shame, indeed, to waste it on the despicable Prince Johan.

One of Ella's numerous attendants approached her, a pearlescent wisp of fabric slung across her arms. "We must measure your veil, Your Grace." She curtsied with her head bowed, averting her gaze.

Ella bristled, deeply uncomfortable with the deferential terms and excessive attention. "You needn't call me that. Please, call me Ella."

"I think not." Johan's tone was frigid, sending all the waiting women into a flurry of activity as he entered Ella's quarters. He moved before her, his eyes trained upon her form in a manner that was highly inappropriate, given their company. "Leave us."

Not one second had passed before they were scurrying out of the room, leaving Ella at the mercy of the spoiled prince.

"You're not to see the bride on the day before the wedding, Majesty." Ella managed a smile, though her countenance was dark. Knots formed in her stomach as she cursed his relentless presence. She'd hoped for one blessed day where she wouldn't have to feign any sort of enthusiasm for Johan. It seemed that was out of the question.

"Superstition is none of my concern." Leisurely, he strode around the pedestal on which she stood, his gaze roving from head to toe in a brazen appraisal. "Not when our marriage is based entirely upon pretense, though it is mutually beneficial. Perhaps in time..." He shook his head, dismissing the thought. "You are truly lovely."

She straightened, too weary from his antics to dignify him with a response. Her obstinance only emboldened him further. Reaching for the corset fastened at the small of her back, he untied it with slow, deliberate fingers.

She clasped the bodice to her chest, her heart rate spiking. "What—?"

"My brother would lose his mind at the sight of you, dearest Ella," he murmured, his breath tickling her exposed neck as he drew nearer, loosening the stays at her back. "But perhaps he already has. I did notice a man bearing a suspicious likeness to him in the town square when we announced our engagement."

She could hear the satisfied smile in his voice, which only served to further anger her. Ella had fervently hoped the ruckus in the square had gone unnoticed, but it seemed, yet again, that Johan had managed to observe everything.

"If it was Ric, then he is well aware of where I stand," Ella declared, desperate to quash his assertions. "It could not be more evident what I've chosen. Maybe it's best that he saw it for himself, firsthand."

"You are extraordinary. I *almost* believe you." The fabric slipped from her back, and Johan chuckled as she shivered where she stood. Never had she been more grateful for her inner corselette, shielding her flesh within the gown.

"I wouldn't be here if I weren't serious." Ella loathed herself for the damnable flush creeping upward from her toes, but she'd never been so bare before any man. With Johan, she'd been exposed not only physically, but mentally as well. It was utterly demeaning, and she meant to make him pay.

"Your game is plain to me, you know," Johan said, coming to a stop before her. His mocking grin spread from ear to ear as he cupped her cheek, pity evident in his eyes. "Ric cannot save you alone, for alas, he has no means. His second writes to me from Chamelaute, awaiting my instructions. I do presume his men believe themselves to have been abandoned."

Ella trained her features, determined to keep them impassive as she lifted her chin defiantly, ignoring the thrill that chased down her spine.

He doesn't know.

Ric's men were on the move. Indeed, she hoped that they were present in Llundyn, ready to wrest control from the usurper at a moment's notice. It was a small fragment of fortune in a competition where she had, as yet, felt very much at a disadvantage.

"It is of no concern to me," she lilted, suddenly filled with renewed faith. She smiled shyly, peering up at him through thick lashes in a manner she hoped to be beguiling. "I will be yours tomorrow."

Johan watched her in silent contemplation, analyzing her as he so often did. He was uncommonly attentive, setting her on edge. "So you shall," he said, after a long moment. "Now, get dressed. I have an early wedding gift for you. You'll have fifteen minutes with Marion — and not a minute more."

"A kindness, Your Majesty. I thank you." Ella curtsied with as much grace as she could manage while gripping her bodice for dear life. She stepped from the pedestal, making a beeline for her daily wear that was sprawled across the chaise near the window before turning. "If you please. I cannot change with you in my presence."

"I see not why it matters. As you said, tomorrow —"

"Yes," she agreed hastily. "*Tomorrow.*"

He bowed, a devilish glint to his eye that told her she was fortunate he was willing to keep up appearances within the castle walls. It seemed he did not wish to marry a woman disgraced, choosing instead to do things by the book, leaving her virtue intact.

And, if he had not, she had a gift of her own, strapped upon her leg in the form of a dagger. She would not submit to him, willingly or otherwise.

* * * *

Ignoring the nagging feeling that told her seeing Marion did not bode well for his future, Ella followed two foreign goons into the cellars for her visit with her dearest friend.

He was sat against the stone wall with his arm slung casually over his propped knee as he stared at the ceiling. To her great relief, he'd been given a threadbare blanket and pillow — better slightly than the complete lack of courtesy given Alan when he'd had his turn in the damp dungeons of Nottinghamshire Castle.

"You will leave us," Ella ordered in her most authoritative tone. She didn't hesitate to command the brigands, given that they had no right to their posts in the first place.

The two men laughed, ignoring her entirely as one opened the cell door. Marion, for his part, was shocked out of his stupor, clambering to his feet as he ran to meet her.

"Why are you here?" His outrage was unmistakable, but it didn't keep him from giving her a lingering hug. "What did you do?"

Ella took him by the hand, moving farther into the dungeon as the hired thugs locked her in alongside Marion, taking up stations on either side of the iron door. They moved toward the rear wall, where Marion took a seat as Ella dropped to her knees beside him, her full skirt a cloud of glossy blue silk as it puffed around her. She leaned toward him, taking both of his hands in hers.

"I've bought us some time is all." She gave him a sweet smile, confident that he was not likely to let her off the hook that easily.

Marion matched her smile with a wry one of his own. He was well aware that her presence within his cell had come at a cost, and he'd known her long enough to witness her doing some rather risky things. "But what, pray, did you do, darling?"

She averted her gaze, unable to look him in the eye. "I've agreed to marry Johan."

"You *what*?" Marion tightened his hands into fists within her hold, shaking as he absorbed the shocking blow. "I am worth no such sacrifice. You will rescind your consent at *once*! Ric must be—" He paused, dropping his voice so that the guards wouldn't overhear him. "Ric must be a walking disaster by now. He loves you, Ella. Don't you know that?"

She sighed. The heir had been much on her mind. It was the thought of him that carried her through the past five days and his face that she'd seen in her dreams each night. "I do. And I've come here for both of you. Now we need only hope that his...his *friends* are on time."

"This is treacherous, even for you. If you're wrong—"

"I'm not. Tomorrow, you'll be a free man once more."

"Not likely, Locksley." Marion met her eyes, finding them earnest and full of tears. She knew, and so did he. His voice was gentle, resigned as he was to his awaiting fate. "Tuck visited today. Gave me my last rites."

"Stop it." Ella clenched her teeth, determined not to become a blubbering mess as she sought to will her own ambitions into reality. "Tomorrow will be a fateful day, that is true. But I will not be marrying that cretin— and neither will you die."

He wiped a stray tear from her cheek with the pad of his thumb, his hand steady, despite his nervous energy. "I know you want that to be so. But in case it isn't"—he paused, warding off her emerging rebuke with a finger to her lips — "I want you to know that you are the truest friend I've ever had. Indeed, I never would've expected such loyalty for someone like myself. You did all that you were able, and that is enough."

"Do *not* speak like this!" she cried, shaking her head as she recovered her senses. "I won't have it. Tomorrow you are free. *We* are free. Please trust—"

"I do, Elle. I do." His voice was thick, heavy as his heart was with the many things he wished to say. "Come here."

She shuffled toward him, casting herself into his awaiting embrace with her tears flowing unfettered as she buried her face into his chest. He held her close, stroking his hand over her hair in a manner he must have hoped was soothing. He usually wasn't good with women.

Well, he wasn't good with women that he cherished.

"I could've loved you," he uttered, smiling as reveries of what might've been sustained his soul. "Maybe I even did."

"I love you, too." A hiccup escaped her, then another, the result of her sudden hysterics. Marion chuckled, drawing a wayward giggle from the lady thief in his arms. Their comradery was as effortless as breathing, sharing an affection that had grown familiar and comforting over two decades of adventures together.

There they remained, quietly enduring as they strengthened one another in the relative privacy of the cold cellar. It would not end here, for Ella simply refused to allow it.

She lifted her head, running her fingers beneath the rims of her eyes as she dried away her tears. She didn't want to give her guards the satisfaction of tearing her away, instead choosing to leave on her own terms.

"This is not goodbye," Ella whispered. She leaned toward Marion, kissing the corner of his mouth before rising to her feet.

"I know." He offered a reassuring grin, her favorite, reaching for her hand, giving her a lingering squeeze. "We'll give 'em hell tomorrow."

"We've always been good at that, my friend." She wandered backward, her eyes never leaving his as she made her way to the door. Offering a timid wave in parting, she turned to go.

Chapter Thirty

Men sparred throughout the early evening hours, Ric's compatriots having made it to the edge of Sherwood only mere hours prior. Doubtless, they were exhausted, after trekking through Wylewoode only to find they had yet another two days' journey to meet their prince. The men were led by none other than Artyrus, journeying to the clearing near the boundary of the forest. There, they began their preparations for war.

General Thorne cleared his throat, stood just beyond the curtain of Riccard's tent. The heir splashed his face with the cold water left for him within his new canvas quarters, raised for him upon their arrival. "You may enter," Ric said, adjusting a clean tunic across his chest. Drilling with his army had left him sore and smelly, providing a much-needed distraction.

Additional gear had been left for him — a chair, a fur rug, a *cot* — each item frivolous, given the new life to which he'd grown accustomed. He would not have given their presence a passing thought weeks before, but since that time, everything had changed.

"You called for me?" Thorne ducked under the flapped entry.

"I wish to discuss the details of our strategy." Ric tossed random trinkets to the side, rifling through his small chest before meeting the general's stare. "You spoke of spies lurking about Chamelaute. How confident are you they've all been detained?"

"Quite, Your Highness, and with the remaining units of your army still present there, if more are found, they'll be captured should they attempt any method of correspondence. The border is being heavily monitored by our men, along with many of King Luther's guard."

"Very good." Motioning the general forward, Ric set out a chair, seating himself opposite his second at a small table. Together, they'd spent many long nights in this same arrangement, agonizing over the most minute details in their battle tactics.

"And your communications with my brother?" Ric pressed, though the very thought of Johan had him livid. Indeed, he preferred not to think of him at all.

"I followed your instruction. With the help of Chamelaute's Seer, I penned correspondence to Prince Johan, explaining that we believed you to have abandoned us, with no indication that you might return. Your brother believes us to be awaiting his direction." The general's smirk suggested a hint of pleasure derived from his deceptions.

"Prince Johan has been given every reason to believe that we remain with our allies," Thorne continued. "Our ships remain anchored at Chamelaute's docks, with many of our ranks sheltered within their borders. He will not be expecting us."

Ric nodded, pleased to be succeeding in his own treacherous measures. The element of surprise was the best offensive tool they could utilize. With it, Riccard and his units would have an opportunity to surround the palace without notice. Though small in number, these were men who could defeat all odds. He had seen them do so firsthand.

"It will be even better yet, once more of our regiment arrives," Thorne persisted, eager to fill the silence that stretched between them. The heir had been quiet and much reserved since the general had returned—a far cry from the cavalier commander Thorne was accustomed to.

"We leave for Nottingham at sunrise, with or without them," Ric decreed with finality. He was long past being deterred, whether he was undermanned or ill-prepared. He would not leave Ella to a fate that damned her to a life with his dangerous brother. He motioned for his second to follow as he pulled the canvas back to exit. "Come... I'd like you to meet my friends. We still have much to discuss."

Outside the tent, Ric found his men scattered across the clearing, many grouped around roaring flames as they told preposterous tales of valor. Others had paired off practicing with swordplay, which was where he soon spotted Will and Little John. Alan observed nearby, shouting obscenities as he watched, while Much stood at his side, chewing on a piece of jerky.

The sight of Ella's ragtag crew brought Ric great peace. He'd spent years training with the royal army, but somehow, these thieves had become dearer companions in only a matter of weeks. In truth, he knew them better than the soldiers with whom he'd been acquainted for nearly a decade.

"Perhaps I should teach them how to properly wield a sword." Catching Ric by surprise, Rory fell in stride beside him opposite the general, smirking as she took in the unfolding display.

"Is this not abundantly more entertaining, *Aurora*?" Ric's use of her full name was met with a blistering scowl, the precise reaction the heir had hoped for.

"You would do well not to trifle with me, *Your Highness*," she teased. "Unless you desire to familiarize yourself with my mastery of the blade as well."

"I should like to see that," Thorne laughed, peeking past Ric at the menacing beauty to his left.

"It very well may be the last thing you see after feeding me to that miserable wolf, Artyrus." Pursing bowed lips, she met Thorne's gaze, her brows raised as if she'd meant every word.

Ric sighed, thoroughly caught in a fit of nostalgia. "Oh, how I shall miss you, dear friend."

"And I you," Rory agreed. She patted the heir on his forearm, each of them profoundly dismayed by the reality within their sentiments.

The trio of observers stopped shy of the clearing, watching as Will pivoted out of Little John's reach, maneuvering as he deftly avoided his opponent's attack. John lunged forward, his footwork effortless as he twisted to meet Will's crouched form. They regarded one another, each with cunning smirks, predicting the other's movements before either could fully execute their charge.

"Watch closely," Much said, surveying their spar with anticipation as he nodded toward Little John.

John stepped forward, only to retreat two steps back. The duo was well-matched, their skillsets equal in both speed and strength, even as fatigue strained their actions. Deliberately shifting his mass into Will's path, Little John paused as his adversary swung, the blade slicing through the air as it clashed against his own.

The shriek of metal on metal rang between them, Will stumbling backward in confusion as he dropped the hilt of his cutlass to the ground, now bladeless in the dirt. Realization colored his features when his eyes fell upon the two separate pieces of his weapon lying at John's feet. "Bloody brilliant!" He grinned, retrieving the hilt and examining it with a laugh, turning it over in his hands.

"The bastard cheated!" Alan bellowed, pointing an accusatory finger toward Little John, whose smile only widened at the minstrel's fury.

"I've done only what my prince requested of me." John beamed, folding into a gallant bow before Riccard. "It worked just as I had intended, holding together through more insignificant hits, only to fail in the heat of battle."

"It was perfect—and properly weighted," Will confirmed through his continuing examination of the blacksmith's trickery. "It's impossible to know it's defective until it's strenuously used—a rather unfair advantage, though I cannot bring myself to regret it."

"Well done." Clapping John on the shoulder, Ric chuckled. "Well done, indeed. How many have been distributed to my brother's mercenaries?"

"Nearly half possess a faulty blade." His words were thick with pride, even as he attempted in vain to hide his smile.

Nodding silent approval, the prince made no effort to conceal the pleasure he found in his friend's clever design. Days before, their lot had seemed hopeless, so much so that Ric had nearly given himself over in what would've proven the single most foolish act of his existence.

They'd come a long way since, not only in physical distance but in confidence.

"And what did you find in the way of support within the villages?" Ric asked.

"Men were hesitant to come with us," Alan admitted. "Bu' they're eager to join the fight. They'll take up arms upon the first ring of the abbey bells, bu' not before."

"No fewer than one hundred men, Your Highness," Will added formally. It was strange, being addressed as such by these pickpockets he'd grown so relaxed around. General Thorne's presence was likely a stark reminder of the company they now kept.

And while Ric doubtless preferred the casual nature with which they'd previously interacted, Ella had always reminded him of his responsibility to the Crown. It wasn't a change or honor he deserved, nor did he crave the authority. But he'd seen the alternative to his rule. He would never allow Johan sovereign power.

Ric longed to leave behind a legacy of service, sacrificial and just — to be a compassionate king worthy of his citizenry.

And it was all within his grasp.

It was Ella who had given him this dream and the courage to pursue it, and it was for her that he would achieve it. A single night is all that separated them.

Yet somehow, it felt like an eternity.

Chapter Thirty-One

It was time. Ella rose from her bed, prepared to meet the day that she'd looked toward, both with trepidation as well as promise. There would be no more games with Johan after today, for she would either be safely in Ric's arms once more, else dead.

A mass of women entered her quarters without so much as a knock, preparing to primp and paint Ella for her impending nuptials. Little did they know their efforts would be for naught, as she would much prefer to present herself to the wretched Prince Johan in sackcloth.

"Your Grace, if you please." Her lady's maid helped her into her slippers, gesturing toward her breakfast laid upon a small table. "We must make haste. There is much to do."

Ella moved to eat her breakfast, choosing to fuel herself rather than protest, despite her nerves. She'd need strength to free Marion as well as herself. Her plans were an amalgamation of hastily conceived schemes and hopeful gambles. Nothing substantial to speak of, but then, she'd scarcely had a moment to herself in the past week. She would be armed with nothing more than her intuition and the dagger strapped to her ankle.

The odds were not in her favor. She'd known that going in. Would that Ric and her crew would arrive, along with his men, making her task far easier to complete.

Ella hated to pin all their fortunes upon Ric's men, but the truth was, if they did not or could not show, there was no doubt that every last one of them would die. For as much as she wished that her crew would simply leave her to her fate, she knew better. They would be there, come hell or high water.

She shot up a silent prayer, a plea for each of their lives and safety.

Time passed her by, some hours or days. It might've been weeks for all the attention that Ella paid, diligently ignoring all the women who fashioned her into the image that would be most pleasing to Johan. When she glanced in the mirror, a mere courtesy to all her attendants, she did not even recognize herself.

"How lovely," she uttered, bowing her head.

"It was an honor...to serve the Hood." Ella turned to find the quietest amongst the women peeking up at her with a fierce expression.

"Make him grieve your very presence, Your Grace," another urged, a knowing gleam to her eyes. "Your courage is noble beyond measure."

The women curtsied in unison, a seemingly impromptu act that brought Ella to tears. They'd been on her side the whole time, but she hadn't had the mindfulness to notice. "Oh," she breathed, gathering herself. "Thank you. Your encouragement is heartening, indeed." Curtsying in return, she knew she was prepared at last to meet her destiny, come what may.

She made her way down the empty corridor, flanked by her retinue of domestics. The palace was eerily still, and Ella did not doubt that every soul who dwelt within the castle walls would have made their way to the chapel long before. At the end of the hall, she was met by Prince Johan's regent.

"You're needed in the courtyard, Your Grace," he growled, none too taken with the traitorous Hood. He'd been the only one on the Council of Lords to lobby his sovereign, beseeching Johan to bind himself to a more worthy woman than she.

Ella was very much in agreement. If only the brutish man realized.

"Why must I go to the courtyard, when we're to wed in the chapel?" Ella asked, only to meet with a long-suffering sigh from the portly gentleman. He scowled, refusing to answer her query. Instead, he took off down the adjacent hallway, gesturing for her to follow.

Something isn't right.

She willed herself ahead, moving along behind the ill-tempered regent with her heart in her throat. Ella was eager to be within the chapel walls, for that was where Ric and her crew would expect her to be. Diverting had her nerves on edge, adding wrinkles to her already tenuous plans.

Had her band already made a move? Perhaps they had, leaving Johan somehow on the defensive. Or could it be that he was prepared to release Marion? She hadn't dared to hope for that, but it was possible. Such a move would doubtless inspire a degree of goodwill on a day that the heinous prince knew full well Ella was dreading. Might he wish to foster a more amicable alliance? If he did, he was a fool, but she would welcome it just the same.

Such a turn would make the chaotic scenario that lay before her much easier to execute. If Marion were present, rather than confined to the dungeons as she participated in the farce of a wedding, it would eliminate the most complicated portion of her plot.

She shook her head, dismissing the prospect altogether. Lulling herself into any sort of false notions at this stage was a fool's errand. Johan did not give anything freely, with every act deliberate.

Besides all that, Marion's words from yesternight readily rang in her ears. He'd all but kissed her goodbye, having already received a visit from Tuck for his last rites.

No. The day ahead would be a struggle until the bitter end.

They rounded the corner before wandering down a staircase at the rear of the palace. Meandering through another series of winding corridors, Ella found herself wondering if they would ever arrive at their destination. The castle was more substantial than it looked from the outside, and she was not at all acquainted with the labyrinth within its walls.

Coming to a stop before a massive pair of oaken doors, Ella waited with great impatience. She was rapidly tiring of the endless mind games. Indeed, if Johan meant to slowly wear her down, he would find himself at a loss.

She would not break. She would not fail.

The surly regent threw his shoulder into the door, and it gave way with a groan. Ella entered the courtyard, shielding her eyes with a raised arm as her vision adjusted to the bright sunlight. The chapel bells tolled in the distance, a harbinger of all the bitter struggles yet to come.

"Ah, my darling Ella, welcome to the show." Johan stepped before her, kissing her cheek as he took her by the hand. "Join me, won't you?"

He moved to her side, towing her toward the center of the courtyard, and what she beheld was nothing short of a nightmare. For there, the gallows sat, built from freshly hewn lumber. The raised platform stood high above the heads of those gathered in the silent crowd, with a post and crossbeam as solid as a sturdy tree trunk. Hanging from the arm was a single rope, a knot with a generous loop at its end swaying in the breeze of the clement morning. It would be an innocuous construction, were it not commissioned to kill.

As they approached, one of Johan's mercenaries dropped the floor, a trap door at the heart of the assembly. They stopped beside the staircase leading to the dais, and Ella swallowed hard, determined not to tremble as her gleeful companion surveyed her. She schooled her features, tilting her head indifferently. "Is this your final wedding gift for me?"

"Not hardly. We're awaiting another guest." Johan smiled, snapping his fingers. On his signal, another door from across the courtyard swung open, revealing none other than her dearest friend.

Striding toward them with his wrists and ankles bound by rope, Marion was impassive. Spying Ella, he gave a half-smile. He'd made his peace with it all, and so, this was no burden. "Locksley, you are a vision," he proclaimed, their eyes meeting in earnest. If this were to be their end, at least they'd conquer it together.

"It's all rather too sensational for me," Ella said, gesturing toward her gown. "Seems we're to be a part of a spectacle, though I do hope there will be more guests." She tossed a meaningful look Marion's way, and he shook his head, convinced that they were now on their own.

At least if that were so, they were not altogether alone. And while each of them felt far more desperate than either was willing to let on, teasing one another was a surefire way to keep their anxieties hidden while also irritating the mad prince, who felt very much ignored as he stood alongside them.

It was a win on all fronts, save for the implications for each of their futures.

"I'd forgotten how charming the pair of you are when you're together," Johan spat, already chafing with their good-natured ribbing. "Alas, you will soon be coming to terms with a life free from one another."

"Oh, I don't know about that. Certainly, we will meet in the afterlife, will we not?" Ella drew nearer to Marion, linking her arm through his as she sought to draw from his steady strength. "Though it might've been more impactful had you erected two posts side by side."

Understanding donned as Johan realized Ella's meaning. "That would be true, had I intended for you both to die. But you, my dear, will remain very much alive."

Ella shivered, her knees nearly buckling as Johan's meaning registered. "But I...you said — "

"I *said* that we would marry today. I *said* that you would bring the kingdom to kneel under my rule. You are the means by which I will gain their loyalty. Why would I hang you?" Johan's eyes narrowed, his irritation ever-growing. In his mind, he had orchestrated a flawless performance for the masses, only to be thrown off course by the flippant duo.

"But why would you hang Marion?" Ella was barreling toward disaster, in danger of losing her tightly held control. "You were to release him after we marry this day! Why would I follow through on our bargain when you will not?"

"You will, for this day is to serve as a warning," Johan hissed, wresting her away from Marion as he jerked her by the arm. "Today, you lose Marion, but tomorrow it could be Ric. Follow through...or my brother will be next!"

Ella stilled, her panic suddenly threatening to strangle her. She knew Johan couldn't possibly have Ric, for doubtless, it would be he in bondage before her instead of Marion if he did. Yet, Johan would never yield, never cease in his quest for total power.

Marion's tender gaze fell upon Ella, rapidly unraveling her remaining composure. "Hang on and do what you must. All is not lost. And you, *friend*," he continued, his tone crisp and cold as he shifted his attention to Johan, "get on with it. I'm tired of your tedious machinations. You always did have a flair for the dramatic. Too bad I'm not interested in playing along."

Moving toward Ella, he leaned down to kiss her cheek. "Ric will love you well, darling," he whispered, the scruff of his chin brushing against her ear. "Do not lose heart." Backing away, Marion smiled without an ounce of contempt, his wide grin bringing silent tears to Ella's eyes as he made for the stairway leading to the platform.

"Don't," she rasped, her voice nearly inaudible as she staggered after him. Johan held fast, keeping her rooted to the earth by his side as Marion reached the dais.

Without a word, he lifted the noose, looping it around his neck as he stood stock-still above the gathered crowd. The hangman threw a burlap sack over Marion's head before stepping aside with a shrug, evidently unneeded for an execution that would be met with no resistance.

But Ella had had enough, struggling against Johan's grasp for freedom. She punched him in the chest, earning a derisive scoff from the prince as she dropped to her feet, her breaths coming in ugly, fitful gasps.

All around, Johan's mercenaries snickered, their mirth driving her to the end of her senses. Reaching beneath her skirts, she retrieved her dagger. In one smooth motion, she rose to her feet, her dirk tightly clasped with both hands as she thrust it toward Johan's gullet. A speck of red beaded up upon his skin where she nicked him with the tip of her blade, but she wasn't fast enough.

Johan stepped back, throwing Ella off balance as he grasped her by both wrists, twisting her arms painfully as he spun her toward himself. In a matter of seconds, he had her overpowered, with her back pressed firmly against his frame, her arms clamped against her sides.

"Do not trifle with me, dearest." His hot breath washed over her as she struggled against him in vain. "I've trained for years. Accept this loss as fate and stand by my side."

Ella calmed, allowing only a moment to simply *breathe*. Her vision spun and tilted as she fought to regain control. Nothing was right, her entire world shattering around her as everything seemingly fell into slow motion.

She blinked, her eyes fixed upon her stoic friend, standing brave and true as he awaited his lot. Again, and she watched as a breeze whirled through, rustling the hoods of those gathered. Once more, and she realized that every person in the crowd was cloaked, their heads concealed by their mantles.

And there, right at the fore of the gathering, was her band. Ella met Ric's gaze, finding both mercy and desperation in his eyes. He nodded once, his features gleaming with determination. They were ready, and they were *there*.

"I'm glad we have an understanding," Johan growled, returning her to herself. "Do it." He waved his hand, with a mere flick of his wrist signaling an end to a life that was as precious to Ella as her own.

All at once, it was bedlam. The mercenaries milling about the courtyard straightened, falling in place around the dais as the hangman moved to pull the pin from the trap door beneath Marion's feet. The floor dropped, taking him along with it as it swung freely from the underside of the structure.

Ella screamed, her bloodcurdling cry piercing the silence of the courtyard as she kicked and bucked, beating against Johan's strength to sever his hold. Collapsing, she caught the prince off guard as she slid from his grasp.

He lunged for her, but she was ready this time, plunging her dagger into his side as he dove toward her. Rolling from his reach, she leapt to her feet, making a beeline for the dais. An arrow whizzed past her head as she climbed the steps, finding its mark in the hangman's heart. He crumpled to the platform in a heap of limbs, clearing the way for Ella.

Marion hadn't fallen far, for beneath him, with his arms bound tightly around Marion's legs was Ric. "Hurry!" he cried, heaving the lord upward to alleviate the pressure on his neck.

Teetering on the lip of the opening, Ella leaned as far as she dared with nary a thing to support herself, sawing the rope that was stifling the life from her friend. With a *snap*, it broke free.

She glanced at the executioner, slumped before his pull with an arrow burrowed fatally into his breast, while underfoot Ric removed the covering from Marion's face. When he laid him down gently, it was clear he was still breathing, the heir slicing through the restraints knotted tightly around his wrists with care.

Staring over the edge on her hands and knees, she watched Marion closely while Ric tended to him, wielding his knife with dexterous accuracy. Issuing a faint wheeze, the lord sucked in a breath, the rise and fall of his chest causing Ella's eyes to flood with tears of relief.

The instant Marion's hands were freed, Ric turned to Ella, his gaze burning with unmistakable solace. He took hold of her waist, drawing her to him, holding her near for the briefest of moments before stepping aside so she could go to Marion.

Kneeling beside him, Ella stroked his cheek, examining the damage to his throat. A deep, purplish bruise had already formed, but he had survived.

Streaks of battle raged in blurred forms outside their fleeting calm, metal clashing against metal followed by groans of agony as men were delivered into eternal rest. Catching a glimpse of Much facing off with an opponent matched closely in size and ability, she gasped when his challenger's sword broke from its hilt, the man raising his hands in surrender as Much placed the tip of his saber to his heart.

Marion, propping onto his elbows, readied himself to rise as chaos ensued around them. "I'm all right," he croaked. When he moved as though it were true, he steadied his eyes on hers. "Help me to my feet, or we will all surely die."

Nodding, Ella hastily surveyed their surroundings, watching as the legs of a merchant she'd known for years buckled beneath his weight, his body collapsing onto the dirt. The mercenary retrieved his sword from the man's belly, his bloodlust falling to Ric as he sneered.

Carrying a sword on either hip, the prince unsheathed the first, tossing it to Marion, before swiftly removing Ella's bow from over his shoulder, handing it to her along with a quiver full of lethal arrows.

She swung the weapons onto her back, eager to join the fray, even as she cursed the confining gown and absurd slippers restricting her movement.

Ric charged a foreigner, pivoting to one side to evade the man's massive claymore before knocking the wind from his foe's lungs, lunging toward him with all the force he could muster. Marion joined the prince, both of them grappling against the hulking figure as another drew nearer from close behind.

Beyond Marion's shoulder, an obsidian streak swept through the bloodshed as Rory's elegant form clashed with its barbarous surroundings. Holding her broadsword with the confidence of a warrior, she threw herself into an unsuspecting victim. Swift and unforgiving in her attack, she slipped steel across the brute's midsection, felling him. The mistress of blades stepped through his pooling blood, wiping the spattered memory of him from her cheek with the hem of her cloak as she moved farther into the fray.

A towering figure approached her, dwarfing Rory's petite frame where he stood at her rear. Without hesitation, Ella nocked an arrow, prepared to fire just as the man halted his pursuit. Rory reached for him, drawing him to her side where he covered her, watching Rory's fierce dance as she cut her way through her enemies. Wordlessly, the pair shifted, standing back to back, creating a unified force as they shredded through every threat that dared approach.

Ella retreated, spying the father of Little John as he struggled against a far younger opponent. Though John must've outweighed the man by dozens of pounds, he was no match for the agile soldier. In the space of a single breath, she released her bolt, the quarrel burrowing deeply into the flesh between the man's shoulder blades. He didn't fall, but his movements weakened, offering John the opportunity to gain the upper hand.

"Seems an awful waste," a brawny hireling hissed through decaying teeth, eliciting Ella's attention. His empty eyes stripped her bare under their scrutiny. "Such a pretty dress."

Nearly twice her size, he moved forward, closing the gap between them all too rapidly. She ducked out of his reach, him narrowly missing her neck. With a heavy blade still hung at his waist, it seemed he meant to toy with her.

Clutching her dagger firmly, she swung, the sharp edge leaving a shallow slash of crimson across the soft flesh beneath his jaw. Without so much as a wince, the man laughed, squaring his shoulders to continue their brawl.

Her pulse throbbed in tandem with her steps, an exercise of endurance and artifice, frustrating her adversary. Perhaps if she could weary him, she might have an opportunity to catch him off guard, though he was equal in speed thus far. He met each footfall, striding forward as she pulled back, neither gaining ground.

"Stupid girl," he spat, his patience clearly waning as he drew his sword.

Sunlight glinted off its surface, the honed edge piercing the space between them before making contact with Ella's flesh. Pain shot through her thigh, the slit through her gown soaked with blood. Stumbling backward, she hit the ground, crawling, desperate to keep herself from him.

Raising his sword overhead, he pursued her, his eyes glowing with battle-born zeal. Combat was in his blood and marrow, his very essence as he stalked her, sending Ella scrambling.

Her last hope was pinned between her back and the dirt beneath her.

Again, his sword cleaved the air, driving through the vacant expanse that would mean her end. In a final effort of defense, Ella reached for her bow, and by a hair's breadth, brandished it before herself.

It was enough.

The rapier glanced off her bow under the force of his swing as Ella rolled out from under it, the wicked metal grazing past her arm as it settled into the earth where she'd lain.

She found her footing as the brigand lost his. He staggered, and Ella rushed him, reaching over her shoulder in feral pursuit. Leaping onto his back, an arrow in hand, she secured her arm tightly around his head, thrusting the tip of her arrow into the crook of his neck.

He reached for the shaft with dwindling strength, draining each passing second. Before he could grip it, his arm dropped, and he became nothing more than a heaped obstacle atop the ground beneath him.

Pushing off his lifeless form, Ella rose, her focus shifting to where Ric and Marion were met against a third rival. Riccard had positioned himself behind their assailant, the prince's elbow anchored unflinchingly across his windpipe. His opponent's face reddened from the pressure of his squeeze, holding fast as Marion sank his sword into the man's ribs, his body still struggling within the heir's arms.

Before Ric had finished the foreigner, Ella watched awareness seize Marion, his eyes suddenly lit with determination. In what seemed less than the singular beat of her heart, he sprang to action. A muted shriek passed Ella's lips, the scream suppressed by incredulity. Running to stop him, she scooped up the blade that had slipped from her attacker's possession, its hilt still warm with the heat of vitality.

She'd not crossed half the distance parting them before the lord braced himself at Riccard's back. An errant sob proclaimed Ella's horror, Marion's intent firmly established. With no alternative but to watch as cold steel penetrated his core, she broke.

Shaking her head, she cried, not knowing if the words were audible or in her head alone as she begged for it not to be so. And if it were not already enough, she gaped as Prince Johan withdrew his weapon before driving it through Marion once more.

Yet striving to get to them, her feet failed her. Her stride was clumsy and sluggish as she stumbled forward, wrestling against despair and yearning to make it to Marion, though she knew it was already too late.

Ric hurled the man that had demanded his concentration after what was only mere seconds too long, the mercenary having expired. Alarmed by Ella's screams, Riccard turned, his saber tightly clutched. When their eyes met, all that existed was terror, her gaze fixed upon Marion's suffering. Johan closed in on his lifelong friend, his arm jerking Marion toward himself as his wrist twisted with a final statement of contempt.

With no other options, Ric sacked his brother from the side, breaking Johan's contact with Marion, his blade left buried in the lord's abdomen. Johan righted himself, eagerly engaging with his brother in a bitter battle of wills. The pair grappled savagely, trading blows that did little to quell the fury welling between rightful heir and usurper.

Throwing Johan into the broad cedar pillar underpinning the gallows, Ric clasped his hands around Johan's gullet, only to shove his skull against the wooden support behind him.

"*Please*, brother," the serpent sputtered, his voice thin from the pressure of Ric's tense grasp. "One more chance."

"Like you gave our father a chance?" Ric bit through clenched teeth. "Like you gave *Marion* a chance?" His features darkened amid frenzied thoughts, reconciling memories of their shared youth with those of the monster his brother had become. "No. You will die."

Johan struggled, but Ric was too strong, despite his trembling hands. He met his brother's eyes in earnest, seemingly searching for some shred of sentiment, any sign of regard.

He obviously found none.

Rory appeared from the fray, steadying Ella where she stood immobilized by the imperial faceoff. For an instant, they observed, watching as Ric sustained his hold. But it wasn't enough.

Ella understood the division of Ric's mind, with the prospect of ending his own flesh and blood distressing beyond all reason. Unsheathing an arrow from the quiver at her back, she drew her bow, aiming at the despot prince.

Taking a deep breath, she whistled the trill of the Hood, drawing her beloved's attention. Meeting her gaze, Ric nodded once, withdrawing from his brother as Ella released her bolt. The arrow found its mark, settling in Johan's chest with all the force of his inflicted tyranny.

It was for Llundyn. It was for Ric. Indeed, it was for Marion.

Johan buckled, collapsing to the earth at Ric's feet. The heir spared his brother only a passing glance before making his way toward Marion. Collecting herself enough to run, Ella did the same, finding that the lord had removed the saber from his torso. He was hunched, yet still upright, and she eased him to his back, his head resting in her lap. Marion held his stomach, his clothing suffused with blood.

Ric dropped to his knees beside him, his fist pressed to his mouth as he stifled a sob, likely cursing himself over his preoccupation with the foreigner.

"What's happened?" Alan demanded, with Little John at his heels. Reaching for his arm, Rory silenced him, the gravity of their comrade's injury evident in the red pooling around him.

Ric placed his hand over one of Marion's wounds then the other, striving to stanch the bloodshed from his lifelong friend. He bowed his head, gathering himself for a moment as he struggled to understand how it had all come to this.

Marion's pallor grayed as his soul prepared to leave his flesh. Even in death, he was handsome, his features peacefully submitting to providence.

"*Ric,*" Ella breathed, setting her palm atop his. She nodded toward Marion, her message plain. With her other hand, she laced her slender fingers through Marion's as he coughed, lifegiving fluid sputtering from his mouth. Using the sleeve of her gown, she blotted it from his face with tears streaming down her own.

"It's all right." Marion swallowed hard, moisture falling from the corner of his eye. "I feel nothing."

"No, Marion, *please,*" Ella pleaded, her whimper smothering her words. "Don't make me say goodbye, not when we've come so far."

Much knelt behind her, resting his hand on her shoulder as Will joined him at his side. Her entire crew was present, but this wasn't how it was supposed to end. Circling their friend, they grieved in silence, his breathing shallow as a low rattle rumbled deep inside of him.

"Damn it all, you saved my life! You can't just — " Ric cursed under his breath, his heart plainly breaking anew as he watched his dearest friend slip away. They'd always been closer than brothers, neither of them able to remember a time before their lives had converged. All for the better, it had changed them both, with Marion having made the ultimate sacrifice for Ric without a second thought.

Closing his eyes, Marion drifted, his final breath passing through parted lips.

"A good man was he. He will be profoundly missed," Alan uttered. Rory reached for him, squeezing his hand while Alan's lip wobbled, though he tried to remain steadfast in the face of their pain.

Together they remained, gathered around the shell of a man they'd each dearly loved. Resting her head over his quieted heart, the ache within Ella's chest was more profound than she'd ever known.

All around them, the conflict dwindled. With minimal loyalty to be had amongst Prince Johan's men, many of them began to surrender, throwing down their weapons in defeat. Others ran to save themselves after their swords had failed in the heat of strife. Ric's men had arrived in force, making use of their battle-hardened savvy as they took prisoners and chased down defectors. Yet, it felt not like a triumph with Marion lying without spirit in Ella's arms.

Clearing his throat, Much rose, taking in the evidence of brutal combat from across the palace grounds. "Your Majesty." Dipping into a bow, he addressed Ric, who'd not yet acknowledged anything beyond his mourning.

Riccard garnered the attention of all who were present, Ella lifting her eyes to meet those of their new leader. His future rule had been threatened, but no more. It was now unequivocally his.

"This, Ric," Ella managed, her voice gentle as she combed through Marion's hair. "He did this for you...for his king."

"It will be over once you speak." Encouraging the heir to address his people, Will stood at Much's side, offering his hand. Ric clasped it with both of his, allowing Will to haul him to his feet. The prince squared his shoulders, acknowledging Will's statement with a nod.

"I must tell them my brother is dead," he said with finality, sparing a somber glance at his fallen friend. His palms still covered in the lord's blood, Riccard hoisted himself up onto the dais.

"Go," Rory said to Ella, urging her toward the edge of the platform with a nod. "Your sovereign needs your strength."

"Thank you," Ella whispered as Rory took her place, tenderly seeing to Marion in her stead as Alan offered his aid. Moving to the front of the dais, Ella stood before her king, her gaze pinned to his.

He stood alone in silent victory that had come with too high a cost. Without a word, the eyes of Llundyn were drawn to the heir. Set upon the gallows, his solitary presence told everyone assembled which side had prevailed.

Ella studied him, a man transformed. He was damaged and worn — but not broken. When he stood before his army and the citizenry in a moment of still regard, exclamations of glory rang out from amongst the crowd. Fists pumped into the sky, while echoes of acceptance poured over him.

It was a new beginning, an awakening of hope and healing.

Chapter Thirty-Two

Ric sat alone, draped in the finery his father had once worn, and his grandfather before him. King Riccard was, at long last, regarded by his country as the sovereign leader of Llundyn. Within sight of the kingdom's most prominent, ermine furs covered his shoulders as he grasped an ages-old scepter while sitting atop the throne.

His throne.

It was not a role he relished, nor desired, but it seemed that precise attitude of mind was what had destined him for it. The crown was heavy and more burdensome than he ever could have anticipated, and with it, the welfare of a nation was his to determine.

It was the faces that did not belong, the faces of his friends that made him feel at home there — not those of stodgy nobles or the monarchical relics from allied regions whom he'd known since birth. New roles had been dispensed, and longstanding traditions altered to accommodate Ric's wishes, but he would not have it any other way.

With the ceremony having met its completion and his coronation made official, the newly established herald cried out for the attention of all who had gathered.

In blessed solace, awaiting Alan's announcement, Ric watched from his father's seat of state. Though through title it was now his, it never should have been passed to him so soon. The day always would have meant sorrow for him, but he had dared hope it not be so vast.

He had never been one to enjoy the tedium with which the affairs of legislation or propriety were conducted. Nevertheless, he would endure it for the memory of his father and for Marion. They had always held themselves with the expected composure warranted by their positions. For Ric, it had always felt contrived.

With arms outstretched, his new role suiting him as well as Ric could have imagined, Alan addressed the assembled guests. "People of Llundyn, I give you King Riccard!"

They were the most affluent, self-absorbed men and women he'd ever met. Yet, with Alan's words, they applauded and cheered, "Long live King Riccard!" in one resonant voice throughout the hall.

He rose to his feet, remaining in place just as advised by his recently named viceregent, Will Scarlet. Taking to Ric's side, Will prepared to usher guests forward according to family or title, each desiring to find favor with the new king.

But the first to greet him was Ella.

The morning had been so full of preparations and tradition that he had not seen her until then. Loosed curls of mahogany framed the delicate features of her face, her cheeks lightly flushed with color. The emerald necklace lay gracefully over her collarbone, set above a gown that accentuated her curves in a seductive silhouette, and the lovely smile upon her lips told him that she was all too aware of his desire for her.

He grinned, a woefully unkingly response, but he simply couldn't help himself.

She is remarkable beyond words.

Dipping into a low curtsy before him, Ella met his gaze at last. "Your Majesty." Her voice was level, despite the burden each of them bore, conveying in only two words that she felt every bit of his confliction. In the past week, they had laid bare to one another their mutual grief, for not only were they suffering the loss of their beloved friend. Life, as they'd grown accustomed to, had also been brought to an abrupt close.

"I've missed you." His confession uttered in a mere whisper, Ric descended the few steps parting them to meet her, taking her hands in his, decorum be damned. While they couldn't go back, he hoped with every shred of his being that she would agree to live their remaining days together.

"I'm pleased you've not yet forgotten me, given all the revelries surrounding your ascension," she teased, her eyes sparkling with warmth.

"Never, my love," Ric replied, pressing his mouth to her knuckles. He longed for a moment that would belong to them alone, but opportunities had been scarce amid the preparations preceding his coronation.

Clearing his throat, Will reminded them of the company they kept. They were being watched closely, but Ric couldn't find it in him to care. He caught Ella's hand before she could step out of reach, drawing her to himself. "Meet me at the chapel gardens in one hour." His nose brushed the silken flesh of her temple as she inclined her head, acknowledging the request with a subtle nod.

Slipping out of his grasp, Ella withdrew into the assembly, leaving Ric and Will to manage those vying for their chance to speak with the new king.

Grouping by grouping, Riccard acknowledged them, keeping conversation to a trifling minimum. From his father, King Edward, he had learned that to speak little was to leave those seeking undue partiality unnerved, a lesson for which he was endlessly grateful. To confound a man was to be his master. It was a statement that had proved true in matters of war, parliament and love.

It wasn't long before Ella's estranged family stood at his feet. He had seen them keeping to themselves at the edge of the room, and Ric found he had to steel himself for their encounter, for in them, he found no redeeming qualities at all.

Sheriff Dane had been relieved of his duties, his lands stripped from him. Margaret had remained faithful to their engagement and Locksley had been re-assigned upon the announcement of their pending nuptials.

"Your Majesty." The former sheriff bowed in reverence, alongside curtsies from his bride to be and her two daughters. "We wish to proffer both our loyalty and thanks for your clemency. You have been most gracious to us." With a fist to his heart, he feigned sincerity.

While Ella had not yet met the age requirement to take hold of the estate, she and the king had found a solution, redistributing the lands to Will Scarlet. He was not a lord, but as acting viceregent, the property could reasonably be given him, and he would preside over it until Ella was of legal age to hold it herself.

"It is not me you should thank, but Lady Locksley," Ric asserted coolly, and he did not miss the way Margaret's lip twitched at the mention of her stepdaughter. "For it was she who convinced me that you had merely acted as directed by my brother. Were it not for her goodness, I would have left you with nothing. Your cruel treatment of the people of Llundyn was disgraceful. You are fortunate, indeed."

Inclining his head, he dismissed them in silence, and they left his company, shamed and incensed as they departed for their dwelling that had been established on the fringes of Locksley in an abandoned cottage. It was better than they deserved, in truth.

"Ella was wise to suggest we keep them under a watchful eye," Will said, his voice low. "They are not to be trusted."

"Agreed. I've already appointed a personal keeper to oversee our dismissed sheriff, though we've yet to find Gisbourne." Ric was perturbed by the disappearance of the former Lord of Clun. The man was due his own form of justice, should they ever find him.

"He won't evade us forever, sire," Will settled, nodding the next individuals forward.

On went the monotony of sovereign duty, dragging as each minute passed. With one-quarter of the hour left before he'd promised to meet Ella, Ric was pleased to have concluded all the required pleasantries.

Excusing himself from the throne after some time, he sought one last guest. Rory had waited for him at the back, stood by her escort, Artyrus, to depart for Chamelaute.

"I'm sorry I can't stay," Rory lamented when Riccard reached the duo. She took his hands, her face creased with sorrow. Their friendship had been unlikely but true, and one neither would soon see lapse.

"Your Seer has been right thus far," Ric admitted, bringing an appreciative smile to Rory's face. He'd never yet acknowledged the madman's accuracy in her presence, and it pleased him to witness her delight.

"Merlin warned we mustn't tarry in our return, and I fear we have already stayed longer than we should." Artyrus was stoic, his tenor laced with an air of agitation.

"We will make it up in our travels," Rory grumbled, scowling at the inference that she'd prevented them from adhering to the soothsayer's instruction. "But he is right, though I am loathe to admit it. We cannot put off the journey any longer. I will miss all of you more than you know."

"Thank you for all you've done, Rory," Ric said. "Should you ever wish to return, there will always be a place for you. Take care on your trek, my friend."

"You know I will." She smirked, releasing the king's hands, offering a parting bow. Without a word to Artyrus, she turned on her heel, departing on her own terms.

The mammoth man followed in her wake, and Ric wondered at the journey they faced. Rory had, indeed, made his own trek through Wylewoode a trial, but at least she hadn't seemed to despise his very presence. For Artyrus's sake, he hoped the man was resilient. Aurora would test his limits without question.

Ric's knowledge of the palace halls served him well, evading attendees as he slipped into darkened corridors and out of sight. Having left his cumbersome regalia bundled in the arms of his second, he had ordered Thorne that his men were not to follow him. He'd received reluctant compliance from the general, which was the best he could expect now that he'd taken the throne.

Wandering into the chapel gardens, Ric was immediately grateful for their solitude. The flowers bloomed with vibrant life, their colors rich from the springtide showers with which the days preceding had blessed the kingdom, standing in stark contrast with the lifeless bones buried in the dampened soil underfoot. It was there that Marion had been laid to rest beside his father and mother, reunited at last.

Before the lord's headstone stood Ella. She had met Ric there each day for the past week, affording them the only privacy to be found. It was peaceful and quiet where Marion lay, and to be there with both he and Ella had felt right to Ric in every way. Together, they shared memories of their dear friend, sometimes with laughter and others, tearful valediction.

Through mutual grief, they had clung to one another, keeping the steadfast Lord of Knighton alive in their hearts. There, Ric had suggested that, should he and Ella one day be blessed with a child, they would name their issue in Marion's honor.

Ella smiled upon Ric's approach. "Marion would have been so pleased to have seen you today."

"And he would have been lost for words having seen you." Ric took in the vision that was his beloved queen of shadows, his eyes roving over the exquisite ivory and gold of her gown—finely woven silk hand-picked by the royal clothier.

"Your attempts at flattery founder, Your Majesty," she quipped, her features alight with mischief. "For Much has been made lieutenant to one of your naval captains, training to rise within the ranks. Little John and his father are to be taken on as your royal armorers, and our very own Alan a Dale has become your personal herald, living within the castle walls. So what of me?"

The corners of Ric's mouth rose with her assessment, her ribbing proving to be more nosy in nature, rather than harboring any sort of scorn. "You've forgotten Will as my acting viceregent," he teased, pulling her into his arms as she giggled.

"Oh, yes. Yes, of course." Ella pulled away just enough to gaze into her sovereign's eyes, a subtle smile playing upon her lips. He took her hand in his, lacing their fingers.

"I've some thoughts on the matter at any rate. Walk with me?" Ella nodded as Ric drew her toward the refuge of Sherwood. Turning briefly, she pressed her fingers to her lips and extended them out to their departed brother before she wandered hand in hand into the thicket with her king.

Sheltered by the surrounding trees, the creek gently trickling alongside their steps, they continued deeper into their safe-haven. Sherwood felt more like home to them than either of their current arrangements, but no longer could it be. Venturing beyond familiar landmarks not far from Nottingham, the hustle that had taken over their lives dissipated, leaving only the birds and chittering creatures moving about the woodland floor to interrupt their peaceful interlude.

Lightly squeezing her hand within his, Ric slowed his stride, facing Ella as he closed the distance that parted them. He reached for her face, brushing his thumb across the curve of her cheek with tender regard. She leaned into his touch, the warmth of her porcelain skin demanding from him what he was all too willing to give.

"Ember," he breathed, rustling the strands of her free curls. Tipping her face upward, he kissed her. Cautiously at first, his hunger for her only grew with each heartbeat as she melted into his hold, their lips meeting eagerly as they savored one another anew. Her fingertips threaded through his hair as she tugged him closer still, unraveling him under her captivating influence.

"Ella…" Ric withdrew, nuzzling her temple as he fought against the desire to lose himself in the entanglement of her affections. She studied his face, with ember eyes fixed upon him as he took both of her hands.

"For years, I have watched you, fascinated by your courage, your beauty." Nerves made his voice falter, his pulse quickening with the gravity of his sentiments. "The hood of your cloak fell to your shoulders the eve you took me as your hostage, and you had me rapt, mind and body. I was… I *am* yours." Her eyes glistened with moisture as he spoke, his intent enveloping her as dusk settled in around them. "You already command these woods and the villages, but I've dared hope to give you more. Be my queen, my wife, and rule by my side until we've no more breath in our lungs."

He fell to one knee, presenting her with his mother's ring — the very one she'd had the pleasure of stealing alongside him only weeks ago — and her breath caught at the sight of him, earnest and passionate in his appeal. Ella's tears spilled over, slipping over her cheeks as she drew him to his feet. "Yes! I will marry you!" She laughed through sobs of joy as Ric lifted her off her feet, holding her to him as he kissed her once more.

Ric beamed, steadying her on the earth beneath them. "Cover your eyes," he uttered, his enthusiasm prompting an errant giggle as she raised slender fingers to cover them, her smile bright against the pending twilight.

Guiding her through the bushes and ample timber into the depths of Sherwood, Ric plucked her hands from her face. Ella's features lit with understanding, their band gathered together before her.

Fresh leaves lined a petal-laden aisle leading to where Friar Tuck awaited their arrival in front of an arch of twisted vines and branches, adorned with fragrant wildflowers.

Will, Alan and Little John were in position, standing opposite one another across the makeshift aisle, each watching and waiting expectantly while Much advanced to her side.

"If it's not what you wanted —" Ric began.

"It's perfect," Ella murmured, her eyes pinned to her beloved in wonder.

Ric grinned, leaning downward as he pressed his lips to hers, only for Much to clear his throat in exaggerated fashion from beside them.

"I believe that's to be saved for the end of the ceremony, Your Majesty," Much said with a raised brow, his features rife with unmasked amusement.

With the exchange of vows, their lives would always be bound. It was a promise, a future, that only a week earlier had seemed unattainable. But there, in the presence of family, they were joined as one forevermore.

Want to see more from these authors? Here's a taster for you to enjoy!

The Chronicles of Fayble: Mistress of Blades
Britt Cooper & Erin Dulin

Coming October 2022

Excerpt

Try as she might, Rory couldn't bring herself to trust Artyrus. Suppressing her misgivings, she ignored the brigand, though every rational impulse within her told her to turn and run the other way. Merlin had sent him — or at least, that's what he'd claimed — and he'd stolen away with her, dragging her back to her duties in Chamelaute.

It wasn't as if she wouldn't have gone anyway. She was well aware of her obligations, the needs of her people. She'd have made her way home regardless, but the bastard was so *insistent*. Even now, her aggravating companion led the way astride his midnight black horse, who was every bit as colossal as he was.

Resentfully, she eyed the back of his half-shaven head, the ash-blond hair sprouting from the top of his skull forming a short tail that bobbed in time with the beast beneath him.

Rory groaned. There were worse ways to travel through Wylewoode. There had to be, though she was hard-pressed to think of any at the moment.

"We're stopping," she shouted to her escort several yards ahead, slowing her horse. Her civility was a courtesy Artyrus didn't deserve. She offered her compliance out of the goodness of her heart, all despite her disdain for her supposed guardian.

"No." Artyrus continued onward without sparing her a glance, his broad shoulders as stiff and unyielding as his ornery disposition.

Tempering her rising fury, she followed him, willing herself to be reasonable where he refused. Someone had to behave like an adult if they were to survive their trek, and that would be a monumental undertaking.

Now she understood the plight of her former sidekick Ric, the newly coronated king of Llundyn, for she had done the very same thing to him. She'd joined him by force and very much against his wishes. That arrangement had worked out better than she'd hoped, but she was under no illusions. Lightning wouldn't strike twice.

"Mind your pace," Artyrus added, his tone dripping with condescension. "We're still days behind schedule."

Rory tugged the reins, her horse rearing as she came to an abrupt halt. "Who put you in charge?"

"Aurora —"

"No!" Her steed turned in an anxious circle beneath her as she met his gaze, her eyes burning with unrestrained anger. "I'm through taking orders from you. I'm hungry, I'm tired and I want a break. We'll get there when we get there. Why all the urgency?"

He turned to face her, his patience apparently waning. "I was more than generous with you and your friends in Llundyn, and we stayed far longer than was reasonable, given your circumstances."

"Ah. How benevolent of you." Rory took a fortifying breath, all the while reconciling the little she knew of Artyrus with the seemingly endless knowledge he possessed about her. She smiled brightly, steeling herself for the inevitable battle of wills. "You may go at your own pace, but I'm going to set up camp. You'll make excellent time without me."

Trotting away, she eased her horse into the tree line, aiming for the stream that ran alongside the roadway. To her satisfaction, she didn't hear her captor tailing her. Perhaps he'd seen sense after all.

At last.

For the first time in days, she began to recover herself, reveling in the peace their rare separations afforded. It would undoubtedly be short-lived, but she wouldn't let that ruin the moment.

So what if she was a bit petulant?

Running away from Artyrus was childish, a far cry from the commanding manner in which she typically acted, but she'd had enough. He'd destroyed her restraint.

"Well, that's better," Rory sighed, patting her mare, Briar. Doubtless, she was temperamental like Rory was. Only somehow, *she* managed to get away with it. For even Artyrus, God's steadfast gift to bravery, was apt to steer clear of Briar's moody escapades and snapping teeth.

Throwing her leg over the broad mare's back, Rory dismounted, guiding Briar toward the stream for refreshment. The familiar thrum of rolling waters soothed her stormy spirit, the crystalline flow deceptively languid as she plunged her canteen into its depths. Briar wasted no time, easing in at Rory's side and sating her thirst.

To any onlooker, the pair made for a hapless duo. But they were all they needed, making the ubiquity of Artyrus an utter nuisance.

Drying her mouth on the arm of her sleeve, Rory reached into her satchel, feeding Briar a handful of oats and taking care not to catch her fingers in the overeager horse's mouth. "This will do, will it not?"

Her newfound freedom was intoxicating, bringing a small, satisfied smile to her face. Why it had taken her so long to assert herself, to demand control of the situation, was beyond reason. Perhaps it was Artyrus's unsettling reticence that had unnerved her — that, or his sullen disposition. Somewhere along their journey, she'd decided not to poke the bear, unwittingly leaving the brute in charge of their odyssey.

She wouldn't make that mistake again. Better yet, she'd simply rid herself of him altogether.

Or perhaps not.

From beside her, Briar started, spooking only a moment too late for any resistance. Swiftly secured from behind, Rory was swept away from the tranquil waters, thrust headlong into the relentless embrace of her most formidable nemesis.

Rory thrashed about like a beached fish, arching and kicking furiously to no avail. "You've got to be kidding! Leave me alone!" Wielding her heels as a weapon, she struck, her foot whacking its target with vicious accuracy. Artyrus's sharp intake of air was of little consolation, however, as he managed to hold her fast.

In one quick motion, he released her, but not before he'd somehow managed to capture both of her arms, deftly securing them from before her with a leather thong. He stepped away, doubling over for one precious moment to catch his breath. "You're *ridiculous*," he wheezed, regaining his composure.

"You're playing a game you cannot possibly win. This is child's play," Rory snapped, holding her bound hands in front of her. He was sorely mistaken if he thought a simple leather strap would bring her in line. She wriggled her wrists, maneuvering one against the other to free herself. He'd gone too easy on her, leaving the band with plenty of slack. Twisting her wrists, she gave them a final tug.

Artyrus only smiled, an evil little smirk that had Rory itching for all-out war as he'd merely given her the means to entrap herself. He stepped toward her, plucking her sword from its sheath, seemingly unfazed by the hatred surely evident upon her face. "Your cooperation, if you please," he urged, his dark eyes meeting hers. "I do not wish to report such juvenile behavior to Merlin. Certainly you'd like to prove yourself worthy of your obligations."

Rory scoffed. "Tattling as if we're a pair of children. Why am I not surprised?"

"You are, indeed, behaving like one." Artyrus folded his arms across his chest before raising a single eyebrow.

A challenge.

Infuriating.

His assertion was annoying in its own right—but making matters worse was the sinister truth that he'd somehow hit a mark she hadn't realized existed. Her life had been one trial after another, with duty ever looming in the back of her mind and obscuring every facet of her future.

Perhaps some piece of her did crave the freedom of youthful irresponsibility, and being held to account was the last thing she needed. Rory closed her eyes, the fight she'd been harboring within her suddenly dissolving. Her sentiments hadn't changed, but taking a stand in the middle of a booby-trapped forest wasn't good headwork.

Artyrus nodded, wordlessly turning to lead the way back toward the roadway. Sighing, Rory grasped Briar's reins, guiding her along as she followed in Artyrus's shadow.

The man was at least aware enough to maintain a healthy distance, quickly reaching his horse where he awaited Rory, who was traipsing toward him slowly. "Up you go." Clasping his hands before him, he indicated his monstrous midnight steed with a bob of his head.

"No, thank you." Rory raised her bound wrists. "I can manage my horse well enough, even without the full use of my hands."

His grim features softened as he bent at the waist, beckoning her forward. "Nonsense. And besides, traveling together should help prevent any further detours."

Rory huffed, willing herself to ignore his provocation, finally having tired of the ceaseless back and forth between them. Making her way toward him, she mounted the devilish stallion without protest, settling into the saddle.

Clasping her boot as he rose, Artyrus extracted a dagger before moving around the front of his horse. Rory eyed him with growing suspicion as he reached for her other one, plucking a second dagger from its sheath. Still, she was armed to the teeth. Losing a pair of blades was of no consequence.

"Are you through?" Rory asked. "For one so concerned with making good time, you're certainly wasting enough of it."

Artyrus ignored her, instead jamming his foot into the stirrup before swinging his leg over, seating himself behind his unruly passenger. He retrieved two more daggers with maddening calm, which were concealed beneath a thin layer of linen, set between her shoulder blades.

"In case you wish to slit my throat," Artyrus gruffed, urging his steed onward with Briar following at his heels.

Rory fumed, even as she refused to acknowledge — at least outwardly — that he'd succeeded in disarming her entirely.

His ability to annoy her was truly unparalleled.

Their journey proceeded without disruption, providing Rory with an opportunity she'd always loathed — time to think. With Artyrus firmly in command of their route and horses — and even greater control over her from where he sat with his arms encircling her form, though he dared not touch her — she allowed her mind to wander for the first time since she'd left Chamelaute.

Planning had never been a strong suit for the wayward woman, taking on each obstacle only as it arose and never before. It was a way of life and not a bad one, though it sometimes led to a close call now and then. Rory eyed her surroundings, eager for a distraction.

The woods themselves were nothing special. Indeed, they were no different from any other woodland terrain. But their ordinary nature bred complacency, leaving one vulnerable to all the perils within Wylewoode. Deadly plants, quicksand and creatures that defied the imagination all resided within the confines of the forest. And though it was difficult to fathom, there were people there, too.

Rory had no interest in them, for only a loon would remain in Wylewoode by choice.

"Perhaps it's time," Artyrus said around a yawn after a time, guiding his horse through a gap in the foliage toward the water's edge. Lifting his arms, he shielded Rory from the tangled mess of branches as they ambled through to the nearby bank.

At first glance, the riverbank was pleasant enough, though the poisonous brambles lining the opposite shoreline reminded them that they were not in friendly territory. Soft light from the fading sun filtered through the canopy of greenery overhead, bringing a chill to the early evening air as shadows veiled the warm glow of day.

"Very well," Rory replied, reflecting an indifference she didn't feel. She was bushed and ready for a break. Artyrus dismounted first, turning to assist her as she did the same.

"Your hands." Pulling a blade from his breeches, Artyrus gestured toward her bound wrists. She offered them, palms up, avoiding his steady gaze as he cut cleanly through the strap in one slice, his brusque manner never failing to peeve her.

Artyrus excused himself then, striding into the brush and out of Rory's eye line. He had disappeared periodically to relieve himself, but it had never lasted long enough for Rory's liking. In truth, he could continue his trek and vanish altogether and there'd be no complaint from her lips.

She set to work, unpacking their meager belongings from each of their horses before sending them to the water's edge to graze. Minutes later, she'd gathered more than enough fodder for a fire and had a small blaze underway.

The burgeoning flames crackled as she prodded them to life, and before long, she had the makings of a tolerable meal, none of which she had any intention of sharing. Rory looked up, suddenly mindful of the blessed solitude in which she'd completed her tasks. How long had it been?

Rising to her feet, she stretched, casually surveying her surroundings as she worked to hide her concern. Artyrus's stallion, Magnus, remained nibbling the bracken creekside. All his possessions sat untouched, neatly lain alongside her own.

Much as she wished to ignore her unease, Rory knew something wasn't right. Recovering several blades from among his belongings, she wandered in the direction of her absent chaperone. Leaving him to survive the ills of Wylewoode was tempting, of course, but the havoc it would wreak upon her conscience wasn't worth it.

Creeping through the boughs, Rory moved quietly, following the sporadic traces of Artyrus's presence. He was somewhat ghostlike—his ability to obscure his tread leaving her reluctantly impressed, particularly in light of his size.

She hadn't gone far when she sighted him, the whole of his body suspended mid-air from where he hung by his ankle. Gently swaying in the mild twilight breeze, he issued curses too numerous to count as he contorted his body, attempting to grasp the rope as he folded himself in half.

Being too top-heavy for success, he heaved one final obscenity, collapsing as he seemingly conceded defeat, swinging like the tail of an irritable cat. The spectacle was equal parts pitiful and humorous.

Rory laughed, giving herself away as he twisted to meet her gaze. "Maybe a little help, if you wouldn't mind," he muttered, his face becoming a concerning shade of red.

"Poor fellow!" Glancing up at her captured keeper, Rory placed her hands on her hips, relishing a moment of fortune. She wasn't about to let the occasion end without a bit of chiding. "I imagine this is what you deserve, in light of your ridiculous strong-arming earlier. The pitfalls of these woods are vast. You'd be wise to allow me the lead."

After a brief deliberation, he merely sighed. "As you wish. Now, *if* you *please*." Gesturing at his ensnared ankle, he was nothing short of resigned from where he swung in an interminable arc.

And while Rory should've been reveling in her minor victory, she was oddly dissatisfied. Unsheathing her reclaimed dagger, she made for the tree that anchored her companion in the heavens. "Tuck and roll," she admonished before severing the rope.

Like a sack full of bricks, he plummeted to the earth, his strapping form landing with a wicked *thud* as he turned to his back, exhaling in a mighty burst that twisted Rory's insides. Flopping an arm across his eyes, he lay in the dust, recovering himself. "My thanks," he managed.

"It's nothing," she uttered, backing her way through the path she'd come. Shaking her head, she dismissed the entire episode, refusing to allow empathy to bloom, instead returning to her forgotten meal.

He reappeared slowly, plodding through the foliage as he made for his belongings, and it was no surprise that Rory found herself suddenly preoccupied with her feast, though her appetite had since expired.

The weight of her hefty cloak melted over her shoulders, providing warmth she hadn't realized she was in want of. She glanced up at Artyrus, who offered only a shrug in acknowledgment. "It's getting cold."

"Here," Rory replied, proffering her plate as he seated himself nearby. "Eat."

He took a hearty bite, gagging slightly as he forced piece after piece down his gullet. "Whew. Let's hope you lead better than you cook."

"Forgive me," she scoffed. "Culinary arts are among the least of my priorities." Scowling, she turned away, though not before she caught a hint of a smile upon his face.

About the Authors

Britt Cooper

Brittany has been a cosmetologist for over a decade, an occupation that continuously explores fresh avenues of creativity and beauty. She is a new mother, learning to balance the reality of what it means to be a mom, wife, stylist, and author. Reading has always been one of her passions and writing an endeavor she refuses to leave behind.

Erin Dulin

Erin is a wife and mother who loves spending time with family. She's an enthusiastic fan of all things sports, experimental baker/chef, and amateur gamer in her free time. Writing has been a passion since her childhood, and while finding peace and quiet in which to write never comes easily, she knows it worth every ounce of chaos when the stories take shape.

Britt and Erin love to hear from readers. You can find their contact information, website details and author profile page at https://www.finch-books.com

Sign up for our newsletter and find out about all our romance book releases, eBook sales and promotions, sneak peeks and FREE romance books!